PRAISE FOR
ANTOINETTE STOCKENBERG

**Winner of the 1993 RITA Award for *Emily's Ghost*
and for her previous novels**

Time After Time
"As hilarious as it is heart-tugging . . . Once again, Antoinette Stockenberg has done a magnificent job."
—*I'll Take Romance* magazine

"A richly rewarding novel filled with wrenching loss, timeless passion and eerie suspense. A novel to be savored."
—*Romantic Times*

"Antoinette Stockenberg is a superb contemporary writer . . . *Time After Time* is that rarest of works—a satisfying treasure for a vast variety of palates."
—*Affaire de Coeur*

Embers
"Terrific!"
—*Romantic Times*

"Stockenberg cements her reputation for fine storytelling with this deft blend of mystery and romance . . . Sure to win more kudos."
—*Publishers Weekly*

"A moving work involving obsession, betrayal, and thwarted passions . . . A book that has 'classic' written all over it."
—*Affaire de Coeur*

Beyond Midnight

ANTOINETTE STOCKENBERG

St. Martin's Paperbacks

BEYOND MIDNIGHT

Copyright © 1996 by Antoinette Stockenberg.

All rights reserved. No part of this book may be used or reproduced in any manner whatsoever without written permission except in the case of brief quotations embodied in critical articles or reviews. For information address St. Martin's Press, 175 Fifth Avenue, New York, N.Y. 10010.

ISBN: 0-312-95976-1

Printed in the United States of America

St. Martin's Paperbacks edition/August 1996

10 9 8 7 6 5 4 3 2 1

For John, with all my love.

Acknowledgments

My gratitude to Sgt. John Jodoin and Officer Paul LeBlanc of Salem; to staff naturalist Robert Speare of the Ipswich river Sanctuary; to Director Kathleen Nelson of the Garrettson Memorial Day Care Center in Newport; and, as ever, to Dr. Howard Browne.

This is the place to drop into a deep curtsy to Steven Axelrod for his steadfastness and to Jennifer Enderlin for her enthusiasm. Thank you both so much.

Chapter 1

March.

Helen Evett dropped a log into the jumpy flames of her cozy hearth, then went over to the sitting room window and closed the heavy drapes of faded rose, muting the sound of sleet that tapped against the panes.

This March will be different.

She poured herself a glass of sherry, settled into a deep-cushioned chair in front of the fire, and cracked open the cover of a brand-new biography of Freud that she'd been meaning to read since Christmas.

It's been four years now. Long enough.

Five minutes into the book, Helen looked up and began staring at the flames, unable, after all, to shake herself free of the mood. March in Massachusetts was long, cold, and cruel, full of false hope. March was a liar. March couldn't produce a damn thing except April first, the anniversary of her husband's death.

For four years in a row, Helen Evett had tried to convince herself that spring would be less painful. She had planted hundreds of snowdrops and burned cords of wood, and yet here she was, facing April again with dread. The memories of that fateful day had burned deep and left scars:

the somber troop commander standing at her front door, the slow-motion ride to the hospital in a state police car, the shocking sight of Hank's gray, lifeless face.

She hadn't dared pull the sheet farther back than his face; part of his chest, she knew, had been blown away.

Helen sighed heavily. Things would get better after April first. But tonight it was still March.

"Mom! I'm home!"

In the hall outside the sitting room, Helen heard the satisfying thunk of the heavy oak door falling into place. One child back, one to go.

"How're the roads?" she called out. Becky had good instincts and a level head; but her driver's license was so new it still smelled of plastic.

"No problem," the girl said in a voice that Helen knew was being deliberately upbeat. Becky was as aware of March as her mother was, but she had her own system for dealing with it: she shopped.

"Look what I found at Filene's Basement." The girl strode into the room, still in her black hooded trench coat, and nudged the cat off the hassock with her shopping bag. "Cashmere. And dirt cheap."

She flipped the hood of her coat off her head, revealing straight gold hair that took its glow from the fire, and beamed at her mother.

Helen, still marveling at the whiteness and straightness of Becky's teeth despite the fact that her braces had been off for over a year, frowned and said, "Cashmere? Since when can you afford cashmere on a baby-sitter's wages?"

"Well, it's not all cashmere. Just twenty percent."

"I hope you put gas in the car."

"Five dollars worth," Becky said, wrinkling her nose. "I'll put in another five when I get paid."

"Becky, this won't do. You can't go spending money like there's no tomorr—" Instantly Helen regretted having said it. Who knew better than they did that sometimes there *was* no tomorrow? For Trooper Hank Evett, writing out a routine speeding ticket, there had ended up being no tomorrow.

Becky was shrugging out of her rain-spattered coat; she let it fall where she stood on the worn Oriental carpet. When she faced her mother again the look in her green eyes was as calmly agreeable as the smile on her face. "You're right, Mom. This is the last thing I'll buy for a while."

It's March, Helen reminded herself. *Let her be.*

Rummaging through a wrap of tissue, Becky pulled out a smart turtleneck sweater for her mother's perusal.

Helen smiled ironically. "Oh, good. More black. Just what you need."

"It's not black. It's blackish charcoal."

"It's charcoalish black."

"It'll look terrific on you, too, Mom. With your black hair and gray eyes—"

"I'd look like a lump of coal. Why all the black, anyway?" Helen added, unable to keep the protest out of her voice. The color of mourning held no allure for her.

"It's just cool, Mom," said Becky with an edge in her own voice. "For no other reason."

Helen had to leave it at that. She stood up, automatically retrieving her daughter's crumpled coat from the floor. On her way out to the hall clothes tree, she asked, "Did your brother say when Mrs. Fitch was picking them up?"

She heard Becky mumble something about Mrs. Fitch's car being at the mechanic's.

Surprised, Helen said, "So how are Russ and Scotty getting home?"

She turned around in time to see Becky sprinting for the stairs. Without pausing, the girl said, "Russ told me a friend of Scotty Fitch was gonna meet them at the mall and drive them both home.''

"Rebecca!" Helen said, more angry with her daughter than with her son. "How could you leave him to come back on his own?"

Becky was taking the stairs two at a time. "We live in *Salem,* Mom," she ventured over her shoulder. "Not Sarajevo."

"You know what I mean! He's fourteen," Helen snapped. "All feet! No brains! I don't want him hanging around with kids who drive."

Turning at the top of the stairs, Becky looked down at her mother and said quietly, "I don't see how you can stop him, Mom."

"Oh, really?" Helen answered in a crisp, dry voice. "Wait till he gets home, then, and watch."

"Oh-h . . . don't take it out on Russell," Becky pleaded. "It was my fault. I'm the one who let him." In self-defense she added, "When I was fourteen you let *me* get chauffeured around by girls older than I was."

"That was different. You were level-headed. I could trust your judgment—up until tonight, anyway," Helen said with a dark look. "And besides, times are—"

"I know, I know: *totally* different," Becky said with a roll of her eyes. "Even though it's—what?—a year or two later?"

"You don't know who's out there, honey," Helen said, ignoring the sarcasm. "There are nutcases . . . madmen . . . psychos . . ."

"Mom. Stop."

The expression on the girl's face was wise and tender and weary all at once. She knew, and her mother knew, that the one madman who mattered most had rolled his car in a fiery, fatal end to a spectacular police chase on Route 95. He was out of the picture, out of their lives.

But that didn't mean there weren't other madmen out there.

"Hey," Becky said, more cheerfully. "I almost forgot. This is for Russ." She reached into her shopping bag and pulled out a Pearl Jam baseball cap. "It's wool. Ninety-nine cents. Can you believe it?"

She tossed the cap down to her mother with a last, quick smile and beat a retreat to her bedroom at the end of the wallpapered hall.

Helen sat the cap on the newel post and sighed. Becky was rolling through the tough teen years so painlessly that she'd almost managed to convince her mother that fathers weren't all that critical. It was Russ who was the reality check: The boy was angry, moody; sloughing off responsibility right and left.

"Pretty typical," Helen's friends all said.

But no one else could pin down, to the day, exactly when her son had begun the transformation from nice kid to beast in the jungle. Helen could. On the evening of his father's funeral, Russell Evett had withdrawn into his room, and when he came out three days later he wasn't Russell Evett anymore. It was as plain as that.

Helen was roused from yet another replay of that time by the piercing ring of the hall phone. The voice that answered hers was fearful and tentative and had the effect of jangling her nerves still more.

"Mrs. Evett? You don't know me—I'm sorry to call you at home—but I have an important request, more like a favor—no, wait, let me start over. I got your name from a friend who has a little girl in your preschool, Candy Greene . . . that's the mother's name, not the little girl's . . . the girl is called Astra? You remember? A little blond girl, very fluent?"

"She's not in my Tuesday-Thursday class, but may I ask who this is?" said Helen, impatient with the meandering voice at the other end of the line. What if Russ were trying to call?

The woman sucked in her breath in a broken gasp. "Oh! I'm sorry . . . it's this vicious headache." She took a deep breath, obviously trying to organize herself.

"My name . . . is Linda Byrne," she said with new deliberation. "I've heard such good things about your school, and I want my daughter to go there. She's *so* bright. She gets along well with children and she's pretty good about sharing and taking directions. She doesn't bite." Hurried and edgy despite herself, she added, "Is there anything else you need to know?"

"Well, yes," said Helen, surprised by the woman's naiveté. "We like to sit down with the parents and the child—"

"Oh, but my husband couldn't possibly be available for that!" the woman said at once. "He's so busy!"

"One parent would be fine. I'll tell you what, Mrs. Byrne. Why don't you come visit the school tomorrow at about five o'clock with your little girl, and we—"

"But I can't. Don't you see? That's why I'm calling. From my bed. That's the favor I'm asking. Couldn't you possibly come here instead?"

Her voice betrayed rising panic. Helen, wishing to reassure her but mostly in a hurry to get off the phone, said, "There's no urgency, Mrs. Byrne. If you're not feeling well, we can certainly meet on another day. Registration has only just opened for the next term. You have plenty of time—"

"I don't! Candy said you fill up overnight!"

Helen laughed reassuringly and said, "Mrs. Greene was exaggerating. Really. Why don't we agree on a day next week—"

"Please . . . next week won't be any better," the woman said, suddenly weary. "I've been so . . . I have to nail this down . . . this one thing, at least. I can't go on like this . . . drifting . . . please, won't you come? We live on Chestnut Street, not all that far from your school. It wouldn't take long . . . really . . . I don't see why you can't. . . .'' she argued, practically in tears.

If Linda Byrne was trying to make a good impression, she wasn't succeeding. She had a top-drawer address, but she sounded like the kind of spoiled, idle woman who routinely takes to her bed when things don't go her way.

On the other hand, something in her tone sent a shiver of sympathy through Helen. Whatever the reason for her headache, it was obvious that Linda Byrne was in real agony. No one could fake that kind of pain in her voice, not even a prima donna.

"All right. I can make time tomorrow evening. Shall I come by before dinner? Say, five o'clock?''

"Oh, yes, thank you,'' Mrs. Byrne said, her voice becoming suddenly faint. "Peaches will be so pleased.''

She gave the number of her house and hung up, leaving Helen somewhat bemused over the whole thing.

Peaches. In Helen's mind the name conjured up everything from a bunny rabbit to a striptease. She'd never taught a toddler by that name, not once in the fifteen years she'd been in day care. From the cozy groups of six she'd cared for in her home to the larger classes who'd passed through the preschool she later founded, Helen had never come across a single, solitary Peaches.

In any case, Helen's plan was to present herself to little Peaches and—with any luck—to talk Linda Byrne into visiting the preschool before she signed up her child.

Helen was immensely proud of The Open Door, proud of the way she'd risked a modest inheritance on an old building in need of rehab and, with tax credits and a lot of sweat equity—hers and Hank's—turned it into a stimulating center for creative kids. She didn't need to chase down

Linda Byrne's business; the class would be full by May first, tops.

She didn't *need* Linda Byrne's business. But oddly enough, she seemed to want it.

Helen was debating whether to throw one last log on the fire or call in the militia when she heard the front door being slammed.

"Russell Evett, get in here!" she yelled. "*Now.*"

After what Helen knew was a deliberate delay, she heard Russ shuffle into the sitting room. She herself was smacking the last of the fire into helpless embers with the poker, trying to get her relief and anger under control. When she was done, she turned to confront her son.

The boy-man who faced her looked like any other fourteen-year-old: baggy clothes, scary haircut, a zit or two on his chin to be followed someday soon by stubble. He was tall, as tall as she was, and growing weed-fast. He'd got an ear double-pierced recently without her permission. She knew he always took out the earrings or safety pins or whatever they were before he walked through the door, and tonight was no exception.

She searched for signs of remorse or hints of fear in his face; it had been so long since she'd seen either. He'd inherited Hank's green eyes and her black hair, a pleasing combination. But somehow, neither Hank's self-discipline nor her hypersensitivity had got passed on. If Russ had either, he wouldn't be standing on the carpet in front of her right now.

"The mall's been closed for an hour and a half," she said quietly. "Where have you been?"

Russell shrugged and looked away. "Hangin'."

"Well, I don't want you 'hangin',' young man. When we agree on a plan, I expect you to follow your end of it."

He shrugged. "Mrs. Fitch couldn't come."

"Your sister was there."

"That wasn't the plan either, Ma."

"Well, she was the obvious alternative."

"Becky said it was okay," he threw out sullenly.

"Becky is not your mother. You know the rule: no cars.
You had plenty of time to reconsider."

"How was I even supposed to find her?"

"Filene's Basement is some big secret? Listen to me: I
don't want you driving around with kids older than you.
Not without my permission, and don't hold your breath for
that. Do you understand?"

His answer was a defiant look of boredom.

"That's it!" Helen snapped. "You're grounded for the
weekend."

The boredom turned to instant indignation. "Grounded!
Why? *I* didn't blow a gasket!"

Helen wasn't sure whose gasket he was talking about,
and in any case she didn't want the bickering to drag on
any further, so she said, "Good night, Russell," in the
calmest possible voice and left him to stew in his own
teenage hormones.

The last of the sad thoughts that drifted through Helen's
head that night was that "Ma" didn't sound nearly as win-
some as "Mommy."

The Byrnes lived on a street that was not only the jewel in
the crown of Old Salem, but arguably one of the finest
avenues in America. Less than half a mile long, Chestnut
Street was lined with perfectly preserved three-story mansions dating from 1800, many of them built for Salem's
early aristocracy: the merchants and sea captains who
reaped mind-boggling wealth from whaling and the China
Trade.

The entire avenue, east end to west, was now a National
Historic Landmark and a mecca for history and architecture

buffs. They could stroll virtually alone along its brick-lined sidewalks and cobblestoned gutters in the imposing shadows of the mansions, and dream about the clipper ships that braved high seas to bring back unimaginable treasures.

It was a great street—but nobody really cared. Not the bread and butter of Salem's tourist economy, anyway; those people were far more interested in Salem's darker, uglier past. The witch trials of 1692, in which nineteen innocent victims were hanged and the twentieth was pressed to death under a crush of rocks—*that* was the story that busloads came to hear.

Who cared if the Peabody Essex Museum contained a priceless slant-top desk carved entirely of ivory? It was much more fun to stand with a cluster of tourists in a pitch-black room around a luridly lit pentagram and hear the tale of Salem's shameful, sinful past.

Helen Evett ought to know. Whenever visitors came to see her—depending on their ages—they wanted to go to the Witch Museum or the Witch Dungeon Museum or the Wax Museum or the Witch House. If they were the pensive type, they sometimes wanted to sit and reflect at the witch-trials memorial.

Rarely did they wish to take a walking tour of Chestnut Street.

Helen drove slowly down the one-way street, searching for the Byrne mansion. She hadn't been on Chestnut Street in a long while, long enough to be impressed all over again by its magnificence. Salem had plenty of historic houses, of course; but there was something about the way Chestnut Street's mansions stood shoulder to shoulder, united against the outside world, that seemed exceptionally exclusive. Chestnut Street did not permit slaggards. No peeling paint, no sprawling privet here, by golly.

Stuffy little street, Helen decided. Automatically she sat up straighter in the seat of her Volvo.

She had dressed in keeping with the neighborhood, pinning her hair in a knot at the back of her head and wearing a suit much more tailored than her usual soft, flowing dresses.

The preschoolers had noticed the change the minute they saw her. One of them, whose mother was a lawyer, had looked up at her and said, "Do you hafta go to court, Mrs. Evett?"

Helen didn't, but she felt as nervous as if she were appearing in her own defense. It was an illogical, bewildering response to the telephone plea of the night before.

Just who was this Linda Byrne, anyway? She sounded too disorganized, somehow, for such a formal neighborhood. And what about Byrne? Had he been surprised to realize that he'd married a dysfunctional neurotic?

Now, now, Helen told herself. *Give the poor lady a break. Headaches can be paralyzing.*

The problem was, Helen had never had the luxury of dropping everything to nurse one. Like most other working women, she could only pop a couple of pain relievers and keep on moving.

She pulled up in front of one of the grandest of the grand houses, a brick three-story mansion with an Ionic portico framing a door painted the deepest of greens. Like most of the houses on the street, the Byrne mansion was set back only a few feet from the brick sidewalk and was fronted by an elaborate painted fence; this one curved back to two urned pillars on each side of the portico.

From the copper downspouts to the fittings on the deep green working shutters, everything about the house suggested taste, discretion, and affluence—and a severity that Helen found strangely off-putting. This was no charming ramshackle cottage; no rambling, whimsical Victorian like her own. The painted ivory shutters on the inside of the windows facing the street were all closed, as if the place were put up for the season. Obviously the owners weren't fond of sunshine.

If Helen had seen a rosebush about to leaf out, or a pot of early pansies on the step, then maybe she would've felt less wary. But except for the ivy tumbling discreetly through the spokes of the fence, and the thick, gnarled branches of an old tree nodding close to the second-floor windows, she saw nothing that seemed relaxed or welcoming. If houses reflected their owners, then Helen wasn't sure she'd like these owners.

She got out of the car and slammed the door. It was a simple, mindless act.

But it changed Helen's life forever.

The noise of the car door spooked an owl that apparently had been roosting in the tree. The bird swooped down in front of Helen, then headed directly for her, locking its gaze on hers. Helen froze. Her heart jumped to her throat. The hair on the back of her neck stood up. Just as suddenly, the owl broke away and bounded off erratically.

It had happened so fast, in the blink of an eye. Helen was left shaking and weak-kneed, as if a mugger had jumped out of nowhere and grabbed her purse. She tightened her grip on her shoulder bag, not altogether convinced that the owl wouldn't be back for it, and hurried up the three steps to the door of the mansion.

Before Helen could lift the heavy brass knocker cast in the shape of a square-rigged ship, the door was swung open for her. An attractive, thirtyish woman stood in the doorway, oblivious to the raw March wind.

"Ah! You made it!" she said to Helen with a warm, vivacious smile.

Helen was caught off guard at the sight of the slender, auburn-haired beauty. "Mrs. Byrne?"

I knew it, she thought. *There's nothing wrong with her.*

The woman laughed and shook her head as she stepped

aside. "No, no, I'm just the nanny. Peaches Bartholomew. Come in. Mrs. Byrne is dressing to come down. In the meantime, come and meet Katherine. She's been so excited all day."

So. Wrong on two counts. Well, one of them was an honest mistake. Peaches Bartholomew looked and acted like the mistress of a mansion. She was beautifully dressed in a calf-length skirt of fine-spun wool and a sweater that had a lot more cashmere in it than poor Becky's. The apricot color highlighted the delicate flush of her Meryl Streep cheekbones; it was easy to see how she'd got the name Peaches.

A poor and distant relation was Helen's first, old-fashioned thought as the two women made their way down the soaring hall, lit by a wonderful chandelier, to one of the reception rooms. Helen stole a glance at the nanny in profile and realized how striking her beauty was: straight nose, high cheekbones, delicate brows and lashes, makeup artfully applied. Her auburn hair was pulled back in a French braid, more elegant, somehow, than the cleverest cut.

Helen responded to the woman's pleasantry about spring being just around the corner, but she was thinking, *I wonder if I would've had the confidence to hire a nanny this pretty.*

They entered a room of lofty proportions which clearly served as a music room. A grand piano was strategically placed beside full-length windows that opened to a view of the garden; a deep, well-thumbed assortment of sheet music was scattered across the top of an obviously valuable Federal sideboard with a serpentine table-edge.

"Katie, come see who's here," Peaches called gaily. She had a beautiful voice, rich and musical. No doubt she accompanied the pianist in the family, whoever that was.

"Katherine?" Peaches said again in apparent confusion.

It was obvious that a game was being played. "For goodness' sakes . . . I thought she was in here."

Suddenly a brown-haired moppet in Oshkosh overalls
popped out from behind a Queen Anne armchair and
shouted, *"Boo!"*

The child broke into a fit of giggles as Peaches reached
down and wrapped her arms around her, half-tickling, half-
turning her to face Helen. "Do you know who this is?"
said Peaches to the child.

Without looking up, Katie giggled again and said, "Yes.
Mrs. Evett. She teaches preschool," the child added, in case
there was any doubt.

Helen crouched to the little girl's level and said, "Hi,
Katie. I'm glad to meet you. Your mommy said that you're
a very smart little girl."

Katie fixed her bright blue eyes on Helen's gray ones.
"I know my ABCs, and I can count to twenty," she said.
This she proceeded to do on the spot, except for seventeen,
eighteen, and nineteen.

When she was done, Peaches tucked one of her curls
back and said, "We've been practicing a lot, haven't we,
honey?"

"Uh-huh. And I know how to draw. Want me to show
you?"

Helen said yes and Katie ran to the other end of the room
where she'd been coloring at a low table, then fell to her
knees and began sorting through her pile in search of her
best pieces.

"She's determined to make a good impression on you,"
Peaches whispered to Helen. "I'm not sure what Linda told
her, but Katie seems to think she may not get into the
class."

"Oh . . . no, I wouldn't say that," Helen said vaguely. It
was awkward to be put on the spot that way, which is why
Helen preferred to do the interviews at school.

The reference to "Linda" rather than to "Mrs. Byrne" did not escape Helen. Over the years she'd met hundreds of nannies picking up their charges at the end of the day. Very few of them referred to their employers by their first names. Maybe Peaches was a relation after all.

To fill the void while they waited for the child to make up her mind, Helen said softly, "Does Katie have many friends to play with?"

Peaches pursed her lips thoughtfully, cocked her head in the little girl's direction, and sighed. "I wish I could say yes. But all the children in the neighborhood are in pre-schools, getting ready for Harvard and Yale. Linda was determined to hold out, but the pressure got to be too much.

"Oh, good, Katie," said Peaches to the girl as she came skipping back with a crayon-drawing in her hand, "that was *my* favorite, too."

Without a word the child handed the sheet to Helen, apparently preferring to let her work speak for itself.

Helen didn't have a clue what the brown and red scribbles were supposed to be. Nonetheless, she was impressed with the little girl's command of shapes. "Oh my," she said enthusiastically. "You must come sit next to me and tell me everything that's in it."

Helen took the girl by the hand and led her to a small camelback sofa opposite the piano, glancing at the entrance to the room as they passed it.

The nanny took the hint. "I'm sorry for the delay," she said at once. "I'll just go see—"

She never got to finish the sentence. A man's voice—loud and urgent and somehow ghastly—cried out from a floor above them, *"Peaches! For God's sake, up here!"*

Chapter 2

The nanny threw down the words "Excuse me" like a discarded tissue and rushed from the music room, leaving Helen alone with the child.

Whatever had happened wasn't good, but Helen knew better than to let a child see that she was upset. In her calmest, friendliest voice she said, "Now. I was wondering what . . . hmmm . . . this is," she said, pointing to one of several brown cigars. She was surprised to see that her hand was shaking as she did it.

Katherine, unhooking her forefinger from her lower lip, gestured in a squiggly circle that took in all the cigars at once and said, "That's Daddy's plane. And this is his other plane," she said, pointing to a blue scribble in one corner. "Only I coulddent fit it."

"And this?"

"This is fog. Daddy doesn't like fog because he can't fly his plane. But I like it," she added in a hushed voice. "Because, well, I like it." It seemed reason enough.

"And this?"

The child's blue eyes crinkled above a smile. "That's Polly Panda," she said, slapping the heels of her hands on the edge of the sofa cushion. "Daddy bringed Polly Panda on the plane. She sat in a seat. Mommy was mad.''

Helen decided not to follow up on that one, so she asked Katie to show her some more of her work.

It was a hard slog. Katie, true to the artist's temperament, had no desire to explain every last smudge, especially in the more abstract pieces. She began to fidget and demanded to know where Peaches was.

Good question, thought Helen. Really, it was shaping up to be an extraordinary interview, with one odd surprise after another. From the owl to the real Peaches to the elusive Linda Byrne, Helen had been kept continuously off balance. She didn't like it at all.

She'd managed to get Katie working on another creation—though it was clear that the muse had flown—when Peaches suddenly reappeared.

The woman's face was as white as a new porcelain sink. Her eyes were red-rimmed, her nose still runny; clearly she'd been crying. She forced a pale echo of her earlier smile and said, ''I really am sorry . . . but something's come up. I'm afraid we'll have to end the interview here. I'm—''

She looked around the room blankly. ''Did you bring a coat?'' she asked in a dazed voice.

It was Helen's turn to sound blank. ''I left it in my car,'' she said automatically.

''Oh . . . of course. Well. I . . . someone will be in touch, then. Thank you so much for coming.''

And that was it. Helen was given the bum's rush out the door.

She stood beside her car, keys in hand, staring at the imposing brick house with its shuttered air of disdain, and thought, *What the* hell *was going on in there?*

A car or two passed on the street. Bankers and lawyers were coming home to their suppers. Helen roused herself and stuck the key in the lock of her door, all too aware that her kids would be clamoring for their own meal. A light snow was beginning to fall. More snow, more March, more waiting.

Somehow the interview seemed to fit right in.

By the time Peaches hurried back from seeing Helen to the door, Katie had climbed halfway up the unbarred stairs. The nanny raced to intercept her.

"I wanna go by Mommy," the child said, trying to wriggle out of her nanny's grasp.

"You can't right now, honey," said Peaches, carrying her quickly up the rest of the stairs. The stairs wound another flight to the nursery around the massive center hall, itself highlighted by a large crystal chandelier that hung from the third floor ceiling. Peaches made sure the child's face was to the wall, away from the open hall—the heart of the house onto which all the rooms opened. "You know how it is when Mommy has a headache."

"I *don't* know," Katherine said, frustrated and impatient. "I don't I don't I don't. I want to see her now."

In the distance Peaches heard the sound of sirens. Her heart lurched in her breast; by sheer force of her will, she made it return to a steady, untroubled beat.

"You can't see her now, Katie," she said evenly.

Not now. Not ever.

Helen ended up waiting a week for the call. More than once, she'd considered calling Linda Byrne herself; but after all her assurances that there was no urgency, she couldn't quite justify picking up the phone.

Besides, it had been a godawful week: A nasty strain of flu was making the rounds, and kids and staff were dropping like flies. Helen had been one of the few left standing, despite a brutal week-long sinus headache.

But Friday had come at last, and Helen was able, finally,

to collapse on the sofa with an ice pack on her head. She was dressed in comforting sweat clothes, gazing listlessly through the wood blinds at the last of a bloodred sky and wondering whether she should close the school for a few days, when the phone rang.

"Russ, answer that, would you?" she begged.

She heard his grudging "H'lo" on the hall phone, followed by an assortment of monosyllables: "Yeah . . . no . . . 'kay . . . no . . . I'll tell her . . . bye."

Russ hung up and came into the family room, which was identical in size to the sitting room on the opposite side of the hall but upholstered in more rugged fabrics. He was buried under fourteen layers of plaid, dressed to go out.

"So? Who was it?"

"Some woman with a weird name," he answered. "She said some kid won't be signing up for preschool that you thought was going to."

"I don't suppose you'd happen to remember the child's name either," Helen said dryly.

"Yeah . . . that one wasn't weird . . . Katherine, that's it!" Russ said, lighting up in the kind of endearing grin that Helen so rarely saw anymore.

"Oh-h . . . Katherine Byrne. So it must've been Peaches Bartholemew who called? Well, that's too bad. Katherine's a sweetie." The sadness lingered in Helen's voice as she said to her son, "Going out?"

"Yeah. Over to Mickey's house. Him and Scott and me were thinking of going to a movie. Um . . . could I have five dollars?"

"He and Scott and I. You spent your allowance?"

"Yeah."

It wasn't all that easy to do, since Russ had had to stay home the previous weekend. Because of the grounding—not despite it—Helen decided to give him the money. "Hand me my purse," she said, sighing.

She fished out a bill from her wallet and gave it to him. "I want you home by nine-fifteen."

"Ma-a!"

"Nine. Fifteen."

"That doesn't even leave time for a Coke!"

"The fridge is full of Coke. Have your friends over after the show. I'll be glad to drive them home."

He shrugged, which under the circumstances meant, "Naturally you must be insane," and took off.

Broke again. Russ was always out of money, which was a good-news, bad-news thing for a worrier like Helen. The good news was, he couldn't be dealing drugs. The bad news was, she couldn't be sure he wasn't using them.

Don't be dumb. You know the telltale signs; you've memorized them from the public-service ads. Russell Evett is not on drugs. He wouldn't betray his father's memory that way.

Before she could run through the litany of symptoms again, she heard the front door slam. Russell had come back.

He poked his head into the family room. "I forgot. She said someone died."

Helen whipped the ice bag from her head and bolted up. "*Died?* Who?"

Russ frowned in concentration. "I forget."

"Not—" But she knew the answer would be yes before she said the name. "Not Linda Byrne," she said softly.

"Yeah. That was it. Bye." He pivoted on one Nike.

"*Hold* it. Miss Bartholemew didn't say anything more than that? What exactly did she say? Think."

This was an utterly pointless demand, similar to many Helen had made of her son. He shrugged and said, "I dunno," with a hapless look. "She died. That's all. Or maybe she didn't say 'died.' Maybe she said 'death.' I'm not sure."

Russ left his mother in a state of shock. Helen began pacing the room in her stockinged feet, wondering whether there was anything she could or should do at this point. Acting on her first impulse, she ran to the phone and dialed the number of the Byrne mansion. She got an answering machine, which she hadn't expected; like a fool, she hung up.

Who should receive her condolences? Poor little Katie? Obviously not. But Helen didn't know the husband. For that matter, she hardly knew Peaches—and anyway, there was something irreverent about offering one's condolences to someone named Peaches.

Besides, the fact that Peaches had given the message directly to the first person to pick up the phone suggested that the call had been the merest courtesy rather than a social event.

Okay, so that was that. Helen Evett and Linda Byrne were simply two ships that had passed in the night. It was sad but hardly extraordinary. Helen picked up her ice bag from the floor and lay back down on the sofa. The pacing had made a horrendous headache worse.

Inevitably, her thoughts focused on her conversation with Linda Byrne. Helen regretted not having been able to satisfy the woman's last request. Not that it was Helen's fault, really. After all, she'd gone to see Linda Byrne the first chance she got. She'd been prepared to accept Katherine into the class. There was nothing more she could have done.

So where's all this damn guilt coming from?

"Oh, God . . . this hurts," she said, interrupting her own reverie. She remembered that Hank had once had a sinus infection that had leveled him for two or three days—and Hank had been as big, as strong, and as stoic as they came.

Yeah, but this one's lasted all week, a voice kept prodding.

It was the headache, she decided, that was making her feel such deep remorse; before it, she hadn't felt nearly enough sympathy for Linda Byrne. All that was different now.

She tried to siphon off some of the pain with a low, prolonged sound deep in her throat. It was neither moan nor whimper, but a kind of pleading pant—as if she were begging for mercy. After a moment, the sound came out again.

But this time it wasn't coming from her.

Instantly Helen held her breath, listening. There it was again: a soft pant, with something like a shiver underlying it. Someone crying? But no one else was in the house.

She sat up on the denim-covered sofa, trying to track the source of the sound. It seemed to evolve into another, sharper noise—as if someone were trying to jiggle a locked door.

Helen turned off the light, tiptoed to the big bay window, and peeked through the lace curtain on the side window nearest the front stone steps. The night was inky black: a streetlight had gone out the day before, leaving the house in a big black hole. She thought of flipping on the porch light, but it was obvious that no one was jimmying the lock of her front door. Unsure now whether she'd dreamed the whole thing, Helen lay back down on the sofa. And listened.

Again the panting . . . again the jiggling.

She sat back up. Someone was in the house. God in heaven. Someone was in the house.

"Helen? Dear? Are you home?"

Ah. "In here, Aunt Mary," Helen said, relieved. Of course someone was in the house. When you give your key to a kindly old aunt who lives in the apartment in the back bumpout, you can reasonably expect the aunt, sooner or later, to be in the house.

With soup. Into the room walked Helen's seventy-three-year-old relation, a gentle, gray-haired bundle of quirks and good intentions. "How're you feeling, dear?" the old woman asked, sitting next to Helen and patting her hand with her own veiny, wrinkled one. "I brought you something to clear your sinuses. It's on the stove, on low. You want me to bring you a bowl, dear?"

The soup fumes—aroma seemed too kind a word—were turning the corner just about then. "Gee, Aunt Mary, I don't know...," Helen said feebly. "What's in it?"

"This and that. Sauerkraut ... pigs' feet ... I fiddled with the recipe your Uncle Tadeusz taught me."

Tadeusz Grzybylek, a member of Salem's spirited Polish community, had wooed Helen's spinster aunt late in her life. No kids, but plenty of amazing food, had come out of the union.

Helen smiled wanly. "Only a taste. It doesn't have the blood of anything in it, does it?"

Her aunt gave her a little laughing pinch and said, "No, no, you're thinking of *czarnina*—duck soup. You just lie there, dear. I'll be right back."

With a mixture of affection and dread, Helen watched the elderly woman scurry out of the room for a bowl of her brew. Aunt Mary had given up a life of her own to raise Helen after Helen's mother—Aunt Mary's sister—had died; Helen owed her everything. Now that Uncle Tadeusz was gone, it gave Helen great pleasure to give her aunt the back apartment and let her have the run of the house.

Nonetheless, she could do without the soup.

Helen sighed. It came out in a shudder, and that reminded her of the deeply distressing sound of panting that she thought she'd heard. The jiggling—okay, that was because Aunt Mary's cataracts made the back-door keyhole hard for her to find. But the sound of panting—that, Helen couldn't explain.

Ironically, the panting could just as easily have been of someone in the throes of passion as someone in the throes of distress. Helen ought to know. In bed with Hank, she used to make the sound regularly. And yet . . . no. This sound had been too full of pain. Something deep inside Helen had responded the way a mother would . . .

Becky! Had something happened to Becky? Helen jumped up, terrified that she'd had some kind of premonition. At that instant the phone rang.

It was Becky, calling to ask whether her mother was interested in a set of Liz Claiborne sweats at seventy-five off.

"Thanks, no, I'm all set," said Helen, buckling with relief onto the sofa. "And, Becky? Please drive carefully. You know how intense you get when you're yakking with your pals."

"*Yes*, Mother," Becky said in an exaggerated way.

Obviously her girlfriends were near the phone: Helen heard giggling. Becky said good-bye and Helen, reassured, was left waiting for her medicine.

Aunt Mary came bearing a galleried brass tray on which a bowl of *kapusniak* sat like a queen's coronet. Helen made herself sit up straight to receive the tray across her lap, then took the round-shaped spoon, part of the old set her aunt had foisted on her when she moved in, and skimmed a bit of clear liquid into it. "Here goes nothing," she said with a game smile.

Aunt Mary sat perched on the edge of one of the corduroy chairs and shook her head. "You look so pale. I don't know . . . maybe you need more protein. Say what you will about *czarnina*, it's high in that, at least. It would put some color in those cheeks."

"Don't even think about it," said Helen, shuddering. The one time her aunt had made a batch of *czarnina*, a neighbor had called the police.

"She was overreacting," said Aunt Mary, reading Helen's mind.

Helen grimaced. "Well, what do you expect when you throw a quart of blood in a vat of water? It doesn't smell like anything normal."

Aunt Mary gave a little tuck to her single long gray braid and said with great dignity, "I'm glad your uncle Tadeusz isn't here to hear you say that about Polish cuisine. He'd be very hurt."

And so, obviously, was Aunt Mary. Her pale brown eyes were glazed over in tears and her rather small, once pretty mouth was trembling in distress.

"I'm sorry," Helen said at once, closing her eyes. "It's this stupid, stupid headache. I wish it would go away."

"Maybe that's what I should do," her aunt said, pushing herself up from the chair with a sigh. She gave the bowl of soup an appraising look, then shifted her gaze to her suffering niece. "Eat it," she said, and then she left.

Helen, feeling honor-bound, finished the serving and then lay back down, closed her eyes, and dreamed of ducks being hunted, their quacks dissolving into panting sounds as hunters with bloodied hands wrung their necks.

She woke with a start at the sound of the front door opening.

"Mom!" yelled Becky up the stairs. "It's me! How're you feeling?"

Helen sat up, groggy and tentative. "I'm in here, Becky. And I'm feeling . . . better," she said, surprised and pleased that the headache had retreated, if ever so slightly.

Becky came in—mercifully free of shopping bags—and Helen smiled a greeting. "I guess that last decongestant kicked in," she explained. "What time is it?"

"Eight-thirty. So what's going on?" asked Becky, flopping tiredly into one of the corduroy chairs. Obviously she expected her mother to answer "Nothin' much."

But the death of Linda Byrne was uppermost in Helen's mind. She related the call that Russell had taken, then said, "I feel unbelievably bad about it."

"Yeah . . . I can see. I'm surprised you didn't notice something in the obituaries," Becky added. "You always read them."

"Ah, but not this week," Helen realized. "It's been so crazy, I've hardly had time to scan the headlines."

She went to the butler's pantry and fished out the week's copies of the *Evening News* from the iron recycle rack, then dumped them in a pile on the claw-footed, round oak table in the center of the kitchen. She pulled the chain on the red, green, and gold stained-glass lamp above the table, throwing light that was more quaint than bright across the walls and high ceiling of the carefully restored room.

Becky came in with the big brass tray and left it on one of the marble counters—Helen's one indulgence when they redid the kitchen—and pulled out a carved-back oak chair.

"Why do you want to look her up, anyway?" Becky asked, dropping her chin onto the cupped palms of her hands. "Isn't that a little ghoulish?"

"When you're older, you'll understand," Helen said, flipping through Monday's obituaries without success. She picked up Tuesday's paper and went straight to the deaths, then sucked in her breath. "Here it is. It's true, then," she added rather stupidly.

She read the headline aloud—" 'Linda Byrne, thirty-two; former art teacher' "—and then scanned the rest. "Born in Geneva . . . graduated from Wellesley with a degree in art; taught at Boston College before she was married . . . member of a couple of art societies . . . survived by her husband . . . one child . . . a mother and two brothers in Geneva . . . a couple of nieces and nephews. *Huh.* It's not much to go on."

"What do you mean, 'to go on'?"

"Hmm?" Helen looked up in a daze. "Did I say that?"

"Mom. Get a grip," said Becky, laughing. She slid the paper over to her side of the table and studied the obituary. "Y'know, I think I've seen this name Nathaniel Byrne somewhere," she added, tapping her multiringed fingers on the page.

"The husband? Can't say I have," Helen decided.

"Yeah ... wait ... somewhere in the house ... I know!" Becky dashed out of the kitchen, went flying up the stairs, stomped across Helen's tiny but efficient home office overhead, and came roaring down again.

"Ta-dah! 'Nathaniel Byrne, Mutual Fund Manager of the Year,' " Becky said, holding up an investment magazine that Helen subscribed to but never had time to read.

"If he's the same Nathaniel Byrne," said Helen. She took the magazine and studied the cover of the magazine. "And anyway, since when are you interested in mutual funds?"

"Who cares about those? *He's* what caught my eye when I dumped the mail on your desk. It was like, when you walk into a supermarket and you see John-John's picture on the cover of *People?* It was like that. You can't help but look."

She was right. The Fund Manager of the Year was a dark-haired, steely eyed, square-chinned, unsmiling male who wasn't the least bit shy about looking straight into the camera and daring it to expose his inner self. His brows were thick and straight, his hair, attractively unruly. He was wearing a heavy wool shirt, khakis, and work boots and was sitting on a massive tree stump in an autumn setting, with his thighs pulled up to his chest and his arms slung loosely across the knees. A gold band adorned his left ring finger and, if Helen wasn't mistaken, that was a Rolex on his left wrist. He was the kind of man that women described as intense rather than hunky.

Near the tree stump was a woodpile with an ax leaning against it. Helen took in the man, took in the setting, and shook her head. "Wrong guy. The Byrne I heard about is a workaholic who ignores his family, flies his own plane, and is never at home. He wouldn't have the time or inclination to chop wood. Besides, look at his boots. They're brand-new."

"Mom, you are so naive," Becky said, rolling her eyes. "The ax and shoes are just props. If he's Fund Manager of the Year, obviously he can afford to get his wood split and stacked. Look him up, look him up," she urged. "See if they say he's from Salem."

Helen did as she was told. The cover article was long, and it finished up, as all such pieces do, with a few scraps of biographical information. "For goodness' sake," Helen said. "You're right. It says he lives on a 'prestigious street in Salem.' "

"Oh, like he's gonna live on a slummy one? What else? Let me read it."

"When I'm done," said Helen, pulling the cover away from her daughter's pesty, hovering grip. She read aloud: *"Byrne and his wife, Linda Bellingame Byrne, to whom he's been married for eight years, have one three-year-old daughter and another child on the way. Mrs. Byrne, an art historian who lectures occasionally in the area, abandoned a professorship at Boston College when her husband began putting in eighty-hour weeks after his promotion to manager of the Columbus Fund. In the five years since then, they have taken no vacations.*

" 'Nathaniel Byrne has made a lot of money for a lot of investors,' Mrs. Byrne told us. 'After the new baby's born, I'm hoping that they let the poor man have a week or two off now and then,' she said with a teasing smile at her husband.

"So she was pregnant," Helen mused. "How sad." She

added, "It's funny that the article lets her have the last word."

Becky, meanwhile, was impressed. "This is so cool. You know this guy, Mom!"

"Number one, I don't know him," Helen reminded her daughter. "And number two, there's nothing cool about it. The timing of this is tragic."

With the ruthless indifference of youth, Becky shrugged and said, "It sounds like Linda Byrne wouldn't've been all that impressed by an article about him anyway."

"Rebecca! A little less cynicism, please."

Brought up short by her mother's sharpness, Becky defended herself. "I only said what you just told me, Mom. Why are you taking this so seriously?"

"I don't know," said Helen, staring at the man on the cover.

What she did know was that her headache had retreated even further. She lifted her hand to the back of her head, just to make sure her head was still there. Yep. And hardly any pain.

Well, for Pete's sake, she thought with a bemused smile. Was it the soup, the pill—or the sight of his face?

Chapter 3

*H*elen went to bed immediately after Russ came home (twelve minutes late, which fell within an acceptable range of defiance). She'd read the entire article about Nathaniel Byrne, twice; but except for a few principles for making sound investments—and the revelation that Linda Byrne had been pregnant—the story had left Helen none the wiser about either Nathaniel Byrne or his wife.

In the meantime, one thought, and one thought only, rolled back and forth through her head: *I wonder what she died of?*

Obviously not the headache. The headache must have been a symptom. But of what? Linda Byrne had not sounded like someone near death, that's all there was to it. On the other hand, she'd sounded in a desperate hurry. So maybe she knew.

And yet Peaches hadn't sent off any such signals. But then, Peaches would be discreet, of course. As for Linda Byrne's husband . . . it's true, he'd been home early that day, which was odd for an eighty-hour-a-week man. Had he known that his young wife was dying? Would he have let a stranger come to the house if he had?

I wonder what she died of?

Half-asleep, half-ruminating, Helen burrowed more deeply into the down pillows that she liked to pile high on her four-poster bed and pulled the blue plaid comforter more tightly around her shoulders. She always kept the room cool for sleeping—a throwback to Hank's preference—but tonight she'd cracked the window way too wide. A damp breeze was blowing briskly from the northeast, foretelling another raw day.

In fact, the room felt extraordinarily clammy and cold. Far from being fresh and bracing, the air seemed dank, almost fishy, as if she were walking along a beach in the off-season rather than tucked in a cozy warm bed. She shivered under the covers, oddly repelled by the odor. Her house was not so close to the water that she could smell low tide; but low tide, with its washed-up seaweed and occasional dead fish, is what this smelled like. She wanted to close the window, but her limps seemed paralyzed with fatigue, her very thoughts frostbitten around the edges. *I wonder what she . . . ?*

A brain tumor?

Helen resolved to find out exactly how Linda Byrne died, and that made it easier, somehow, to fall asleep. But the respite didn't last long. Late in the night, when she was deep in sleep, she was roused by a high-pitched call that sounded like, "A fire, fire!"

Helen shot up in bed, heart pounding, adrenaline surging. What in God's name was *that?* A screech, a bark, a cry? Before she had time to figure it out, she heard it again, only farther away: a not-quite-human, not-quite-animal sound. Whatever it was, it wasn't someone yelling fire.

Eyes leaden with sleep, she listened for a moment, then fell back on her elbows, waiting. After a little while she heard it again, from yet another direction. *Something with wings,* she decided at last. Raccoons, even cats, weren't fast enough to cover that much ground. Another owl? Salem seemed suddenly overrun with them.

Snuggling back under the covers, still too cold to make a sprint for the window, Helen tried to calm her nerves. But images and thoughts, all of them disturbing, kept pounding away at her determination to drop off into blissful, headache-free sleep.

Nathaniel Byrne. She remembered vividly the sound of his voice as he yelled down to Peaches to get upstairs— the voice, hoarse and urgent, that seemed such an odd fit with the cooly confident financier posed on the stump. Helen remembered the voice so well that, for the first time, she realized that it had held more shock than surprise, more anger than grief. It was not the voice of a man expecting his wife to die at any moment of some terminal disease.

Nathaniel Byrne. Helen's heart went out even more to little Katherine.

By morning Helen's headache was back, worse than ever. It didn't seem possible. It took all the strength she possessed to get out of bed and on with the day. She was making coffee and halfheartedly arguing with her son over whether or not he could go to a performance by a really vicious rock group when they were interrupted by the arrival of Helen's aunt.

The elderly woman took one look at her niece and clucked in distress. "It didn't work?" she asked, apparently incredulous.

"For a while it did," Helen said, managing a limp smile. She pulled her terry-cloth robe a little more tightly around her and padded over to the fridge for cream. "But then I guess the potion wore off."

"You'll have to get your head x-rayed then," Aunt Mary decided without any more ado. "It could be a brain tumor."

"Ma, can I go or not?" asked Russ, annoyed by the interruption. "Mickey hasta know to buy tickets."

"I'll tell you what," said Helen, ignoring her son. "I'll have my brain tumor looked at if you have your cataracts fixed. Do you want some coffee?"

"I don't have cataracts," said Aunt Mary stubbornly. "Just half a cup."

"Ma-a," whined Russ.

"One of these days you're going to fall down the steps and break a hip. Then where will you be?" asked Helen over her shoulder as she half-filled a mug. "Careful. Hot," she said, sliding the mug across the table to her aunt.

"I wish you wouldn't treat me like a three-year-old," said Aunt Mary, working up a head of steam of her own.

"I wouldn't, if you'd act like an adult. But this *thing* you have about real doctors—"

"Ma, I wish someone would listen to me because—"

"Hi, everybody," said Becky as she strolled, yawning, into the kitchen. "You making breakfast, Mom, or are we on our own today?"

"On your own, I guess. I got up late."

"Okay," Becky said with a shrug. She pulled a box of Cheerios down from the cupboard. Moby, the stray cat they'd found hanging around The Open Door, heard the rattle of cereal and hopped onto the marble slab, where he began to whine piteously for a handout.

"Becky, how many times do I have to tell you," said Helen wearily, "no cats on the counter."

Aunt Mary came to the poor black cat's defense. "He goes on the counter when you're not in the room, anyway, dear. Why fight a hopeless battle?"

"Ma, even Moby comes before me. All I want is—"

"Some Cheerios?" asked Becky. "Here, twerp, have a handful," she said, threatening the box over his head.

"Screw you, Becky," said Russ, shoving her arm away.

"Russell Evett! Is that how your mother raised you?"

"Why don't you ask her," snapped Russell to his great-aunt.

"*Stop it!* Everyone just—*shut up!*"

Helen hurled the words at her family like a hand grenade, blasting them all into stunned silence. Immediately she realized that she'd never told any of them—much less all of them—to shut up before. Not in the lean years; not in the sad years; not in the first six days of the headache. But today, Saturday, the seventh day . . .

"I have to call a doctor," Helen said abruptly, pushing back tears of remorse. She turned on her heel and walked out of the kitchen.

"Well, Mrs. Evett, I really don't know what to tell you," said Dr. Thomas Jervis. The ear, nose, and throat specialist whom Helen had begun to see two weeks earlier was a kindly man of late middle age, heavily set, with twinkling blue eyes and thick gray hair that would someday turn white, at which time he'd be able to moonlight in malls as Santa Claus.

His looks alone made him easy to trust; but more than that, he had come highly recommended, which is why Helen was so dismayed when he confessed to being baffled.

"As we know, nothing in your medical history suggests a predisposition to headache," he said. "Nor did the preliminary X-rays turn up anything. Now that we have the MRI results, you can definitely dismiss those fears of a brain tumor," he added with a gently ironic smile. "I'd consider blaming your headache on a 'sick' building, but you say you've worked there for years with no ill effects."

Sitting across from her at his paper-strewn desk, the physician rubbed his chin thoughtfully. "You also say you're not stressed, but—have you had counseling since your husband's death?"

Helen shook her head gingerly; the pain was too intense for her to do it vigorously. "I'm not stressed," she said once again. "The preschool's doing wonderfully; I have no money problems. My daughter's a treasure and my son— well, he's fourteen. What can I say?

"It's true I have no love life," she added, fiddling with the handbag in her lap before she looked up again. "But that doesn't mean I'm sexually frustrated," she said forthrightly.

Dr. Jervis nodded, then said, "Since you watch your diet, don't smoke, and exercise regularly, it's my opinion that psychotherapy is the most logical avenue for you to pursue. I wish you'd think about it. You sound as though you have a lot on your plate. You could be more frazzled than you know, young lady," he said with a fatherly smile.

"I don't need a psychologist," Helen said simply.

Dr. Jervis sighed. "You've lived through a horrible experience, Helen. There's no shame in wanting to deal with it."

Helen shook her head, convinced that a shrink was the wrong way to go.

"In the meantime," said the physician without arguing further, "I'm going to prescribe something for the headache." He slid a prescription pad in front of him, then scribbled something on it as he said, "We'll start with a very low dose; I want you to read the precautions carefully. If you have any numbness, unusual coldness, or pain in your fingers, let me know at once. Do you know whether you're allergic to ergotamine?"

Shocked, Helen cried, "Oh my God!" and stood up so suddenly that she knocked over her chair. "How dare you?" she shouted, slamming her purse on the astonished doctor's desk. "Are you insane?"

Unaccountably, she burst into tears. "How could you!" she croaked, and then she ran out of his consulting room, through the waiting room, past the receptionist, down four flights of stairs without even thinking about waiting for an elevator, and out to her car.

Helen was shivering too violently to line the key up with the ignition slot; only then did she realize that she'd left her coat behind. Somehow she got the car started and the heat going. Utterly shocked and dismayed by her bizarre behavior, she sat parked in the lot of the medical building for a full ten minutes, too angry—and mortified—to go back for her coat. Once she stopped shivering, she put the car into gear.

Once she stopped shivering, she realized her headache was gone. She was convinced it was for good.

"Aunt Mary? These are for you. I'm *so* sorry for the way I've been acting. But that's over now."

Helen handed her aunt an armful of scented pink tulips and kissed the surprised old woman on her fuzzy cheek. "It's gone. The headache's gone," she explained, beaming. "Dr. Jervis said there was nothing wrong with me. It must've been psychosomatic—because ten minutes after he told me that, I felt fine."

She'd sent a second batch of tulips with a note of apology to Dr. Jervis, who seemed far too kind actually to have her hunted down and arrested for assault.

That left Becky and Russell and poor uncoddled Moby. Helen made a double batch of chocolate-chip cookies for the kids that night, humming the whole while, and offered the cat a mound of chopped liver.

It felt so good to feel good again.

Chapter 4

𝒫eaches Bartholemew gave Katherine a glass of warm milk, read her *The Cat in the Hat*, and sang her an extralong lullaby. For the thirtieth day in a row, there would be no kiss from Mommy tonight, no snuggle-buggle in the rocking chair with her. A peck from Daddy, once again, would have to do.

"Daddy will be right in to say good-night," said Peaches, tucking in the bathed and sweet-smelling child with a kiss of her own. She turned down the Snow White lamp next to the crib, and the room dissolved into soft shadows and glowing light. "Night-night, sweetie."

Katie rolled her head to face the wall. She blinked once, twice. And that was all.

Leaving the door ajar, Peaches tiptoed away and stood outside the nursery, relocated on the day after the funeral from the third to the second floor. She waited long enough to be sure that Katie wasn't going to try escaping from her room again—lately the possibility that the child would hurt herself was very real—and then she went downstairs to tell Nathaniel Byrne, working in the library, that his daughter was in bed.

It had been the father's practice to kiss his daughter

good-night before she got ready for bed, but after his wife's death, Nathaniel Byrne moved the kiss to after Katie was all tucked in. That way, he told Peaches, her father would be the last thing Katie saw before she slept. It never occurred to him to take over the bedtime routine altogether.

Peaches knocked softly on the heavy paneled door. When there was no response, she knocked again.

"Yeah," came the preoccupied voice on the other side of the door. "Come in."

She opened the door part of the way. Nathaniel Byrne was parked behind a stack of reading material piled high on a Regency mahogany library desk that sat, flanked by leather armchairs, alongside a gas-fueled fireplace burning with a small, dull flame.

Peaches had been at the Central Park Zoo watching Katie on the day the Byrnes won a bidding war at Christie's for the desk, one that had topped out at twenty-six thousand and change.

"Nat had it coming," an exhilarated Linda had said to Peaches afterward. "That was our cancelled trip to Aruba—and, of course, the cost of the guilt trip I laid on top of that."

So there he was, twenty-six thousand dollars poorer and apparently none the wiser: handsome as a movie star and brilliant at buying and selling stocks, but dumb as a doughnut when it came to family.

Peaches waited, as she always did, for him to break from the spell of his charts and reports. She admired that in him, that ability to lock on to a subject with such intensity; it's how you got things done.

"Ah . . . Peaches," he said at last. "What's up?" He pitched his pen on the glossy publication that was spread out before him, took off his reading glasses and rubbed his eyes tiredly, and ran his hands through his thick dark hair.

"Katie's all tucked in," Peaches said softly. "Just wanted you to know."

"So early?" He looked at his watch and muttered in surprise. "Uh-oh. Or not. Okay. Just give me a couple of minutes to finish running this screen . . ." He began tapping the keyboard of a computer humming at his elbow.

"Just so you know," she repeated, smiling.

He looked up and returned her smile with a remarkably boyish one of his own, and Peaches pulled the door carefully closed. After that she went to her private quarters—which had been relocated to the second floor along with the nursery—and opened the book she'd been studying for the past couple of weeks, an in-depth study of stock-market theories. She was halfway through a chapter on the Elliot Wave when she heard the telltale creak of the top stair at the second-floor landing.

Finally, she thought, and went back to her book.

A couple of minutes later, there was a soft knock at her door.

"Peaches? Are you dressed?"

She got up from the tufted damask chaise that sat in front of a pretty, unlit fireplace and opened the door to him. "Is everything all right?" she asked, reflecting the concern on her employer's face.

He didn't bother to answer her question. "Can you come downstairs?" he asked quietly.

She went out into the hall with him and they walked in silence over the magnificent Oriental runner that spilled down the steps to the main hall, itself highlighted by a large and priceless Persian rug that had been in the family for generations. As she expected, Katie's father did not lead her to the library—reserved exclusively for his work—but suggested instead that they go into the music room.

The music room was Katie's favorite: It was the sunniest in the house, and it was where she and her mother had sung

Raffi songs at the piano. Ever since the funeral, the child had more or less camped out there; the evening's toys were still scattered at one end of the room. Automatically Peaches began picking them up, but Katie's father said, "Never mind those now."

He went over to a built-in, glass-front cupboard that he'd had the cook convert to a liquor cabinet. His idea had been to have his nightly cocktail in the music room while Katie played with Peaches before dinner; but that plan, like all the others he'd devised to spend more time with his daughter, had gone by the board. He *was* managing to get home earlier since the death of his wife—but inevitably he took his briefcase straight to the library and didn't emerge until halfway through dinner. If he emerged at all.

"Anything to drink?" he asked Peaches, taking down a decanter of whiskey. Peaches declined and he half-filled a tumbler for himself, then began pacing the room. He was clearly upset, which only made him look more handsome: Intensity sat well on his chiseled face.

He paused to down his drink, then went back to the makeshift bar. "Katie was asleep—obviously," he said as he poured himself a refill. "The time got away from me. Did you know that she keeps a dog-eared photo of Linda under her pillow?" he asked. "You had to know about it."

Peaches, addressing his back, said, "I didn't see how it could cause any harm, Mr. Byrne."

He turned around and gave her a wry look. "For god's sake, Peaches, call me Nat. You and Linda were thick as thieves. I don't see why I have to continue to be given this formal treatment."

"No, sir," Peaches said evenly. Her cheeks flushed pink; she looked away.

"Well, whatever," he said quickly. "If it makes you feel uncomfortable." He came over to the cushy, slipcovered sofa where she was ensconced and dropped into the Queen

Anne wing chair opposite. "Katie was sucking her thumb," he said as he leaned forward with his forearms on his thighs, his hands cradling the tumbler. "Did she used to suck her thumb?" He was surprisingly intent on the answer.

Peaches hesitated, then said, "Not before—"

"*Damnit,*" he said, with a sharp nod of his head. "I should have seen this coming. I can lose myself in my work, but what's a three-year-old supposed to do? My instinct was to keep her home, keep her safe . . . away from prying questions."

He didn't take his eyes from Peaches's face. "You can tell me this if anyone can, Peaches: Have I screwed up by keeping her isolated?"

He looked so unsure of himself that Peaches allowed herself a reassuring smile. "No. Keeping Katie around familiar faces was the right thing to do—for a while. The trouble is, there aren't that many faces here," she said, gently alluding to his chronic absence. "With all the best intentions in the world—"

"I'm blowing it. I can see that." He put his drink down and fell back in his chair, deflated. "I thought that bringing my work home would make the difference. So much for the fax-and-modem age. You still have to read; to concentrate. Tell that to a three-year-old," he said in a rueful mutter.

"At that age she needs stimulation . . . engagement," Peaches said gently.

He dropped his head back on the armchair and closed his eyes, then sighed. "I'm not shipping her off to Switzerland, no matter what her grandmother says."

He didn't care for his mother-in-law, Peaches knew. Linda used to shrug and say, "His choice," and go off herself to visit her mother. It suited them both.

"Too bad *my* folks are gone," he mused, still without opening his eyes. "They'd have gotten a kick out of Katie.

She's so much like her mother. Oddly enough, they were nuts about Linda.'' He smiled dryly and said, ''I remember one time Linda was shopping with my mother on Boylston Street when some punk grabbed my mother's purse and took off. Damned if Linda didn't take off after the creep, screaming for help the whole time. A couple of good Samaritans helped her tackle the guy—Boston's like that—and she got written up in the *Globe* as a feisty citizen. She never showed you the clipping?''

Peaches said, ''She never even mentioned it.''

''No. She wouldn't,'' he decided. ''Linda never had time for looking back. For that matter, she never bothered about the future, either; she lived entirely in the present . . .''

His voice turned suddenly dark and cold and furious. ''. . . which is probably why she didn't give a shit about consequences!''

He snorted and said bitterly, ''Sorry. It's the whiskey.''

With a visible effort he pulled out of his foul mood and sat up straight. ''You're a good listener, Peach,'' he said with a tight smile. ''I don't know where Katie and I would be without you.''

Color flooded her cheeks again. She looked down, then made her eyes meet his. ''Don't hold those last strange months against her. Even if she wasn't the perfect wife . . .''

Peaches paused to compose herself and went on. ''Even if she wasn't, she was still a devoted mother to Katie. That's what we ought to focus on,'' she said softly. A tear broke loose and rolled down one cheek. ''We have Katie.''

Nathaniel Byrne's jaw settled into a firm straight line, a kind of underline to the resolve in his sea blue eyes. ''Yes,'' he reminded himself. ''Katie.''

He took a deep breath, apparently to clear his head. ''So: preschool, do you think?'' he asked in a different voice altogether. "Can we risk it? Katie should be okay there—probably. Wouldn't you say?"

Peaches had to smile; her employer could be charming in his helplessness when he wanted to.

"Katie would be fine," she said. "Maybe I can even put in a few hours as a teacher's aide. Sometimes the schools allow it. I assume you want to try to get into The Open Door preschool."

"If that's the one Linda was so keen on."

"I still have the application somewhere. I'll call Helen Evett first thing tomorrow; I hope we're not too late."

She added, "They may still want to test Katie—although, maybe not. Mrs. Evett saw samples of Katie's work when she was here."

Katie's father became indignant. "For God's sakes, we're not talking about med school here. Besides, Katie's as bright as a new copper penny. It's obvious."

Peaches smiled and added, "You also have to realize that Mrs. Evett may insist that someone visit the facility before she accepts Katie."

"Whatever it takes," he said, resigned. "Just tell me when and where."

"I will."

Relieved to be done with the subject, he glanced at his watch. "Huh. It's not all that late," he decided. "I think I'll work a little longer."

He excused himself with a quick smile and was halfway down the hall when he backtracked and ducked his head through the door of the music room. "Peach? You will come with us, won't you?"

Peaches, cradling an assortment of stuffed toys and plastic parts, laughed and said, "Wild horses couldn't keep me away."

* * *

Helen Evett was in the middle of an argument with her plumber when the phone rang.

It was Peaches Bartholemew, who accepted Helen's belated, awkward condolences with reassuring grace. "I'll be sure to pass on your sympathy to Mr. Byrne," the nanny said. "It's awfully nice of you to be so concerned about Katie; I can see why your preschool has a reputation for caring."

"But I really do mean it—truly," Helen insisted, somehow managing to imply that the preschool's reputation was a fraud. Frustrated by the sound of her own babble, she added, "I can't begin to tell you how . . . how upset I was."

"Yes . . . of course," said Peaches vaguely, sounding a bit put off by the fierceness in Helen's voice. "You knew Linda, then?"

"Well, no."

"I see," said Peaches, although clearly she did not. She cut short the confusion by explaining her mission: to get Katie into The Open Door preschool. "I hope we're not too late," she added, almost as an afterthought.

In fact, registration was full and there was a waiting list. No matter. "You're in luck; we have one space left," Helen lied. She made a decision on the spot to squeeze Katie in, even though it meant exceeding the limit she herself had imposed on class size at The Open Door.

Ashamed but unrepentant, Helen added that she had only one requirement, and that was that an adult responsible for Katie come to see the preschool, preferably when it was in session.

Peaches said, "Mr. Byrne has promised to be there."

Yeah, right, thought Helen. Aloud she said, "That would be best, under the circumstances."

They agreed to meet on the day after next and Peaches hung up, leaving Helen free to return to her battle with the plumber.

He was a big man with red cheeks and wiry hair, a long-time employee of the outfit who'd redone the baths during the makeover of Helen's house two years earlier. She was pleased that Tony had been the one sent to solve her maddening mystery. She remembered him as being more approachable than the others, more inclined to explain why there was never enough water pressure upstairs and why the sink backsiphoned into the dishwasher every once in a while.

But that was then, and this was now.

"I'm tellin' you, Mrs. Evett, it's not the pipes you hear knockin' all the time. I've just bled every last one of the radiators, and look," he said, handing her a paper cup. "Practically no water. It's not the pipes. I'm tellin' you."

"Well, *something's* keeping me up every night," said Helen in an equally testy voice. She was tired and irritable after two weeks of interrupted sleep. What good was it to be over the sinus headache if she was going to be awake all night anyway?

Shaking his head, the plumber chewed on his lip and mulled the possibilities while he stared at his shoes. "Wood can shrink and expand with temperature changes, especially in spring and fall." He looked up at her from under bushy eyebrows. "You could be hearing beams."

From outer space, you mean. Plainly he didn't believe her. And in fact, the house had been predictably quiet the whole time he was there.

Tony turned to Russ, who'd ventured out of his room in search of milk and cookies. "Do you hear anything in your bedroom at night?" he asked the boy.

Russell—who was singlehandedly supporting half the dairy co-ops in New England—shrugged as he filled a sixteen-ounce tumbler with milk. "Nope."

The plumber tried another tack. "So it would be—where?—in the livin' room that you hear these noises?"

"Nope. I don't hear that stuff."

"Why are you asking *him*?" Helen said, rescuing the Oreo bag from her son and handing him four cookies. "He walks around under a set of headphones all day."

Not that she'd given the boy a choice. The latest rap group whose spell he'd fallen under was so loud, so vile, so guaranteed to put Helen's teeth on edge, that she'd bought him a top-of-the-line personal CD player that he wore strapped to his hip at home.

In any case, Tony didn't have any answers, so Helen gave the joyless plumber a soothing smile and said, "I'm sure you solved the problem, whatever it was," and asked him to send her the bill.

But that night as she lay sleepless in her bed, waiting for the sounds she knew would come, Helen gave in to a bout of self-pity.

If Hank were here, she thought, *I wouldn't care about the sounds. If Hank were here we'd make cute jokes about ghosts in the attic. But Hank isn't here.*

Unless?

No. Hank was gone forever. Too stoic ever to indulge in false hopes, Hank had always said, "When you're dead, you're dead." It used to distress Helen whenever he said that, because she knew that sooner or later one of them would be dead and one of them would not. She'd wanted to believe that somehow they'd be able to bridge the great divide of mortality. And yet here she lay, cold and alone, without Hank; without hope.

She fell asleep in a state of depression, fully expecting to be awakened at three A.M. She wasn't disappointed. The first knock, barely audible and yet somehow thunderous, woke her instantly. In the dark she listened without moving her head on the pillow, without breathing, as she waited for the sound to evolve into the next phase.

There it was: the jiggle. After the knock always came

the jiggle. It sounded exactly as if someone were trying a door, finding it locked, then rattling the doorknob back and forth impatiently. Whether the someone was locked in or out—that, Helen could not say.

There was another long pause, as she knew there would be, and then came the knock . . . the short pause . . . and the jiggle. Over and over and over again, starting at three in the morning, Helen had endured the maddening sequence of sounds night after night after night. The plumber had been her last hope.

In a deep and mysterious part of her soul, Helen understood that the sounds were unrelated to the pipes and radiators. In the last two weeks she'd turned the heat up, down, and off, with every possible variation between, until the kids had begun to beg for mercy. Becky had accused her of entering premature menopause. Russ had threatened to move in with a friend. Everyone was miserable, Helen, most of all—because she was the only one who could hear the sounds.

A couple of nights earlier, when the heat was off entirely, she'd actually dragged Becky into her bedroom to bear witness. It made Helen groan with pain even to think about it.

"Listen!" Helen had hissed to her sleepy daughter. "Can't you hear it?"

Becky, a shivering waif in her nightgown and bare feet, had stood in the near dark with her head bowed and her hair tumbling over her eyes and had mumbled, "Mom . . . please . . . I've told you."

And then Helen had grabbed her daughter by the arm and swung her around to face first one wall, then another. "There! Now—there! That jiggle! And then the knock!" she'd insisted. When Becky had continued to droop and shake her head, Helen had grabbed her other arm and cried, "What's the matter with you? Are you deaf?"

And Becky, the laid-back, well-adjusted, go-with-the-flow darling of her mother's eye, had broken down into a fit of sobbing. "Don't do this, Mom, don't do this," she'd said through her tears. "You're scaring me. Please . . . don't!"

The next morning, despite the futility of the gesture, Helen had called the plumbers.

Chapter 5

On Thursday Helen made her coffee extra strong, put on a simple lavender dress that she liked to think of as subtle, and resolved again to put the noises of the night behind her. Squirrels, the echo of a ticking clock, a demented woodpecker—the tappings could have been any of those things.

The fact that Becky hadn't been able to hear the sounds meant nothing. Who's to say whether her hearing was as good as her mother's?

In any case today was not the day to be tired and dragging. Nathaniel Byrne—or, more likely, his proxy Peaches Bartholemew—was bringing little Katie to school during the last class. It was absolutely critical to Helen that they be impressed. She felt as nervous as a schoolgirl herself, with a stomach full of butterflies and a heart that wouldn't stay quiet.

What if they didn't like the facility? What if they decided to shop around a bit? What would she do without Katie?

She wanted Katie there.

Helen blinked at the thought. Where had it come from? She didn't need Katie, really; as it was, it was going to be awkward to bump one of the twelve children already accepted—probably that bratty Merielle who'd wedged open the paint closet during Helen's interview with her mother.

So why the anxiety? Why was it that as soon as someone mentioned the name Byrne, Helen felt an unease that amounted to queasiness? She might have pondered the question forever if the irate driver behind her hadn't blasted her out of her reverie with one long lean on his horn.

She turned the Volvo quickly into the parking lot of the preschool and pulled into one of the reserved slots. There were many others available for parents dropping off and picking up; space was no problem at The Open Door.

The preschool operated out of a charming nineteenth-century brick building that once had been a small bank. Helen, catching a wave of renovation that was sweeping over historic downtown Salem, had timed her purchase well. Despite the fact that bringing the building up to code had not been cheap—and even without the dollar value of the school's reputation—the place was now worth far more than she and Hank had invested in it.

Even if it weren't, Helen would still love it. She and Hank had sunk so much of their time and emotions into their little brick bank. Together they had hired the contractors, working side by side with them sometimes; together they had prowled tree farms and nurseries for Arbor Day sales and midwinter specials. The Catawba rhododendrons, barely up to her knees once their root balls had been buried, now grazed the six-foot wood fence that separated the north side of the property from the street. The mountain laurels, the junipers, the replanted Christmas trees—every one of them had a story to tell, and she loved them all for the memories of them.

Helen wished she could let Hank know that his favorite mountain laurel, the red one, had managed to survive that blistering summer after all. It was now as bushy and bud-covered as the pink and the white ones, thanks to Hank's skill and patience. The wish to tell him was surprisingly sharp—as if she suddenly realized she'd left the iron on. With a start, Helen realized that it was April first.

The anniversary.

She sighed and tried to shake herself free of the memory of it, at least until after school, and hurried up the flagstone path that led from the parking area to the attractive main entrance, set diagonally across one of the front corners of the building.

She slipped a key through the lock of the plate-glass door topped by an attractive Palladian window and stepped inside to a cheery reception area dotted with bright-colored chairs and low-hung posters of fairy tale characters and— far more interesting to Helen—samples of the children's latest art projects. The Little Mermaid was all very well; but little Davey Mersten's sense of color was nothing less than sublime.

Disengaging the alarm, Helen walked past the huge steel vault that remained from the building's life as a bank and went directly to her office opposite the reception area. She scanned the messages that had come in after she'd left; with any luck, there'd be one from Merielle's mother wanting her deposit back.

Just the opposite: there were messages from two more eager-sounding parents of three-year-olds. Helen shook her head in wonder. Where were all the kids *coming* from?

"Yoo-hoo!" came a voice Helen knew well. "Who's in?"

"I'm in the office, Janet," said Helen to her long-time secretary. Janet Harken, now fifty-eight, had taken the job on the day her daughter and son-in-law had packed up their kids and moved to the West Coast. She needed surrogate grandkids, she'd told Helen, and she needed them fast.

It was a match made in heaven: Janet's office skills were good, her love for children, boundless. She was the one who stayed, if the late-afternoon person didn't show, when a parent was held up. She was the one who was first to notice if a child came in sad or sick or—on several depressing occasions—with suspicious bruises.

Nothing got past Janet. She was Helen's extra eyes and ears, a guardian angel at the gate of the preschool. Steady as a rock, Janet never got ill, angry, or flustered. In three short years she was planning to retire with her husband to California. Helen dreaded the day.

But for now she was in Helen's office, filling it with her usual aura of warmth and security. She was like a pair of soft mittens, a cup of hot tea. "You saw the messages?" she asked, unbuttoning her plain wool coat. "Where on earth will we put two more?"

"On the waiting list; it's all we can do," Helen answered, sighing.

"For goodness' sakes, why so glum?" asked Janet. "This means that word is really getting around about The Open Door."

"We're going to have to bump Merielle Hawkins," Helen confessed. "I may have to honor an earlier commitment I made," she added vaguely. "I'll know more later today."

"Merielle? Good," Janet said with a comically grim smile. "In that case, I won't have to padlock the paint locker." She folded her coat over her arm and gave Helen an appraising look.

"You look nice today," she said with her kindest smile. She knew very well what day April first was. "You have some color for a change. You got a good night's sleep, then? Finally?"

"Sure did," Helen lied. A little makeup had given had given her what a rotten night's sleep could not.

"So it was the pipes and not squirrels?"

"Apparently," said Helen, lying again.

"Huh. But why," Janet asked, "would the sounds return

every night at the same time? It doesn't make sense. You'd almost think—''

"It was air in the pipes," Helen said in a testy lie. She brought herself under control and said far more pleasantly, "Janet, be a dear and bring me Kristy Maylen's lesson plans for next week, would you? I want to see what kind of tie-in she's planned to the field trip."

With that, Helen closed the subject of the nighttime knocks and jiggles once and, she hoped, for all.

At three in the afternoon the little brick bank began to empty out. As usual at that time, the energy level was high: Excited children poured out of their classrooms bursting with Most Important News about their day, while harried mothers made themselves pause long enough to listen to their stories. Everywhere there was coming and going, laughing and calling, punctuated by sharp little reminders to hurry up, hurry up.

The children looked especially sweet because today was the day they'd had their photographs taken. Helen, substituting for a teacher, was explaining to Stephanie's mother why Stephanie was wearing emergency pants (she'd fallen partway into the toilet—after the photo, thank God—and her jumper had got wet.)

During the conversation, Helen chanced to look out the windows of the classroom and caught a glimpse of a black Porsche pulling into one of the reserved parking places. Since neither she nor any of her staff could afford a Porsche—and wouldn't pick black if they could—her curiosity was aroused. She said good-bye to Stephanie and her mother and waited to see who it was who could be so successful and still not be able to read two simple words: *Staff Only.*

Ah. He was taller, she saw, than the magazine photo of him sitting on the stump suggested, and he was dressed far more authoritatively in a dark business suit and a brightish tie that got lifted in the afternoon wind and plastered against his lapel. His hair was long enough to be tousled, though he didn't seem the tousleable type; she suspected he left it a little shaggy by design, to make himself seem more down to earth.

And he was late.

He went around to the other side of the car and opened the door for Peaches, who slid out of the low-slung seat with enviable grace and then unfastened Katherine from the backseat while her father glanced around, taking his measure of the place. After that, each of the adults took one of Katie's hands and the three—looking like an average Ralph Lauren ad—began walking toward the building.

Helen could have flagged them directly into the classroom; but she preferred that they come in through the rather grand entrance, so she went quickly around to her office, dodging little ones and their mothers along the way. Though she felt instinctively at an advantage on her own turf, she was amazed at the thunder of her heartbeat. It didn't seem like her own heart at all.

Too much caffeine, she decided as she whipped open the door of the closet-sized bathroom in her office and checked her hair and makeup in the oval mirror above the pedestal sink. Surprise: She didn't need the blusher after all; her cheeks looked downright feverish. But her black hair was smooth and straight, thanks to a recent cut, and her dress had managed to make it through the day without a speck of pee or paint on it. So far, so good.

But what if Katie doesn't know me? she realized in a sudden panic. *What then?*

Again she surprised herself. Why should Katie know her? Their only contact had been brief, and a month had passed since then. To Katie, Helen would seem like just another lady who was way, way taller than she was.

Helen took a deep breath. Katie had to know her, or she wasn't sure what she'd do.

She stepped into the hall in time to see Nathaniel Byrne get the door for Katie and Peaches. The child and her beautifully dressed nanny went through and, after holding the door for two mothers leaving with their kids, Katie's father stepped inside for his first impression.

Alas, his first impression was not the best impression. From out of nowhere chubby little Alexander Lagor, an impressionable three-year-old, ran up and ambushed him from the rear, screaming, "Stranger! Stranger!" and hurled his little metal Thomas The Tank Engine at him.

Nathaniel Byrne whirled and said, "What the devil—?"

By now Alexander had retreated behind his mother's skirts, still screaming at the top of his lungs and pointing at the interloper; it was far and away the child's most violent reaction to someone new. In the meantime one or two other kids began screaming in sympathy, like crows mobbing a hawk. The rest of the mothers, instinctively cautious, held their children's hands more tightly and gave Nathaniel Byrne a wide berth as they hurried out, throwing him hostile glances as they passed.

Nathaniel Byrne, coloring deeply, bent down and picked up the little blue train engine and began walking toward Alexander and his mother with it. "Your son seems to have dropped this," he said dryly.

Alexander's screams were rising by decibels and octaves; he was on the verge of true hysteria. Byrne dared not approach any more closely. He placed the toy carefully on the floor in front of the boy and his mother, stood up, and began walking away from them toward Peaches and his daughter.

"C'mon, Katie," he said abruptly, extending his hand to her. He glanced at the door.

Leaving. He was leaving and taking Katie with him.

"Mr. Byrne! Good heavens, you can't just go!" Helen called out to him. "Wait right there. Hi, Katie!" she added in her cheeriest voice, pivoting her hand back and forth at the child.

She ran up to Alexander's overprotective mother and after a short struggle was able to reassure her that Nathaniel Byrne wasn't really the bogeyman, despite the dark suit and the scowl. "He's just someone's father. Really, Mrs. Lagor," she added in an undertone, "we're going to have to discuss Alexander's fear of strangers. It's getting worse. Please call me tomorrow to arrange a time."

"My son is not afraid. He's . . . cautious," the mother said in a voice wound tight. "As he should be."

"Yes, but—please. Call me." Without waiting for her response, Helen turned to her thoroughly offended client.

There they were, face-to-face: Helen Evett, director of what she thought was the best darn preschool in Salem; and Nathaniel Byrne, who looked as if he'd just tripped and stumbled into the seventh circle of hell.

She stuck out her hand to him and said, "Hello, I'm Helen Evett," before Peaches had time to make the introduction.

Byrne was obviously still smarting from his treatment by little Alexander. "So this is The Open Door," he said as he watched the toddler being carried out, still sniffling, by his mother. "That means—what? That you take anyone, including baby psychopaths?"

Helen didn't approve of flippancy in front of little ones. She gave Katie a cheerful hello and then said in soft warning to Byrne, "Some children are more fearful than others. We don't belittle them for it."

Blue eyes—bluer even than Katie's—looked into her gray ones without remorse. "That kid needs work," Byrne said flatly.

"He needs reassurance. That's what we're here for."

Helen turned to Peaches with relief; here, at least, was a friendly face. The look in her eyes was as sympathetic as the half-amused smile on her lips. "Ignore the guy," she seemed to say. "What does *he* know?"

"Nice to see you again," Helen said, extending her hand to Katie's beautiful nanny.

"What a wonderful location you have! I love all the little ones' artwork," Peaches said, looking around her with pleasure. "Aren't the drawings fun, Katie?"

Katie, like all egocentric three-year-olds, could care less. It wasn't her own stuff that was hanging on the wall. She yawned and looked around without seeing.

The last of the mothers were straggling out; Helen couldn't help noticing how drawn they were to the strikingly attractive trio standing next to her. By far, the biggest draw of the three was Katie's dad. There was no shortage of attractive Mommies or adorable toddlers at the preschool; but to-die-for men like Nathaniel Byrne didn't walk through the open door of The Open Door every day.

In the meantime Byrne, hands in his pocket, seemed immersed in his own line of thought. "I mean, right now Katie is pretty outgoing," he said, oblivious to the mothers' stares. "But I'd hate to see her come out of preschool acting like—"

With a lazy nod toward the exit Alexander had just passed through, Byrne made it clear that he thought The Open Door could do more harm than good for Katie.

Helen's eyebrows went up ever so slightly. It was too ironic, giving Katie preferential treatment just to be told the school might be a bad influence on her.

"The subject of how toddlers should deal with strangers is a bit complex, Mr. Byrne," she said. "Perhaps now is not the best time to go into it."

She inclined her head toward Katie, who was hanging from Peaches's hand and pivoting on one foot as she swung her other arm in a wide arc for extra momentum. Everything about the child said bored, bored, bored.

"Fair enough," said Byrne, taking Helen's rebuke in stride. He looked at her for a second or two longer than he needed to; she had the sense that it was a quick and easy form of intimidation with him. "Suppose you take us on that nickle tour, then," he suggested.

"My pleasure," said Helen coolly.

Damn, he was a pain! She'd been expecting a certain amount of arrogance from Byrne; the man was a stock trader, after all. But his reluctance to sign Katie up had caught her by surprise. She didn't know how to handle him. It had been a long time since she'd had to sell someone on The Open Door; most parents arrived hats in hand, eager and sometimes desperate to get their children into the school.

Not this fella.

Helen took a deep breath. *Whatever it takes to get Katie registered,* she told herself, no longer questioning why. Feeling a little like a snake-oil salesman, she began selling her school as hard as she could. First stop: reception desk.

"This is Janet Harken, our administrative assistant and the school's guardian angel," Helen said with obvious affection. "Janet does everything around here but walk on water."

Laughing off the compliment, the youthful grandmother handed Byrne another brochure on The Open Door and offered Katie a big pink flower-shaped sticker that said "Visitor" on it. Byrne slid the brochure into his inside suit pocket without a glance. But Katie, staring at the huge hot pink sticker on her chest, was ready to sign up then and there.

One down, two to go.

They stepped across the hall to Helen's office, a calm and cozy environment decorated in celadon tones and rich woods, with a potted palm on the floor and tumbles of ivy dotting the bookshelves. A vase stuffed with cheery supermarket flowers adorned the walnut partners desk, the desk for which Helen no longer had a partner.

"I just need to get the keys to the kitchen and the lunchroom," Helen explained as they went in.

She was retrieving a key ring from her top drawer when Katie made a dash for a heavy glass globe that Helen used as a paperweight. "What's this?" the child asked, reaching up with both hands for it.

"Careful, honey!" Helen said, whisking the clear glass ball out of her reach. "You wouldn't want this to fall on your toes!"

"What is it?"

"I use it to keep the wind from blowing my papers everywhere," she explained. She relocated the ball onto a high shelf and said, "Shall we continue our tour?"

As they approached the classrooms Helen began ticking off the school's solid credentials. "We're accredited by the national associations, of course, and by the FIDCR, in addition to OFC. It's in the brochure. You'll notice also that we have an even better ratio of adults to three-year-olds than is recommended by the conservative AAP and NAEYC—"

"Sorry, you're losing me," Byrne interrupted.

"It's in the brochure," she said, realizing that his world was AMEX and NASDAQ. She added, "I'm proud to say the turnover rate of our teachers is very, very low. The staff have been thoroughly screened, and all of the teachers have degrees in early childhood education. I should warn you that that isn't always the case."

"I'm not really interested in other cases," he said flatly. "I'm here to learn about The Open Door."

Stung, Helen colored and said, "I understand." He was right. Why was she resorting to scare tactics? Again this desperation! It was utterly beneath her. Embarrassed and off balance, she tried to rally her wits—which would've been a heck of a lot easier if he weren't being so arrogant. And, of course, if he were less damn good-looking.

"Ah—Miss Maylen," she said as they all stopped and peered into the first classroom, where the young teacher was tidying an open row of colored storage cubbies that lined one wall. "May we have a look around?"

Helen made the introductions while Katie headed straight for the neatly organized bins of toys, each one labeled with big block letters, and settled on the one filled with plastic FOODS: milk and bread and fruit and cheese, and uncanny versions of pizza slices. From the bin marked DISHES came plates and cups and saucers as Katie began laying out a picnic on the floor.

In her tartan-plaid jumper and white frilly blouse, the child looked absolutely adorable.

But her father had to try hard not to frown. "Food. Dolls. Stuffed animals. I suppose it'd be too much to hope she'd head for the Legos and actually start constructing something."

"The girls often do," Kristy said reassuringly. "It just depends."

Byrne sighed and shook his head. "Not *my* little girl. Can you do something about that?" he suddenly asked, fixing a hopeful look on poor Kristy. "Steer her away from the domestic stuff and more toward skills that pay?"

The teacher glanced at Helen, who rolled her eyes from behind Byrne's back. They got this question all the time: Can you turn my sweet little three-year-old into a rocket scientist, no matter what?

Kristy said carefully, "Well, we work hard at stimulating the children in a number of ways—not only intellectually but physically; not only socially but individually. But—"

"But we don't push the children where they don't want

to go," said Helen, interrupting. "And we don't subject them to formal learning," she added, more willing than Kristy to be blunt about it. "It's too soon. Some of them would suffer burnout."

"But some of them wouldn't," argued Byrne, switching his attention from Kristy to her boss. It was unsettling, the way his demeanor instantly changed. His voice took on a taunting edge; his look became confrontational.

"So there are no reading lessons?" he asked unnecessarily. "No math? Isn't that approach a little quaint for the computer age? What do the kids do all day, besides play with plastic pears and cheese wedges?"

He was trying to pick a fight. Maybe he was testing her mettle; maybe he was looking for an excuse not to sign Katie up. Helen didn't know. But she couldn't misrepresent The Open Door, no matter how good she thought it would be for his daughter.

"If you look around you, Mr. Byrne, you'll see that we expose the children to numbers and letters, to music and nature and science," she said with more asperity than she'd intended. "But we don't have a rigidly structured program. And that's by design."

"What do you do with precocious children?"

"We encourage them."

"That's what you said about the timid ones."

"And I meant it. We have quiet corners; we have active ones."

Byrne seemed to be waiting for more. Helen looked him in the eye and lifted her shoulders in a tiny shrug. "I will not promise that Katie will be able to read or write at the end of the term, Mr. Byrne."

Byrne declined to argue further. He turned to Katie's nanny, who'd been watching the verbal sparring with interest. "Well, Peach? Whaddya think?"

Chapter 6

$\mathscr{P}$eaches went over to one of the toddler chairs and surprised everyone by sitting down in it and looking around the room from a three-year-old's vantage.

"It's a very attractive room," she said to Byrne. "Colorful without being overpowering . . . lots of interesting, low-hung posters . . . good light. And it smells"—she took a deep breath—"clean," she said, smiling. "Are the classes reasonably quiet?"

Helen was impressed. Here were lots of shrewd, practical observations.

"No preschool will ever be completely quiet," she said honestly. "It would be bad if it were. But the noise is *good* noise, if you know what I mean. And the sounds don't bounce around; we've insulated as well as possible."

She said to Byrne—because she knew he was responsible—"It's a shame you weren't in time to see the classes in session."

Unlike some schools and despite the security complications, The Open Door was available for observation, even during the tricky times: right after arrivals and just before naps.

Byrne said snappishly, "I did the best I damn well could."

She saw his cheeks flush. She'd hit a nerve. Good. He was a single parent now; with or without a nanny, he was going to have to work twice as hard. The sooner he figured it out, the better for Katie.

"I'm sure you did," Helen said with a serene smile.

He thought he was a hero, showing up personally at the school. The fathers often felt that way. It would be sweet if it weren't so sad. Still, he *had* shown up, late or not, and for that he deserved some credit. Helen resolved to give him the benefit of the doubt.

"It can't be easy," she said, "trying to fit a preschool screening into your terribly hectic pace."

It was supposed to sound sympathetic, but somehow it came out snotty. Helen couldn't believe it. She seemed to have no control over her own sentiments. Embarrassed by the sneer in her voice, she looked away, only to see Kristy and Peaches staring at her. Even more flustered now, Helen threw herself at little Katie's mercy.

"Katie? Would you like to see the rest of the school?" she asked in a nervously high-pitched voice.

Katie was busy trotting from DOLLS to PUZZLES to the big one—BOOKS—and wasn't all that interested in leaving. "No. I wanna stay here," she decided.

In the meantime, Byrne had taken Helen by the elbow and was saying, "May I speak to you alone for a moment, please?"

"Of course," Helen answered all too faintly. "Miss Maylen, would you mind explaining to Ms. Bartholemew the various scheduling options available? Thank you. We'll be right back."

She rallied and lifted her elbow pointedly out of Byrne's grip, then walked ahead of him into the hall. "We can use my office, if you like," she said cooly.

"Fine."

They walked in testy silence to Helen's office.

Helen dropped into her swivel chair and pinched a droopy leaf off one of the freesias in the vase on her desk. "Have a seat," she said, reasserting her authority in the situation.

Byrne stood. "What the hell's going on here?"

"*Excuse* me?"

"Why should I do that? I haven't been subjected to that kind of attitude since my—well, let's say I know that tone when I hear it. You have a grudge against me." He parked his fanny on the edge of her desk and folded his arms across his chest. "May I ask why?"

" 'Grudge' seems strong, Mr. Byrne," she answered, trying to sound ironic. Nonetheless, she was thinking that *grudge* was a darn good choice of words.

"What's it all about, then—that sarcasm back there? You don't know me from Adam."

"True enough," she conceded. "But I could say the same about you. You seem to have shown up here loaded for bear."

"Not true," he said, visibly annoyed. "It was hard for me to make the decision to put Katie in preschool. If you think I'm just dumping her—"

"Of course I don't." She did. "It's obvious that you want what's best for her." It wasn't. "The difficulty will be in choosing from several fine preschools." Easy as pie. "Naturally we think The Open Door has the most to offer." *Dope.*

"My wife wanted Katie to come here," Byrne said with an odd little twist in his voice. He dropped his gaze to the cut flowers and began fiddling with a yellowed leaf.

"Yes . . ." Helen said, relenting. "I was so sorry to hear . . ."

"Thanks," he said without looking at her. He pulled

away the leaf so forcefully it bent the stem of the freesia. "It was rather sudden."

"I know."

He looked up sharply at her. "What do you know?"

Helen felt a *ka-thump* in her breast. She didn't know a thing, and yet her heart was pounding wildly.

"I mean, she sounded fine when she spoke to me on the day before she—"

Actually, Linda Byrne had sounded anything but fine. How could he not argue the point?

In any case, he didn't. He said quietly, "It was a big blow to Katie. I know three-year-olds are resilient, but I'm worried about her."

"She knows about Mrs. Byrne's death?" It should've been a silly question, but Helen knew from experience that it was not.

"Well, actually," Byrne said, embarrassed, "at first I told Katie that her mother went away for a while. It seemed the kindest thing. Peaches put me straight about that, though. I had to go back to Katie and . . ."

He took a deep breath of air and shook his head. "I'll tell you, it was rough. Katie seemed to accept it, but lately she's become listless . . . cranky . . . she keeps asking when Mommy's coming back. It's my fault, I guess, for having programmed her to expect it."

"It's not your fault," Helen found herself saying. "It's very hard for children that age to grasp the permanence of death. Even I—" She stopped herself from bringing Hank into the conversation; this was about Katie's bereavement, not her own.

Byrne hardly noticed her hesitation. Now that he had opened up about his daughter, he seemed eager to go on. He was so clearly, painfully in the dark about what to do, despite the good advice he seemed to be getting from Peaches.

He said, "I thought the best thing would be to keep Katie's routine as normal as possible—isn't that what you're supposed to do?—but without her mother, her life is hardly normal."

Helen had a thought. "I presume you're keeping Peaches on as her nanny?"

"If she left us now I'd die," he said simply.

"In that case, you might consider trying to talk her into putting in a few hours occasionally as a teacher's assistant. That way, Katie's new environment would still be reassuring."

He seemed amazed, as if Helen had just guessed the combination to his safe. "Exactly what Peaches suggested! Great! If you two are both on the same wavelength—well, that's great. It must be the right thing to do. Y'know, suddenly I feel a hell of a lot better about this."

Oh, how glad he was to be relieved of making more decisions. Helen could almost see the weight roll off his back as he stood up and flashed a devastatingly attractive grin at her.

Wow. It was one thing to be handsome, another thing altogether to be seductive when you weren't even trying. Wow. She had to catch her breath. What an irresistible grin. Wow.

Helen found herself returning it. There they were, suddenly happy about who knows what, when Peaches appeared at the door with Katie in tow. The nanny seemed upset.

"Hey, kiddo," Byrne said easily to his daughter. "How would you like to come to school here and have Peaches around to play with, too?" He winked at Peaches, who tried to tell him something, and then he did a knee-bend down to Katie's level and said, "I'm pretty sure you can do that."

"Mr. Byrne—I don't think so," said the nanny in an unhappy voice.

"No, it's all right, Peach," said Byrne. "In fact, it was Mrs. Evett who suggested it," he added with another grateful smile at Helen.

"No, no, we misunderstood. The opening is for September, not June."

"September." Byrne stood up again and turned to Helen. The joy, the relief, the unwitting charm—all gone. In their place was a look so cool it bordered on contempt. "Do you mean to say that we're standing here on April first to register for a class that's almost half a year *away*?"

"I'm sorry," Helen said, wincing under his baleful look. "The staff is reduced in the summer and Summercamp slots are much more limited."

"What the hell good is half a year away?" he said in an undertone through clenched teeth. "She needs the school now!"

"I know that, but—"

"June was bad enough!"

"But you can have a nurturing home environment with relatives and friends—" Helen checked herself and stood up abruptly, determined to head off any more discussion in front of Katie. "Ms. Bartholemew, perhaps you'd like to take Katie—?"

Byrne cut her off with a short, bitter laugh, as if the joke were on him. "Never mind," he said, turning on his heel and taking his daughter's hand. "Forget the whole thing."

Someday he'll kill us all.

Peaches gripped the door handle, her standard hint for Nathaniel Byrne to kindly remember his cargo was precious, and turned back to Katie, cocooned in her custom-made car seat.

"Are you all right back there, honey?" she asked pointedly.

The child, feeding off her father's frustration, was edgy

and uncommunicative. "I don't know," she answered.

Byrne was driving the way he always drove: expertly, and much too fast. His wife used to blame his habit on the long commute that he had to make between Salem and Boston every day. Linda had begged him to shorten the commute by moving closer. He'd compromised by moving faster.

"She led me on, damnit."

Nathaniel Byrne's thoughts were bubbling up like tar over the edge of a pot. "Who does she think she is?" he barked.

Peaches doubted he wanted an answer, so she shrugged and said, "Who knows?"

"I mean, if I misled someone like that, I'd be hauled in front of the SEC in two seconds flat."

"I was as surprised as you were."

"Why couldn't she just say she didn't have a space this summer? She could've told you when you called. Why waste my time?"

Peaches sighed and said, "We'll never know."

"She should've moved heaven and earth to get Katie in. She knew the situation."

"Yes. She did."

"God. What a coldhearted, unrelenting. . . ."

His disgust was music to Peaches's ears. She hadn't liked seeing sparks fly between them. Sparks were all too capable of starting a fire.

"Some women are like that," she said in a pensive voice. "They haven't become successful by being kind. The bottom line for them is always business. They'll do anything to get it."

He downshifted and took a corner hard. "She didn't sound like the type. She certainly didn't look like the type."

It was a tense ride home.

*   *   *

The cook, who drank, had been keeping supper warm for them. Father, daughter, and nanny sat down to a meal of overdone three-cheese lasagna.

Byrne poked at the dried-out, curled edge of a noodle and scowled. "This isn't edible. I've got half a mind to fire her."

Peaches thought the cook—sixty-two, hard of hearing, and uninvolved—suited the household perfectly, so she said, "Well, we did tell cook we'd be in and out."

"We *were* in and out," he snapped. "Or didn't you notice?"

He was acting far too upset over the failed attempt to get Katie settled somewhere. Peaches was beginning to fear that he might make some rash decision.

"It's not the end of the world if Katie can't get into The Open Door," she said soothingly. "We'll just look for another preschool."

"What's the point? Anything that's any good will be filled."

"We don't know that. I'll get on the phone tomorrow and see."

Katie, who'd refused to let anyone cut her food tonight, was busy separating the layered noodles with her fingers and rearranging them into a fort. Byrne watched her effort morosely, then said, "Finally. An honest effort to make something."

"She's going to surprise you someday," said Peaches, smiling.

He snorted. "And in the meantime?"

He leaned forward on his elbows and cupped a fist in his open hand, lost in thought.

"Uh-oh, Daddy," said Katie, wagging a messy finger at him. "You diddent finish."

Smiling grimly, he said, "Oh, yeah? And what about

you, tomato-face? How about eating some of that instead
of playing with it?''

Katie giggled at the notion that she was a vegetable and
said, "I'm not a tomato face.''

Peaches took the damp cloth that she kept by her side
and reached over to do some preliminary mopping up.
"How would you like some cereal and bananas instead?''
she asked the squiggly, resisting child.

"Yes, with jimmies on it,'' Katie demanded, twisting her
hands above her head in sleepy petulance.

"Ha-ha. That's a funny joke,'' said Peaches as she got
up and began heading for the kitchen.

"Peach?'' said Byrne quietly. "Switzerland: Would you
go if I sent her off to her grandmother for a while?''

It came out of the blue. Peaches had considered many
scenarios, but not that one. Up until that afternoon Nathaniel Byrne had been determined to avoid reaching out to his
mother-in-law at all cost. They did not get along—even at
Linda's funeral there had been coolness—and that, so far,
was that. Switzerland! She'd be baby-sitting half a world
away while he . . . who knows what he'd be up to?

She turned to him, lasagna fort in hand, and said softly,
"If you think it's necessary, of course I will. But let me
have tomorrow first. Absolutely, we'll do whatever is best
for her. But . . . Switzerland?''

Peaches didn't have to point out the obvious: That with
his schedule, he wouldn't see Katie the entire time.

"I know, I know,'' Byrne said, giving his restless daughter a brooding look. "I'd hate it, too. But I don't know
what else to do, where else to find family.''

He'd ignored them all in the course of his career, and
this was where it had got him: alone, with only hired help
for comfort.

"Leave it to me,'' Peaches said, resolutely upbeat. "I'm
not going to let you down.''

He gave her a tight, bleak little smile. "Thanks. You're a doll."

He was letting her see him at his most vulnerable, which was progress; he was a proud man, after all.

But the downside was that he was so vulnerable.

He's easy pickings right now, Peaches decided as she brought out a box of Cocoa Puffs from the pantry. All it would take was one good woman. Several of Linda Byrne's female friends had called during the past month, offering their sympathy—and worse, their help.

She had to move fast.

Chapter 7

*H*elen Evett drove home in a state of dismay. Somehow she'd let them slip through her fingers. Nathaniel Byrne was right, of course. Without actually saying so, Helen had let them all think that Katie was being considered for the summer session. Who could blame him for being angry?

She could argue that he had overreacted. But she remembered her own edginess after Hank's death far too well to blame Byrne. His wife had only been gone a month. He was still in shock.

So that was that. Surprisingly, Helen felt no guilt over the confusion; all she felt was a terrible emptiness that Katie wouldn't be coming to her preschool.

She hurried up the front steps of her shingle-and-clapboard Victorian, anxious to check her answering machine: Maybe Byrne had changed his mind about September. Inside, the house was pulsing to the sound of heavy-metal music. Dropping her trench coat over one of the hooks of the oak hall tree, Helen cupped her hands and yelled, "Russ! Turn it *down*!" to absolutely no avail. "Beck-eee! You home?"

"In the kitchen, Mom, making tea," came her daughter's voice.

"*Russell!* I'm *begging* you!" Helen shouted. She detoured into the kitchen and said, "Any calls?"

"Don't know; just got in," said Becky, lighting a burner under the teakettle. "I'm in kind of a hurry; French Club tonight."

She was wearing her blackish-charcoalish turtleneck and a long black shirt. Helen had to admit that her daughter looked terrific in black. With her shining gold hair and the flush of youth on her cheeks, Becky was able to pull off the simple severity of the outfit very well—even with Doc Martens clodhoppers on her feet. She was turning out to be a beautiful, very together young woman. If only Hank . . .

"Make sure you eat something before you go dashing off," Helen said on her way out to the answering machine in the sitting room. If a call had come, Russ couldn't possibly have heard it over the din in his room.

No calls. It was disappointing. Helen was about to go upstairs and cut the electric cord to Russell's amplifier into tiny pieces when the phone rang. It was Alexander's mother, still upset over the Thomas-The-Tank-Engine episode in the lobby of the preschool.

"I've decided that Alexander won't be coming back for the summer session," Mrs. Lagor said firmly. "In the first place, we'll be away the whole time."

"Oh, but—" They weren't doing any such thing. Mr. Lagor was a contractor; summer was his peak season. But Helen could hardly point that out, so she said, "I'm sorry to hear that, Mrs. Lagor. But we'll be looking forward to seeing Alexander again in the fall."

There was an utterly meaningful pause before Mrs. Lagor said, "I'm not sure about fall. I think Alexander should stay home until kindergarten."

Which was the exact worst thing for the overprotected child. "I see," Helen said. Very carefully, she laid out her argument against the idea. "It's true, some children are better off at home until then," she said. "If they have siblings or neighborhood friends close in age to play with, then staying at home can be every bit as enriching as attending preschool; in fact, more so."

But Alexander was an only child and Mrs. Lagor was very aloof. Helen hoped the disadvantages would be obvious to her.

Apparently not. Before Helen could pursue her case further, Mrs. Lagor said vaguely, "Don't worry, I'll be sending you a letter," and hurried off the phone.

Poor Alex. She's going to hold on to him until they pry him loose with a crowbar. And yet, Helen could hardly blame the woman. She herself had to fight an almost constant urge to keep her own kids under lock and key. It was a scary world out there.

Helen was halfway up the stairs when it hit her. She now had room for Katie Byrne in the summer session. It seemed too good—and too eerie—to be true. After all the handwringing, after all the back-and-forthing between Nathaniel Byrne and her, all it had taken was one quick phone call and suddenly Katie was safe.

Safe?

Helen frowned as she pounded on Russ's door with loud and empty threats, then retraced her steps down the hall to her bedroom. *Safe from what?*

She opened the door to her room and went in, intending to change into jeans and a shirt, but stopped dead in her tracks and sniffed.

Perfume. The smell of *Enchantra* pervaded the room, distinct and overbearing, as if someone had spilled the bottle that stood on her old walnut bureau. The pearlized decanter was round and roly; Helen had knocked it over herself in the past. But the stopper had never fallen out, which is what had to have happened for the scent to be so strong.

She picked up the bottle and checked it: The stopper was still in hard. Annoyed without really knowing why, she went back to Russ's bedroom, banged on the door, and opened it. Russ was now under his headset; she motioned him to take it off.

"Were you in my room earlier?"

His green eyes went blank. "Whuffor?"

"Someone spilled my perfume."

"Well, it wasn't me," he said, snorting. "Ask the ditz."

That was a little more logical, but only just. Helen knew that her daughter would never use *Enchantra*. Becky preferred younger, lighter scents. For that matter, Helen never used it, either; it had been a gift from her aunt. She threw open a window, despite the chill, and called her daughter upstairs.

Becky walked in and made a face. "Whoa, Mom—go easy on that stuff."

"You weren't in my *Enchantra?*" Even as the words left Helen's lips, a small dim bulb seemed to go on in the cluttered closet of her mind.

Becky was plainly puzzled by the question. "Why are you asking me?" she said, picking up the bottle. "You're the one who reeks."

"I'm not wearing *Enchantra*," Helen said bluntly.

Becky pulled on the stopper, which made a little *puh* sound as it came out. "In tight. It couldn't have evaporated." She bent her face close to the embroidered linen that covered the bureau top. "I don't smell anything there."

"Right," said Helen tersely. "It's in the air around us."

Becky spied the open window. "Oh—*well*—if you're gonna leave the window wide open . . ." She walked over to it, parted the lace curtains, and took a deep breath, testing the outside air. "Nothing," she said, baffled, and turned around to face her mother. "Definitely, it's in this room."

So was the knocking. And the jiggle. And the cold rank smell of the sea.

"I know that, Becky," Helen said in a pale echo of irony. She tried to shake away the unease that was ambushing her routinely nowadays. "What I don't know is why."

They were standing in the most open area of the room, between the four-poster bed and the oak armoire that dominated one wall. It was where they'd stood two nights ago when Helen lost it in front of her daughter, and her daughter lost it in front of Helen. Surely Becky remembered.

The girl went over to a far corner of the bedroom and sniffed. "Maybe I don't smell it after all," she said in an edgy, hopeful voice. "We need another opinion."

She left the room and returned in a few seconds with her irritated brother in tow. "Do you smell anything?" she asked Russ.

"Yeah. Girls." The boy shrugged out of her grip and escaped back to his room.

Becky whispered, "Do you think we were broken into?" The blood had drained from her face, leaving her a wan version of her former self.

"There's no evidence of it," Helen said as she turned on the brass swing-out lamp above her bed. She wanted light. Lots of it. The deepening twilight would soon be night.

"Could someone have a key?"

"Only Aunt Mary has a key."

"She could've been here!" said Becky. "She could've been cleaning your room or looking for something or, I don't know, just wandering. She's getting really weird."

"She's just the same as she's always been!" Helen said sharply.

"Oh, Mom. She's not. She can't remember anything very well and she gets flustered all the time. Yesterday when I came home from school she was in the yard sitting on the bench with a trowel in her lap. She called me over and said, 'What's this thing? I used to know.' "

Helen made an impatient tisking sound and said, "Everyone forgets the name of something once in a while."

"It wasn't just the name she forgot," said Becky. "She didn't know what the trowel was *for*—and she's been a gardener all her life! I wasn't going to tell you because I know how much she means to you," Becky confessed. "But that was before this bit."

Helen was caught between two agonies. She could assume that the "bit" was the work of her beloved aunt or she could assume . . . something else entirely. Neither suspicion could possibly lead anywhere satisfying.

She swore under her breath, then sighed and put her arm around her daughter as she led her out of the bedroom. "Look . . . honey . . . don't mention this to anyone, okay? Or about Aunt Mary. Just don't say anything to anyone about anything. Let me look into this. There has to be a simple explanation."

Helen could see how relieved Becky was to be let off the hook of responsibility. She was still a kid, for all her apparent maturity. "I'm glad you're being so normal about it, Mom," she said, kissing her mother on the cheek.

She took off and Helen was left to figure out what a sixteen-year-old considered "normal" in a mother. One thing was certain: She couldn't let Becky know she was upset, much less afraid, of the unexplained events around them. One more disaster like the night before last, and Becky would lose confidence in her mother altogether. A wall would go up, and there they'd be: just another mother and daughter who couldn't communicate. Helen had managed to stay standing—emotionally speaking—after her husband had been gunned down. Now was not the time to trip and fall.

Throwing a second window open, Helen shivered and hurried out of the room. She closed the door behind her with the thought that whatever was inside would eventually go outside, and then she went downstairs to make dinner for Russ and her.

She wanted to call Nathaniel Byrne at once with the good news about the opening at the preschool, but two things were stopping her: one, it was the dinner hour, and she suspected that they let the machine take their calls; and two, she wasn't all that sure that Katie's father would consider an open slot at The Open Door to be good news.

At eight o'clock that evening the phone rang at the Byrne mansion. Peaches picked it up. It was the director of The Open Door, Helen Evett, which didn't surprise her at all. So she was right. There *had* been sparks.

Her voice was deliberately cool as she said, "How can I help you, Mrs. Evett?" It was an idle question. The point of the call was all too obvious; Helen Evett was going to muscle Katie into her preschool.

"I . . . this is almost embarrassing after the misunderstanding we had this afternoon, but I have some very good news for Mr. Byrne. It seems we do have room for Katie in the summer program, after all."

"Really."

"Yes. I wonder if I might speak to Mr. Byrne about it."

"I'm afraid it would be a waste of your time, Mrs. Evett. We've made other arrangements."

"Oh." There was a confused pause. "So quickly?"

"Yes," said Peaches. "But we do appreciate your efforts."

The director's voice sounded bemused as she said, "It was nothing *I* did, really. We had a last-minute cancellation. It seemed almost fateful."

My ass. "We appreciate your thinking of us. Thank you so much for calling."

"Well, naturally I thought of Katie. She made quite an impression on me," Helen remarked. Clearly she was stalling. She sighed and said, "I wonder—could I have a moment of Mr. Byrne's time if he's free? Our leave-taking was so awkward," she explained.

"I understand your concern, Mrs. Evett, but it's unwarranted," Peaches said, throwing her a bone of reassurance. "It was a simple misunderstanding. Mr. Byrne never thought twice about it afterward."

"Are you sure?" Helen asked guilelessly. "He seemed so upset."

"Not at all," Peaches answered. She glanced up in time to see Nathaniel Byrne come into the music room, looking for a report she knew he'd left behind.

Peaches motioned silently toward the low table where it lay mixed in with Katie's coloring books, and then she said briskly into the phone, "I'm sorry. We're simply not interested," and hung up.

"Who was that?" Byrne asked, picking up his document.

"Another telemarketer," said Peaches with distaste.

Helen had no intention of letting Peaches Bartholemew speak for her employer.

"Call me a snob," she told Becky later that night, "but I'll be darned if I take a 'no' from the baby-sitter. This is too important to Katie's welfare. If Nathaniel Byrne doesn't want her in my preschool, he's going to have to tell me that himself."

Becky was in her pajamas, scouting the kitchen for a bedtime snack. She settled on a banana, although her sigh seemed to say potato chips. "You're really into this Katie kid, aren't you," she said, peeling back the fruit.

"I guess," Helen agreed. "I feel so sorry for her."

Becky took a big bite of her banana and said with a full mouth, "You talk to Aunt Mary?"

"As a matter of fact, I did. She's been inside all day, finishing an afghan for the Senior Citizens' Jumble this weekend. She wasn't on our side of the house—and she seemed absolutely fine."

Becky shrugged. "Oka-ay." Obviously she didn't believe it.

Helen was well aware that her aunt had been slipping a bit; but it was normal slippage for someone her age. Absolutely normal. And today she seemed vital and enthusiastic. Yes. Normal.

"So what do we think the smell was?"

Helen was ready for that one. "Between you and me, I wouldn't put it past your brother to pull a stunt like that. He's still mad at me for going through his room on that search-and-destroy mission for moldy clothes."

Blame it on Russ. It was the easiest thing for now.

Helen preempted any more questions by fishing noisily through the silverware for the can opener, which she used on a can of gourmet fish blend for poor starving Moby. The cat was brushing relentlessly back and forth against Helen's stonewashed jeans, leaving a swath of black fur on her pant legs.

"All right, all right; hold your horses," Helen scolded. "God. The more I feed her, the thinner she gets. I wonder if she's hyperthyroid?"

"Maybe she's bulimic," Becky quipped.

Helen looked at her daughter sharply. "Why do you say that? What do you know about bulimia? Are your friends doing that? Are you—?"

"*Muh*-ther! I am not bulimic. And yeah, I know people who're into that. I think it's disgusting," Becky said, sliding off the marble countertop where she'd been perched.

"Good. You just stay disgusted," said her mother as she rinsed the smell of fish from the can opener. She wiped her hands on a checkered towel and said softly, "You know how you want a normal mom? Well, I want normal kids. So please, honey," she said with a wistful smile. "Stay just the way you are."

"I will if you will," Becky said without missing a beat. She tossed her banana peel and resumed her search through the cabinets. "I'm still hungry," she whined. "How come we never have anything good to eat around here?"

Smiling to herself, Helen hung up the towel and threw the bolt on the kitchen door. There was nothing more normal than a ravenous teenager.

Helen went to bed in her freshly aired-out room, slept soundly through any tappings and jiggles that may or may not have occurred, and the next morning drove to the preschool filled with determination to pin down Katie's arrogant, misdirected father.

After calling the Columbus Fund and picking her way through a bewildering maze of electronic directions, she was finally delivered over to a live human being at the other end of the line. Helen gave the assistant her name, along with a brief—and no doubt unprofessional—message that the call concerned Katherine Byrne. Sometime after lunch Byrne returned her call.

"I'm sorry I wasn't available earlier," he said without sounding sorry at all. He was definitely still angry. It occurred to Helen that Peaches was either unobservant or very diplomatic. "What can I do for you?" he asked.

Helen had decided beforehand not to mention her call to his house; it was simpler just to plow forward in ignorance.

She cut right to the chase. "One of our three-year-olds won't be able to attend the summer session. The slot is available for Katie if you'd like it. I'm referring, of course, to the summer of this year,'' she couldn't resist adding through a grim smile.

He surprised her by saying in a halfway friendly voice, ''Gee, that's too bad. I've just made plans to send Katie for a stay with her grandmother in Zurich.''

''Zurich, *Switzerland*?'' said Helen, hoping for his sake that there was a Zurich in Massachusetts.

''Yes. Linda's people are from there.''

Helen knew that, of course, from the obituary, and still she couldn't believe it. His own daughter! She tried to keep her tone reasonable as she said, ''No doubt you've thought about this long and hard.''

''It's a safe assumption.''

She could picture him so clearly as he said it: the clean-shaven jaw set in annoyance; the intense, laser-beam focus on the subject at hand. Damn his blue eyes!

''How can you *do* that?'' she blurted, despite herself. ''How can you just ship Katie across an ocean?''

''Oh, I won't box her up or anything,'' he said with brutal irony. ''I'll probably pay for a plane ticket and let her sit with Peaches and me.''

''Don't do it! It's a mistake!''

''Says who?'' he snapped. ''Look, Mrs. Evett. I read your brochure. I understand that your preschool is approved by every organization in America except maybe the U.S. Artichoke Association. I understand that you have dual master's degrees in education and psychology. I even understand how little I know about childrearing. What I don't understand is how you get off butting your nose in my business.''

''I—''

She sucked in a breath of air, then let it out in a deflated sigh. ''I don't know either. I have no right to say any of this, but . . . I just know that Katie needs to be around you.

It's very important," she said with soft urgency. "You must believe me, Mr. Byrne."

Something in her voice—probably her begging tone—made him actually try to reassure her. "You know, Katie's grandmother sounded genuinely thrilled when I called this morning," he said. "She has a house on Lake Constance with dogs and a cat and swings . . . Katie has some cousins over there; they all speak English. I think. It'll work out. You'll see.

"Besides," he added, "it'd be embarrassing as hell to call it off now. I'd really look like a jerk."

"You don't have to call it off, then," Helen said, seizing on the opening. "Just go for a short time. Then come back. Before you know it, the summer session will have begun."

"Hmmm."

It was all she needed, that "hmmm." It meant he was coming around to her view. Helen had no idea why she was being so pushy. But something deep inside leapt up in joy at the thought that Katie would be snug with her father instead of shunted far away from him.

"I wouldn't be able to stay with her there, no matter how short the visit," he confessed. "It can't be done."

"Oh."

"But I reckon Katie'll survive a two-or three-week stay. I'll go out and bring her back, naturally. And after that, well . . . you're sure you have a slot?" he added in a voice that was amused, skeptical, and persuasive all at once.

"As sure as April means rain," said Helen, overjoyed.

The plane took off in a torrential downpour, then bumped its way through its ascent to smooth air above the clouds.

"Next stop, Switzerland, Katie-pie," said her father as he opened a carton of chocolate milk that Peaches had brought in her ample carryall.

Katie, dressed in daffodil yellow, was leaning out of her

car seat next to him with her hand flattened against the window. "I can't see it," she said, disappointed.

"That's the ocean," said Peaches. "It doesn't look like much from up here. Switzerland is still kind of far away. You'll know we're there when you see big, big mountains sticking up in the clouds."

"In the clouds!" said Katie, scandalized. "What if we could hit them!"

"Not a chance, punkin," said her father. "We'll just fly around them and between them. C'mon, turn back around and you can have your milk and—oh, shit!"

He'd knocked the milk from his folded-down tray directly into his lap, leaving a giant stain. *Good*, thought Peaches. Let him know how inept he was at nurturing. It made her that much more indispensable.

"What's 'shit,' Daddy?" asked Katie with wide-open eyes.

She'd never heard the word before; Linda wouldn't allow it.

Byrne, frantically dabbing his crotch with a handkerchief and paper towels that the first-class attendant had produced out of nowhere, said, "What? Oh, that. It's not a nice word, Katie. I shouldn't have said it."

In his haste to contain the mess he knocked over the carton again. "Oh, *shit!*" he said. "Ah, sorry, Katie. Peaches, trade places with me while I go off to hose myself down, would you?"

Peaches let him go. By the time he returned, carrying his jacket strategically across his arm and over his pants, Peaches had got Katie nicely settled in with an oatmeal cookie and a carton of white milk.

Somewhat sheepishly, he took the aisle seat. Heaving a sigh, he said, "Tell me this isn't an omen."

Peaches laughed and said, "You'll get the hang of it."

He shook his head. "Obviously I should leave this stuff

to more experienced hands.'' He added unnecessarily, ''Like that Evett woman. I have to admit, I feel good about Katie going to The Open Door this summer. How about you?''

''It couldn't have worked out better,'' said Peaches with a careful smile.

''That's what I thought.'' He stretched his legs and said, ''I had my doubts there, of course. But I have to say, she wasn't about to take no for an answer.'' He let out a short, bemused laugh. ''She was pretty feisty on the phone, though she doesn't look the type at all. Funny . . . something about her reminds me of Lin—''

He glanced at his daughter, then shrugged and said, ''Anyway, all's well that ends well. I'll get to score some points with Katie's grandmother. You'll get to visit a gorgeous country for a couple of weeks. And Katie will get to meet her family, which is only right.''

''And we won't be gone so long that Katie will have—quite—forgotten you, sir.''

He winced. ''*Et, tu,* Peaches?'' he joked. In a more serious vein he said, ''I'm sorry I didn't consult with you before setting up the trip. I meant the call to be exploratory; but Linda's mother just took the ball and ran. The way she always does. At least I was able to cut back the length of the stay.''

Peaches said softly, ''It's not a problem, Mr. Byrne. Really.''

''For pity's sake, call me Nat,'' he said. ''It's so much easier than this sir-and-Byrne business.''

Peaches glanced shyly at him, then looked away. ''All right,'' she said, her cheeks coloring attractively. She took Katie's empty carton away before the child could rearrange it into an alpine cottage. ''I will.''

*   *   *

Katie's grandmother liked to sleep in, and her grandfather liked to hike in the morning. The maid had cleared away the breakfast things; Katie and Peaches would have the next hour all to themselves.

The child had slept badly the night before. Peaches sat in a rocking chair and held her in her lap and they gazed languidly at the serene lake, framed by budding trees, that lay shimmering in the morning sun like a picture postcard.

Peaches said softly to the child, "Who has crystal balls, Katie? Do you know?"

"Um . . . no-o . . ." said Katie.

"Do you remember in the Wizard of Oz? Who had the crystal ball in the Wizard of Oz, Katie?"

"Um . . . the witch. And she was bad. She wanted to catch Dorothy and . . . and . . ."

"And what did she want to do to Dorothy? Do you remember?"

"She wanted to do bad things to Dorothy."

"That's right. Very, very bad things. And what did she use the crystal ball for?"

"I don't know."

"What did she see in the crystal ball, Katie? Remember?"

"She saw . . . she saw when Dorothy and the lion and the other ones were coming."

"That's right. She could tell because she saw it in the crystal ball. Who else has a crystal ball, Katie? We saw one in real life, didn't we? You wanted to pick it up, but she wouldn't let you. Who wouldn't let you touch her crystal ball?"

"Um . . . Mrs. Evett."

The child looked distressed. She became quiet. After a long, thoughtful moment she snuggled closer to Peaches and said, "Is Mrs. Evett a witch?"

Peaches wrapped her arms around Katie and drew her closer. "I'm afraid she might be, sweetie," she said, running her fingers through the child's brown curls. "Mrs. Evett might be a witch."

Chapter 8

$\mathcal{H}$elen was losing a game of Scrabble to her aunt Mary—and feeling tickled to bits that her aunt was so sharp about it—when the phone rang. It was ten o'clock, too late to call for a lighthearted chat.

Russell.

She was right. Over the thundering of her heart, Helen listened to the measured reassurances of a Salem police officer calling from the emergency room of Salem Medical. Her son had been in a car accident, her son was fine, the young driver was not so fine, but the others were okay and so was her son, really, a sprained ankle is all, nothing to worry about, could she pick him up, he was fine, her son was fine. It's good he belted; too bad the driver hadn't. But you know kids.

Helen's hand was shaking violently as she hung up the phone. "It's Russ," she said to her aunt in a zombie voice. "He was in an accident. In a car. I can't believe it."

Her aunt slapped a hand to her chest. "Oh, dear lord. Is he all right?"

"Yes. A sprained ankle. He twisted it climbing out of the passenger window when the door wouldn't open," Helen explained in the same vacant tone. "He was wearing a seat belt. The officer seemed to think he deserved a medal for that. He could have been killed. Russell could have been killed.''

"But he's all right.'' Aunt Mary sprang up shakily and said, "We've got to go get him. Where are my shoes? Didn't I wear them here?''

Her shoes were under the table on the rag rug, where she'd taken them off because her corns hurt. It was no big thing, that panicky lapse of memory—but Helen seized on it because it was actually easier to think about her aunt's senility than the thought of her son lying in a ditch.

"Your shoes are right there, Aunt Mary,'' she said, pointing to the black Cobblers. "But you can't come with me. When Becky gets back you'll have to explain—no, on second thought, you should go home. It's better if you don't—no. Becky will wonder where I am. Can you tell her without frightening her?''

The old woman was plainly trying her best to understand Helen's rush of instructions. She nodded vigorously, if cluelessly, at the end of her niece's hurried speech.

And meanwhile Helen wanted to fly, not drive, to her son's side. "Just sit still. Right here,'' she said in a general's voice. She added more gently, "Make yourself a nice cup of tea. I won't be long. There won't be any traffic this time of night. I have to go. Really. I have to go.''

Leaving her shoeless aunt to fend for herself, Helen grabbed her trench coat and ran out the back hall steps to her car, parked on a cobbled square they'd carved from the garden. Thank God Becky wasn't using the Volvo tonight; what would she have done then? She drove through the streets like a madwoman, aware that this time she didn't have a troop commander to escort her, aware that a kid with a sprained ankle was not the same as a trooper shot dead.

Russ had defied her. There was no other word for it. He'd

done exactly what she'd told him not to do, and done it spectacularly well. Her heart seesawed between pity and rage. How terrified he must have been when the car hit the guard rail, then skidded across both lanes into the median ditch. It was a miracle they hadn't hit another car. What were they doing? Horsing around? She didn't even know the driver; how dared Russ get into a car with him?

Tonight, a friend's car; next time, a borrowed car; the time after that, a stolen one. In the mood she was in, it seemed inevitable. And she didn't know what she could do about it.

If he had a father. Boys needed them so much. Ten was an awful age to lose one. At ten, Russ had been old enough to understand, young enough to resent the loss. Ten was awful.

How would Hank handle this? She could almost hear him in the car alongside her: "I'll beat the living crap out of him, that's how." Not that he'd ever do it. He'd never raised a hand to his kids. Not once. But he might say it to her, to let off steam.

She wished *she* could say it. She wished she could say to someone, "I'll beat the living crap out of him." It would make her feel so much better. But there was no one. All she could do was slam her hand on the wheel in frustrated fury.

By the time Helen got to the emergency room she was a wreck. After the inevitable directions and delays, she found him: sitting on a blue plastic chair, his cool haircut looking mussed and uncool, with two aluminum crutches—crutches!—propped up beside him. Her little boy. Black and blue and lame. The sight of him ripped her heart in two; she could feel it tearing inside her breast. Her Russ. Their Russ. He might have died.

"Hey, kiddo," she said quietly when he saw her. Striking a pose of nonchalance, she kept her hands in her coat pockets. She didn't dare throw her arms hysterically around him, not with Scotty sitting in the chair next to him, looking even more wary than her son. "Did they say you're gonna live?"

His chin trembled. "I'm fine, Ma. Just a twisted ankle. I didn't even want it bandaged, but they wouldn't listen." The lips firmed into a macho sneer, then began to wobble again.

She thought he might cry, which would've been a delight and a disaster, so she said briskly, "Well, then, let's get home."

She turned to Russ's pal. "I assume," she added dryly, "that the sleepover at your house is off for tonight, Scotty?"

Scott stared at his Nikes. "Yeah, I guess so."

"Is someone picking you up?" she asked him, looking him over. He was tired but unhurt. He must've been wearing his seat belt, then. Another hero.

Without looking at her, Scotty said, "This is the hospital my mom works at. I'm waiting for her to get off her shift."

"Where's your dad?" It was an intrusive question, but Helen didn't care.

"He had to fill in for someone at the mall."

So having a father didn't make a difference after all. A kid could screw up brilliantly with or without one.

"You should've let me know that your parents weren't going to be home tonight, Scotty," she said sternly.

The boy squirmed. "It wasn't for long."

"It doesn't *take* long!"

"Ma-a-a . . ." came Russ's tired bleat of protest.

Helen brought herself up short. Best not travel down that road tonight. She was upset. They were upset. It was all she could do not to bang their heads together. "I'll be—"

She was going to say, "in touch with your mother," but

she denied herself the satisfaction of even that small threat. "Good night, then," she said wearily.

After hobbling to his feet, Russ made a fierce attempt to keep ahead of her as they began the long process of checking themselves out of the hospital. She decided he was keeping his distance because he didn't want to risk a reprimand in public, which was fine with her. It gave her the breathing space she needed to get herself under control.

Once he was settled in the car, however, he surprised her by saying, "I suppose you want all the gory details."

The truth was, she assumed she'd have to pull the gory details out of him one by one. Nonetheless, she said, "No. Not tonight."

They drove in silence for a bit. Then he blurted, "Oh, why don't we just get it over with! What's the sense of dragging it out?"

Did he really want to confess and apologize? She wished. No, it was more likely that he'd worked up a defense worthy of F. Lee Bailey, and he wanted to use his material while it was still fresh in his mind.

She wasn't going to give him the satisfaction. "No. Tomorrow, I said."

He fell back into sulky silence. Once home, he refused her help managing the front steps; but he had such a hard time with them that Helen insisted he sleep on the sofabed in the family room.

"Either that, or go up the stairs on your fanny."

"No *way!*" he said with a truly offended scowl.

So that was that. The family began to disperse. Aunt Mary's tense vigil was over; pale and exhausted, she headed across the hall to her own apartment. Becky had the wisdom to confine herself to a brief word or two of sympathy for her brother. Her only question was: "Would you like your CD player?"

"Yeah—no," Russ said. Everyone knew he didn't allow Becky in his room.

Still, the deprivation showed in his face, along with the flat-out pain. Before this, Russ had never suffered anything but bumps and scrapes in his life. This was new, this fleeting brush with his own breakability.

"I'll get you a pair of shorts and a T-shirt," Helen said briskly, though she wanted desperately to hug and comfort him. "And I'll put them in the downstairs bathroom for you. Do you want your own pillows?"

"No—yeah." It meant his mother would be going into his room, but it couldn't be helped. He did want those pillows.

Helen went upstairs and, ignoring the DO-NOT-DISTURB sign on his door, into his bedroom. The room was a mess, of course, but even she could see that the mess had a rhythm to it. When you threw open the door you saw closet, bookcase, desk, computer—things you were permitted to see. Over in the corner, far to the right of the door, that's where the bed, the music, the locked trunk, and the shrine were. It was almost a room within a room, a place where Russ Evett could be himself, away from any possible ambush by nosy relatives.

She walked over to his bed, resisting the urge to pick up dirty clothing along the way, and got both pillows, cased in a black and purple pattern that Russ had picked out himself. She lifted the pillows to her nose and smelled: They were due, but not overdue, for a wash.

She began to leave, then paused in front of the shrine. It was all still there, more or less as Russ had arranged it after his father's funeral. The candid eight-by-ten shot of Hank in uniform, arms folded across his chest, as he leaned against the hood of his state trooper's car; the badge; the Ray-Ban sunglasses; even the flag that the family had been given at the funeral, still in its reverential folds—it was all there, carefully arranged atop the small three-drawer chest that once held Hank's handkerchiefs and socks and not-quite-worn-out wallets.

He loved you so much, she thought, touching her fingers to her lips and then to the photograph. *What if it's not enough?*

She sighed, then scooped up Russ's CD player and a few scattered CDs from his desk and went downstairs.

"Here you go," she said, tossing the pillows on the opened-out sofa bed. "And I thought you might want this," she added, placing the player and disks on the small table alongside. "Is there anything else I can get you, Russ?"

"No."

"A sandwich?" she ventured. "You must be hungry."

"No."

It was her cue to get out and leave him with his thoughts, but she kept on hugging the stage. "A glass of milk? And some cookies, maybe?"

"No."

She should leave. Truly. "I'll bring you a glass of water, in case you get thirsty in the night."

"No."

Wincing, she said, "Suit yourself. If you need anything, just yell. I'll keep my bedroom door open tonight. Don't worry about your medication. I'll wake you when it's time."

He was silent. She couldn't begin to imagine what he must be thinking. Suddenly exhausted by the scope of his willingness to shut her out, she began to leave the room at last.

"Ma?"

Helen stopped in the doorway and glanced back casually. "Yes?"

"Thanks. For the player."

She smiled, despite her resolve not to. "It was a toss-up between that and your math book. Good-night, Russ."

A week later, Helen was in the Tuesday-Thursday class for threes and fours, subbing for a sick teacher, when she spied Nathaniel Byrne through the glass square of the closed classroom door.

It was only by chance that she happened to glance up from the circle of children that fanned out to her left and right. She was on her knees, too immersed in the lesson to have noticed him before; but she had the sense that he'd been standing there a while.

Nobody had told her that Byrne was coming to observe, which meant that Janet must have arranged something on the spot for him. Helen at first assumed that he was on his way to the observation deck, discreetly tucked alongside another of the classes, so that he could get that close-up look he'd missed his first time around.

But no. Once he made eye contact with her, he decided to let himself in—which simply wasn't done. Not in her preschool, anyway. As he came inside Helen shot him a warning look, meant to keep him in the shadows, and went back to her finger-puppets. She was teaching a lesson in toddler-science, which meant that the children were joining in and asking questions; she had no attention to spare for the casually dressed dad with the big pink "Visitor" flower stuck on his windbreaker.

The kitty finger-puppet on Helen's left hand was hunched over a seagull feather and a tablespoon. "Hmm," the kitty puppet said, scratching its head, "I wonder which is heavier, the feather or the spoon?"

Naturally all the children had opinions, not all of them correct (the feather was a really big one that Helen had found on the beach during her first walk of the year there). The kitty finger-puppet lifted the objects and appeared to weigh first one, then the other, then passed them around for the boys and girls to do the same.

It was a hands-on experiment in weights and measures; but if Nathaniel Byrne was expecting to see Helen teaching the difference between grams and ounces, he'd come to the wrong place.

She stole a look at him every so often as the kitty and puppy puppets picked up different pairs of objects—cotton balls and ball bearings, baseballs and Wiffle balls, carrots and wrenches—and then tried to guess which weighed more between them.

Byrne, hands in his pockets, had taken up a post alongside a big plastic castle with its knob-headed knights and cone-gowned princesses, the most popular toy in the class. Probably he wouldn't want to know that every boy-child in the room enjoyed the jousting knights, and every girl-child there loved the fairy princesses—but it was a fact. Helen considered telling him later, then smiled grimly to herself and thought, *Better not. He'll tell me it's my fault.*

The teacher's assistant, one of the children's mothers, was at Byrne's end of the room gathering up the floppy stuffed toys for their periodic run through the washer and dryer. Not a shy woman, she went up to Byrne and whispered a few words to him. He gave her a not-quite-friendly smile—probably she'd demanded to see his social security card as well as a picture ID—and then he stepped aside to let her pass with her armful of stuffies.

Disaster. He backed straight into the plastic castle, with its knights so carefully positioned on the parapets, its ladies so safe and secure inside the walls, and sent the whole damn fantasy flying.

The noise wasn't as bad as little Jeffrey's dismay when he saw someone mucking up his project. Jeffrey got to his feet with a horrified look and slapped his fists to his thighs. "You *bwoke* it!" he cried.

He turned to his teacher and, just in case she hadn't noticed, reported the crime directly to her. "He *bwoke* it!"

"He didn't really, Jeffrey, he just knocked it over a little," said Helen. "I'll tell you what. Why don't some of us spend the rest of the time setting up the castle again? Okay? That way we'll know that everything is fine. And the rest of us can have extra toy time today."

It was called going with the flow; either that, or struggle through science time with a bunch of upset, distracted toddlers, thanks to Mr. Bigfeet.

The guy just doesn't have the touch, Helen decided. *Some fathers did—Hank did—but others . . .*

She returned Byrne's sheepish look with an unamused one of her own and proceeded to settle the children into the new routine while the assistant, sighing, unpacked the hamper of stuffed toys for them.

Obviously Byrne was a hotshot in his chosen career; you didn't become Mutual Fund Manager of the Year by sitting around on Saturday morning making balloon animals for all the kids in the neighborhood. But generally, it was Helen's experience that young children and Type-A personalities didn't mix. To relate to a three-year-old, you had to believe—or be able to pretend—that life went on forever and that you could linger over the fun parts and run away from the scary parts.

She suspected that Nathaniel Byrne wasn't good at lingering and that he didn't have much fun. Even more disheartening was her sense that he might actually enjoy the scary parts: the risk, the uncertainty, the impossible situations that his career threw his way. Who else could thrive in a world where financial ruin was a real possibility? She shuddered at the thought of what he did for a living with people's hard-earned money; that kind of responsibility was not for her.

In the meantime Byrne had the sense to keep out of her

way. Until the end of the session he didn't make a peep. After their first curious glances, the children paid no more attention to him than they did to the broom locker. Eventually the buzzer sounded, the door was thrown open, and the mothers began to collect their own.

Only after the last of the children had exited did Helen turn her attention to Byrne.

He came up to her with hand extended. "Thanks for putting up with me," he said seriously. "I learned a lot."

His courtesy disarmed her completely. She'd been about to say, "Don't you ever crash a class again without express permission from the teacher." Instead, she practically apologized as she said, "I wasn't expecting you," and shook his hand.

"I know. That's my fault. A meeting got cancelled and I decided to head home early to catch up on some research; it's a luxury to have the place to myself. Somehow or other, I ended up detouring here instead. I don't know whether it was guilt or insecurity driving me."

Instantly Helen said, "So Katie did end up in Switzerland, then?"

It wasn't the best choice of words. Some of the light went out of his eyes as he said defensively, "It's not as if I sent her off to Siberia. Her grandmother has a fabulous place. And Katie has Peaches at her side all day long."

Helen shrugged unhappily as she loaded her science props into a canvas carryall. "You know the situation better than I do, of course."

So why did she feel so convinced it was wrong?

The cleaning lady came in then, with her disinfectant and her sponges, to wipe down tables and toys and anywhere else that germs liked to play.

Byrne and Helen were in her way, so Helen said, "If you have any questions . . . ?"

"Just one," he said. "Will *you* be teaching Katie?"

"Unfortunately, no. I'm a full-time administrator now, unless there's a pinch, like today."

He looked genuinely disappointed, which sent a funny little surge through Helen, and then he said, "That's too bad. I can see that the kids like and respect you."

"They trust me. But they trust the other teachers too, Mr. Byrne; we have a wonderful staff." She began to ease him out of the room so that the cleaning lady could get on with her job. At some point he too was going to have to trust Helen and her staff; she wondered whether it would ever happen.

They stood for an awkward moment in the hall while he peeled off the giant visitor sticker from his windbreaker. She was able to study his hands. Becky was right: He didn't chop his own wood.

"I've never worn pink before," he said lightly as he folded the sticky side onto itself. "Do you suppose your secretary did it on purpose?"

There was no doubt. "Oh, it was probably a random choice," said Helen as she marched him along.

But he dug in his heels. "Look, Mrs. Evett . . . since I'm here, I wonder if you'd—look, can we go somewhere for a cup of coffee?" he asked, obviously at a loss as to protocol. "I'd love to be able to talk to you about Katie, about some of the things I should do to make the transition easier for her."

Helen glanced at her watch and said, "Ah, I'm afraid I can't. My son was injured in an accident the other day, and we're due at the doctor's before long."

He looked appropriately concerned. "Nothing serious, I hope?"

"It looks worse than it is," she admitted. "He's on crutches, but the last I saw, he and his sister were having a sword-fight with them."

Byrne laughed then, a sudden, nervous explosion of

sound, as if he somehow felt guilty about it. "They sound close," he said.

"Only in the sense that their bedrooms are across the hall from one another," Helen quipped. "No. I shouldn't say that. They're close, I think. I've seen each of them defend the other fiercely, but they do it behind one another's backs, you know?"

"Actually," he admitted, "I don't know. I was an only child. You?"

"I had a brother, but he was raised with my father in L.A. He died twelve years ago."

It was odd, to be standing in front of her office sharing family history with a stranger. Even Janet didn't know she'd had a brother. What exactly was going on here?

She glanced at her watch again, then said, "You know, I have some books in my office on toddlers. It sounds silly to have to read up on how to handle 'em—parents are convinced they should know this stuff instinctively—but really, you'd find the books a great help."

"Madame, I would be forever in your debt," Byrne said, bowing low. It was an ironic, grandiose gesture and, considering that it turned several mothers' heads, an annoying one. She would've preferred a simple thank you.

Helen led Byrne into her office and quickly pulled down several books on the toddler years and swung around to hand them to him. But she did it so hurriedly that the top book slid off the others and dropped to the floor. They both stooped down to retrieve it, nearly knocking their heads together in the process. It was an awkward, but hardly extraordinary, little incident. Helen was not prepared for the look of pain on his face when they stood up again.

"*Enchantra?*" he asked.

"*Ench*—? No, no," she said. "I don't use that."

The pain turned to puzzlement. "Funny. My wife always

wore it. I thought I knew the scent. I was sure I caught a whiff just now.''

"No. I wear plain old Chanel No. Five," Helen said faintly. "Here's your book," she added, all but kicking him out of her office. "Enjoy the reading."

"Yeah . . . well . . . thanks again," he said with a distracted frown. "I'll return these as quick as I can."

Byrne left then, but Helen stayed behind for a few minutes, because her heart was pounding far too wildly for her to think about hitting the road.

She'd thrown out her bottle of *Enchantra* days ago.

Chapter 9

It must've clung to this dress, Helen told herself. *When it spilled out of the bottle last week.*

It was a reasonable theory until she remembered that she'd picked up the dress from the cleaners the day before and had left it hanging on the downstairs peg-rack overnight.

The scent wasn't on the dress; it wasn't on her underwear. The smell of *Enchantra* wasn't from Helen. Period.

From whom, then?

She pushed the question violently away. It landed in the same creepy, crawly corner as the others for which she had no answers.

Who was doing the tapping?

Who had screamed at the doctor? (It couldn't have been her.)

Who had railed at her family?

Who had given her the vicious, unbearable headache that had battered her for weeks?

Who?

Helen didn't know. She decided she didn't want to know, as she drove the historic one-way streets from the preschool to her house. More accurately, she didn't want to believe that someone—or thing—was behind the series of unexplained events that had come and gone over the last two months. It was much more rational to believe that those events were random and ordinary and most of all, unconnected.

Yes. Unconnected. A series of coincidences. What did they have in common, really? Nothing. What did the smell of the sea have to do with the smell of perfume? What did the knockings have to do with the headaches? Nothing, nothing, nothing!

No, that wasn't true. There was one thing. And damn it, it was a big thing: They'd started on the day that Linda Byrne died.

For Nathaniel Byrne to have smelled *Enchantra*—for his wife to have used *Enchantra*—went beyond coincidence. But what was the connection, then? Did the spirit world communicate with people who shared their brand of perfume? What about lipstick, in that case? And shampoo? It was absurd.

Helen believed—as her husband had not—in an afterlife. What kind of afterlife, she wasn't sure. But she believed that men and women and children and their love for one another were too wonderful for it all to end at death. And so she expected—truly expected—to be reunited somehow, somewhere, in some form, with those she loved in the course of her life. And it would be *nice* if Hank would cooperate.

But this! This didn't fit in with her theory at all. She didn't know Linda Byrne—if that's who was behind all this—from Hillary Clinton. A single phone conversation wasn't enough to form a basis for haunting, not according to Helen's system, anyway. What possible connection could they have to one another?

Katie. It must have to do with Katie. Linda Byrne had been so fierce, so dedicated a mother that her spirit was hanging around to make sure that Katie was well taken care of. It made a crazy kind of sense. It would explain the extraordinary concern Helen had been showing for Katie's welfare. Maybe all mothers were connected on some mystical plane. In that case, Linda Byrne had come to the right place. Her little girl would be in good hands at The Open Door.

"You can rest easy, Mrs. Byrne," Helen whispered rather whimsically to the air around her. "Truly."

Somehow, in her naiveté, Helen thought the reassurance would be enough.

As she pulled up in front of her house Helen saw her son hunched on the bottom step, waiting for her. His denim jacket was no match for the sharp sea breeze that was blowing in off the ocean. She thought about running in for something warmer for him to wear, but what would be the point? He wouldn't put it on, anyway.

She swung the car door open while Russ, an expert by now with crutches, deftly tossed them into the back and slid into the seat alongside her. "Sorry I'm late," she said to him. "I got held up at school."

Russ shrugged. "It won't be my fault if Dr. Welby's pissed."

"Cool it, would you?" she said tiredly.

He was still angry over the grounding she'd imposed after the accident: one full month, with no hope of parole. It was the stiffest punishment he'd ever got, and the sad thing was, Helen was sure she'd be upping the ante in the future. She glanced at her son, his chin set in stony silence, his hands slapping his thighs to an imaginary beat.

She wanted to say things like, "It's for your own good," and "You'll thank me when you're older"; but, again, what would be the point? They'd hashed all through that on the day after the accident when she'd thrown every parental cliché she could think of at him and had got only sullen nods in response.

One thing was depressingly true: he'd already had his first ride in a stolen car. The sixteen-year-old driver, who'd suffered broken ribs and internal injuries, had taken his cousin's car without permission and now the cousin was pressing charges. The police had gone easy on Russ and the other two passengers (who all thought the driver had permission) but there was nothing they could do about the angry cousin's legal vendetta.

Russ had been scandalized at the thought that a man would turn on his own relation and had muttered darkly about friends being the only blood you could count on. That sounded ominously like gang talk to Helen, but when she grilled her son further she was satisfied that he was talking through his Pearl Jam hat.

In the meantime, the grounding was in force. And after Russ got rid of his crutches—which he surely would do today—it was going to be a lot harder to make it stick. God, he was exhausting to raise.

If only he'd stayed on the basketball team. Or kept up with his keyboard lessons. Or agreed to work on the school paper. He had the talent to do any and all of those things well, but he was scorning them as too demanding or too wussy. So here he was, smart and bored. It was a scary combination.

They had to wait forty-five minutes for the doctor, but fortunately for both of them there was a dog-eared copy of *Sports Illustrated* in the reception room. Russ scooped it up and hid behind its pages the whole time, leaving his mother to scan an even more battered copy of *Good Housekeeping,* its pages stripped of recipes, its Christmas ideas too late to use for the past holiday, too early to remember for the next one.

When their turn came, Russ was pronounced fit to roam

and was allowed to leave on his own two feet.

It was anybody's guess where he'd go from there.

The next evening Russell decided to drag out his electronic keyboard, which made Helen as happy as if he'd made the honor roll. He was doing something at home. Today, the keyboard, tomorrow, who knows? Maybe even his homework.

Tortured notes and fractured chords competed with the moody Beethoven sonatas that Helen played in the kitchen as she busied herself with a little homework of her own. She was determined to find out all she could about Nathaniel Byrne's wife, the devoted mother who wore *Enchantra* and who died so premature a death.

Helen had saved Linda Byrne's obituary. It was in front of her on the kitchen table, along with a copy of the funeral announcement that had come out two days later, and an old volume of *Who's Who in the Art World* that she'd borrowed from a friend. She also had copies of the original engagement and wedding announcements from the *Evening News*. And that, unfortunately, was it.

Helen picked up the copy of the grainy engagement photo. Unquestionably, Linda Byrne had been a beautiful woman. Her face was a perfect oval, with wide-set eyes under thinnish arched brows that gave her face a delicacy only blondes seem to possess. It was hard to tell the shape of her nose from the frontal photograph, but there was no doubt about her smile: Her teeth were wide, her lips full. Everything about her was perfect; everything about her radiated confidence. You'd expect a woman like that to run a Fortune 500 company, and possibly to own it.

Which was what made the funeral announcement so troubling.

Helen picked up the clipping again and reread the last

line of it: "Memorial contributions may be made in her name to the Good Buddies Hotline."

Why a suicide hotline? Good Buddies was a volunteer organization dedicated to steering people away from whatever abyss they were peering into. Drugs, depression, bereavement, abuse—anything that could push people over the edge was the Good Buddies' concern. Their phone number was posted alongside most of the high bridges in the state.

Memorial contributions were nearly always directed toward charities that were related to the manner of death. It didn't seem possible that Linda Byrne could have taken her own life, and yet . . .

The front door slammed, ending Helen's uneasy reverie, and Becky yelled out, "Oh, no, he's gone back to his music? Gross!"

Her voice, half-joking, half-groaning, sounded like sleigh bells on a cold dark night. Helen grinned and called out, "You should've heard him an hour ago!"

Becky popped her head in the kitchen doorway and rolled her eyes. "I mean, give me a break! I can't possibly study here."

"The Celts are playing in half an hour; he'll be winding down," said Helen. She added, "I kinda like it. It lets me know he hasn't climbed out his bedroom window to escape."

"Not with that ankle," Becky decided. "Give him a week." Still in her caped black trench coat, she came over to the table and looked over her mother's shoulder. "More Byrne? Where'd you get all this?"

Coloring, Helen leaned back in her spindled oak chair and feigned a casual stretch. "Oh, just some stuff I picked up at the library."

"Are we doing criminal background checks on the parents, too, now? I thought that's what you only did with the staff,'' Becky quipped, matching her mother's light tone.

"Don't laugh,'' Helen said grimly. "Some of the parents probably wouldn't pass.''

But Becky wasn't about to be diverted. She picked up the copy of Linda Byrne's wedding photo and studied it. "Pretty,'' she said. She put it down and picked up the engagement picture. In a quiet voice she said, "Does all this have something to do with the way you've been acting lately, Mom?''

Helen had to think about what she should tell her daughter. Except for the time two days earlier when Nat Byrne had smelled *Enchantra* in Helen's office, Becky was clued in to every weird event so far. She may not actually have heard the tapping in Helen's bedroom, but she certainly understood that her mother had suffered a crushing headache. And even she had smelled the perfume. The temptation for Helen to confide in her levelheaded daughter was irresistible.

But—resist she must. Becky wasn't versed enough to take part in a discussion about psychic phenomena. Helen had an academic background in psychology; her daughter had, at best, a couple of tabloid TV shows under her belt.

"Mom?'' Becky persisted. "Does it?''

Helen decided on a half-truth. "In a general way, yes. Linda Byrne's death *has* affected me. Maybe it's because of that phone conversation we had. There was something in her voice that must've set me off, something that I must've picked up on.''

"Like what?'' asked Becky, slipping off her teddy-bear knapsack and letting it drop to the kitchen floor. Her face was wide-eyed and innocent as she sat down in the chair alongside her mother's. "You said she was upset. You said she was sick. Was there more?''

Without directly answering her daughter's question,

Helen shoved the funeral notice at her. "Look at where they wanted contributions to be made."

Becky understood at once. "Oh. She killed herself."

Helen was shocked at the ease with which Becky accepted the idea. "Oh, honey," she said, reaching out to stroke her daughter's hair away from her face. "Don't be like that—don't be so blasé about suicide. I know it's a sign of the times, but God, I wish you wouldn't."

Becky picked up the wedding shot again. "What else could it mean?"

"I don't know; maybe she called the hotline once and they talked her out of . . . doing something rash. Maybe she was in a postpartum depression after Katie was born," Helen said, struggling to come up with a less downbeat view. "Her hormones could have been out of whack. It happens."

"And her husband was thankful to the Good Buddies for saving her?" Becky frowned at the black-and-white image, twice removed from reality, that she held in her hand. "I guess it could be the reason. But then why are you so bothered? You should only be sad that she died so young."

Damn. Her logic was impeccable. This is what happened when you took someone only halfway into your confidence. "Well, look at the circumstances," Helen said lamely. "I was there when she . . . died. It was very unusual."

"So it was the melodrama that affected you?" Becky asked, scrunching her nose in an unconvinced way. "I guess."

She got up slowly, then picked up her backpack and slung it over one shoulder. "I'll be in my room." She looked at the ceiling after an especially sour note came wafting down from Russ's room. "Trying to study."

After a step or two she turned around and said to her mother, "If you want to tell me what you really think, you know where to find me."

*   *   *

The next couple of weeks proved to be passable, all things considered. Russ, while not happy, wasn't as disagreeable as Helen feared he'd be during his confinement. He divided his time between the electric keyboard and the TV and spent long hours on the phone with Scotty and one or two other friends. The melodious *bong* of his computer going on and off filled Helen with the hope that he was using it for something besides games. He was reasonably civil to Becky and positively courteous to his great-aunt Mary. Helen began to feel that the pain of disciplining him was going to pay off, after all.

She shortened his term by a week.

In a way, she had no choice; it was getting harder and harder to ride shotgun on the boy. Administrative chores which she'd been putting off were beginning to pile up. Deadlines loomed. Helen needed to be at the preschool more and more, which meant pressing poor Aunt Mary into baby-sitting service more and more. Russ saw the problem for what it was: a question of trust.

Helen didn't have much of that. It was actually easier to grant Russ his liberty than to hope that he'd keep himself under lock and key.

I'm pathetic, she decided one afternoon as she plowed through a pile of paperwork. *I'm supposed to be an expert on child-rearing, and sometimes I haven't got a clue.*

Her hand reached out to the phone. Russ should just be getting home from school. If he stopped long enough for Oreos, she might be able to catch him before he took off to join his pals at the basketball court. She punched in her home number but got the machine.

He's come and gone, she decided. Unless he hadn't bothered even to come home first. Maybe she should just slap his face on a milk carton and be done with it, she thought wearily. He was making her nuts.

Clutching an evaluation form and an OSHA checklist, Helen walked out of her office to Kristy Maylen's classroom. She needed to ask Kristy whether she'd taken the CPR refresher course, and while she was there she thought she'd check the tags on the fire extinguishers in the room.

Kristy had left. Helen was inside the empty classroom, out of sight of those in the hall, when she heard one of the mothers cry out in surprise, "For heaven's sakes—Nat Byrne! What on earth are *you* doing here?"

The voice that answered—the voice that made Helen's heart go banging up against her rib cage—was cooly polite. "Hello, Gwen. Actually, I'm looking for the director."

"Did you check the playground?"

"No. Might she be there?"

"She could be anywhere. Ask Janet to page her."

"Thanks . . . I'll just try her office again."

Instead of stepping out into the hall to greet them all, Helen hid in the shadow of the door. It was hard enough keeping Becky from learning her off-the-wall suspicions about Linda Byrne; what on earth might she say to the widower? Let him drop off the books—if that's why he was here—and be on his way.

But in the meantime, Gwen and a woman whose voice Helen didn't recognize were lingering in the hall outside the room. Helen stayed breathlessly quiet as Gwen said, "I hope he's not too grieved to manage my money properly."

"Him? He's married to his work."

"They say his wife was gorgeous. Did you know her?"

"I didn't know her. I knew of her. I heard . . ." Here the woman's voice dropped low. "I heard she was in the middle of an intense affair right up until the time she . . . you know."

"Get out. Why would anyone cheat on *him?*"

"I can't imagine. And I can't remember who told me. I might've overheard some gossip at a party. Anyway, it doesn't matter; he's a free man now. And rich as sin. She had tons of money of her own, more than he had, I think.''

"How promising. I know someone who might enjoy going out with him.''

"I'd wait a decent interval first. I have a friend in mind myself, but I'm not rushing it.''

They changed the subject to something safe and moved on. Helen was left clutching her OSHA list in a state of shock. Linda Byrne—a cheat? It wasn't possible. She was far too . . .

Too what? Too devoted to Katie? Maybe so, but that didn't mean she adored her husband. All Helen knew for certain was that Nathaniel Byrne spent a lot of time away from home and that his wife resented it.

Or maybe not. The brief phone conversation seemed so long ago now. Helen had a vague recollection that Linda Byrne had wanted to get something settled—presumably Katie, into the preschool—before something else happened. It was maddening not to be able to recall what it was.

Linda Byrne may have had motive. She definitely had opportunity. A toddler could be a full-time job, but Mrs. Byrne didn't have a career and she did have a nanny. It wouldn't have been hard to slip away if she wanted to. Despite her own best instincts, Helen found herself admitting that an affair was plausible, given the state of the marriage.

Who could the lover have been? Not the gardener or the handyman; the affair couldn't have been conducted at home. Besides, Linda Byrne was a woman of intellect, an art historian, who was being neglected by her husband. Maybe she was looking for a soul mate. Maybe she sneaked out once in a while to debate the merits of Impressionism over a cup of cappuccino. It could've been entirely platonic.

An *intense* affair, the woman had said.

Helen grimaced. There was only so intense you could

get over a bunch of dead artists. And anyway, let's say Linda did meet regularly with some professor to talk about art. Professors had more affairs, per capita, than anyone else on earth. So Gwen's friend was probably, sadly, right on the money. Linda Byrne had been involved in an affair. The question was, had she killed herself over it? Who the hell knew? With a sigh of frustration, Helen swept the endless speculations from her mind.

They were giving her a headache.

Two hours later, tired of paperwork, Helen decided to pack it in and head for home. It was a shame, really; she used to love the job so much that she had to drag herself out of the little brick bank. But in the past couple of years she'd begun to realize that she was spending far more time with forms and rules than with boys and girls. Often, when she was up to her eyeballs in correspondence, she'd hear the laughs and chatter of children in the halls and feel like the boy at the piano who hears the crack of a baseball bat outside: hopelessly trapped.

She stood up and stretched, then packed her attaché with must-be-done work for after supper, which was going to be late again. Glancing at the stack of books on toddler care that Nat Byrne had left on her desk, she peeled off the Post-it note on the top book and again read its terse message: "Thanks."

It was oddly disappointing. A personalized note or memo with the same one word would've seemed so much more grateful. She studied the handwriting—what there was of it—for clues to the man's character. Upright letters, barely more than a squiggle of shapes. The *t* was two lines, the *s* wasn't closed. A man in a hurry. A man with a goal.

Money. It always, always came down to money in life. She'd known that since the day she'd showed up for the reading of her father's will and her angry stepsister had shoved her into the lawyer's arms. Money. People debased themselves for it.

The preschool was eerily quiet, the sound of her footfalls unnaturally loud as Helen walked the empty hall through the lobby, then paused at the door to activate the alarm. It had been the first warm day of a cold, hard spring. No wonder no one was around.

Still feeling like that boy at the piano—only with supper to cook after the piano lesson was done—Helen hurried along the flagstone path to her Volvo, parked in its allotted spot behind the building.

Next to it, like a sleek black cat stretching its paws into a carpet of bluestone, sat a very new Porsche.

Chapter 10

*H*ere, still? She could see him behind the wheel, not sleeping, not reading, just . . . sitting. Waiting. For her? When he could be at home or the office, buying and selling and making scads more money for everyone?

Helen was deeply impressed. He must be taking Katie's welfare very seriously indeed to be able to make himself sit like a bump on a log for two whole hours. She was nearly to the parking lot when Byrne climbed out of the Porsche's low-slung seat and stood beside the car, attentive and alert, a half-rueful smile on his face. Despite the dropping temperature he wore no jacket, which she could see was thrown over the passenger seat. He'd rolled his white shirtsleeves to the elbows and loosened his tie, as if he were preparing himself for a knockdown, drag-out negotiation.

What, exactly, did he have in mind to negotiate? He wasn't due at the preschool until Orientation Day, more than a month away. Unless a parent was on the fussy side, it was unusual to have any contact before that time. Even then, it would be by phone.

She walked directly up to him, remembering well their last encounter. The whisper of *"Enchantra"* seemed to hover in the air. Her heart began tripping erratically, out of fear that the scent would waft between them again. What if it did? What could she say?

"Hello, again," she murmured, feeling the heat rise in her cheeks. She felt obligated to apologize. "I had no idea you were out here. Why didn't you ring? I would've got the door."

"I didn't want to interrupt you at work," he explained. "Obviously you stayed late because you had plenty of it to do."

Ah. Work. Naturally he'd respect that. "I saw you returned the books. Did they help?"

"Helped a little; scared me a lot. I had no idea what I didn't know until I read them," he said candidly.

"That's all right. You're not alone," Helen reassured him, but she was wondering where he'd *been* for the past three years. Hank had learned to change a diaper faster than she could, and Hank was the one, not her, who'd potty-trained Russell. Could a stock trader possibly be more macho than a state trooper?

Byrne had cocked his head and was looking at her briefcase. "Uh-oh. I recognize a workload when I see it. Not done yet for the day?"

Helen sighed and lifted the attaché, weighing its contents. "Nope. The paperwork never ends." She opened the door to her car and dropped the briefcase on the passenger seat, then turned to him. If he had a reason for being there, now was the time for him to state it.

"Okay, here it is," he said, as if she'd spoken the thought aloud. "I was hoping to steal some of your time. Hoping to pick your brain about Katie. I'll be bringing her back from Zurich next week and frankly, I'm not any forwarder on what to say or do about Linda."

Linda. He used the name as though she were a mutual friend. It sent a shiver through Helen, as though he'd thrown open a door to a vast, cold place.

"Mr. Byrne—"

"Nat."

"Nat," she said automatically, "I don't think my advice can possibly top what you read in the Fendelstine book."

His brow came down in a sharp crease of impatience. "That one assumes the child attended the funeral. It doesn't apply."

Which Helen knew but had forgotten. "You're right, of course," she allowed, feeling less like an expert than before. "Did you look at the section on terminal illness in the book by Carey?"

"I did," he said, "even though Linda didn't suffer from terminal illness."

Here was new information.

Helen nodded and said, "Even a brief illness would warrant the same response."

She shivered again in a sudden, rippling wave. It was cold. She was tired. Russ and Becky would be waiting like hungry cubs back at the den. She was torn between helping him and serving them.

He folded his arms across his chest and leaned back on his gleaming car, then looked down at his shoes. He cleared his throat. Then he looked again at her.

"I don't know about you," he said with a half-smile, "but this conversation, as much as I want—need—to have it, seems a little on the bizarre side for a parking lot. Can't we just go somewhere for a while, have a cup of coffee and a piece of pie, and talk?" he pleaded.

Put another way, the question might have gone something like: "Is your time really so all-fired precious?"

The short answer to that was: yes. Helen had a career and two kids. The pie-and-coffee part kind of got lost in the shuffle. Despite that, she decided on the spot to file him under "career" and have the pie and coffee. It was, somehow, the least she could do.

"All right. I just have to call home and have my kids order a pizza," she told him. "They'll be faint with hunger by now."

"How old are they?"

"Fourteen. Sixteen."

"They don't fend for themselves by then?" he said, surprised and obviously alarmed.

Helen gave him a grim, wise smile. "Not unless I leave notarized instructions on the kitchen table. I'll be right back."

She turned to head for her office, but he caught her arm. "Wait. Use my cell phone," he suggested.

Heat. The warmth of his touch shocked her. Here it was, twilight in May in New England; but it felt like noon in July in the Bahamas. "I . . . oh . . . yes. That makes sense," she stammered. "I've been meaning to get one of these things."

He reached in his front seat for the phone, activated it, and handed it to her with the kind of pleased expression that boys reserve for their best-loved toys. She took the phone, dialed the house, and was thrilled—*thrilled*—when Russ answered.

"Hey, kiddo, I'm going to be later than I thought," she said, turning away from Byrne. "Is Becky home?"

She took his grunt to mean a yes. "Good. You two can send out for pizza. You'll find a few dollars on my dresser if Becky's broke. I want everybody staying in tonight. Are you clear on that?"

She could hear him rolling his eyes. "Natcherly."

"I should be home in—an hour?" she asked, looking at Nat for his best guess.

Nat bobbed his head from side to side in comical consideration, then pursed his lips in a reply of "more-or-less."

" 'Kay. Bye," said Russ, devoid of curiosity.

Helen handed the phone back to Nat and said, "Where to? I'll follow you in my car."

But Katie's father simply shrugged. "Damned if I know. I haven't eaten around here in years."

"But you live right—" Helen bit off the observation, not wishing to remind him what a rotten, uninvolved husband and father he sounded like, and said, "Genevieve's is nice. Besides the restaurant, they have a pub with lighter fare. It's on Derby Street, near Pickering Wharf. Suppose you follow me."

They got in their respective cars and Helen led the way, with Byrne nudging her along. She frowned repeatedly into her rearview mirror, trying to keep him a safe distance from her bumper. But Type As weren't like that; Type As would much rather breathe down the back of your neck. Not for the first time, Helen had to wonder how any woman with a sensitive, artistic temperament could have married a man so hard-driving—literally—as Nathaniel Byrne.

She glanced in her rearview mirror again. There he was, his dark brows knit in concentration, his full lips set in a line more grim than eager. If she hadn't known the man, she'd have had the uneasy sense that he was stalking her. *Damn*, but he made her feel on edge. One minute he was disarmingly casual; the next minute—well, this.

It wasn't far to Genevieve's. Helen pulled into the restaurant's parking lot and Byrne whipped into the spot alongside, slipping out of the Porsche in time to get her door for her. Suddenly things were looking and feeling very much like a date, which left Helen poised between sudden guilt and murky pleasure.

It's not a date, not a date, she reminded herself as she got out of the Volvo. *It's a tax-deductible snack.* She'd make certain of it by paying for it.

He slammed her door for her while she waited uncertainly in his shadow. He turned. She was in the way. They bumped shoulders.

"I'm sorry," Helen said, truly distressed. "I'm used to getting my own door."

Byrne smiled that damnably disarming smile of his. "That's the problem with career women today: too competent by half. How do you expect us to impress you with our chivalry?"

They were very close. *Oh, I'm impressed, all right,* she wanted to say. *With your smile if not your chivalry.*

Suddenly he cocked his head and said, "Are you sure you don't wear *Enchantra*?"

"You can't possibly smell it again," she said, begging the question. She began walking quickly toward the restaurant's side entrance.

Falling in with her, he said, "I don't smell it, exactly. But—laugh if you must—I'm finding this undeniable *aura* about you. Of *Enchantra*." He shrugged and said, "You must remind me of their ads or something. I expect they use a raven-haired beauty like you."

Raven-haired! Beauty! What could she say to a remark like that? Nothing. She let the wave of pleasure that had rolled across her nerve endings recede, and then she spoke. "I hope Katie is enjoying herself in Switzerland," she said, determined to keep the conversation tax deductible.

She watched him in profile as his brow creased again. He compressed his lips and shook his head uncertainly. "She doesn't sound happy when I talk to her. Three-year-olds run hot and cold on telephones, I know. But in general, I think maybe Zurich was a mistake."

"What does Peaches say?" Helen asked as she stepped inside the restaurant ahead of him.

"Ah. Peaches. She wasn't crazy about the idea in the first place. I plan to give her a big, fat bonus when—"

A hostess approached with a smile. "Two for dinner?"

All thoughts of a simple piece of pie and coffee seemed to go by the board. Suddenly Byrne was starved, and so was she. They had no reservations and the restaurant side was crowded, but they were in luck: A table for one could be made into a table for two. They eased their way behind the hostess through the pub section and were seated in a dark snug corner with a view of the wharves through the mullioned windows. A waitress came by to replace a flickering candle inside its amber hobnailed globe and promised to return with menus.

More than ever, it was feeling like a date. Helen glanced into Byrne's sea blue eyes, then out at the darkening sky above the harbor, before returning again to his comfortable smile with an awkward one of her own. He seemed perfectly normal. She, on the other hand, felt as self-conscious as hell.

She pressed forward with her plan to take a tax deduction. "You were saying about Peaches and Katie?"

Some of the smile left his face as he said, "I was wrong about the cousins. The good news is their English is decent. The bad news is they're boys, and older than Katie. They've pretty much ignored her."

"And Katie's grandmother?"

"Just the opposite—she's spoiling Katie rotten. Candy, presents, indulgences—hell, that's my job," he quipped. "It's a strain on Peaches, as you can imagine. She doesn't say so, of course; you have to read between the lines. She's in an awkward position. She's not Katie's mother, after all. And my mother-in-law is a big believer in blood being thicker than water."

"And you aren't?"

He thought about it for a moment. "On balance," he said carefully, "I think kids belong wherever the most love is. A parent's love is a wonderful thing; but it's not the only thing."

His voice was sad and pensive and unsure. Helen had to wonder whether he felt truly enlightened or was just rationalizing. He did love that career, after all.

"You have lots of faith in Peaches, then."

The waitress brought wine, which he had wanted and Helen had not; he sipped it appraisingly, then answered her question. "It was Linda who had all the faith. She and Peaches were uncannily close. I've never seen two women hit it off like that."

"Really. How long had they known one another?"

"Let me see. I guess, about three and a half years. They met when Linda was pregnant with Katie. Peaches was Linda's Lamaze partner, in fact," he said, coloring.

Helen wasn't fast enough to hide a double take. "I know, I know, I should've been there," he acknowledged. "But I was getting the Columbus Fund up to speed: seven days a week, eighteen hours a day. I wanted Linda to hold off on starting a family, but she—"

He smiled ruefully at the memory. "She had a mind of her own," he said softly. "And I'm glad, because otherwise I wouldn't have Katie now."

But you don't have her, knucklehead, Helen wanted to say. *Your mother-in-law does.*

Still, the deed was done and his daughter would soon be home, so Helen settled for saying, "Katie's going to blossom at The Open Door. I hope you'll be there to see it happen; it's one of life's more joyful miracles."

It was a warning shot across his bow. Helen didn't want him thinking that he could dump Katie off at The Open Door and go back to moving money from here to there and back again without another care in the world. Single fathers didn't get to do things like that.

He lifted one eyebrow. "You don't think much of me, do you?"

Now it was her turn to flush. "I didn't say that. You seem concerned, if a little at sea."

The waitress arrived before he got a chance to respond. After she left with identical orders of chicken breast in raspberry vinaigrette, he said, "Let me be blunt. I haven't been a hands-on father, partly because Linda never forced me to. She was perfectly happy, with Peaches's help, to do the parenting on her own.

"All right," he corrected, "maybe not perfectly happy. We were fighting a lot over my absences at the end . . . fighting over everything, actually," he muttered as he fiddled with his bread knife.

He stared out the window, and it seemed to Helen that he was somewhere else altogether. "There was increasing . . . hostility. We didn't seem able to communicate at all. I thought it was about Katie, but it wasn't. It was about Linda . . . or me . . . or both of us. I don't know. We just lost it. In the space of a few months, we just . . . lost it," he said with a bleak little sigh. "It happened so fast. All of it."

Caught completely off guard by his candor, Helen made a big deal of buttering her roll. She had no idea what to say. He seemed to want to talk, not about Katie so much as about Linda. It was natural, of course. He was bereaved; and Peaches, his sounding board, was in Zurich.

Helen felt obliged to say something. "No one is ever really prepared for the death of someone close." It sounded so trite.

He swung his gaze back to her. "Are you married, or divorced?" he asked, implying that there were only those two choices.

"Neither. Like you, widowed."

He looked bewildered, as if she'd accused him of joining a cult. "*Widowed*. It's a funny word. I don't feel widowed. I feel as if Linda's just gone off in a snit. That she'll be back and we'll hash it all out. The end was so . . . God. Brutal.''

He looked up at Helen, genuine pain in his eyes. "We hadn't been speaking for three days before. . . .''

Three days. Helen had hardly gone three hours in anger at Hank. "That makes it much worse, then," she conceded.

"If I could only have the days back!" he said fiercely. Then he focused on Helen once again, with an intensity that left her drained. "How did you deal with it? Was it a hard loss?''

His question, so blunt, so naive, took her breath away. "Very," she said.

"Was it unexpected?''

She didn't like this at all. He was a fellow sufferer—but she didn't like this at all. "You might say that," she said faintly. "My husband was a state trooper. About four years ago, he pulled someone over for speeding. He . . . he was shot point-blank by the motorist.''

Byrne slumped back in his chair, as if he himself had taken the bullet. "Oh, God. I'm so sorry.''

"It's all right," Helen said, forcing a tight smile of forgiveness. "It was a long time ago.''

"I'm sorry," he repeated. "I'm so caught up in Linda's death that . . . I'm sorry.''

"No, really, stop. You may not believe it right now, but people do work through their grief, some better than others." She added, "I had a hard time because Hank died violently—''

"I understand, I understand completely," he said.

Somehow she resented that. "I don't see how you can," she argued. "When someone *takes* a life, it's always worse—''

"Right.''

Something about his look, his voice, sent a shiver through Helen. He had refused to stick to the subject—his daughter—and had gone lurching off onto an unmarked path. As curious as Helen was to know the fate of Linda Byrne, she wasn't sure she wanted to walk down that path just then. Not with him.

She hesitated before she said, "I . . . don't understand you."

He picked up on her reluctance. "Of course you don't understand me," he said with forced lightness. "I'm babbling. Chalk it up to nervousness. I haven't been out for a meal with a woman since . . ." He shrugged. "I can't remember." He glanced around for their waitress. "Where the hell is she?" he wondered irritably. "The service here stinks. Oh, miss," he said, commandeering the nearest one he could find. He held up his wineglass to her.

Edgy and nervous herself, Helen watched him fume as he waited for the refill. He was making no effort to pick up the thread of their original conversation about Katie, apparently leaving that burden to Helen.

Well, nuts to you, she decided. *First you need me, then you don't.* This was a waste of time. Surely she should be home minding her own family instead of second-guessing the hotbed of emotions that was sitting opposite her. She resolved to wait him out. He had come here to talk about Katie. Fine. Let him talk.

But waiting was easier said than done. Something about him—something about the pain and anger and confusion that she saw in his eyes—made Helen want, suddenly, to comfort him. Whatever had happened, however Linda had died, he didn't get it. Helen remembered all too well the sleepless nights when she had asked herself, asked God, asked the sun and the stars and the moon: *why?* Why did Hank have to die?

The only answer she'd ever got was: because. Because he had to. Which was no answer at all.

Completely on impulse, Helen reached across the table

and put her hand over his. "Don't punish yourself," she whispered. "It won't change anything. I know."

She felt his hand curl into a tight fist beneath the blanket warmth of her own. He locked a burning gaze on her. "What was your husband like?" he asked out of the blue.

Helen blinked at the question. "The best," she said simply.

Byrne shook his head. His lips firmed into an unrelenting line. The muscles in his jaw flexed. But he made himself respond.

"Then you *don't* know," he said in a black voice.

Stung, she withdrew her hand.

The waitress came with the chicken and more wine, which at least gave the two of them something to do. By now Helen was an emotional wreck. They had come here to talk about Katie and had ended up talking about Linda— but they hadn't really talked about Linda, either. It was all so cryptic. All Helen knew about Linda was that in some way she had failed her husband.

By having an affair? And then dying before she and Nat could thrash it all out? Undoubtedly that would account for his bitterness.

But it wouldn't account for the anguish Helen was feeling for Linda's sake. That's where all her sympathy had begun to flow—to Linda. Despite Nat's anger, despite his own sense of loss and betrayal, Helen wanted to rally around Linda. The feeling astonished her. She didn't even know Linda. How could she possibly want to defend her?

And meanwhile they hadn't talked about poor Katie at all.

Helen put aside the odd, deep sense of injustice she was feeling for Linda's sake and said, "When do you fly to Zurich?"

"This Friday," Nat answered in a more civil voice. He seemed grateful to get off the subject of his late wife. "We fly back to Salem on Sunday. I don't mind telling you, I'll be glad to have Katie home where she belongs."

"That's great," said Helen warmly. "Before you know it, she'll be be making a dozen new friends at The Open Door."

Mollified, he said, "When she gets back Peaches is going to arrange for some of those—what d'ya call 'em?—play-dates at the house." He laughed softly. "It's all such a hassle. Whatever happened to spontaneity? Does it all have to be done with appointment books and stopwatches?"

"Supervised play," said Helen. "It's the buzzword of the times."

"Well, the times suck."

She was thinking of Hank; worrying about Russell. "Amen to that."

Their gazes met. She saw in his face an unspoken apology for being a jerk. It was enough. She smiled and said, "This vinaigrette is pretty good."

"Mmm," he agreed, but she saw that he was being listless about his food.

"I want you to know," he blurted, "that I never really considered another preschool besides yours. Linda was so adamant about it. And whatever else, I trust her judgment completely in that."

Blind faith: It was the easy way out. Helen decided to give him a little lecture about it.

"As busy as you are," she said, "I still urge you to check out one or two other schools—for your own satisfaction, if not for mine. Sizing up the building and the playground is fairly easy. I can give you a list of things to look for, although I'd guess that Peaches has done that homework for you. What you need to pay attention to is the staff. Watch how they relate to the children. Pay attention to how clean they keep the children's hands and faces. Look at how much stimulation they offer to children's senses. Watch to see how nurturing they are, and how the kids respond to them. It's those intangibles that count.''

He'd begun to smile halfway through her little lecture. When she was done he said, ''I saw enough when I saw you on your knees with the finger-puppets. You were great. Patient, focused, lighthearted . . . I saw enough,'' he repeated softly.

A slow burn of pleasure began washing over Helen. She'd been complimented on her childcare techniques many times by satisfied parents, but never—never—had she responded with such visceral, aching pleasure. Not even close.

''I'd feel better if . . .'' she began. But she wasn't sure anymore what it was that would make her feel better, so she let the thought drift away, like goose down in a summer breeze. She was becoming overwhelmed, and she had no idea why.

''You make it look so easy,'' he pursued in the same soft voice. ''Whereas I . . .'' He sighed. It seemed to bring up a lump in his throat, because his voice cracked with emotion as he said, ''What am I going to do with a three-year-old who depends solely on me? What if I screw up? What if I wreck her for life?''

If you could see your own face right now, Helen thought, *you'd know you weren't going to do that.*

But he couldn't, and so she said, ''Have you told her anything more about Linda?''

He groaned and said, ''Before I left Zurich we had a long talk. I explained that Mommy went to heaven. She wanted to know where heaven was. I said, in the clouds. She wanted to know why we didn't stop off and visit Mommy when we were up in the plane.''

Grimacing at the memory, he said, ''You can see what a mess I've already made. I said, God wanted Mommy to be with him because he loved her so much. Obviously that was the wrong thing to tell her. She was scared God was going to take me, too, or Peaches. So then I changed my story altogether and decided to go with the facts. I said, Mommy swallowed something that made her very sick. Katie said, 'Medicine?' I said, yes, which turned out to be an even dumber move. Katie got a touch of the flu after I left and refused to take anything to break the fever because she thought she'd die and get hauled off to this heaven place.''

Medicine. An overdose. The thought came and went through Helen's mind; she'd think about it later. For now, her smile at Nat's confession was utterly sympathetic: there wasn't a parent alive who hadn't been put through the wringer with his kids over the concept of death and dying.

"How did you finally leave it with her?" she asked him.

"Bottom line? I cut and ran. I think I muttered something about our being healthy and having nothing to fear—you can see how well that logic fed her fever later—and then I just . . . got out of there. Thank God for Peaches. She's been straightening it all out for me."

It was disconcerting, how much he relied on Peaches. It was disconcerting that he had cut and run. Over coffee, Helen decided to give him the most profoundly simple advice she could.

"Katie is young enough to get over the loss of someone, Nat, no matter how close," she said, leaning forward with an urgency that surprised her. "But she'll never, ever forget hugs. Reassurances. Warmth. Simple expressions of love. Those are the things she'll remember forever. Believe me when I say that."

Helen was thinking of her own mother, who had died when she was four. What she remembered about her mother and then Aunt Mary were the hugs, the reassurances, the warmth, the simple expressions of love. For one brief instant she was thrown back in time to her early years. A tear broke loose from the secure vault of those memories and rolled down her cheek.

Embarrassed, Helen wiped it away and said, "I love to wax emotional over childhood."

He was watching her with a soft, appraising look. "Because you had a good one," he ventured.

"Yes. And, to be honest, no. I was raised by an adoring mother and then her older sister; but my father left when I was Katie's age, and I never saw him again. I still regret it."

"Well, I'll be there for Katie from now on," Nat vowed. His cheekbones, high and almost fashionably gaunt, flushed dark with emotion. "On God's honor, I'll be there."

Chapter 11

*H*alf an hour later, Helen was at home, ducking under a barrage of questions from her daughter.

"Mother!" Becky said, scandalized. "Dinner—with a man? A rich, good-looking, famous—single—*man?* Awesome!"

"Not so awesome, dear," Helen said calmly, even though she was thinking it was pretty damn awesome indeed. "We talked about preschools almost the whole time."

Becky was following her mother around the kitchen like a hungry seal. "What's he like, what's he like? Was he, like, cool—or was he geeky? Wall Street can be geeky, I bet."

"Not cool. Not geeky. Somewhere in between. Confused about parenting. I told him to join the club." Helen tossed a soggy filter filled with coffee grounds and replaced it with a new one in the coffee machine. "Russell!" she yelled as she pried open the plastic lid to a can of Hills Brothers. "I can smell the litter box from here! Didn't you change it?"

"So, like, did you talk about sex or anything interesting?"

"*No*, we didn't talk about sex. What's the matter with

you? I told you. It was a business meeting. Pure and simple.''

Not so pure. Not so simple. All the way home, the very nearness of him had clung to her like the essence of perfume. She found herself surrounded by him, immersed in him, thinking, thinking, thinking of him. It was more than a little terrifying.

"You know what, Mom? I don't believe you. You look too . . . excited," Becky said.

"Excited!" Helen felt her cheeks getting more excited than ever. She'd never been much good at concealing her feelings—Hank had always been grateful for that—and now was no exception.

Scooping coffee out of the can as if she were digging a hole to hide in, Helen laughed all too spontaneously and said, "You know what your problem is, Beck? You're bored. I can fix that in a hurry. Have you cleaned the downstairs bathroom yet?"

"Why?" Becky said instantly. "Who's gonna pee there that's so special?"

"As I thought. Just do it. What did you two do while I was gone besides make a mess of this kitchen? Fold up that pizza box and put it out with the trash. Honestly. Do I have to leave a list for every little thing?"

Suddenly Helen could see it all: every dirty fingerprint on the cupboards, every muddy footprint on the floor. The stainless hood above the stove—when the hell had *that* been scrubbed last? My God. The place was a pigsty. She began a headlong pass through the kitchen, doing everything at once.

But not without raising Becky's suspicions. Becky was by far the most observant one in the family. Not a whole lot got past her, which was going to make her one heck of a mother to reckon with someday.

"What's going on here, Mom?" she asked with a sideways look and squinty eyes. "You only run around like this when company's coming. Who're you expecting? Is *he* coming over?"

Russell, responding at last to his mother's shrill summons, arrived through the kitchen door in a clunky shuffle. "Who's comin' over?" he said, heading for the cookie cupboard.

It was the most interest he'd shown in someone else in a year and a half. "Nobody," snapped Helen. "Basement. Litter box. *Now*," she commanded.

With a beleagered sigh and a mournful look, Russell trudged through a door in the kitchen and down the cellar stairs while Becky folded the pizza box on itself, then on itself again, and stood on the edges, flattening them with her hiking boots.

Helen stopped to stare at her daughter's feet. "Why do you wear those in the house, Becky? You know they drag sand in by the beachload."

Becky shrugged and said, "I forgot."

"Forgot? How can you forget ten-pound weights on your feet?"

The girl tried to joke her way out of it. "This way, if there's a fire I'll be ready to run."

"You know what? I'm not laughing."

"Ma-a? We're outta litter," yelled Russell from the foot of the stairs.

"You didn't put it on the list," Helen yelled back down.

"I forgot."

"For pity's sake. Becky, go out and pick up a bag, would you?"

"Now? It's almost nine o'clock!"

"I don't care. The smell of cat pee is overwhelming."

"I don't smell anything."

Helen had the Windex out and was cleaning up the marble counters. She poked furiously at something dried and crusty and said, "How can you smell *Enchantra* from a hundred miles away, and not be able to smell urine strong enough to set on fire?"

Becky was at the back door, pizza box under her arm. She unhooked a black silk windbreaker from the peg rack and slipped it over her black jumper, then paused long enough to fire one last shot. "*Some*body's coming. You're only like this when somebody's coming."

"I'm only like this because I'm so very tired of cleaning up after the two of you. You have your assignments. I shouldn't have to beg, bribe, or nag you to do them."

"*Who's* coming over?" said Russ with mind-boggling persistence.

Becky turned to her brother and said, "Oh . . . this guy. He's one of the parents."

"Becky!" said Helen, practically apoplectic by now. "Will you let it go?"

Becky shrugged and off she went. That left Russ, who seemed inclined to seek answers.

"What parent did she mean, Ma? They never come to our house."

Without missing a squirt, Helen went from the counters to the black dishwasher panel, continuing her hand-to-hand combat with drips and stains. "I had to see one of the parents tonight about a little girl whose mother died recently. It's kind of serious and the conversation was too long for us to have over the phone."

"Oh. So why's Becky so upset?"

"Upset? She's not upset," said Helen testily.

"So why're *you* upset?"

"Oh, for—I'm not upset, either," Helen said without daring to look at her son. "If you don't have anything else to do, Russ, I can think of lots of things."

Mumbling something about homework, Russ backed out of his mother's grip and escaped to his room.

Half an hour later—having changed the litter box her-self—Helen retreated to her book-lined sitting room and scanned a shelf or two in search of a popular paperback that she'd once bought and scanned. Yes, it was still there: *What Every Toddler's Mom and Dad Should Know: A Basic Primer.*

Helen had been assuming that Nat Byrne would be most helped by scholarly treatises on child care and had lent him some of her college texts. After tonight, she decided that he wouldn't be insulted, after all, with a little help in plain English.

Still following some new and compelling urge, she went to the phone and dialed his number; the phone was ringing before she realized that she must've memorized it from the single call or two she'd placed right after Linda's death.

He picked it up on the second ring. "Nat?" she asked unnecessarily. She realized that she'd know his voice any-time, anywhere. "This is Helen Evett."

"Helen!" he said warmly. "I was just thinking of you."

It made her heart sing. "I hope I'm not bothering you at too late an hour," she said. "But it occurred to me that I might have just the book for you."

She told him the title and added sheepishly, "It's . . . a paperback. But it's awfully good, anyway. Really."

He laughed, and she knew from the sound of it that they'd moved onto some new level of intimacy or friend-ship or just plain ease. Again she felt her heart lift in song. It was as if a new symphony were about to be played, and the orchestra had begun to tune up. Each little off-beat note was thrilling in its own way.

"I wanted to thank you again for hearing me out; I re-ally, really needed that time with you," he said frankly. "I—well, you inspired me, that's all. Katie deserves more than me, but me is who she's stuck with."

"All grammar aside," said Helen, smiling, "I think you're going to do great."

He laughed again, embarrassed this time, and said, "This is ridiculous. We're spending all this time on me when it's Katie who needs the attention."

He was right, which Helen found sobering. What had he actually done for Katie, other than express a certain amount of enthusiasm? Helen tried hard to rein in her warmth, but it was like slowing down a buckboard with two runaway horses.

"Well . . . I have the book, anyway," she said, shyly now. "Would you like me to mail it?" She hoped desperately that he would not.

He didn't fail her. "Please, no, don't go through the bother. I could pick it up at the preschool, if someone's going to be there tomorrow at, say, eight?"

"Eight?"

"Too late," he agreed. "Hmm. I gather from something you said that you don't live far from me. Would you mind if I picked it up at your house? At eight? You could throw it out the window or leave it in your mailbox, or—"

"Don't be silly. Ring the bell. I'll—we'll—be home."

"Great. I appreciate that, Helen. And again—for tonight—thank you."

"It was my pleasure."

She gave him her address and they hung up; and Helen understood, really for the first time, why she'd seized the Windex. Company *was* coming. It *was* Nathaniel Byrne. She *was* excited. Becky was right on all three counts.

And Helen, so deluded, so in the dark about her own motives, was suddenly afraid.

The following day was one of mixed blessings. The good news was Helen knew exactly where the kids were. The bad news was they were home and bored.

She was feeling absurdly self-conscious about seeing Nat Byrne, and both Russell and Becky had sensed it instantly. They were like hungry cats circling the lady with the can opener.

"What's with the lipstick, Ma?" Russ asked when Helen came back down after supper. He was slouched on the family room sofa, watching a horror flick on cable. "You goin' out?"

Too obvious a shade, thought Helen with regret. But it was too late now.

"Yeah," said Becky with a penetrating look. She tossed a copy of *YM* onto the massive seaman's trunk that served as a coffee table. "What's up?"

"Can't a person try to look nice around here?" Helen asked, turning the question around. "Speaking of which, it wouldn't hurt you to tuck in the shirt, Russ. And is there *nothing* better on TV?"

"Nope," said her son placidly. "This is the best I could find." Nonetheless, he began lazily surfing up and down the remote.

"Is your homework done?"

"Didn't get any."

"He did, too, Mom; I saw him working on it after school," Becky said with a *nyah-nyah* look at her brother. "Only he's too ashamed to admit it."

"What d'*you* know, dip?"

"I know you turned down an invitation to be on the chess team, little bro."

"Chess sucks. I'd rather play Doom."

"What invitation—?"

The doorbell rang and Helen let out a little gasp, which brought an abrupt end to the haggling. "I'll get it," she said quickly.

Automatically she straightened her hair—aware too late that she'd done it in front of the kids—and left the room.

She considered closing the door on them; it would be so, so much easier than having to go through introductions.

She let out a jittery sigh and went to answer the bell. Here she was, a so-called expert on child rearing, and the best she had to show for it was a boy who looked like something the cat dragged in, and a girl who considered black a pastel color.

Her kids were utterly typical; she knew that. And yet she'd give up half her soul to have them look—just for ten measly minutes—like the Brady Bunch. With a mental note to quiz Russ about the chess team invitation, Helen threw open the front door to the man who'd turned her life inside out and upside down in the course of one chicken vinaigrette.

"Hi," she said in a voice that was far too happy. "You're right on time. Come on in."

"Thanks," he said, stepping over the threshold. "It was touch and go whether I'd get out of there on time. And then that commute! It's beginning to wear thin. Tonight it felt like weeks."

It was a perfectly innocent remark, but Helen was in no mood for innocence. "You need to get a job in Salem," she said lightly.

"No, I need to get a house in Boston."

Suddenly she was like a kite in a tailspin. "Well, that's a more obvious option," she murmured, trying to sound impartial and hating every syllable of it.

"Problem is, the house was built for my great-great-grandfather. I can't imagine selling it."

They were at the door to the family room. "Come meet my brood," Helen said skittishly, "and then I'll fetch that book for you."

Helen led him inside. Her son was where she'd left him, attached to the remote control. "Russ, I'd like you to meet Nathaniel Byrne. His daughter, Katie, will be attending The

Open Door this summer." She threw in the part about Katie to give Nat some kind of legitimacy in being there.

Nat said, "Hi, Russ, how's it goin'?"

Russ barely threw him a glance and a "Hi" before reimmersing himself in his movie. The sounds of blood-curdling screams would've drowned out more substantial chitchat, in any case.

"And this is Becky the Elder," Helen said, resolving to ship the TV to Goodwill as soon as Nat left.

Becky came forward with a bright smile and wide eyes. "Hi. I'm glad to meet you," she said in a way that made her mother proud.

And then, of course, Becky blew it. "*Wow*. You look just like the cover," she blurted.

"Excuse me?" he said.

"I mean . . . wow. You really do."

"I subscribe to *Mutual Fund Magazine*," Helen explained. It wasn't a bad save. This way it looked like she understood financial planning.

"An overblown story," Nat said, embarrassed by either it or Becky or both. "Don't believe all you read."

He looked ill at ease. She said, "Well . . . I don't want to hold you up . . ."

Hurrying him out of there was not what she wanted to do. All day long she'd been savoring the thought of the assignation—she thought of it as an assignation and not a parcel pickup—and now here she was, practically running him out of the house on a rail. And why? Because she was afraid to have him under the same roof with her kids for more than three minutes.

They're spoiled, she realized. *They think they have sole possession of me. And I play right into those expectations.*

Well, damnit, it was time for all three of them to do a little growing up.

She led Nat into her sitting room and got the book for

him. He began flipping through it hungrily, like a man who thinks there's a simple formula for winning at blackjack. Helen didn't mind. She enjoyed watching him unobserved; enjoyed studying the way he furrowed his brow and chewed his lip in concentration. She wanted to say to him, "You're raising a three-year-old, silly, not Lazarus from the dead."

But the plain fact was, it was hard. The stakes were high. And the challenge only got harder. Ask any parent of teenagers.

"Would you like a cup of coffee while you do that?" she suddenly asked him.

"Hmm?" He looked up at her with an open, guileless gaze that made putty of her bones. "Yes . . . thanks," he said, smiling. "If you have the time."

"I'll be right back," she said softly, suppressing an idiotic urge to grin.

She hurried to the kitchen and cleaned out the filter basket, then ground some beans to make coffee good enough to seduce him into seconds. Becky walked in at the height of the noise and said over it, *"He is so—"*

Instantly Helen stopped grinding.

"—cute!"

"Shhh," Helen hissed in horror. "For God's sakes, put a sock in it, would you?"

"Ooo, I'm sorry," Becky said, matching her mother's whisper. "He seems younger than forty. I could go out with someone like him. I really could," she said in a silky sigh.

"I think Michael is plenty old for you," Helen said, shuddering at her daughter's fantasy for more reasons than one.

"Oh, *Michael*." Becky compressed her lips in a pretty pout. "Michael's a *boy*."

"And you're a girl. You match. Besides, the earth revolved around him as recently as yesterday," said Helen, flipping the brew switch on the coffeemaker.

"And today I found out he asked Chelsea to homecoming. Do you think he'd buy a raffle ticket?" Becky asked. "Mr. Byrne, I mean?"

"Leave the poor man be."

"What's the prize?" came a voice from behind them.

Both heads swung in unison. Nat Byrne, book in hand, was standing in the doorway to the kitchen, an amused smile on his face. It was anyone's guess how much he'd heard.

Becky had the decency to blush; but that didn't last long. Warming to the idea of a sale, she said promptly, "First prize is a propane barbecue and a resin patio set. Six chairs and a picnic-sized table with adjustable feet, and two little tables. And an umbrella in your choice of three colors, either solid or stripes. With a base, of course. And nothing will ever need painting!"

Nat nodded, suitably impressed. Helen pictured the plastic chairs in the exquisitely understated elegance of his brick-walled garden with its ancient vines and weeping specimen trees, and had to repress a shudder.

"Since I don't have time to paint," Nat said with a deadpan face, "I guess I'd better buy a couple of tickets. How much?"

"Five dollars each. By 'a couple,' do you mean two or do you mean three?" asked Becky, hawking shamelessly.

He smiled again. "Say, three."

He reached into his suit jacket and took out a slender billfold. Besides a Platinum credit card or two, Helen doubted that it held much. No photographs, no unfiled receipts. Just the essentials to get through situations like these.

He handed Becky a twenty. She said, "Oh, sorry, I don't have any change."

"Let's call it four tickets and we'll be even, then," he said with a wry look.

"Rebecca!" her mother said sharply. "Bring me my bag. I'll find the the change."

"Mother—we already have a deal. Thanks, Mr. Byrne. I'll get the tickets for you," Becky said, and she bounced out of the kitchen.

Nat turned to Helen and said, "Remind me to offer her a job when she graduates. She'd make a helluva broker."

"She's never been shy," Helen noted dryly.

"Is that what Russ is?"

So Nat had noticed the short shrift he'd got from her son. But then, he'd have to have been in a coma not to. Helen turned away to retrieve a couple of mugs from the cupboard. "You know how boys are at that age," she said vaguely.

"I thought I did, having been one myself," Nat answered. "But I don't remember the . . . hostility."

Helen winced, then turned to him and said in an upbeat but lowered voice, "It's all a front, really. Behind that tough-guy facade is a soft little marshmallow."

She filled one mug, then set it on a wooden tray along with cream and sugar as Nat pondered her words. He surprised her with his next question: "Do you date much?"

"For goodness' sakes, why do you ask?" she said in a ridiculously carefree voice. In the meantime she misjudged the distance between the coffee decanter and the second mug, smacking the glass on the rim of the cup. The decanter didn't shatter, but the crack made it unusable. New decanter: twenty dollars. Now they were even.

"Okay, it's none of my business," he admitted. "I just thought that maybe . . . you know . . . he wasn't crazy about having father-age figures around. That he might have a problem with it."

"None that I know of," she said, which was true, as far as it went. She hadn't dated at all. How could she know how Russell would react? She added softly, "You're only borrowing a book, Nat."

He was embarrassed by the implicit reproach. "You're right, you're right. Too much Oedipal theory. It's your fault," he said, rallying. "You're the one who lent me the books."

She laughed at that and the moment passed. After that she took him back to her sitting room, the most private room in the house. It was Helen's sanctuary, a place where generally she was left undisturbed.

Or not. Before they had taken two sips of coffee, before they had decided on an arbitrary topic of conversation, Becky was back with the raffle tickets.

"Here they are," she said, thrusting them at him. "The drawing is in three weeks."

He took them and slid them into his wallet. "Would it be impolite to ask who benefits?" he asked gravely.

"No, it wouldn't be impolite," said Becky, giggling. She plopped down on the big tufted hassock that sat between the deep-cushioned chairs that held her mother and him.

"It's for the soccer team," she explained. "We need new uniforms and jackets and stuff . . . and, like, one of the girls has a dad who owns a hardware store, and he agreed to donate the prizes. We thought it would be easier than a bake sale. Nobody knows how to bake."

"More's the pity," said Helen to her daughter's back. "It would give you something to do evenings."

But Becky wasn't taking the hint. She wanted to talk, and talk she did—about the team's record, about the team's chances, about the team's last and best game. After that she felt at ease enough to tell Nat all about the injury she suffered a year earlier when someone kicked her—absolutely accidentally—in the kidney. But now all the doctor's re-strictions were off and she was back to being a goalie again. And she baby-sat when she wasn't playing soccer or meeting with the French Club or prowling the malls. She was really a *very* busy person.

Except tonight. Nat, having drunk his coffee, stood up at the first instant that could reasonably be considered a pause and thanked Helen for the book and for the coffee, and then beat it.

Helen was, to put it mildly, in a state. She had raised her daughter to be politer than that. She marched through the front hall back to the sitting room where Becky was sitting, still on the hassock, with her head in her hands. Becky looked up when her mother came in.

"Mom! Why didn't you stop me? It was like, I couldn't shut up. I started and then I just kept going. He made me feel so nervous! I could die. I could just . . . die." She dropped her head back onto her hands.

Preempted of her lecture, Helen said, "It's probably be-cause we don't often have visitors who're so cute."

Becky moaned. "Do you think he heard me?"

"I think his daughter in Switzerland heard you."

"Don't *say* that!"

Helen ended up by feeling sorry for her inexperienced, impressionable daughter. Putting aside her own feeling of being robbed of a treat, she said, "I guarantee that he didn't notice you were acting goofy. You sounded just like any other sixteen-year-old. Just don't do it again. After all, nor-mally you sound like an eighteen-year-old."

It was the right thing to say. Reassured that on her worst day she was still a cut above average, Becky kissed her mother and went to her room, probably to record the entire humiliation in her diary.

And later, when Helen was in her nightgown and almost

asleep, Becky knocked softly on the door and came inside and sat in the dark on her mother's bed.

"So why did he come, if not for the book?" she whispered.

"He came for the book."

"No, really, Mom. You two acted like old friends."

"Friends! How could you possibly tell? We hardly got a word in edgewise."

"But when you did. You just seemed to know each other. To trust each other."

Which is exactly how Helen had felt. "I . . . suppose it's because we have Katie's interests in common," she said, hedging.

"Is that how it is when you meet someone right? You feel like old friends without hardly knowing each other?"

"Becky . . ." Helen reached for her daughter's hand in the dark, and then she sighed. "Yes, honey. That's something how it would be like."

"Is that how it was when you met Dad?"

"Oh, *well*, with your dad it was entirely different."

"Different, how?"

"For one thing, he was available," Helen said, smiling.

"Mr. Byrne is available."

"Mr. Byrne is in mourning."

"He didn't look in mourning. He looked perfectly normal."

"Men don't show their grief the way women do."

"Maybe they don't grieve the way women do."

"Maybe."

"Maybe they don't grieve at all."

It was a startling hypothesis from one so young.

"I suppose the cruel ones don't," Helen admitted. "The cold ones. The con-men—"

"And the murderers. The serial killers."

"Now we're talking nonsense. My point is, Mr. Byrne came by because he wants to be a better father. Not because—"

"Of you? I think he came by because of you."

"Well, you think wrong. Go to bed, honey. I'm beat."

Chapter 12

It was just as she feared: He never looked better.

Peaches Bartholemew, dressed to kill in a suit of rust silk, smiled and waved and then said to Katie, "Here comes Daddy, sweetheart!"

She released Katie's hand as Nathaniel Byrne emerged into the SWISS AIR boarding area, and the child went running into her father's outstretched arms. He scooped her up in a high-flying arc before hugging her to him. She squealed with pleasure as he laughed and called her funny names like Katie-Bobbaroo and Little Swiss Miss.

Someone's got her clutches in him, Peaches decided as she walked up to her employer. He looked happier, younger, altogether more lively than the day he'd left Zurich three weeks earlier.

She hardly had to ask herself who it might be.

"You're looking fit," she said as they got close. She managed to position herself so that he couldn't shake her hand. But her cheek was available to be kissed and that's what he did, quite without awkwardness, which made her think, again, that he was feeling much more at ease than before.

Still grinning, he said, "You look pretty darn spiffy yourself. That color suits you."

As well it should. Peaches had spent a great deal of time and money in the couture shops of Zurich, outfitting herself for the coming campaign. Her shell of blue silk, in a shade that flattered the rust, had been shipped from Paris expressly for her.

She blushed prettily and said, "I spent a little mad money during my stay here. I hope you don't mind lugging the extra parcels back with us on Sunday."

"Not at all," he said, but his attention was on his daughter. "Are you having a good time at Nana's?"

"Sometimes I am," Katie said dutifully. She studied the well-loved teddy bear that she clutched in one arm. "But sometimes I'm sad."

"Oh? Katie-bear, sad? That's not right."

"Because I want to come home."

She laid her head on her father's shoulder in an inexpressibly poignant way. The effect it had on him was profound. He sighed deeply and laid his hand on his daughter's cheek, and smoothed the brown curls that had tumbled over her forehead. "And that's where we're going, darling," he said, kissing her soft pink cheek. "Home. As soon as we get you packed."

With his free hand he slung his carry-on bag over his shoulder, and they fell in with the rest of the smartly dressed passengers moving through the pristine international airport.

Nat had a hundred different questions for his daughter; but Katie would not be drawn out about her vacation at Nana's. Her answers, when they came, were in languid monosyllables.

Nat turned to Peaches and said over his daughter's droopy head, "She is over the flu, no?"

"Definitely. No temperature, no symptoms. She was running around like a monkey all morning long," Peaches added in a lie. "I expect she's worn herself out, that's all."

Or maybe she's tired after the nightmares about witches all night.

"So how are things back in Salem? You've been busy?" Peaches said, changing the subject.

"Yeah, the usual," he said, obviously distracted. "Sweetie?" he murmured, cocking his head to meet his daughter's averted gaze. "Are you all right?"

Katie shrugged uncertainly.

He laid the palm of his hand against her forehead. "You feel okay. Hmmm. Do you think if we stopped for an ice cream, that it would perk us all up?"

Katie sighed and said, "Maay-be."

Reassured, he smiled and said, "I think maybe it would, too." He turned and winked at Peaches, convinced that he'd managed to turn his daughter's spirits around.

Peaches smiled back. He was so naive.

Three days without him. Presumably it could be done. On Friday night Helen worked late at home. On Saturday morning, she cleaned out her closet and made Russ and Becky do the same. On Saturday afternoon she boxed everything up for the Salvation Army and made a list of it all for her accountant. On Sunday afternoon she went antiquing on Pickering Wharf and came home with a set of silver butter knives and, for her aunt Mary, a pair of Victorian needlepoint pillows. On Sunday evening she dragged the kids off to a restaurant with their great-aunt to celebrate her seventy-fourth birthday. On Sunday night she drank a tall glass of warm milk to help her fall asleep quickly, so that she'd be all rested for Monday.

And on Monday morning she opened her eyes and asked herself, "What the heck does it matter if I'm rested or not?"

It was as if a spell had been broken. Somehow—blame it on Becky—Helen had got it into her head that she and Nathaniel Byrne had established a relationship of some kind. It may have been based on a mutual concern (Katie) or shared grief (loss of a spouse) or even mutual admiration (she understood preschools; he understood finance).

But lying in her bed in the clear bright light of Monday morning, Helen knew: The one thing the relationship was *not* based on was mutual attraction. It would be too . . . unseemly.

She smiled unhappily at the old-fashioned word. *Unseemly.* The idea seemed almost quaint. In these days of instant attraction and overnight courtships, what was so unseemly about a widowed man being attracted to a widowed woman? And yet there it was: unseemly. Nathaniel Byrne's wife had recently been laid to rest, and nothing but the passage of time could create a decent interval where there was none.

You're a fool, Helen Evett, she told herself. *He's implied nothing, said nothing, done nothing even remotely out of line. You're the one who's having the damned unseemly fantasies.*

Fool.

She dressed and went to school, disappointed in herself for having let her imagination drift into places where it could not go. And yet, despite all her efforts to focus on the bleak reality of the situation, Helen found her imagination . . . drifting, all day long.

Every time Janet passed a call through to her, she imagined. Every time she heard the sound of a high-strung car engine out in the street, she imagined. Every time she heard footsteps in the hall, a male voice, or a woman's surprised laugh, she imagined. For that matter, every time she saw a stupid little Post-it note—and her office had them everywhere—she imagined Nat there again, with her again.

She remembered his intensity at Genevieve's; his warmth on the phone; his wry, quick glances over coffee while Becky babbled. *Was* there something there besides simple civility? In her heart of hearts Helen had to say: yes.

But what did *she* know? She was out of touch with that whole scene. When was the last time she actually had someone come on to her? She hardly ever went to parties, and she hadn't been at a bar with friends in a long, long time. As for those fixed-up dinner partners—well, the less said about them, the better.

One thing Helen did know. People were much more blunt than they used to be. The modern, interested male probably said something like, "Hey, babe—how about it?" and if the babe said, "Cool," that'd be it: into the sack they'd go.

If Nat had asked, Helen thought wryly, she'd probably have remembered.

Still, at the end of the day as she walked to her car, the memory of him sitting behind the wheel of his black Porsche was so vivid, so utterly thrilling, that Helen had to shut her eyes and bite her lip and blink back tears.

It was absurd. She was absurd. She resolved to get on with her life.

She managed to do that pretty well until she hit Friday night, which she spent within pouncing distance of the phone. On Saturday she paced. On Sunday she moped.

And then it was Monday again.

Three weeks later, Helen was in the garden with her aunt Mary, knee-deep in six-packs of newly bought annuals: pink cosmos and white cleome and deep yellow sunflowers (if the picture-tags ran true), and a whole flat of white impatiens to brighten up the shadier parts of the yard.

The morning was sunny and warm, the kind of May day that people write songs about, and the mood of the two women was as mellow as the temperature. Two Bufferin had knocked back Aunt Mary's arthritis, and a rare Bloody Mary had done the same for Helen's lingering sense of disappointment over Nat.

Pretty faience plates with croissant crumbs, empty majolica fruit bowls, and half-filled cups of rich, dark coffee were all that remained of their outdoor Sunday brunch. It was their first of the year, a ritual that dated back to the days when Hank took the kids to the Salem Common to play catch or fly kites, giving aunt and niece some time alone with their Memorial Day plantings.

"Lena," said Aunt Mary, slipping into a pair of soft cotton gloves, "whatever made you buy sunflowers? Where will we put them?"

"These are dwarfs—they say. We'll stick 'em behind the birdbath. How much trouble can they get into there?"

"That might work."

"And the cardinals will be thrilled."

"If the squirrels don't get there first."

"Okay," Helen said, taking a pair of lime green gloves and a trowel from her ancient trug. "Let's start digging."

The women worked contentedly for several hours, filling in the gaps left by faded spring bulbs and fickle perennials. The work was easy and satisfying. Scoop out two spoons of dirt, pop in a tiny root ball, and there it was: a young, eager annual just bursting to take off.

They're like kids, Helen mused as she patted warm, crumbly earth around the stems. *Reckless, energetic, desperate for attention.*

"Lena, dear, is Russell all right?"

Helen looked up across the kidney-shaped bed at her aunt who knelt opposite her, on a pad set in a sturdy metal frame to help her get up and down.

Helen laid the six-pack of cosmos on the grass and leaned back on her haunches. "Why do you ask?"

"Well, yesterday when I was in the back hall fiddling for my keys, I heard someone arguing with him. Very loud, he was."

"Scotty? Was it Scott?" Only two or three others had permission to be there when she wasn't home.

Her aunt brushed a gray-white strand of hair back over her forehead, leaving a streak of moist earth on her face, and shook her head. "No. I didn't recognize this voice. Didn't care for it, either. The boy's language was terrible. I know they swear and such when they're not around us, but—"

"Did you go in to see who it was?"

"I knocked. They clammed right up. I thought, they're embarrassed to be heard. It seemed enough. I went on my way."

Disturbed by the news, Helen frowned and said, "I'll ask him about it."

"No, no, don't," her aunt said, scandalized. "He'll think I told on him."

"You did tell on him," Helen said with a grim smile. "But that's all right. He has to understand that if he's broken the rules, he can expect—"

"Mom, Mom!" came Becky's excited cry behind them. "Guess who I just saw!"

She came running up to them, then dragged over a small metal bistro chair and sat down in it with an eager expression on her face. She leaned forward. "Guess!"

The girl was dressed in her version of spring: crushed pale linen hat with the front brim pinned back; black sleeveless jumpsuit. She'd been too long in the sun without sunblock, Helen noted; her nose was burned, and the tops of her shoulders. She looked whimsical, charming, vibrant, and—like the annuals—ready to explode.

"I haven't got a clue," Helen said, smiling, as she returned to her cosmos. Pink or white? There was no tag.

"Nathaniel Byrne."

That got Helen's attention. Down went the little six-pack again. Helen looked up with what she hoped was a mild expression. "Really? How did you manage that?"

"I was walking on the Common with Michael—he didn't want to ask Chelsea to homecoming, by the way; she forced him to—and there he was: flying a kite. This big, huge, enormous kite with Snow White on it. And a tail that must have weighed twenty pounds. There wasn't any wind; the kite just kind of sat there. Once in a while it went up a few feet, then dropped back to the ground. It was hysterical."

"He saw you snickering at him?"

"No, he was too busy."

"He was flying a Snow White kite on Salem Common by himself?"

"Of course not. He had an adorable little girl with him. I guess it was his daughter?"

"Brown curly hair? Fat bowed legs?" Becky nodded and Helen said, "That was Katie, without a doubt." The image of them together with the kite tugged at Helen's heart. She would have loved to have been there.

"And someone else," Becky added.

Something in her voice washed over Helen like an ocean wave in January. "Beautiful?" she asked quietly. "Great figure? Dressed for a fashion show?"

"Yeah," said Becky, her face a mirror of her mother's disappointment. "She sure wasn't dressed for a day in the park."

"That was the nanny," Helen said dryly.

"No way! She was giving him these adoring looks . . . no *way*," Becky repeated, unconvinced. "The woman I saw had a thing for him, Mom. Really."

"Nannies can have things for their employers," Helen said, remembering the way Peaches had looked once or twice at Nat when they were at The Open Door. "Haven't you ever watched *Upstairs, Downstairs*?"

"She didn't look very downstairs to me. How can she dress like that on a nanny's wages?"

"How do you manage on a baby-sitter's wages?"

"That's different. I shop for bargains. I guarantee she's never been in an outlet store."

"Obviously Peaches is good at what she does. She must get paid well," Helen said, trying hard to be less catty.

"She has a nice laugh," Becky added glumly. "She laughs a lot. Then again, it was funny, the way he tried and tried."

"I wonder if he got it up."

"Mother!"

"The *kite*."

"Of course the kite," said Becky, reddening under her sunburn. "Yeah, he did, eventually. Someone went over and told him to shorten the tail."

Helen could feel a fine flush of color in her own cheeks. In the meantime poor Aunt Mary was utterly lost amid the double-talk.

"Who're we talking about?" she asked over her spectacles. She leaned into the side handles of her kneeler and pulled herself up with an effort. "Whoever he is, you both seem fixated on him."

"No, we're not," said Helen.

"Yes, we are," argued her daughter. "Except Mom won't admit it. Well, I'll admit it: I wouldn't mind having him hang around here."

"Don't hold your breath."

Becky sighed and pulled off her hat. "Too bad about the nanny," she said. With droopy shoulders, she hauled herself out of the bistro chair and went inside, forlornly smacking her hat on her thigh as she walked.

Whatever Becky had witnessed, it was enough to convince her that Nat and Peaches were either an item or on the way to becoming one. The thought wrapped itself around Helen's heart like rusty chain.

What's this? she thought, amazed. *Jealousy?* If so, it was a brand-new emotion. She'd never been jealous in her life; with Hank there'd been no need. And yet the thought of Nat and Peaches laughing over how to fly a kite for Katie ripped at Helen's soul. She felt her heart pound, her cheeks burn, her body flood with adrenaline.

I can't believe this, she thought. *This is really scary.*

Aunt Mary had pulled off her gloves and, with a grimace, was arching her back.

Helen had to pull herself together. "It's getting chilly out here," she said to her aunt. "Why don't you go in? I'll finish up."

"I think I will, dear. Thank you. What's left? Only the one six-pack?"

"That's it, and then we're done."

"Well, it was a good day's work. In a month this will be a magical place." Smiling, Aunt Mary took one last, lingering look around, and then she left.

Helen took her trowel and made six sloppy holes, then threw in the last of the cosmos. Pink, white?

Suddenly she didn't care.

The heart-wrenching feeling that Helen called jealousy stayed with her throughout the week. She couldn't shake it. It dogged her, just like the headache that had ruined her days and haunted her nights. She walked around in a tangle of anger and melancholy.

Russ was the first to feel the heat. She blistered him for having someone over without clearing it with her, and then abruptly changed course when she learned that the new friend's name was Dale. A Dale couldn't possibly own a weapon or smoke marijuana. As for Dale's language, Aunt Mary had probably overreacted.

For now she was giving her son—and Dale—the benefit of the doubt. Her angry scolding ended up in a melancholy apology. Russ obliged her with a half-angry, half-melancholy apology of his own.

The jealousy continued. After a week of sleepless nights, Helen did what she never thought she'd have the nerve to do: picked up the phone and called Nathaniel Byrne herself.

She had an excuse, sort of. After an exchange of greetings—his warmer than hers—she said, "Orientation Day is next week, Nat, but we haven't had a response from you. Will you be able to come? I think you'd enjoy meeting the other parents. Look at it as the first meeting of a twelve-step program in parenting," she added lightly.

It was said in the most professionally pleasant voice she could muster. She was determined not to sound clingy. And besides, what she said was true. He hadn't RSVP'd to The Open Door invitation.

He had no idea what she was talking about. "It must've got lost in the mail," he said. "Honest. I never saw it. Of course I'll be there."

"In that case," she said, hard-pressed to keep the joy out of her voice, "I'm glad I called." She gave him the day and the time and was about to ring off, reluctantly, when he said, "Helen—wait."

Two words, both music to her ears. "Yes?"

"I've wanted to call you but I wouldn't let myself."

Her heart started a free-float. She was responding to his tone more than his words. She smiled and said softly, "You're not under any obligation—"

"I decided I couldn't go running to you for advice about every little thing," he explained, "like some kid in his first chemistry class who's afraid he's going to blow himself up. So I'm toughing it out with Katie. I've made some progress

. . . it does seem to feel a little more natural, although— hell, who'm I kidding? I have a notebook filled with questions for you."

Helen laughed and said, "That's all right. Fire away."

"Wait, let me just close the door," he said.

She heard him walk across the room, heard the sound of a heavy door slipping into place. His voice dropped to a low, concerned tone. "Katie seems to have changed her mind about The Open Door."

"Because . . . ? Is she having that hard a time with her mother's death?"

"She has her bad days," he admitted. "But it's more than that. She seems to be afraid of the school itself. Afraid of the teachers there. Afraid," he said finally, "of you."

Peaches waited until she heard him hang up the phone, and then she eased the extension into its cradle. Sooner or later she had expected Katie to voice her vague fears to her father. Sooner was better, actually. It might keep Katie out of The Open Door and away from Helen Evett.

But now she'd been thrown a curve. She'd just heard him invite the Evett woman to the house so that she and Katie could get to know one another. The direct approach: how very typical of him. It was his greatest strength and his most exasperating weakness.

Well, she'd have to deal with it. There were angles she could play. Helen Evett had been at the house just once before, and when she left, Katie's mother was dead. It was an easy, frightening association, one which Peaches had been pointing out to Katie whenever she could.

How would it be, if she ratcheted up the fear? What if Katie were made to understand that the next time Helen Evett showed up, someone else might disappear?

It could be Peaches. Perhaps Daddy. Maybe even Katie herself.

Chapter 13

On Saturday morning Katie's father was in his office on the first floor of the mansion, running the numbers on a possible stock acquisition. A national HMO was rumored to be eyeing a regional HMO, and he had to decide if there was money to be made for his shareholders in the process. Quite obviously, he did not want to be disturbed.

Quite obviously, Peaches would have Katie to herself until the arrival of Helen Evett.

"I'm expecting Helen at two, but don't mention it to Katie," Nat had remarked. He didn't explain the reason for the secrecy and Peaches, of course, had no need to ask.

She took Katie, sluggish from a big breakfast, upstairs to the nursery to wash her and change her and poison her mind. Time was running out. Although Katie had been sad and vulnerable on Thursday, Thursday had felt too soon. Friday hadn't been any good, either. The child had been cranky and unreceptive all day. It was now or it was never.

"Come, sweetie, time to get dressed," said Peaches in her most caressing voice. "Would you like to wear the pink top, or the yellow one?"

"Pink," said Katie, sitting on the carpeted floor of the dressing room, busy with her feed-and-wet doll.

"And which jumper? The blue one, or the green one?"

Katie looked up and pointed emphatically to the apple green gingham frock that Peaches was holding in her left hand.

"Good choice! This will make a pretty outfit," said Peaches to the child. "Would you like to wear a ribbon in your hair today?"

"Uh-huh. Can my dolly have one, too?"

"Oh, for sure," cooed Peaches. "Let's see. What would be a nice ribbon for dolly? I'll look through the basket."

Peaches poked around in a basket of bows that lay on top of one of the painted white chests and pulled out a pink bow for Katie and a red ribbon for her doll.

"You know, it's a good thing I'm here, isn't it, Katie? Because I'm big enough to reach things on this dresser."

"But I'm not," agreed Katie, taking the red ribbon from Peaches. "I'm just liddle." She fussed with the ribbon, twisting it around the doll's blond hair without being able to tie it.

"And I'm big," Peaches repeated, "so I can do things for you, and take care of you." She knelt down next to the child and gently took the ribbon from her. "But sometimes I'm afraid that I won't be here to do things like this; like tying this ribbon in dolly's hair."

"Why?" asked Katie with a surprised—and alarmed—look on her face.

"Well, you remember how we talked about when Mommy went away so suddenly? Do you remember what we said?"

Somewhere in her subconscious, the child obviously remembered that there was a distressing connection to her mother's disappearance. Her fine, dark brows drew down in worry; her round cheeks got a little bit rounder as she pursed her lips in concentration. "When Mommy went away she diddent say good-bye," she murmured, hurt all over again.

"That's right. She didn't. And do you know why?"

Katie started to say something, then stopped. Her mouth was a little open, as if her words were too afraid to make the leap.

Peaches wanted Katie to come up with the name of Helen Evett on her own. "Katie? You remember," she coaxed.

Whether Katie remembered or not, she never got the chance to say so, because an ear splitting alarm went off just then on the first floor.

"A fire!" said Katie, responding to a much more obvious association.

Who could tell? Peaches had no choice but to grab up Katie and rush her down the stairs to safety. Nine chances out of ten it was a false alarm, but Nat wouldn't want his nanny making that judgment on her own.

At the door to the kitchen, they discovered the cause: billowing smoke from a pan on the stove, left to burn by the Cook Who Drank.

Damn!

Nat had got there first and was pulling the safety on a large fire extinguisher as they watched. Unaware of their presence, he worked quickly to put out the flames, spraying chemical foam over the pan and some nearby newspapers that had also caught fire, not stopping until the extinguisher was emptied.

After he was done he turned to the cook, who was leaning against the wall, weaving in place and staring at nothing. Peaches wasn't sure the woman even knew there'd been a fire.

"That's it. You're fired," Nat said with repressed fury. "Get out. Now."

The smell and the mess were horrendous. The commercial range and the butcher-block counters were covered in sticky white goo. Nat was clearly about to let loose with a stream of invective when he saw his wide-eyed daughter, clinging tightly to her nanny.

"Katie," he said soothingly. "Isn't this a mess! I guess we won't be eating chicken nuggets for lunch, will we? Maybe we'll just have pizza."

With impressive sangfroid Katie said, "It isn't even lunchtime."

Nat threw a deadly look at his retreating, staggering ex-employee and said, "You're absolutely right, punkin. But when it *is* lunchtime, that's what we'll order."

He took Katie from Peaches and said apologetically to the nanny, "I hate like h—the dickens to ask you, Peach, but can I beg you to make some kind of pass over this mess? After that, call in some professionals to finish the job."

"Think nothing of it, Nat," she said reassuringly. "I'll be glad to do it."

"Thanks. You really are a Peach. And one last thing," he added, lowering his voice. "Make sure she leaves. Pronto."

"Where is she going?" piped up Katie. Her voice was high and strained, on the way to panic.

Excellent. Peaches bent her head sideways in a tender way and said with a soft smile, "Shhh . . . no place very far, honey."

In a painfully jovial voice Nat said to his daughter, "How about a little horsie ride into Daddy's office? While Daddy works, you can draw or paint or . . . something. Whatever. God—the timing!" he moaned, and marched off with Katie on his shoulders.

The timing stinks, decided Peaches, surveying the mess.

At exactly two o'clock they heard three strong whacks on the brass-ship door knocker.

Most visitors rang the bell. Peaches, who'd barely had time to peel off her rubber gloves and change back into decent clothing, allowed herself a startled gasp.

Katie picked up instantly on Peaches's reaction. "What was that?" she asked, staring with big eyes into the hall.

"I'll get it," said her father quickly. He threw down his unread newspaper and walked out of the music room, leaving Peaches alone with his daughter.

"Goodness," she said to Katie when Nat was out of earshot, "that scared me. Who could it be that doesn't ring the doorbell? Someone mysterious, I'm afraid."

Picking up on the key words, Katie whispered, "Me, too."

But then she heard her father's voice in the hall, low and friendly and laughing. Something in the sound of it made her face light up. "Mommy's back!" she cried, and scrambled to her feet.

She hears intimacy, Peaches thought calmly.

She intercepted the child, then decided to let her run. Katie shot off toward the hall, with Peaches moving swiftly behind her. She was in time to see Katie come to a screeching halt in front of her father and Helen Evett, who was dressed in an amazingly ordinary dress of yellow challis patterned with blue cornflowers.

Clearly baffled, Katie whirled around to Peaches, then back to her father. Peaches thought she'd want to know where her mommy was, but the child surprised her by not saying anything at all. Instead, she seemed to be studying Helen Evett.

Helen stooped down to Katie's level; her off-white linen jacket skimmed the antique Persian that carpeted the entry hall. She wore pale stockings and bone shoes, probably Brazilian, certainly not Italian. Peaches was interested, as before, to see that she still wore her wedding band and a small solitaire engagement ring. Her black hair was pulled away from her face and pinned in back; the rest fell straight and loose on her shoulders.

Plain, plain, plain, despite her good color, thought Peaches. *She can't possibly have his attention.*

She certainly had Katie's. The child's hands shot up to the bow in her hair—a band of pink roses on white—as she said, "I'm all dressed up for my tea party."

"And you look very pretty," said Helen. Her smile took in Peaches, who returned it, but it dwelled on Katie. "Did you pick your clothes out yourself?"

"Uh-huh. How did you know that?" asked Katie, wondering.

Because that's what three-year-olds do, thought Peaches, suppressing her irritation behind an amused and loving grin.

"Well, when my daughter was as old as you, she always wanted to pick her own clothes out."

"And I can even dress myself," Katie said. She looked up at Peaches. "I can," she insisted. It didn't happen very often; her nanny discouraged such acts of independence.

"You can do lots of things," Peaches said as she straightened the bow in the child's hair.

Nat had his hands in his khaki pockets, as if he were strolling among guests at a garden party. Nat being Nat, he should've felt harried and out of place; but he was clearly interested in the way Katie and the preschool director were relating.

More than that: He was interested in the preschool director herself. Peaches watched as his gaze moved from the top of her head to the hem of her dress, which lay on the carpet in a puddle of cornflowers. He came back to Helen Evett's face, and suddenly Peaches saw what he saw: high cheekbones kissed with natural color, green-gray eyes rimmed in thick lashes, full lips barely touched by lipstick.

She didn't like what he saw.

He seemed to have to shake himself loose from his reverie. "Katie and I were just about to have tea," he said with a fond glance at his daughter.

"Uh-huh," said Katie, nodding her head. "And you could come, too. Okay?"

Nothing in Peaches's carefully planned campaign had prepared her for the child's about-face. Tea with Helen Evett! The little brat had forgotten everything. And then the morning—wasted. Because of that stupid, damned drunk of a cook.

"Well, thank you," the Evett woman said to Katie. "I'd be very happy to have tea with you."

"But we don't know where to have it," Katie said with a fretful sigh. "Daddy says it's too wet outside. And that silly ahl is in the tree. What if it could eat up all our cookies?"

Peaches noted that some of the color drained from Helen Evett's face. Interesting: Suddenly she wasn't quite so pretty. The nanny smiled; a little makeup would've prevented all that.

"An owl?"

Helen's heart took a dive at the mention of the word. She hadn't thought about the owl since the day Linda Byrne died; but the owl and the death were entwined in her memory, and the memory was disturbing.

"Uh-huh. It lives in our tree. And it eats all the mouses."

"My goodness!" Helen said to cover the faintness she felt. "And does it say 'who, who'?"

Katie shook her head. "But sometimes it sneezes."

Nat smiled and said, "Our neighbors have a potting shed filled with sacks of birdseed. The shed's not tight; every mouse in the county has figured it out. In the meantime the owl's figured out about the mice."

"I thought owls hunted at night," Peaches remarked.

Nat shrugged. "Not this one. Well, where do we set the

table, Katie-kins? Music room or your room?''

Katie clasped her hands together and lifted them over her head. ''Mine!'' she said, reaching a decision at last.

''Yours it is, then,'' her father said solemnly, extending his hand to her.

Katie and her father led the way; Helen fell in behind with Peaches. The nanny, who'd taken Helen's purse and jacket, was going on in a pleasant way about a Monet painting that hung in a lighted alcove at the foot of the grand staircase, but Helen wasn't hearing much of what she said. Her attention was focused on two things: father and daughter.

Her emotions, already wound tight before she got there, had corkscrewed still further when Nat had answered the door instead of Peaches. Had he any reason to do it besides laughing off the grease fire earlier? Or was Helen looking for meaning where there was none? He'd greeted her warmly; but then that was his way.

And the owl. What was that all about? Was it the association with Linda Byrne's death that had set Helen's heart thundering? And yet Katie didn't seem to be afraid of either the owl or Helen right now. So maybe none of it meant anything.

Helen tried to erase her mind of preconceptions and simply enjoy the moment. By now she'd given up trying to fight the deep, deep sense of attraction she was feeling for Nat. Appropriate, inappropriate—it really didn't matter. She could hide it, but she couldn't deny it.

In the meantime, Katie had taken it upon herself to explain the floor plan. ''And this is Peaches's room and that's my room and over there is Daddy's room. It's all different now,'' she added.

For one brief second Helen saw a kind of haziness appear in the child's face, as if she were losing focus. Then she snapped out of it with the same kind of determination that an old, old woman uses when she speaks of offspring that have passed on before her.

It was a remarkable feat for a three-year-old. *It's because she's so excited to have someone new to play with. But we're not enough; she needs playmates her own age.* The sooner Katie began at the preschool, the better.

They all filed into the nursery, which Nat explained had been converted from the master bedroom, and Katie conducted a personal tour for Helen's benefit.

"These are my clothes," she said, dragging Helen over to the first door, which led to a dressing room walled on one side with painted white bureaus and lined on the opposite side with enough racks of clothing to stock a fair-sized Junior Gap store.

"And this is my bafroom," Katie said, rushing off to the second door. The walls of that room were charmingly hand-painted with images of Snow White, her seven pals, and—not surprisingly—no witch. A red step stool with the name "Katherine" in blue letters on it was pulled up to a porcelain basin imprinted with trumpet vines and hummingbirds. A slew of toothbrushes in every known color and cartoon character jammed a bright plastic holder alongside. The towels, red and yellow and blue, were all embroidered with the name "Katie."

Who had bathrooms like that besides royalty?

A third door led to a small library—"small," as compared to, say, the New York Library. Helen couldn't believe it. There were hundreds, perhaps thousands, of books, many of them out-of-print collector's items, lining three walls of shelves. Arranged on top of the low wrap-around bookcases was a staggering collection of stuffed animals, all of them with hopeful expressions on their faces. *Take me, hold me, love me,* they begged.

One little girl. All those toys. It couldn't be done.

"I will set the table now," said Katie, finished with the

tour. "You can wait right here. Okay?" She turned to her nanny and said in a stage whisper, "Peaches, you help me," and hauled her by the hand into the nursery proper.

That left Nat and Helen surrounded by a hundred pairs of prying stuffed-animal eyes.

"Well! This is really ... something," said Helen, not having any idea what to say about the almost mindless ostentation. There was something not right about it. The place looked like a toy warehouse.

She couldn't keep herself from murmuring, "You spoil her."

"I can afford to," Nat said without taking offense.

"You can't afford to. That's just it." God, she was lecturing. She didn't want to lecture. She tweaked the ear of a four-foot stuffed panda that filled a tufted spoonback chair and said, "Polly Panda, I presume?"

"You've met?" he asked, smiling.

Helen remembered too late that the toy was somehow tied in with an angry outburst by Linda Byrne. "Katie did mention her."

"It was a bribe," Nat admitted, "pure and simple. I missed Katie's third birthday. I was in Phoenix, checking out a pipe manufacturing company, and I brought back the biggest thing I could find, thinking it would look like the biggest apology I could offer. Didn't work."

"Ah. So this would be—?" Helen asked, tickling the neck of a six-foot giraffe.

"A cancelled trip to Busch Gardens. But Katie was really too young then, anyway."

"And this?" She stroked the soft, fuzzy ear of a bunny the size of Harvey.

He sighed. "Easter. Who celebrates Easter anymore?"

On a hunch, Helen went up to an incredibly dumb looking Santa Claus that had flopped over on its nose. "Surely you didn't miss—?"

"Can you believe it? I got snowed in on Christmas Eve in Denver. That was the old airport, though. It wouldn't happen now."

She shook her head. "It's a regular rogues' gallery, isn't it?"

"I'm the damn rogue. I know it." He sat the Santa back up, muttering, "But it's not as if she cared."

Something in his voice made Helen say, "Who, Katie?"

He clenched his jaw, then answered, "No. Not Katie."

Linda Byrne. He knew about his wife's affair, then. Helen felt her cheeks flooding with color. Obviously he'd just figured out from her question that she knew about it, too.

The brutal silence felt downright bizarre as they stood there surrounded by soft fuzzy creatures and waited to be summoned to tea.

"So many books!" Helen said, searching for a subject. She laughed and added, "Have you considered opening a preschool of your own?"

"It may come to that," he said in his new dark mood. "Unless we can figure out what the hell is bugging my daughter."

"I know what you're saying, Nat," she responded, seriously now. "But Katie seems fine with me so far."

"Yes. But she runs hot and cold."

And you don't?

Helen said quietly, "Has she been any more explicit about her fears?"

"No. Only that she's afraid of your office, as I told you. She goes on and on about 'that room we were in.' "

"That's so odd. But nothing else?"

"Just this morning she asked me, 'What if the preschool gets on fire, Daddy?' "

"That's understandable," Helen said thoughtfully, "after the fire in your kitchen."

"I guess." He seemed to scowl at the memory of the morning. "I don't know why I ever let the woman stay on as long as I did. Peaches pointed out that we don't need a cook. She can fix Katie's meals; and as for me, I'd prefer to grab something on the run—"

"Oh-ka-a-ay," sang Katie. "You can come out now."

"Shall we?" he asked, offering Helen his arm.

Smiling, she fell in with his whimsy and laid her hand on his forearm. He was wearing a long-sleeved polo shirt of a soft rose color, a surprisingly gentle choice for a man with a black Porsche.

For Katie's tea party, Helen decided. She liked him the more for it. His forearm felt sinewy to her touch; she decided that he chopped his own wood, after all. She tried not to think any further about it than that.

They arrived at the table, a sturdy little affair with a varnished top around which three fifteen-inch-high chairs had been arranged. Bright plastic cups and dishes had been set out on the tabletop, and a little white teapot. A plate of very edible chocolate chip cookies lay in the middle. A plastic crystal vase with plastic flowers supplied the necessary touch of elegance.

Katie sat down and said excitedly, "You sit here, Daddy. And you may sit here," she said to Helen, pointing to the other empty chair.

And Peaches? Once Katie got everyone in place, the nanny smiled and said to Nat, "I'll be in my room if you need me."

It could have been awkward, but it was not. Peaches had a way of putting everyone at ease. No wonder Nat relied so much on her.

She left and suddenly Helen wished she'd stay. What if Katie became frightened of Helen without her nanny close by, and went screaming off to find her? Helen would die of humiliation.

But as it turned out, Helen had no need to worry. Katie was on her own turf and in her element. She was chatty, animated, eager to please. Even Helen, who got along exceptionally well with children, was surprised at how simpatico they were.

It turned out that they liked the same colors, the same Sesame Street characters, the same Raffi songs. They even both knew Barney! Before the cookies were half eaten and the teapot emptied of its lemonade, Katie and Helen were like old friends.

When the cookies were done Katie jumped up from her chair. She went around the table to Helen and put her hands on Helen's cheeks, forcing Helen to focus directly on her.

"I will bring you something orange, okay?" Katie said, her eyes huge with excitement.

Helen laughed and said, "Okay," and off the child went, returning from her reading room with a Zoe doll. Daddy, whose back was killing him anyway, got bumped from the toy chair to make room for the Sesame Street moppet. He went off to fetch the spoonback chair from the reading room.

Back to Helen Katie went, pressing the palms of her hands to Helen's face again. *Look at me*, her gesture said. *Please, please, pay attention to me*.

"I will bring you something liddle, okay?"

Off she went again. This time she brought back a tiny worry-doll, one inch high. Helen looked at Nat, who shrugged and said, "Airport. Guatemala."

"I will bring you something pretty, okay?"

"Oh, yes," said Helen, and this time Katie—after reassuring her father that she wasn't going to use the stairs—went out in the hall.

"Probably to get something from Peaches," Nat said, as amused as Helen was by his daughter's frenetic to-ing and fro-ing. Relaxed in the spoonback chair, he was watching

Helen carefully, probably to see how long she could sit on a minichair without getting a raging backache.

"So I was wrong," he added, smiling. "She's wild about you."

" 'Wild' is strong; but she doesn't seem afraid," Helen had to admit.

"I don't get it. One look at you, and that was it. It's as if she'd known you all her life."

"Some kids bond easily," Helen said, "if you give them a chance." She thought of her son. *Then again, some kids don't.*

"*Enchantra,*" Nat said, leaning back in the tufted chair. He was rubbing the bottom of his chin; his blue eyes were narrowed under their pulled-down brows as he studied her.

"Pardon me?"

"*Enchantra.* I can't help it. I look at you, and that's the association I make. It's very . . . powerful," he said, almost baffled now.

"*Chanel.* I've told you," Helen insisted, averting her gaze from his. She felt the heat rushing to her cheeks. Her heart began knocking against her chest. "Number Five," she added, as if that would clear things up once and for all.

Into the room Katie came running, holding something sparkly in her hand. "Here," she said, thrusting a magnificent diamond bracelet into Helen's hand.

Helen's jaw dropped. "Katie! You must put this right back. It's not a toy."

Automatically Helen held the bracelet out to Nat; the strand of diamonds shimmered and shone in the beam of the recessed light above them.

Nat had an absolutely odd expression on his face: cautious, curious, amused, amazed—Helen hadn't a clue what he was feeling.

"Peaches," he yelled, almost in reflex.

The nanny came in at once. Nat said to her, "Katie got

a little carried away with her presents to Mrs. Evett. Do you know where this thing goes?''

Laughing, Peaches said, ''I'll put it back.'' She took the bracelet from Helen, who assumed it was paste, and left the room.

Nat smiled and said, ''Anniversary. Big one. Remembered.''

So it wasn't paste.

In the meantime, Katie didn't think much of being overruled. Like the Queen of Hearts, she turned petulant. She began to fuss and then to cry. Her generosity had been spurned; she couldn't understand it. The wail got louder.

Helen began trying to distract the child out of her disappointment, but Nat seemed convinced that a full-blown tantrum was in the works. He picked up his daughter and began promising her stickers if she'd only pipe down. Instead Katie began to flail and thrash.

Once again he ran the flag up for the nanny.

Peaches returned and took in the situation in a glance. She lifted Katie from her beleaguered father's arms and held her very tightly to her breast. ''My goodness, I haven't hugged you all day,'' she said, and carried the screaming child out of the room.

Nat blew air through puffed-up cheeks. ''Christ, what brought that on?''

''I expect she's frustrated,'' Helen said mildly.

Frustrated himself, he said, ''You're the expert; how do you deal with tantrums like that? They're happening more and more.''

''The way Peaches handled it wasn't bad,'' Helen admitted. ''It works with some children. So does distraction. Or silliness. Or even ignoring it, although I think Katie needs comforting more than anything.''

She added, ''Stickers and other bribes generally aren't such a hot idea.''

He gave her a rueful smile. "I don't know—they worked on Linda."

Helen smiled back, but she was thinking, *You know they didn't. You know she went off and found someone else.*

"Shouldn't we maybe vacate the nursery?" she suggested. "Peaches may want to bring Katie back for a nap. Suppose we put away the tea things—so Katie's not reminded," Helen said, bending over the low table to gather up the toy plates.

That's when it hit with the force of a baseball bat: the headache.

It was back: sudden, violent, and—Helen knew in her soul—there to stay. It was a cruel, vicious blow; she thought she'd got over the headache once and for all, months ago. It had left without warning. And now it was back. Without warning.

In agony, she thought of her purse downstairs. Did it have any aspirin? Not anymore. "Oh, damn," she muttered, straightening up and pressing her hand to her forehead.

Nat, who'd returned the spoonback chair to the reading room, came back, saw her face and said, "Are you all right?"

"Sure," Helen said faintly. "Just a sudden . . . headache." The word seemed so inadequate. Crippling seizure was more like it.

"Katie's tantrums can do that to you," he said lightly. But he looked concerned. "Do you want something for that? God, Helen, you're white as a sheet. You'd better sit down," he said.

"No, no . . . Katie will be . . . no. I'll be all right."

They left the nursery quickly. In the hall, a new and more terrifying sensation seized Helen: nausea.

"I think I'm going to be . . . sick," she said in a ghastly voice. "Where can I . . . ?"

"In here—my room," he said, taking her by the arm. He rushed her through a spacious bedroom furnished in elegant period antiques and into the adjoining bath, then retreated.

Helen closed the door and fell to her knees, poised over the bowl. A wave of ignominy washed over her, hard on the heels of the nausea. She waited, dreading the retching sounds he'd be able to hear.

But nothing happened. The nausea passed. After a while, she stood up. The headache came roaring back. Reeling, she held on to the sink. What on earth could she do? Not drive home, not like this. With rubbery hands she filled a glass with water, then downed it slowly. She pinched her cheeks and bit her lips to give them color.

Then she forced herself to open the door. As she thought, he was waiting: sitting in a big hobnailed wing chair of cream-colored leather. He jumped up from it at the sound of the door latch and said in a voice that sounded taut with concern, "How're you doing?"

It occurred to Helen that he'd witnessed her kind of pain before.

"Oh—it passed," she forced herself to say lightly. "I probably should be going. But I wonder—would you have any aspirin or anything?"

"Oh, yeah, sure," he said, continuing to stare. "In the medicine cabinet. There's Advil, Tylenol—everything."

She turned on her heel and closed the door behind her again. When she opened the beveled mirror of the walnut-framed medicine cabinet, she was startled—and yet not surprised—to see a vast array of pain relievers.

She thought, with almost tearful sympathy, of Linda's headaches. *There has to be something extrastrength in here.*

She rummaged through the bottles. Capsules, caplets,

gelcaps, tablets, time-release, fast-acting—there seemed to
be one of every over-the-counter pain reliever in existence.
There was also, among the clutter of pills, a single bottle
of prescription medication.

Ergotamine. A brand-name version of ergotamine.

She read the label on the brown plastic bottle. Dated nine
months earlier, it had Linda Byrne's name and address on
it. Without knowing why, Helen took the container down
from the shelf and stared at it. Her hand began to shake
violently, too violently to read the recommended dosage or
cautionary label.

Ergotamine. The mention of the drug by Dr. Jervis had
once sent Helen into a paroxysm of anger. She'd called him
a monster for even thinking of prescribing it for her. And
then she'd fled from his office in what she now realized
had been sheer hysteria.

Because of this drug. Seized by a compulsion to flush it
down the toilet, she pressed down on the childproof cap in
an attempt to twist it off. But her hands were shaking too
much; Katie had a better chance of opening it then Helen
did.

With a sense of shame and disgust, she stuck the brown
bottle back on the shelf and shut the cabinet door so hard
she thought the mirror would shatter.

She had to get a grip on herself. Closing her eyes, she
made herself take a deep, long breath and let it go. Another.
Another.

*There is nothing involved here except a logical coinci-
dence. Headaches are often treated with ergotamine. She
had a headache. You have a headache. What's the big deal
about this drug?*

Calmer now, and determined to make no more a spec-
tacle of herself than she had already, Helen opened her
eyes. She had intended to splash her face with water, make

her apologies, and call it a day. Instead, her plan—her life—got knocked completely off track in the brief reflection of an instant.

Instead, came the vision.

Chapter 14

Helen started violently. In the mirror, hovering over her left shoulder, was a shadowy form. More shimmer than substance, more shadow than fact, one thing was undeniable. It was the form of a woman, and the woman was in pain.

Helen felt her chest collapse, as if she'd been punched there with a fist. Though her gaze was fixed on the phantom shape, she was aware in the mirror that her own eyes were wide open in shock.

It's only me; I'm seeing double, she tried to tell herself. *My God in heaven. Please. Let that be so.*

The form drew nearer and then wavered, like a mirage on hot sand. Then the head seemed to fall back, as if in extreme suffering. Helen saw, or thought she saw, a mouth—open, dark, bottomless—crying out. Trying to cry out. In silence.

Oh, God. Oh, God.

Hands gripping the sink, Helen stood paralyzed by the sustained horror of the vision. It would not go away. It held her in its appalling grasp, crushing her, drawing down her energy, supplanting it with languid terror.

She tried to cry out but—as in the vision—no sound

came forth. Woozy with fear, she didn't dare take her gaze from the mirror. Whatever instincts she had were directed at keeping the thing at bay.

The standoff lasted for a long eternity, and then the quivering shape began to surge and recede in place, until finally, slowly, it broke up altogether.

It was over.

Helen stumbled backward from the mirror, still without taking her eyes from her own reflection, and fumbled with the doorknob behind her. She backed out of the bathroom, heedless of how she must appear to Nat, and turned to him to say something. Anything.

As it turned out, the speech wasn't very long. "I—" she began to say, and then she felt comforting blackness overtake her as she dropped, in slow motion, to the floor. Whether Nat was still in the master bedroom, she didn't really know. All she remembered afterward—all that was able to penetrate the thick filter of her oblivion—was Katie's excited voice crying, "Mommy!"

When Helen came to, she was on Nat's bed. Nat was standing at the foot of it, his arms folded across the chest-high footboard, staring at her with a grave look on his face. How long he'd been there—how long she'd been there—she had no idea.

The heirloom coverlet had not been pulled back and she was fully clothed, so apparently she wasn't dreaming. If she were, the sheets would be rumpled and she'd be naked. So would he.

She gave him a forlorn smile and said, "Why do you remind me of Papa Bear?"

" 'Someone's been sleeping in my bed,' " he quoted in a strained voice.

"And I know who it is," Helen said groggily as she

made herself sit up. "The real question is, what the hell is she doing there?"

"You fainted," he said, coming around to the side of the bed and sitting on it. "Feel better?"

In fact the headache had retreated. It was still around, but it was bearable, enough so that she could make it home.

"I don't suppose there's much point in telling you how embarrassed I am," she said, brushing back the half of her hair that had come out of the barrette. She stared at her feet. Her shoes were gone.

"You don't have to feel embarrassed," he said, taking her hand in his. She thought he was going to pat her wrist like some kindly country priest, but instead he turned it over and put three fingers to her pulse—like some kindly country doctor.

She must look like hell. She felt exhausted. Even her throat hurt. If she could see herself in a mirror she'd—

The mirror.

The horror.

Her amnesia had been total, but it had been temporary.

"Yow," Nat murmured without taking his fingertips from her wrist. "You feel like galloping horses." He looked truly alarmed now. "I'm going to call our doctor," he said, standing up.

"No, no, no," she begged. "I'm fine." She staggered unconvincingly to her feet, then promptly swayed headfirst into him. Her forearms were braced against his chest; his hands were locked under her elbows. He was near enough to kiss. She lifted her face to his—and saw piercing blue eyes filled solely with apprehension.

Her mortification was now complete. She said the first thing she could think of.

"I need a drink."

"Really?"

"Please." Isn't that what people always asked for when they were scared to death? A drink?

"I think you'd be better off with a cup of tea."

She didn't argue. Still supporting her by one elbow, he waited as she slipped into her shoes. Then he led her out of his bedroom and down the stairs. Helen reached deliberately for the stair rail; he took it as his cue to let her go.

Still unwilling to acknowledge what she'd seen in the mirror, she murmured, "I thought I heard Katie cry out."

She could not make herself say the word *mommy*.

"You did hear Katie. She came running into the bedroom—God knows why; maybe she heard my cry and saw me carrying you in my arms. My back was to her. I expect she got confused," he explained vaguely.

"I see. Where was Peaches?"

"I wasn't paying attention. Somewhere close, I guess, because she hustled Katie out of the bedroom pretty fast."

They were at the entrance to the music room. He said, "Find yourself a cozy corner. I'll be right back with the tea."

"This is so embarrassing," she blurted again.

He smiled and said, "I heard you the first time, darlin'."

He went on to the kitchen and Helen was left to wonder what he meant by "darlin'" as she sought out the pale shabby-chic sofa at the far end of the room and collapsed into its softness. She pulled the barrette from her half-pinned hair and slipped it into the pocket of her dress.

Darlin'. The word on his lips was almost as shocking as the face in the mirror. Helen could chalk up the ghastliness of her vision to pain and nausea, a kind of projection of her own misery. But *darlin'?* Was it a figure of speech? A comforting endearment? A first, easy foray into friendship? Whatever it was, she hadn't imagined it. The face, yes. The word, no.

Overwhelmed in every way, she picked up one of the

down-filled throws and hugged it to her chest for comfort. She let her head drop back on the cushy sofa and closed her eyes. The minutes ticked by. Eventually her thoughts, like ripples on a pond, flattened into serenity. She was slipping into sleep.

Bam. The face appeared, with its silent scream of agony.

"Oh," gasped Helen, hurtled from her stillness.

Nat walked through the door at exactly that moment, carrying two steaming stoneware mugs. *"What?"* he demanded to know. "It's back?"

"Oh God, yes," Helen said, before she had time to consider the question. Then: "You mean, the headache. No . . . no, not really," she mumbled, sitting up wearily.

He placed the mugs in front of her on the low table where Katie liked to color, then retraced half a dozen steps, picked up a square white pillow from the floor, and returned it to the sofa alongside Helen.

"I guess that's why they call 'em throw pillows," he quipped.

While Helen sat aghast at the thought that she must have flung it across the room to ward off the vision, Nat went over to the glassed-in cabinet and took out a decanter of brandy. He poured a big dollop of it into his mug and, when Helen nodded, a smaller one into hers. Then he sat back and said, "All in all, an interesting day."

Helen laughed weakly. "Oh, yes, we must do this more often," she said, totally ironic.

"I'd like that."

She looked at him for signs that he too was being droll, but he seemed perfectly sincere. Coming hard on the heels of the "darlin'," his remark left Helen once again second-guessing his intentions.

For God's sakes, she warned herself. *He's in mourning. Get a grip.*

Aloud she said, "This hits the spot."

He was polite and presumed she meant the tea. "Earl Grey," he said. "Peaches told me you looked like the Earl Grey type."

"Did she?" It was annoying, being categorized according to tea preference, but Helen simply smiled and said, "What an extraordinary young woman she is."

He missed Helen's coolness completely. "She graduated from a nanny's college in London," he told her. "Half her class is bottle-feeding royalty as we speak. Those girls— women—can write their own tickets, you know. They get paid fabulous salaries over there."

"I'm surprised Peaches didn't stay there, in that case," Helen said, sipping her tea and letting the hot brandy race through her blood. It was the perfect restorative.

"Well, for one thing, there's her accent. Her stepfather was British, but so what? She's American. No Brit wants his children's speech corrupted by one of *them*."

"True enough," Helen said, laughing. The brandy was wonderful. It was giving her perspective. Had she really thought she'd seen a ghost?

She said, "So Peaches came back to the States with her hard-won credentials. But how did you happen to realize how good they were? I didn't know London nannies were so special. And I'm in the business."

"We didn't have a clue, either," he admitted. "Peaches came to us in an entirely different way. She was one of the students in an art class Linda was teaching. Linda—four or five months pregnant with Katie at the time—was having coffee with Peaches and some of the other students after class once, and Peaches happened to describe the training she'd got in nanny college."

He added, "She hadn't even had a chance to use it yet; as it turned out, after graduation she'd taken a pretty good job as a British woman's companion. But then the woman died, and Peaches came back to the States, and took the art history course, and there you go. The rest is history.''

''Serendipity.'' Helen smiled and knocked back some more of her tea. ''So Katie was Peaches's first real responsibility?''

''Unless you count the elderly woman. Which you should.''

There was an edge in his voice that made Helen back away from seeming to question Peaches. And, really, she was not. After all, Peaches was obviously competent. If anything, she seemed too competent. She should've been chairman of someone's board, not baby-sitter of someone's kid.

Helen tried to erase the impression that she was second-guessing. ''Caring for *any*one is an enriching experience,'' she said. It was the best she could do.

''In any case, it made no difference whether Peaches had experience with kids or not,'' Nat said flatly. ''Linda still would've hired her. They were incredibly in tune—like sisters,'' he mused.

He got up and went over to the glass-front cabinet to restock his teacup. ''Sometimes I think about that; about how deeply Linda trusted her,'' he said. ''Peaches knows where everything is around here—the money, the jewelry, the art. And yet neither Linda nor I ever thinks—thought—thinks twice about it,'' he said in some confusion.

He shrugged off what were obviously painful memories of his wife and sat back down with a smile. ''You're looking better. The tea helped. Or maybe it was the pain reliever?''

It was an opening and Helen took it. Without admitting that she hadn't actually swallowed anything, she said innocently, ''I noticed a prescription for ergotamine in the cabinet. Is it effective?''

It was an intrusive question. Miss Manners would've said she had no business noticing any prescription in the master bedroom's medicine chest. But Helen and Linda and ergotamine were tangled up together, and Helen wanted to—had to—sort out the mess. Now.

She was surprised by his response. A red flush of emotion darkened his cheeks as he said with deliberate calm, "Is that still there? I thought I'd tossed it."

Clearly she'd hit some kind of hot button. She forced herself to sound nonchalant about being a snoop. "The reason I ask is, my doctor suggested I take it, but, I don't know, I guess I worry about side effects. You know how scary the fine print can be."

Helen didn't have a clue what the side effects were. It was just the first thing, and an obvious thing, to pop into her brain.

Nat gave her a withering stare that reduced her to ashes. Then he stood up. It was tantamount to a dismissal. If Helen had any doubts, his next words dispelled them.

"I've kept you here too long already," he said in a voice that was utterly stripped of feeling.

"Oh! Yes. I . . . I really should be going," she answered, stung to the quick by his sudden hard tone. Feeling like Alice at the Mad Hatter's tea party, she jumped up and glanced around her. "I'm not sure where I left my—"

"Peaches will know," he said automatically.

This time he didn't even have to call the woman. She appeared, almost magically, at the door. "Ah—you want your things," she said without being asked, and retreated to fetch Helen's purse and jacket.

She's made herself indispensable, Helen realized. From out of nowhere came the question: *Why*? She turned to Nat with a conciliatory smile and said, "I can see why you value her."

"She's very efficient," he agreed in the same cold voice as before.

They waited in silence for Peaches to return, then Helen

accepted her things from the nanny, threw out an awkward reminder about Orientation Night, and bade Nathaniel Byrne good-bye. As for Katie, she was still napping, Peaches said; so Helen let herself be ushered out the door.

Again. On the street, with her hand on the door handle of her Volvo, Helen was overwhelmed by a sense of déjà vu. It was the second time she'd been booted out of the house. She stared at the brick mansion with its windows elegantly shuttered to the street and thought, *What is wrong with this picture? Why the hell am I here, on the street, when I should be there, in that house?*

She did a double take at the thought. On what grounds was she basing her claim? She stood for a long moment on the brick sidewalk under a newly leafed-out chestnut tree, working it through.

Finally, calmly, she admitted to herself what she had known all along. *On the grounds that I'm the one who's seen the ghost of Linda Byrne.*

Peaches was in her room, reading a book, when she heard the expected knock on her door. She slipped her Krantz novel under the cushion of her sofa and opened the latest issue of *Money Magazine*.

"Come in," she said in a serene voice.

Nat looked more haggard, more tense, than he had in a while. It was very comforting.

"How'd you finally get her to sleep?" he said in a tired voice.

"Oh, the usual way: with soothing stories."

"Did she ask about her mother again after you carried her out of my bedroom?"

"No. She just wanted me to hold her."

"Well, good, I guess. Did she ask about Helen?"

"Oh, no, not at all."

He hesitated. "I don't like to interrupt your free time . . ."

"Please," she said reassuringly. "Sit down." She put her magazine aside.

He dropped into a small but comfortable open-arm chair. She could see that he didn't know how to begin. The muscles in his jaw were working, just the way they used to when he was at a loss with his wife. His problem, Peaches had long ago decided, was that he was too well brought up. He refused to speak ill of anyone—women, especially— and he refused to listen to anyone else do it. That made it tricky, but not impossible, for Peaches to do her work. She waited.

"Peaches . . . look . . . I've never asked you this before, but . . . I want to know. Did Linda ever tell you his name?"

Ah. Well, it was bound to come, sooner or later. Peaches looked surprised, then pained, by the question. Shaking her head, she said, "Linda was very discreet."

"As we know," he said bitterly. He swallowed hard and said, "But she never said who he was? Or where he was from? Was he from Salem?"

"Nat . . . truly," Peaches said softly. "I don't know." Her eyes glazed over with emotion. "But I think . . . I somehow had the sense that he was from Boston. And in finance."

"Oh, Jesus. Her lover was someone I know?"

"I don't know," she whispered.

"My God. I'm going to have to try to remember every Christmas party, every cocktail hour . . ." He ran his hand distractedly through his hair and stared without seeing. "This is unreal," he muttered. "Still so unreal. The baby had to have been his. It had to."

"You chose not to prove that," Peaches reminded him gently.

That brought him back to her. "Good God, how could

I? How would it have looked, demanding a DNA test after she died? Wasn't it proof enough that she tried to . . . to . . ."

Abort it? Interesting. He still couldn't even say the word, much less come to terms with it.

Look at you, she thought calmly. *Burning to put it all behind you. Without that there'll just be ongoing pain, won't there? And rage.*

With a look of heartfelt sympathy, Peaches said, "They accepted that it was an accidental overdose, Nat. Shouldn't we leave it at that?"

"How could she have been so dumb? If we hadn't seen the book on her desk with the page on ergotamine turned down . . ." He shook his head. "How did she think she could safely self-medicate? Who did she think she was? God?"

"She was desperate, Nat. Desperate women don't always think straight."

"But why not go to a clinic and have it done? Why take the risk of overdosing?"

"She may have been afraid you'd find out."

"Well, I found out anyway, didn't I?" he said bitterly. "God. I thought this thing would get better with time. It just gets worse. The slightest reference to those last days, and I turn into a psychopath. I just about took off Helen's head this afternoon."

"I'm sure you didn't do any such thing," she said to reassure him. "You couldn't possibly."

"You didn't see the look in her eyes," he said, wincing. He got up and, on his way out, paused behind the loveseat and put his hand on Peaches's shoulder. "Thanks for being there for me, Peach. This has been a dark time."

Not as dark as it's going to get, she thought as she looked up at him with tear-glazed eyes.

"Dark, for both of us," she whispered. Her hand reached

up to cover his. "I didn't want to believe it, either, Nat. Linda—with another man? When he started calling here, I didn't know what to do. I couldn't be certain, of course. I wanted to believe the best."

Peaches shuddered and went on. "But when I heard her tone, her laugh . . . I was in agony. I truly didn't know what to do. Linda was my best friend. If it hadn't been for her, I would never have known—"

She stopped before the "you." Nat looked down at her querulously but did not press. He was exactly where Peaches wanted him to be: confused. Let him puzzle out the possibilities later, in bed, as he was dropping off to sleep.

It was so much more erotic that way.

That evening, Helen carried a plate of sliced roast turkey across the hall for her aunt Mary to divide and freeze. She laid the platter on the old enameled tabletop and said in a teasing tone, "Since you're too stuck up to eat with us, you're going to have to get sick of turkey all by yourself."

"I don't like to impose, Lena," said her aunt. "You know that."

"But you're not imposing," Helen said as she went to the drawer in her aunt's sweet, cluttered kitchen and took out a box of aluminum foil. "How many times do I have to—"

"No, no, don't use new," said Aunt Mary, taking the box out of Helen's hands. "I have some scraps saved up." She went to her secret place behind the Morton's on the open shelf above the stove and pulled out several neatly folded rectangles.

"Such a lot of meat," she said as she began carefully unfolding the foil squares with arthritic hands. "How big was the bird?"

Helen sat with her chin on her knuckles, watching the

aged woman struggle through the simple chore. Her aunt was slowing down, no doubt about it. "I don't know," she answered absently. "Twenty-two, twenty-three pounds? Did you want gravy, by the way? I could go back—"

"Oh, heavens. What would I do with gravy? Gravy would keep me up all night. No, dear, this'll be fine. Now tell me about your day. Were you able to reassure your Mr. Byrne about the preschool? What a suspicious man he is."

"He's having a tough time adjusting to single parenthood," Helen agreed.

Her aunt said, "How's the little girl doing? Is she still scared, poor thing?"

"She's less afraid of me than he is," Helen said wryly, reliving her afternoon antics all over again. "Do you want me to take over wrapping that?"

"No," Aunt Mary said, a little sharply. "I can manage."

She disliked being helped with anything—from slicing bread to filling out her checks—that didn't require raw strength. But lately it was taking her longer and longer to do less and less. It was natural; after all, she was seventy-four.

Helen sighed. Seventy-four wasn't so old. Her aunt's friends at the senior center were all in their eighties and learning to dance the lambada. Seventy-four should be the spring-chickenhood of old age.

She broke off a piece of white meat and nibbled on it, then got to the point. "Aunt Mary, have you ever seen— you know, Uncle Tadeusz?" she asked casually.

"What kind of question is that?" said her aunt, busily rearranging several large slices this way and that to fit on the foil. "He's been dead how many years?"

"I mean, since his death."

Aunt Mary looked up. "In my dreams? Do I dream about him?" she asked her niece.

"No," said Helen carefully. "This would be more like—"

She cleared her throat. "—when you were awake."

Her aunt kept rearranging the breast meat: slowly, deliberately, uselessly. There was no way it was going to fit on the small piece of foil.

"No, Lena," she said mournfully. "I wish I did." She had a thought. "Why? Do you see Hank?"

"No. Not Hank."

"Someone else, then?"

"Yes."

"Do you know who?"

It was an amazing conversation—at least to Helen; God only knew what her aunt and friends talked about at the senior center. *Probably this kind of thing comes up often*, she told herself. Maybe it wasn't so weird, after all. She took a deep breath and plunged ahead.

"You remember I told you Mrs. Byrne—Katie's mother—died suddenly? Well, I think I saw her at the mansion today. Her . . . her ghost, I mean," Helen said, wincing at the word.

Her aunt looked up. "Oh, dear," she said, sad and distressed. "Where?"

"In the bathroom."

"Is that where she died?"

"No. I have the impression he—they—found her in her bed."

"Oh. Then it was probably some other ghost you saw."

"Wha—!" A sliver of dry meat caught in Helen's throat. She coughed and ran for a glass of water, then drank it in one breath and, after she settled down, resumed her surreal exchange with her aunt.

"Is this . . . something that happens to people as they get older?" she asked, folding two scraps of foil to make a larger piece. "They develop an ability to see and hear strange . . . things?"

"Ghosts, you mean?"

Helen winced again at the word and nodded.

"Good heavens, no," said Aunt Mary. "I don't know anyone who's ever seen a ghost. Except now you."

With a preoccupied frown she began piling another load of meat on another piece of foil, with no more hope of making it fit than the first unwrapped pile.

Suddenly she looked up and said, "Did you bring any gravy for this, dear?"

"*Gravy*? Oh—I'll go get some."

Helen didn't know which she found more unnerving: the talk of ghosts, or the talk of gravy. Immeasurably distressed at her aunt's growing ineptitude, she said gently, "I have some much bigger scraps of foil, Aunt Mary. I never remember to use them. I'll bring those, too."

Her aunt's tired, lined face went as bright as the morning sun at the prospect of free foil. "That's the trouble with you young people nowadays: waste, waste, waste," she said in a good-natured scold. "You don't remember the Depression."

But you do, Helen thought, kissing her aunt's cheek on her way out of the kitchen. *Even if that's all you remember.*

"Be right back," she said, cheerful as a robin.

She dashed across the hall to crumple some new foil, then fold it flat again. Uppermost in her mind was the thought that the woman who raised her, the woman who loved to cook even more than she loved to garden—that dear, dear woman, one of the loves of Helen's life, had just lost her ability to wrap up leftovers.

Chapter 15

At the end of the school day Helen left The Open Door and took herself off to the Salem Athenaeum, where she spent an hour poring over a handbook of prescription drugs. She was looking for an answer to a very simple question: If ergotamine was so good, why did she think it was so bad?

With a medical dictionary at her elbow, she waded through pages of mumbo-jumbo and came up with a couple of interesting facts. One: a migraine could be bad enough to cause nausea and vomiting. Two: ergotamine itself, sometimes used to relieve migraines, could cause nausea and vomiting.

So much for modern medicine. At least it explained why Helen reacted so strongly whenever she heard or saw the word *ergotamine*. Somewhere in her past, she must have known someone who'd suffered side effects from it. Yes. It explained a lot. She felt an enormous surge of relief.

She was about to close the handbook and hurry home to make dinner for Becky and Russell when her eye fell on the word *oxytocic* at the end of the description of ergotamine.

That word, she knew.

*   *   *

"It's a drug that induces labor," she explained to Becky after supper as the two were clearing away the dishes. "Sometimes doctors have to rely on oxytocic drugs like ergotamine in difficult deliveries."

Helen wasn't sure whether her daughter really needed to know that, but she was aching to tell someone about her discoveries. And in any case, she wanted Becky to feel comfortable talking with her about sex and babies. Nowadays, that was more important than ever.

Becky understood the problem instantly. "But why would Linda Byrne take ergotamine when she was pregnant? Wouldn't that be dangerous?"

"Definitely. Headache or no headache, any physician would've warned her not to use it," Helen said. "She could easily have had a miscarriage."

Now Becky was caught up in the mystery. She lifted their chronically hungry cat from the counter and draped the slinky black creature across her shoulder, then stroked her fur thoughtfully. Helen could hear Moby's purr from across the room.

"Hey. Wait a minute," Becky said, startled by her own powers of logic. "Like, who says she even took the drug? You said the date on the bottle was nine months ago. She wouldn't have been pregnant then!"

Helen went into the butler's pantry, now a laundry room, and began transferring wet laundry from the washer into the dryer. "You've never had a migraine," she called out to her daughter. "You don't know how desperate . . . how irrational you can become."

"Yes, I do," Becky retorted. "We've seen you with one."

Helen set the dryer controls, then came back out to the kitchen to fill the kettle. "Are you having tea?" she asked her daughter, though she had little hope that her daughter'd be able to linger.

Becky shook her head. "Library." Still, she seemed reluctant to dash out, maybe because she'd developed an emotional stake in the Byrne family. She was in love with the father, amused by the daughter and—now, too late—intrigued by the mother.

She took a seat and draped the cat across her lap, puzzling it through. "Wait! If Mrs. Byrne did take ergotamine, she must've lucked out because we know she was still pregnant when she died," she said triumphantly.

Helen shook her head. "I don't think she took the drug. I'm sure she didn't."

"But, Mom! You just said—"

"She was too smart, too well-informed. Too devoted." *As a mother, if not as a wife*, Helen added to herself. "What I need to do is prove it," she threw in indiscreetly.

That set Becky off big time. "Why? What difference does it make now? She's dead. It's irrelevant!" she said, confused and irritated by her mother's twists and turns.

Poor Becky. She was being so adult, so logical. *Whereas her mother*, Helen thought wryly, *was being an emotional, irrational pain in the butt*. Talk about your role reversals.

Helen's smile was filled with lame reassurance. "When you're older, you'll understand."

"Oh, please," said Becky, rolling her eyes at the tired cop-out. She stood up, spilling the cat out of her lap. "I'm outta here," she said as she headed for the door. "To do some research for a term paper that'll actually make sense."

She slammed the door in annoyance, leaving her mother alone with her theories, and her worries, and her vision of fear.

*   *   *

Katie Byrne, dancing with excitement over her first play date, hid behind her nanny's skirt as Peaches swung open the front door to welcome their visitors.

A young couple with lots of money and nothing much to do except watch it grow had moved in three doors away. They had a bright and noisy daughter called Amy who was just two months older than Katie and, long before Katie, had been signed up for summer session at The Open Door. But preschool was still two weeks away. In the meantime, Amy's mother suggested that they nudge the friendship along with a couple of play dates.

The idea, Peaches felt, had possibilities.

Little Amy Bonham was not shy. As soon as the door was opened, the brown-eyed moppet came marching in, did an end run around Peaches, and said to Katie, "Do you have toys?"

"Uh-huh," said Katie. She began rattling off a list of her current favorites, from Jumpin' Jiminy to Sally's Log Cabin.

Together the little girls made a beeline for the nursery. Amy's mother, thrilled to leave her only child in the care of a genuine London nanny, stayed two minutes and then took off to go shopping.

Peaches would have the girls for the next three hours. She let them get used to one another, while she waited for her opportunity. At the end of the second hour, when it became apparent that the girls were getting a bit tired, she made her move.

"Katie? Amy? Would you like me to tell you a story? We can use the log cabin and we can also use the gingerbread house to play-act while I tell the story. It's a really good one!"

Amy, a chatterbox, tagged after Peaches as she set the stage—the two houses, with a forest of potted plants between them—on the floor of the nursery.

"My mommy tells me lots of stories," the child said, "and Daddy, too, but Mommy tells me more because Daddy doesn't know so many, and Mommy says he tells them too fast and I like it when it's a long story and then I don't have to go to sleep. But when Mommy tells a story she tells them slow and she makes lots of faces and she makes me laugh and sometimes it's even sad. Do you know a long story?"

"Yes, I do, honey," said Peaches. "Has your mommy or daddy ever told you the story of Hansel and Gretel?"

Conceiveably the father had; they liked to scare their young.

"No," said Amy promptly. "What's Han . . . Han . . ."

"Hansel and Gretel were two dear girls who were friends—just like you and Katie," said Peaches, corrupting the fable to suit her needs.

"Are they three years old? Because I'm going to be four years old," Amy warned.

"Well, they were just exactly your age—your age and Katie's age. And they lived in this very nice log cabin," Peaches said, putting two small dollhouse figures in Sally's Log Cabin.

"Who lives in *that* house?" asked Katie, pointing to the charming gingerbread cottage whose outside walls were painted all around with blue delphiniums and pink roses clinging to white lattice.

Peaches had already slipped a black-robed old crone, one that she'd been saving for a day like this, into the gingerbread cottage. She smiled and said, "You must wait to hear the story, Katie."

It was obvious from the way Katie nervously hugged her teddy bear that she wasn't sure she wanted to hear it. "Will it have a happy ending?" she asked with a hopeful look.

"Maybe!" said Peaches cheerfully.

And maybe not.

*   *   *

Helen didn't hear from Nat until Thursday, and when she did, the news was disappointing.

"I've been out of town. Even worse, I'll be gone again for Orientation Day next week," he said on the phone.

Without bothering to explain—and really, what would be the point?—he went on to say, "But I wanted to find out how you're feeling. You looked pretty knocked around last Sunday." His voice was sad and low and frustrated, which wasn't surprising; he must be exhausted.

Helen had been struggling all week long over whether or not to call and apologize for her bizarre behavior. She'd rehearsed fifty different clever speeches, but all she could think of saying now was, "I'm not in the habit of fainting in stranger's bedrooms, you know." She sounded as prim as a virgin librarian.

He laughed and said, "You can't possibly think of me as a stranger."

Which was true, because she didn't, nor had she ever. Everything about their relationship had been too intense for that, starting with the call of anguish she'd heard from him on the day his wife died.

"Anyway, I'm fine," she said softly. "How's Katie?"

"Not so fine," he answered. "She's withdrawn; jumpy. Peaches says she's been like that since Sunday."

"Because of me, you think? Because she saw me—you know—in your arms?"

His voice sounded strained as he said, "You make it sound like I was hauling you off to ravish you."

I wish. The thought came and went like a shooting star.

"I just mean Katie may be having fears that her mother's being . . . displaced," Helen explained. That didn't come out right, either.

"Lord, I forgot," he said without taking offense. "You're a psychology major."

"Yes, and we always look for conflicts where there are none," she said lightly. "So ignore me."

"That's a little hard to do," he shot back.

Helen had the sense that they were straying into deep water, so she said, "And *I* almost forgot. Every year we hold a lovely event on the third Saturday in June to celebrate graduation for the preschoolers, as well as to kick off the summer session for newcomers. We call it our Old-Fashioned Ice Cream Social. It's held outside, weather permitting; otherwise, inside the school. The parents all bring ice cream or fancy toppings—or flowers to decorate the tables, if they're gardeners. The kids love it, and so do the grown-ups. It's a very friendly affair. And brief," she added for his benefit. "It runs from two to four."

"Are we invited?" he asked unnecessarily.

"Of course. The invitation's in the mail."

"Great. What can I bring?"

Bring? Him? Helen had to keep herself from breaking into droll laughter. "Oh, that's all right. Janet has everything under control."

"Okay, I'll call Janet, then."

"No, really, you don't have to do any—"

What was she thinking? He wouldn't be doing anything. He'd have Peaches stop at a Ben and Jerry's and that would be that. "Fine, just call Janet," she said, relenting.

She added, "I'm sorry you won't be able to make Orientation. We always have a nice video showing highlights of the previous year . . . it's very informative."

"You don't have to impress me, Helen," he said in an oddly rueful voice. "I'm already impressed."

"Well . . . but still," she said, tingling down to her socks. Again she moved the conversation into shallower water. "I'm glad you can make the Social, anyway. You sound flat-out. How big is that Columbus Fund you manage?"

"It's not the Magellan Fund, if that's what you mean," he quipped. "But it's big enough for me to lose sleep over. Two billion."

Two billion dollars of other people's money! The size of the responsibility took her breath away. And yet he didn't seem fazed by it. In fact she had the sense that, like Avis, he was trying harder to be number one.

"But don't you get tired of being on the road so much?" she asked.

He laughed. "The truth? It's not that bad. The airlines, the car rentals, the Hiltons and Marriotts all love road warriors like me. We're a big percentage of their profits. They shower us with platinum cards and give us the best rooms, the best views, the best service. Ask anyone who travels constantly. He may not always be greeted by smiles at home, but he damn well is at the hotel desk."

My God, she thought. *What kind of marriage did he have*?

"Katie thinks your office is in an airplane," she said, trying to lay guilt on him.

It didn't work. He laughed again and said, "She's right. Phone, fax, laptop—I have it all in my virtual office high above the clouds."

Helen was surprised to realize how sensitized she'd become to the issue of his traveling. *It's as if Linda has passed the baton to me,* she decided, a little frightened by the realization. *Why do I feel this closeness to her all the time?*

"Well, happy trails, then," she said. "We'll see you at the Ice Cream Social—with any luck."

This time he felt the barb. "I said I'd be there, Helen. And I will."

Yeah, yeah, yeah, she thought. *We'll see*. Aloud she said brightly, "Great! We'll look forward to seeing you!"

She hung up, morose at the thought that she wouldn't

see him until then—if then. She was thinking of him more and more, seeing him less and less. It was all so dumb.

"Lena, dear, why so sad?" asked her aunt when Helen returned to the garden to finish her tea.

They had set out the floral cushions on the Adirondack chairs so that they could enjoy the evening, by far the warmest of the year. The air was lush and still, with a hint of the heat to come. The earliest rose in the garden—a wonderful, scrambling thornless bourbon with the exotic name of Zephirine Drouhin—had opened just that day; its scent, as lurid as its bright pink color, spilled over them, leaving Helen edgy with longing.

"That was Mr. Byrne," she said with an exasperated sigh. "He can't come to Orientation because he'll be traveling. He's always on the road," she added petulantly.

"Where does he go?"

"Wherever the company is whose stock he wants to buy. I don't understand why he can't make his decisions in the office. Why does he have to go out and actually kick the tires?"

She sighed again, more disappointed than ever. "Boy. They used to say that all these modern electronics would make it easier for people to stay home and work. If you ask me, it's just made it easier for them to take their offices everywhere around the world."

"He sounds very conscientious, Lena," said Aunt Mary, tucking her cotton afghan across her spindly ankles. "Why do you hold it against him?"

"Because of Katie, for one thing. He can't just raise her by remote control, you know."

"Well, that's true," said Aunt Mary agreeably. She sipped her tea and then broke off a small piece of her sugary Angel Wing, rationing her pleasure. "You're very taken with him, aren't you, Lena," she said. "Are you falling in love, do you think?"

The simple question hung in the twilight like the moth hovering in the evening primrose. Helen didn't know what to say. Up until then she'd been able to tell herself that the attraction was no more than a physical one. Nat Byrne was knockdown good-looking; who wouldn't be attracted?

But in the sanctuary of her garden, surrounded by sweet scent and soft light, for Helen to admit anything less than the truth seemed profane. Was she falling in love?

"I think I am, Aunt Mary," she whispered. Her voice was an echo of despair. "God help me. I think I am."

"Oh-hh. That's very nice," said her aunt, smiling. "It's been such a long time."

"But I don't know why," Helen added, shaking her head in sorrow. In a way she was relieved to have the confession off her chest. Now, at least, she could come to terms with her feelings for Nat. She could look at them, turn them over, and—with any luck—grind them to dust.

"You know how they always say, 'When it's right you know it'?" she said quietly. "Well, I don't feel that way. Nat Byrne is the opposite of everything I loved and admired in Hank."

One by one, she ticked off her reservations. "He's a man who puts his career before everything. He buys and sells emotions like they're some kind of trading commodity. He considers hotel clerks and parking valets to be his best friends. And God alone knows what he must spend on speeding tickets every year. He's nothing like Hank, Aunt Mary; nothing. And yet . . ." She pressed her lips together, trying to hold back the tears. She failed.

I'm falling in love with him.

"Maybe that's why, dear. Because he's nothing like Hank."

Helen wiped her eye furtively. "You mean . . . I'll never find an exact replica of Hank . . . so subconsciously I've decided to look for something else altogether?"

Ignoring the fancy talk, her aunt said simply, "If his heart's in the right place . . ."

"I have to admit, he means well," Helen said with a sigh. "But so what? The road to hell is paved with good intentions."

"But isn't it possible that someone—"

"Can shape him up and keep him closer to home? I don't know. He's such a workaholic."

"But you work hard, dear."

"That's different! My job has meaning."

"Money has meaning. Most people think so, anyway."

"No, I'm sorry," Helen decided. "It doesn't take my master's in psychology to figure out why he's always away: The man has a fear of commitment."

"Oh." After a moment, her aunt said, "What does that mean, dear—'fear of commitment'? I see it all the time on the covers of magazines when I'm food shopping."

"It means he'd rather be away with his work than at home with his family. It's the number-one phobia that men have," Helen said, working herself into a fine snit. "They're not afraid of heights, speed, guns, fists, or sex; but dangle a commitment in front of their faces, and they run like rabbits."

Aunt Mary made a tisking sound and said, "He did marry the lady who passed away, didn't he? He wasn't living in sin or anything like that?"

"No, no, on paper, he looks fine. It's just that . . . he wasn't there for Linda," Helen murmured. "And now he isn't there for Katie."

The two women lapsed into silence, each with her own thoughts. Aunt Mary, older and with more experience of the glitches and flaws in life, spoke first.

"Piddle," she said flatly. "You're being way too hard on the man."

Helen sighed and said, "Maybe I am. But you know what? It's easier for me this way."

The twilight had deepened, setting the stage for a parade of stars. Already the first and brightest were showing off. It was bedtime for Aunt Mary, come-home time for Russell.

Helen stood up and held out her hands to the elderly woman. "Come on, Aunt Mary," she said with an affectionate smile. "I'll help you climb out of that chair."

"Thank you, dear. First take this . . . this whachamacallit. This bottle," she said, handing Helen the afghan. "And then pull me up."

When the call came, it knocked Helen out of a sound sleep. As she groped for the phone she opened one eye: two in the morning. Probably a drunk. Angry that the house was being roused at that hour, she mumbled an annoyed "Yes?"

As it turned out, she didn't have to worry that Becky and Russell had been rudely awakened. They weren't home. They were, to be precise, in the juvenile holding cell in Salem's brand-new police station, properly chaperoned by a matron who was standing guard outside the cell block.

Helen was speechless. Her mind, barely functioning at that hour anyway, shut down at the news. It wasn't possible.

"They're in bed," she said stupidly. "Wait."

She slammed the receiver down and staggered down the hall, flipping lights on as she went. All she found were rumpled beds in empty bedrooms and one open, screenless window.

Returning to the phone again, she said indignantly to the lieutenant on hold, "What're they doing *there?*" Her tone suggested that they'd been grabbed from their beds by a Salem SWAT team.

"As I said, ma'am, they were apprehended in the act of

spray painting city property: the statue of Roger Conant, across from the Common. In front of the Witch Museum?" he added, mistaking Helen's stunned silence for geographic confusion.

"Are you kidding me?" she asked. "Not *that* statue. The most well-known one in Salem? *Nobody* would be that stupid. It's in the heart of town . . . a tourist landmark. They would've been caught!"

"They were caught," said the lieutenant laconically. "Your two, anyway. Three others got away."

She couldn't get over the choice of targets. "Roger Conant? The founder of Salem? It's . . . unpatriotic!"

Her logic, not very impressive so far, improved as her mind cleared. "And Rebecca would never—*never!*—vandalize something. No, Lieutenant, really. There's been a mistake."

"We checked with the juvenile probation officer," he said without comment, "and neither of your children's been in trouble before, so we're releasing them to you. You can come for them anytime. Juvenile Court convenes on Tuesday; you'll want to be there for their hearing."

Juvenile Court. Hearing. They were words guaranteed to strike agony in a parent's heart. "My children aren't allowed out at this hour," Helen insisted. "You must believe me."

"Be that as it may, they were out, Mrs. Evett," the lieutenant reminded her.

"What will happen on Tuesday?" she asked, humbly now.

"They'll be ordered to pay for the cleanup. Since it's their first offense, the charges will probably be filed for a year." He hesitated, then added, "Ma'am? I know about your husband. I'm sorry about this. We all are."

She thanked him and hung up and burst into tears.

All the lessons, all the love, all the training—useless.

They might as well have been raised by wolves. Where had she gone wrong? How had she failed so thoroughly as a parent? And how could she possibly blame Nat Byrne for screwing up his family life when she was doing such a spectacular job of messing up her own?

After the tears of remorse and self-doubt passed, Helen blew her nose, washed her face, and prepared to head out to collect her delinquents. But before she left, she detoured into the basement and hunted down every can of solvent she could find—thinner, turpentine, acetone—and packed them into a box with rags and a scrub brush. She loaded them into the trunk of the Volvo and, feeling like a terrorist on a mission, drove to the station.

The process was slightly less embarrassing than she imagined it would be; maybe it was because she was getting used to being a criminal's mom. After Becky and Russell were released she hurried them out of the station and threw them into the backseat of her car, where she conducted her own interrogation.

"What the hell has gotten into you?" she demanded to know.

"Nothing," said Russ in a whiny tone. "We were just goofing around until *this* dufus grabbed me by my shirt and wouldn't let go."

"I wouldn't let go because the cop told us to hold it right there!" Becky shouted in her brother's face. She was furious.

"I coulda made it! Everyone else did! But no-o-o, you've gotta be a guardian angel!"

"You are so clueless, you moron! Don't you know what you've done? This could affect what college we go to! You moron!"

"Stop it, both of you! Start from the beginning. Becky, you first. Russ, shut up. You'll get your turn after."

Becky, who was shivering so much that Helen had to

start the engine and turn on the heat, said, "I heard some whispering back and forth from Russ's window down to the side yard. So without turning on my light, I got up and peeked. Russell was climbing out of his window and down the trellis on the house. I saw him go out to the front and get into a black Bronco with wide gold stripes that was parked across the street."

"It was a blue Bronco, snitch!" her brother interrupted.

"Shhh! Go on, Becky."

"I decided to follow him this time."

"*This* time!" Helen said, mouth agape.

Wincing, Becky went on with her tale. "But by the time I got my jeans on and sneaked down the stairs, they were gone. So I got in my car and I started driving around, looking for them. I knew they were up to something because I saw a dusty can of spray paint sticking out of Russ's backpack yesterday. I figured he got it out of the basement."

"You nosy rat!"

"Russell! Not another word!"

"So then," Becky said, more resolutely than before, "I was driving through town and I saw the Bronco and I stopped where they couldn't see me. And I couldn't *believe* it when I saw them spraying graffiti on the statue. So I ran up to them to get Russ away, and then the patrol car came by, and then—well, you know the rest."

Helen nodded grimly. "Russell? Your turn."

"This never would've happened if she just minded her own business."

That, apparently, was it: the sum total of his defense.

"Excuse me? Roger Conant wouldn't be defaced if your sister had just stayed in bed?"

"I don't mean that. I mean this," her son said, nodding sideways at the police station.

"Well, this is about that, Russell Evett! And the sooner you connect crime with punishment, the better off you'll be. Because they don't have GameBoy in the slammer. Or an endless supply of chocolate-chip cookies. Or weekends off. Or sailing lessons. You'll never have your own car. They'll let you earn a high school equivalency, but I'm not so sure about med school," she said scathingly.

He seized, arbitrarily, on that. "I don't wanna go to med school," he said. "That's your idea."

"Well-l-l, I was wrong about that! I think I'll start pushing you into a law degree—because I know at least one fool you can take on as a client."

Helen swung her look, burning with anger, at her daughter. "Make that two," she corrected.

By now Becky wasn't bothering to hold back the tears. "Oh, Mom, can't we just go home? I want to go home."

"Hold that thought the next time you're tempted to play Joan of Arc, young lady. Because furloughs from prison are hard to get!"

"Please?" Becky said, weeping now.

Despite her fury, Helen was in despair. The innocent one was showing remorse; the perpetrator, a sullen defiance. Was he missing a gene of some kind? How could she reach him?

"All right," she said to Becky in a voice shaking with self-imposed calm. "We'll leave the Escort here overnight. You won't be needing it for the next few weeks, anyway."

Resigned to the additional punishment, Becky fell back on the seat and closed her eyes. "Can't we just go home?" she moaned again.

"No," said her mother grimly. "We have a job to do."

Chapter 16

*T*ourist mecca or not, before dawn the corner of Brown and Washington Square was usually empty. Helen hauled her kids, punchy with sleeplessness, out of the Volvo and handed them their tools.

"Start scrubbing," she said in a hushed command.

She helped them climb over the black stakes of the wrought-iron fence that surrounded the monument, an imposing bronze statue of the colonist who in 1626 led thirty men, women, and children to Salem from a failing colony in nearby Cape Ann. Poor Roger Conant. He was a mess.

The graffiti, done in yellow and Day-Glo orange, was mostly confined to the deep folds of the pilgrim's cape. Russell Evett's first initial, done in a rounded, filled-in style, was all he'd had time to execute. One of the other boys had settled on that old favorite, the *f*-word; and some-one else had been about to pillory a girl named Sarah.

Under the lurid red glow pouring from the towering windows of the cathedral-like Witch Museum, Helen took over as lookout while her children cleaned up the damage to the maligned settler.

She was as jumpy as a vandal. "For Pete's sake, hurry up," she said several times. The two did their best, which wasn't very good—not good enough for Helen, anyway. She jumped the fence herself and went at the paint on the settler's fingers with the vigor of an old-world housewife.

When the inevitable squad car approached them on Brown Street, Helen nearly jumped out of her skin. It was too much: the red glow, the scowling pilgrim, the murky night, and now The Law. A career criminal, she wasn't. She climbed out of the fenced-in pen and went rushing up to the patrol car waving her arms in either surrender or apology, she wasn't sure which.

Don't put on the siren, she begged silently. *Don't make this any worse*. She put her finger to her lips as she got closer to the police car; it was the motherly instinct at work.

Mercifully, the patrol officer listened to her story without calling in reinforcements. When she finished, he said, "Be careful over the fence," and drove silently off.

Relieved, Helen went back to gather up her equipment and her children and head on home, a mere mile away from the crime scene.

In the car, Russ, still surging with adrenaline, said, "I bet someone called that cop! Both times!"

Becky said, "Well, *duh*. What do you expect?"

Russ said, "I dunno. It was like, just as exciting this time as before. More, even, b'cause, like, we didn't have to worry about being caught. I mean, not really worry. Because we were, like, on the right side?"

For Russ it was a long, philosophical speech. Helen felt a glimmer of hope. Maybe he had the makings of a sheriff after all. She said, "We're just lucky the patrolman thought so. Or we'd all end up spending the night in the cage."

After a few seconds Russ snorted and said, "Cool."

It was a bonding moment.

They piled out of the car in brighter light than they'd piled into it: Dawn had arrived. Obviously no one, including Helen, was in any shape for school; Helen sent her son and daughter off to bed with the promise that she'd call the school for them. Becky dragged herself off to her room, but Helen told her son to wait.

At the foot of the stairs he turned to face her, wary and unsure what to expect.

Ignoring the fact that he was in his no-hug years, Helen took her reluctant son in her arms and held him in a sighing embrace. If only she could make him understand; if only she could love him into a state of innocence again.

She said, "I want you to promise me that you'll never sneak out of your room at night again." She held him at arm's length and looked into his green eyes, hollowed from lack of sleep. "Promise me? As a man?"

His cheeks went pink; it was the first time she'd ever addressed him that way. "Yeah, okay."

"All right. We've got to get through tomorrow in court. We'll do it together. If your father were here, he'd be there, too; you know that. Now get some sleep."

Russ started up the stairs, then turned. "If Dad were here, he wouldn't have to," he said with depressing insight. And then he went to bed.

The hearing went pretty much as the lieutenant in charge had told Helen it would. No charges were filed; no scarlet letters were issued for her children to wear. Becky was let off the hook altogether; Russell was put in Salem's Diversion Program, intended to redirect troubled youths. His punishment—very fitting—was to raise and lower the flag in front of City Hall for a month.

The results should have been comforting, but somehow they weren't. What if he should slip up? Helen felt as if they were *all* on probation. As a result she was subdued, and her children were subdued, that night at dinner. Helen had grounded them both Until Further Notice while she made up her mind what to do. She wanted to be fair; but she was feeling too dejected to be fair.

All that changed when the doorbell rang.

Helen, dressed for comfort in baggy slacks and an oversized T-shirt, was working at her downstairs desk when Russ came in and said, "It's that guy with the Porsche."

The boy was trying to be discreet, but the guy with the Porsche was right behind him, standing in the doorway. "Thanks, Russ," Helen said, without even looking at her son. Her gaze was focused on Katie's father. Except she wasn't thinking of him as Katie's father. Or Linda's widowed husband. Or the Fund Manager of the Year. He was simply the man with whom she was falling in love. Looked at that way, he was utterly irresistible. It made her spirits soar just to have him in the room.

Russ, who had nothing more to say or do, ducked around Nat on his way out, leaving behind a huge void of silence.

"Hi." The word tumbled feather soft from Helen's lips.

"I brought back your book," Nat said, lifting it up between them.

"The book," she repeated, pretending she understood what the word *book* meant. She had no idea.

"The primer?" he explained. "On toddler care?"

"Oh, the book. Thanks. You've brought it back?"

With a subdued smile, he lifted it up again for her to see.

She'd lost her wits. Never mind Aunt Mary; *she* was the one who was in big trouble. She stood up and said, "You didn't have to rush through it for my sake. Did you make a special trip?"

"Yes and no," he said as he walked over to the bookshelf from which the book had been removed. Sliding the volume into the gap that still remained, he said, "I was driving past your house, anyway—but I take a roundabout route from work so that I can drive past your house."

"I . . . oh. Excuse me?"

He turned and leaned back into the bookshelves and folded his arms across his chest. "Yes. I made a special trip. Yes."

Now her heart was hammering.

Flushing, she said inanely, "Well. Thank you."

She realized that he was still wearing a suit. His tie was loosened and his hair was rumpled; obviously he'd been working late. "Have you eaten?" she asked, at the same time trying to figure out how to change into something more becoming.

"No. . . . Is that an offer or a rhetorical question?"

"Would Katie still be waiting up for you at this hour?"

"Will it make a difference if she is?"

"Is either of us ever going to answer the other's question?"

He laughed at that and said, "Katie's dead to the world by now. I said good-night to her on the phone before I left Boston. I know it doesn't look as if I'm getting any better at this, but there is a light at the end of the tunnel. I'm hiring more help at work. In fact, that's why I'm late tonight; the interview ran over."

"That is good news," Helen said, truly pleased to hear it. "It calls for some kind of celebration. Would a sandwich and a beer be about right?"

With a wry grin he said, "I hate to think what I'd have to do to earn a casserole and a glass of wine."

"Hire three more analysts," she said promptly. "Come on, I think the kitchen's still open."

With a fervent hope that Russ was under his headphones, Helen headed for the fridge with Nat in tow. She felt exactly as if she were sneaking a man into an all-girl dorm.

This is stupid, she told herself. *I'm the boss around here. My kitchen, my food, my—*

Son. "Yes, Russ?" she asked as the boy came skidding to a halt at the door to the kitchen.

Russell glanced from his mother to the cookie cupboard to the man in front of it to the fridge to his mother again. "I'm hungry," he said warily. He looked like a coyote who'd wandered into a Sunday brunch.

"I'm making Mr. Byrne a sandwich. Would you like me to make you one, too?"

"No," he said with distinct coolness. "I'll get something myself." He settled for an unfinished bag of Doritos, grabbed a Pepsi, and went out without a word to either of them.

As Helen emptied sandwich fixings from the refrigerator, Nat said flatly, "He has a problem with me."

"Russ has a problem with everything," Helen said, trying to laugh it off. "It's a stage."

"It's more than that, I think. He tries too hard to pretend I'm not here."

Slicing off two thick hunks of sourdough bread, Helen said, "He's bored. He's angry. He's fourteen." For some unaccountable reason, she added, "He's an *artiste*. They're temperamental, you know."

"Ah. He has artistic talent?"

"He must think so," she said lightly. "He got yanked off the statue of Roger Conant the other night with a can of spray paint in his hand."

"Uh-oh. Graffiti?"

When Helen thought about it afterward, she wondered why she'd felt the urge to tell Nat about it. Maybe she was afraid the police were going to go blabbing to every stockbroker in town. Whatever the reason, she decided to make it all a joke. She described herself scrambling up the boulder and scrubbing the pilgrim's fingernails; her hysteria when she spotted the patrol car; her suspicious loitering the next day as she looked for telltale traces of Day-Glo orange on the statue. She made the story about herself, with Russ merely a bit player in it.

When she finished, Nat was laughing and saying things like boys will be boys. He confessed, himself, to a desperate and so far unsatisfied urge to spray paint the huge Corita tank alongside Boston's Southeast Expressway.

In short, he made Russell sound perfectly normal, and for that Helen would've been willing to go to bed with him on the spot. But that wasn't possible, so instead she placed a thick ham and cheese sandwich in front of him, and a tall, frosty beer, and said, "You've made my day, Nat. You'll never, never know how much."

She sat alongside him, wearing a big, fat grin on her face. "Eat up," she said, drumming the palms of her hands on the wood enthusiastically. "There's more."

He cocked his head and gave her a quirky little smile. "I like you like that. Especially the ponytail. It makes you . . . less official, less authoritative, somehow."

Her hand flew up to the rubber band; she'd forgotten about the ponytail. Damn! At *least* if her hair looked decent!

She pulled the rubber band off and swung her black hair from side to side, freeing it. "I need all the authority I can get around here, Nat," she said, laughing. "Believe me."

He had no answer to that; only a troubled, burning look.

And then Helen's laugh subsided to a smile, and the smile softened to a slight tremble of her lips as he slid his hand behind her head and brought his mouth on hers in a soft, tentative kiss. The touch of his lips was shockingly real after the fantasy of it for so many weeks; Helen made a tiny sound, deep in her throat, mostly to convince herself that this time the kiss was not a conjured act in a silent dream.

No. It was very, very real. No.

"Nat . . ."

"Don't tell me you didn't expect this," he whispered, tracing a soft line of kisses to her ear. "Don't."

Her heart was racing. "If I did," she murmured, dropping her voice to match the secrecy in his, "what diff—"

The squeak of running shoes in the hall brought her up short. She jerked her head back guiltily and sat up straight in her chair, just the way she'd nagged her kids to do a million times. Her cheeks, she knew, were flushed with embarrassment.

Nat, on the other hand, seemed to have no problem being caught making out with a real live mom. He gave Russ a look that was friendly, open, and unconcerned. Technically, Nat was right. They weren't doing anything illegal or immoral.

Technically.

Russell's own face was burning bright red as he finally broke out of his trance, turned on his heel, and fled.

"Oh, perfect," Helen groaned, truly distressed. "Just what Russ needs: another reason to hate me."

"Hey, c'mon—hate? Isn't that a little strong?"

Helen smiled wanly. "Don't you remember how it was, being fourteen? You didn't merely approve or disapprove. You loved or you hated. There were no in-betweens."

She glanced down the hall, somehow expecting Russ to come back with his father's badge and arrest them both. It was crazy, letting her son dictate her life this way. She resented it fiercely; and that made her feel even more guilty.

"It's because of Hank, the way he died," she blurted. "It left us all emotionally crippled, one way or the other. The wounds are healed; but the scars . . ."

She shook her head, not trusting her voice. "The scars will always be there," she said at last. "I'm sorry," she added in a choked voice.

"Shhh," Nat said, stroking her hair away from her

downcast face. "Don't you think I understand? My wife died suddenly; violently."

Helen looked up in pain. "It's true, then?" she asked, dismayed. "From an overdose? Of ergotamine?"

He had to steel himself to answer her. "Yes."

A shudder of revulsion went through her. "It can't be," she whispered. "It's not possible."

"That's what I told myself," he said quietly.

It was odd, the way he seemed to have to comfort her instead of the other way around. Helen murmured, "And yet . . . you seem able to put it behind you."

He sighed, then smiled a smile as bleak as Helen's had been. "I don't know about putting it behind me. I only know that when I'm with you, the pain is eased somehow. It's as if—oh, I don't know," he said, frustrated.

He tried again. Taking one of Helen's hands in both of his, he said, "I feel as if you can explain her to me. Peaches tries—I grill her all the time—but it's you I've come to believe in."

"But I didn't know Linda at all," Helen said, bewildered by his confidence.

"Go figure," he said with a wretched laugh. He lifted Helen's hand to his lips and kissed it. "You're the key," he insisted.

"Tell me about her first, then," Helen begged. "Why would she take ergotamine when she was pregnant? She seemed so devoted to her motherhood."

"I can't tell you that," he said in a voice that tore at Helen's heart. "All I can say is that there was a bottle of the pills, with the cap off, on the floor when I found her in bed."

"Are you absolutely sure that's what—?"

"Yes. They were absolutely sure," he said grimly.

"But—"

He shook his head. "That's all I'm going to say. That's

more than I've said to anyone else except her mother.''

"And Peaches.''

"Obviously.'' He relented a little and added, "Linda was bothered by cluster headaches on and off throughout our marriage. When she became pregnant the second time, they became unbearable. Apparently hormonal changes can do that.''

"But she did understand about ergotamine and pregnancy?''

"Yes. We found a medical manual with a bookmark on the page.'' He let go of Helen's hand and stood up. "I'm sorry,'' he said with a queer little sigh. "I guess I haven't put it as far behind me as I thought. I've been through the denial, vented my anger, worked through my depression. I thought I was finally coming around to acceptance. Apparently not.''

"You're rushing the process,'' Helen said, all too aware that it was folly to try.

He seemed to be thinking of another meaning to her words altogether as he said, "I hope I haven't got you in too deep with your son.''

"He'll get over it,'' she said lightly, remembering the kiss. *But I will not.*

She saw Nat to the door, not so much to protect him from being stoned by Russ as to drag out the seconds of her time with him. Because that's all they ever had: seconds here, minutes there. A night would be—well, pure fantasy.

She swung the door open to a warm, starry night in Salem. June was a month to break anyone's heart, and this June was a bigger heartbreaker than most. Nat stepped over the threshold onto the gray-painted porch. The amber teardrop in the porch light—so dim, so historically correct—made him look young and carefree and, presumably, Helen, too. What did *she* care about a hundred-watt security light? Right now, she felt great with seven.

"I'll see you soon," he promised.

"At the Ice Cream Social . . . if not before."

He lowered his mouth to hers in another kiss—this one, less tentative, less deliciously surprising, than the first. But it had something else, something more: heat.

Too fast, she thought, drawing back reluctantly. *Give it time*.

"Good-night," he said, and so did she, and then she forced herself to close the door rather than stand there smiling and waving and generally making an idiot of herself while he backed out of the cobbled drive.

Inside, she leaned against the door, reliving his kiss. It was safe now to let herself break into an idiotic smile, and she did.

But then she heard the upstairs door to Russ's room slam nearly off its hinges, and the smile died on her lips.

Peaches was in the kitchen, warming a wedge of brie in the toaster oven, when Nat popped his head in. "Just in time!" she said cheerfully. "I was about to make myself a snack. Shall I make it for two?"

"Thanks, no, Peach, I'm all set. I bummed dinner off Helen Evett."

Helen Evett.

"Oh, I'm sorry," Peaches said without missing a beat. "I thought you said you were going to grab something at the office."

"I was, but then I didn't, and—anyway, I'll have a drink while you nibble. Music room?"

She nodded, smiling, and he said, "Meet you there."

That little bitch.

Peaches quickly arranged an attractive plate of the cheese, some crackers, and green grapes. Her mind was working overtime, trying to second-guess his feelings for the Evett woman. *It can't be love*; there was that consolation, at least. Nat was still too full of anger over what he thought was Linda's apparent betrayal to be thinking straight.

He could be trying to get back at his wife, never mind the grave that separated them. Vengeance: It was a powerful motive. Dumb but powerful. Peaches herself had no use for it. It involved emotions. She had no use for those, either. The one thing, the only thing, that made any sense to her was money. Lots of it. Nat had that. Once Linda's will was probated, he'd have even more.

Maybe he was driven by sex. It had been months, obviously, since he'd had any. Men didn't like to go months without it. So there was always that possibility. But no. If he were sexually motivated, he would've come to Peaches, a much better object of desire than that twit at the preschool. It couldn't be sex.

The need to talk about his feelings? There was that possibility, certainly. He and Helen Evett had both suffered losses in a savage way. It was a sobering thought: traumas in common. He could tilt either way—to Peaches or to her—in his need to share. *Damn*.

She set the plate, a glass of wine, and two napkins on a tray of inlaid wood, then checked her hair and makeup in a small mirror in the pantry before going out to join him.

She found him slouched in the biggest armchair, deep in thought, nursing a brandy. She didn't like the look on his face. It was too intense by half, and there was no computer in sight.

Peaches put the tray between them on the low table, then slipped off her shoes and snuggled on the end of the sofa nearest him. Plucking a grape from the bunch, she said, "So how did the interview go?"

"Hmm?" he said, looking up at her with blank blue eyes. He was a million miles away. "Oh. The interview. Pretty well. We're gonna make him an offer. He's a know-it-all hotshot, but we'll see. Twenty-four years old," Nat added, bemused. "A frigging kid."

"You were twenty-six when you took over your first mutual fund."

"Smaller fund."

"Different dollars."

He smiled at the compliment. "Well, in any case I'm older now. Wiser now."

Richer now.

"And a hell of a lot less cocky," he said wryly. "You should've seen this kid. God. Tonight I feel old."

Peaches laughed and said, "Oh, yes; you're ready for *Wall Street Week*'s Hall of Fame, all right."

"I mean it. If it weren't for the fact that I have a three-year-old . . ." He took a sip of his brandy, then said, "Did Katie go off to sleep all right?"

"Pretty well. Every day she seems a little more relaxed."

Every day away from that wild fainting stunt, she implied. And yet the truth was that Peaches admired Helen Evett for it; it was a damn good way to end up in Nat Byrne's arms.

Nat began to smile at some recollection. "She wants me to hire another three analysts so that I have more time for Katie," he said.

No need to explain who "she" was.

"Mrs. Evett is a single parent with a career and two teenagers," Peaches said, slicing into the oozing cheese. She spread some on a cracker and handed it to him. "I expect her children are too much for her to handle. She feels overwhelmed, so she assumes everyone else is, too."

Nat took the offering and said, "Funny you should say that. Helen had the same lament. She's wrong, of course; I could see that she has a terrific relationship with her daughter. The boy's a pistol," he added. "But what the hell. He's fourteen."

"I know fourteen-year-olds who're model citizens," Peaches sniffed. But that was pushing it too far, so she added, "But fourteen *is* a devilish age."

"You got that right," he said, laughing at some other recollection. "The snot just got caught—well, never mind," he added, smiling to himself.

He thought about it some more and laughed. "I can just see her now with the two of them." He shook his head, unable to wipe the smile off his face. "I'm sorry, Peach. I know I'm being rude. I'd love to tell you this story, but I don't think she'd appreciate it. Let's talk about something else."

"Yes. Why don't we?" she said with a smile that was perfectly entitled to look annoyed.

It was time to up the ante.

Chapter 17

For the fifth straight year, the weather for the Ice Cream Social was perfect. Blue skies, puffy clouds, enough warmth to make the ice cream worth eating—it couldn't get any better than that.

At twelve-thirty Helen Evett and Candy Greene were in the basement kitchen of The Open Door, wrapping full-length aprons around their sundresses to protect them from the drips and stains of flower arranging. The work was fun, the fragrance, divine. But that's not why Helen volunteered for the job. Her ulterior motive—her only motive—was to pump Candy about her late friend Linda Byrne.

With the easy intimacy that gardening promotes, they chatted for a bit, and then Helen began a roundabout approach to her goal. "We'll miss Astra at The Open Door," she said. "She was such a delight."

Expertly stripping a rose stem of its thorns, Candy said, "She loved every minute she spent here. Today I had to practically bribe her to stay at home with Henry until two o'clock. I hope she's as happy in kindergarten. Will you ever offer that level, do you think?"

Helen sucked in a deep breath and blew it out slowly. "I've thought about it, but the school keeps me flat-out—

and away from my family—as it is. The fall term is completely booked, and the waiting list keeps getting longer."

"Marvelous. And you don't even advertise," Candy said as she tucked magenta roses among blue-black delphiniums in a parian vase. "Word of mouth—it's so effective."

"Speaking of which," Helen said, seizing her chance, "I wanted to thank you for referring Katie Byrne here; she's a real sweetie."

"Oh—Katie. Yes. *She's* an angel."

Implying that somebody else wasn't? Helen didn't know what to make of the remark. She was mulling a response when her assistant Janet Harken, coordinator of the affair, marched in.

Janet took one look at the stainless steel counters covered with iris and lupines and lilies and said, "What? You're not done with the flowers yet? For goodness' sake. I need those counters. I need the sink. I need the kitchen, and I need it now."

She brushed aside the women's protests that you couldn't rush art. "If you wanted to make a Broadway production out of this, ladies, you should've come earlier," she said, sweeping some of the stems and scraps into a waste can.

"Janet, you're a bloody tyrant when you want to be," Helen said, scowling. The timing was infuriating.

Janet wasn't intimidated in the least by her employer. Fitting a hair net over her curly gray hair, she said, "It's an ice cream party, not a New Orleans cotillion. Mrs. Greene, you can just go ahead and finish what you're doing over there," she said, pointing to a small freestanding table out of the flow of traffic.

Then she turned to Helen and said, "As for *you*, you'd better hand in your apron. You have parents to greet—you do realize that some eager-beavers are already out there, don't you?"

"What! It's only one-fifteen!" Helen made an exasperated remark about early birds and what she'd like to do with the worms, then dumped the apron into Janet's outstretched hand and rushed outside to welcome the newcomers.

On her way, she intercepted Russ and Scotty, who'd finished setting up the tables and chairs on the pea-stone surface of the playground and the adjacent grass. They were sitting on the low-slung toddler swings, looking more gangly than ever as they talked in bored tones while they waited for their next assignment.

Helen felt a stab of pain. It seemed only weeks ago that Hank was pushing his son on a swing like that, and Russ was shrieking, "Higher, higher!"

"Thanks, guys," she said. "It looks good. Now go see if Janet needs you for anything." She waved to the early arrivals, who still had forty-five minutes of embarrassment to go.

"We're not settin' the tables or nothin'," her son warned.

"Or anything," she corrected automatically. "All right. Maybe you should go over and show people where to park. Not by the rhododendrons, make sure. Otherwise they'll block the way."

"Yeah, okay, we can do that," said Russ, acting as shop steward. He nudged Scotty hard in the ribs and they sprinted away.

Forget med school, Helen thought. *Forget law school*. Her son's apparent career of choice was to be a parking valet. He'd been fascinated by cars since his Tonka-toy days. She knew he'd probably sell his soul to sit in Nat's Porsche; it's a wonder he hadn't tried to steal the thing.

She went over to reassure the self-conscious parents that they were hardly early at all, and to tell them that the lemonade would be out shortly. The Baers had opted to make a generous donation to The Open Door's "Scholarship

Fund'' instead of bringing ice cream or toppings, and Helen took the opportunity to thank them again for it.

Every year Helen accepted two local kids into the pre-school without charge. When the Schoolarship Fund fell short, as it invariably did, The Open Door made up the difference. It was Helen's own little Head Start program, and a wonderfully rewarding one; she was explaining how she still kept in touch with most of the recipients' parents, when another car pulled into the parking area.

She watched as Russ and Scotty, with much wild waving, made sure the car parked efficiently. ''Ah. It's Alexander and his mother,'' Helen said, surprised that Mrs. Lagor had bothered to come after withdrawing from the summer and fall terms.

Introductions were made as fat, shy Alexander, clutching his Thomas the Tank Engine, clung to his mother with his free hand. Little Molly Baer, a whole year younger and twice as bold, began coaxing him over to the jungle gym.

The ever-watchful Mrs. Lagor handed an Igloo Cooler over to Helen. ''I brought mint chocolate chip. I've packed it in dry ice, so we won't have to worry about salmonella from melting ice cream,'' she said. ''Alexander! Not so high!''

Without bothering to explain the obvious—that ice cream would melt before it would spoil—Helen thanked her and took the cooler back to the kitchen, where Candy was finishing a magical arrangement of yellow achillea and fragrant white lilies entwined with sweet peas.

''What a pretty combination,'' Helen said. ''I'd never have thought of it.''

''Helen, I am in the business, after all,'' said Candy.

Helen was well aware of it. Candy's floral-design business was a favorite with upper-class Salem. As a result, she'd been in the home of everyone who was anyone—and was privy to the choicest gossip. Candy would know, if anyone would, about Linda Byrne's affair.

They were alone, so Helen jumped in with both feet. "We were talking before about Linda Byrne," she reminded Candy.

"Oh, yes," said the designer, hardly listening; she was intent on her arrangement.

"I was wondering if you knew anything about how she died? I'm asking strictly for Katie's sake; I wouldn't want to pry."

Candy looked up from her flowers. The question *was* intrusive. She knew it, and Helen knew it. Nonetheless, she obliged Helen with an answer of sorts. "It was her heart," she said.

Yeah. It stopped, thought Helen. This was getting her nowhere. Disappointed but determined, Helen let out a sigh of sympathy and tried one last feeler. "She was so young."

"Yes," Candy said coolly. "It was tragic."

Well! Nothing more there. Temporarily defeated, Helen took herself off to see how she could help Janet, who had begun impatiently to spread the tablecloths on her own. Janet needn't have worried: Becky drove up right on time in her Escort—today being an exception to the driving ban that was still in force.

Outfitted in a black spaghetti-strapped dress and a straw bowler topped with a sunflower, Becky emerged from the Escort, whacked her brother on the head over some insult or other, waved cheerfully to her mother, and helped her arthritic great-aunt out of the car.

Helen set up a rocking chair under the maple tree for her aunt, who never missed the Ice Cream Social. She loved to watch the young ones romp while their parents, dressed in summer pastels, mingled nearby. True, Aunt Mary was older now, slower now; but her joy was the same. She always dressed with particular care for the social. In her floral frock, white gloves, and neat bun, Mary Grzybylek gave the event the kind of dignity that only old age can confer.

Janet Harken, on the other hand, supplied the momentum. "Timing is everything," Janet liked to say. She had a mind like a stopwatch and a voice like a starting gun.

In the next half hour she had her ragtag volunteers performing like a crack catering unit. A long table was set with bowls, spoons, and napkins arranged in pretty patterns. A second table was set with several luscious sauces—hot fudge, cold peach, plain chocolate, warm apple, crushed strawberry. Next to the sauces was placed a vast array of toppings: nuts, candy sprinkles, chocolate chips, crumbled cookies, sliced berries, chopped pineapple, chocolate-covered espresso beans and raisins, minimarshmallows, and last of all, maraschino cherries.

In between the tables, in copper tubs that the fathers had filled with dry ice and topped off with ice cubes, the mothers began nestling the ice cream itself. (As always, Janet had insisted on the classics: French vanilla, dark chocolate, butter pecan, black cherry. Mrs. Lagor's mint chocolate chip was unexpected; but room was made.)

By two o'clock the place was rich with the sound of happy squeals and summer laughter. Parents milled, children cavorted, a dog or two barked excitedly. Expectations were high. The place was full. *Everyone* knew not to be late for an ice-cream affair.

Almost everyone, anyway.

Helen, who'd been moving briskly among her guests introducing outgoing sets of parents to incoming ones and incoming ones to each other, had no real reason to expect Nathaniel Byrne to show. The man had a long history of good intentions and broken promises.

If his heart's in the right place ... Aunt Mary had said.

Unquestionably, Nat's heart was in the right place. But

the pressure to make money for his shareholders was intense. He was a wizard at it. Wizards had obligations. How could a bowl of ice cream expect to compete with two billion dollars?

Time is money. It was an old saying.

Money is the root of all evil. That was an old saying, too.

Damn it. You could make a case either way.

Helen put aside her disappointment and turned her attention to a three-year-old whose ice cream was about to slide out of its bowl and into the mouth of a lurking golden retriever. After averting that crisis, Helen stood up and found herself facing another one: Nathaniel Byrne, getting out of his Porsche in the parking lot.

He came, after all. I love him, after all. Dear God, what do I do now?

Heart soaring, she waved giddily, though he couldn't possibly have picked her out in the crowd, and waited while he fiddled in the backseat of his car. She moved away from the guests, the more easily to be seen.

I love you, she shouted to him in silence. *I love you, I love you, I love you.*

''*Him!* What's *he* doing here?''

Helen whirled around. Candy Green was standing behind her, glaring furiously in Nat's direction. She was a pale, blond woman, but right now her cheeks were red with anger, her green eyes dark with outrage. ''He has a hell of a nerve,'' she said, putting down her untopped bowl of ice cream. She began looking around for her husband and daughter. ''Henry!'' she said, calling over across the crowd to him. ''Round up Astra. We're leaving!''

''Wait!'' Helen said, amazed by her vehemence. ''What's wrong?''

''*He's* wrong,'' Candy hissed. ''He made Linda's life

hell, and now he's playing the do-good dad! It makes me sick!''

"What're you talking about?" Helen said, instinctively coming to his defense. "It's true, the man is career-driven—"

"*Career*-driven!" Candy was focussed like a laser beam on the Porsche. "All those so-called business trips? All that time away? He took along some young twit! And Linda put up with it. And for what," she said through gritted teeth. "She was heartbroken. She should've left him as soon as she found out."

"Are you out of your mind?" said Helen, agape with emotion. The grass beneath her sandals began to sink away, like quicksand. "He's not the cheat—"

Candy fixed her burning gaze on Helen. "The hell he isn't. Linda had proof."

"Proof? What kind of proof?"

"Someone she trusted completely saw him at a bar in an airport with another woman before they boarded the plane together. That kind of proof!"

"That's not proof," said Helen, outraged. "That's malice!"

Stung by Helen's reaction, Candy became defensive. "It's true she was too proud to hire an investigator the way I told her to; but she had proof enough. There were other things—lipstick marks, long blond hairs. Not that she'd ever have noticed—she wasn't the type—if it hadn't been for the initial tipoff from her friend."

"Friend! That person was no friend," said Helen, deeply offended for both Nat and Linda.

Candy hardly heard her protest. "Look, there's the nanny. I'm amazed she stayed on; she must be incredibly devoted to Katie. That's something, at least. If she's still around, it must mean he hasn't set up his bimbo at the house." She laughed bitterly and added, "Not that he'd dare. Linda would come back to haunt him if he tried."

Poor Henry was hauling little Astra over to her mother as fast as he could. Candy grabbed her surprised daughter's hand, then turned to Helen with a forced smile. "Thank you for all the care you gave Astra. Do the same for Katie. And please," she added in an undertone, "think twice before you ask that bastard to a school event."

Helen had absolutely no answer to that. Her first thought as she watched the Greene family march off in protest was that someone might have overheard. She looked around her: apparently not. Everyone was having too good a time.

Still dazed, she swung back around to see Nat walking as fast as he could, carrying a big two-handled pan in his hands. He was grinning at his own awkwardness and making apologetic grimaces for being late. Behind him came Peaches, dressed like many of the guests in a flowing dress and wide-brimmed hat; and Katie, in a sky blue dress with a print pinafore over it.

How clever of Peaches, Helen thought with dull irrelevance. *If Katie drips ice cream on herself, Peaches can just slip off the pinafore. She really does plan ahead.*

"Better late than never," Nat said as he got within earshot. He took in the table layouts at a glance and said, "Can you make room for this?"

"What is it?" Helen asked, staring blankly into the pot. It might as well have held fish guts.

"Toasted Almond Sauce," Nat said, not without pride. "Lots of it."

"Why, Nat?" The question had nothing to do with the almond sauce.

"Why? Because one batch didn't look like much. So I made another. Then another. And I burned one. And meanwhile," he said, amazed at the variety of sauces already laid out, "I guess y'all can live without it."

Still having trouble taking everything in, Helen gave

Peaches a vague greeting and Katie a halfhearted one.

Katie looked up at Helen and said, "You fell down. And Daddy picked you up. And sometimes he picks me up, too. When I hurt myself he picks me up. Did you hurt yourself?"

Helen opened her mouth to say something, but Peaches mercifully interrupted her. "Oh, look, Katie—there's Amy."

Katie skipped away to say hi to her new friend. Peaches smiled and said pleasantly, "Helen, I noticed you collect glass globes, and I thought you might like this one. It's spun glass—not solid—but I thought of you at once when I saw it."

She held out a small, palish-pink ball the size of an apple to Helen, who said distractedly, "Well, I don't actually collect . . . but it's very pretty . . . thank you."

Helen held out a still shaky hand to receive it. In the meantime Nat, tired of holding the pot, cleared his throat comically. It was enough to distract Helen even further. Somehow the ball slipped away and caught the back of a folding chair, shattering into many pieces.

Heads turned; the sound was an ugly intrusion. Helen's cry of dismay was an overreaction—it was only a bauble, after all—but by now she was completely off her mettle. "I'll get a napkin to put the pieces in," she said. "Peaches, will you stand guard so that no one steps on the glass?"

"Of course," said Peaches. "Don't think anything of it."

What a stupid thing to bring to an outdoor event, Helen couldn't help thinking as she began making her way through the crowd.

"Hey, hey, hey," said Nat behind her. "Do you want this stuff or not?"

Helen turned around, distracted beyond comprehension.

"Oh . . . you know . . . just . . . stick it somewhere," she said.

Nat cocked one eyebrow, said "Fine with me" in a cool voice, and turned on his heel.

Helen grabbed two napkins, then hurried back to Peaches, who'd already picked up the broken glass. The nanny put the collected pieces carefully into Helen's open napkins, then said, "I'm sure I got everything. I went through the grass with a fine-tooth comb, but we can put two chairs over the spot for extra insurance."

"Good idea. Would you do that for me?" asked Helen, and she went to throw the shards somewhere out of harm's way.

On her way to the kitchen she was accosted by her daughter. "Mom! Taste this," said Becky, aiming a spoon at her mouth.

"Becky, not now—"

But Becky insisted and so Helen tried the sauce. In her present mood it tasted like warm, wet chalk. "What about it?"

"Isn't it fantastic? Mr. Byrne made it," Becky said, dipping into her bowl again. "He's a major hit, y'know. He spoons it on personally for you. Laurie's already gone back for seconds. She is, like, so uncool. I mean she just hangs on him."

"Is that what you ran here to tell me? That your best friend is flirting with Nat Byrne? What do you want me to do? Break it up for you?"

"Uh-oh." Becky rolled her eyes and said, "Never mind. You're obviously stressed out again." She turned and ran back in the direction of the toppings table.

Helen had to get away. She got rid of the glass and fled to her office, where she closed the door and collapsed in her swivel chair.

Nat Byrne, with a lover of his own? Helen refused to

believe it. She'd prepared herself for many scenarios, but that wasn't one of them. His wife had been attractive, accomplished, vivacious. He had no reason to take a lover.

Using that logic, however, neither had his wife.

Maybe, in her preoccupation with her child and her pregnancy, Linda had begun to ignore him. On the other hand, he'd been busy with the Columbus Fund. Would he even have noticed?

He could've taken a lover in retaliation. She could've taken a lover in retaliation. They both had motive. They both had opportunity.

Helen's head began to spin. She sat back in her chair, still convinced that Candy was wrong. Suddenly she remembered that the story she'd overheard of Linda Byrne's affair had also been second-or third-hand. Was it possible that neither story was true?

Helen knew that rumors tended to be false and that they could do terrible damage before they ran their course. But it was a fact, not a rumor, that something had gone very wrong in the Byrne marriage, wrong enough to end Linda's life prematurely and to leave Nat angry and bitter about it.

It was so frustrating. The more information Helen acquired, the more confused she became. There was no light at the end of this tunnel. There wasn't even a tunnel; only a criss crossing meander of allegations. Helen closed her eyes, depressed and distracted by them, and shuddered.

And shuddered again. Violently.

The room had become ice-cold. Not cool, not chilly, not even cold: *ice*-cold. A wet, dank swirl, mixed, improbably, with the scent of *Enchantra*, surrounded Helen, pinning her to the chair as firmly as a set of chains.

None of the manifestations so far had come even close to this exercise of raw, brute power over Helen. The knockings, the jiggles, the scent of perfume—even the vision itself—had not been able to paralyze Helen so completely.

Linda Byrne. She was in the room with Helen—some part of her, anyway—and Helen didn't know why. Breathless, motionless, utterly prostrate under the binding spell of the ghost's power, Helen tried desperately to think without panic.

Her options were pathetically few. She dared not scream—not there, not then. It would be the end of her career.

Nor could Helen try ordering the ghost away, even supposing she'd had the nerve. People were coming and going through the building, and Helen might easily be heard. A director who talked to herself wasn't much better than one who screamed at empty air.

Helen couldn't even make herself open her eyes; there had been too much horror in what she'd seen the first time to try it again. And so she sat, chattering with fear, as the coldness ebbed and flowed over her body, like waves on a beach in May.

I'm so cold, so cold, she thought, stupefied by what was happening. *I'm not crazy, I'm not; but I'm so, so cold. . . .* With her eyes still closed, she sat frozen to her chair, suspended in time, until she became afraid that someone would begin to search for her. Or worse still—that someone wouldn't.

Finally, desperately, she screwed up her courage and, at the risk of being heard, whispered, "I can't help you. Wherever you are, however you got there—I can't do anything. Leave me alone," she begged.

"Please, Linda," she said, saying the dread name at last. "Leave me alone." She cringed in her seat, expecting the worst.

The room got colder. Helen had never felt anything like the killing, chilling atmosphere that surrounded her. It was hard to breathe it into her lungs. When she did, it seemed to scorch the edges of her soul.

What do I do now? she thought, feeling more and more faint. *That was the only trick in my bag. If this goes on, I'll die of hypothermia, if not of fright.*

"All right," she whispered, beaten down by the awesome power that held her relentlessly in its grip. "I'll do it. I'll find out. . . ."

Find out what? She knew now what she was destined to do. "I'll find out why you died."

Suddenly the wave of cold withdrew, like a falling Maine tide, and she allowed herself, at last, to open her eyes.

It was over. Just like that. Helen stood up tentatively and looked around. Nothing seemed out of the ordinary. The room was June-warm and filled with the heady scent of a desktop bouquet that Candy must have arranged for her. Helen had been so upset that she hadn't noticed it when she first came into the office.

Cautiously, she tested her weight on each leg before taking a step or two. No wobbles. Good. There'd be no embarrassing fainting spell this time. In fact she felt oddly, remarkably invigorated—as if she'd just spent a weekend at a spa.

She went over to a narrow window in the corner of her office, one from which she could just catch some of the goings-on outside, and tried to make sense of the encounter.

I was tense; upset, she reasoned. *Becky noticed it right off the bat. So I came in here to decompress. I fell into a deep meditation. I resolved to get to the bottom of Linda's death, a concern I've had since the day she died. Having reached a resolution, I awoke from my self-induced trance. Every day, business men and women do what I did to improve their productivity. Often they pay good money in seminars to learn how.*

It was all perfectly normal, perfectly nineties.

Having convinced herself of that, Helen became eager, almost hungry, to rejoin the crowd that had gathered on the grounds of The Open Door. Almost everyone she cared about was out there: the children, their parents. Her family. Katie. Nat.

Nat. From out of nowhere came an intensely detailed vision of him in his industrial-sized kitchen making Toasted Almond Sauce. It was a joyful, delightful thought. Nathaniel Byrne, career maniac and Fund Manager of the Year, slaving over a hot stove. Who could possibly have known?

Helen hugged the picture to her soul; it was proof, if proof were needed, that Nathaniel Byrne would never have cheated on his wife.

Chapter 18

*P*eaches paused in the shade of a maple tree from which she had a good view of the festivities. The shade was cool and the view strategic; she decided to have a seat.

In a rocking chair close by, an elderly woman in church-wear and white gloves sat with a pleasant if vacuous smile on her face. It took Peaches less than two minutes to figure out that the lady in the neat gray bun was not all there.

It took Peaches less than a minute more to decide that she would stick around, anyway. The lady in the neat gray bun was Mary Grzybylek, the aunt of Helen Evett.

"And which child is yours, my dear?" asked Mrs. Grzybylek.

Pointed to an arbitrary group of toddlers playing in the sandbox, Peaches said, "Behind the little blond girl." They were all blond, but never mind; the old lady didn't see too well, in any case.

But Mary Grzybylek smiled benignly and said, "This has always been my favorite thing. The weather is nice this time of year. On Halloween it often rains; on Christmas— I'm afraid of the snow and ice. But summer and ice cream, well, they go together with the little ones very well."

Peaches agreed, then stumbled over the pronunciation of the woman's name, which led to a short little discourse on Polish culture and cuisine. As soon as she could, Peaches brought the talk back around to Helen Evett.

"I've heard such wonderful things about The Open Door," she said. "You must be so proud of your niece."

It was like saying the words "Open Sesame." Out poured a torrent of praise for Helen Evett's character, backed up by anecdotes dating back to her childhood. All of it was confusing, most of it was boring; but there was one anecdote that stood out from all the rest.

Helen Evett, it seemed, had a thing against graffiti.

Still feeling bizarrely euphoric after her brief but profound ordeal, Helen began making her way back to Nat, who was in the playground with Katie.

She was nearly through the crowd when she overheard an innocent remark that made her pause: "He's not what you'd call a typical executive."

Gwen Alaran, a highly intelligent woman with a career in public relations, could've been referring to any number of fathers there, but somehow Helen didn't think so.

"A typical executive loves to dominate," Gwen was saying. "Donald Trump, Lee Iaccoca—they get off on manipulating people. But him? My guess is that he'd rather be in a room with his charts and his laptop than with a dozen members of a board. You know what I think?" she added. "I think deep down he's shy."

"*Shy*? Are you kidding? He's been flirting with every female here."

"No," said Gwen. "He's been *acting* like he's flirting."

Helen couldn't resist edging into the conversation. "Whoever it is you're talking about," she said, smiling, "I think I'd like to meet him."

Gwen's friend, a bosomy thirty-year-old Helen had never

seen before, said good-naturedly, "Get in line, then, lady. I'm ahead of you."

Helen laughed while Gwen rolled her eyes and said dryly, "Smart move, Carrie. This is the director of The Open Door. Now she knows I've let you crash the party just to meet Nat Byrne."

After introductions, Helen said to Gwen, "You really think he's leery of people?"

"I do," Gwen decided. "He's so intense about his work. I think he's channeling not only all of his ambition but all of his emotions into it. It'll be interesting to see whether someone can reroute that energy."

Helen said softly, "Maybe it'll be his daughter."

"Maybe it'll be me," said Carrie, arching one eyebrow over a seductive smile.

All three women turned to give Nat Byrne the once-over. He was pushing his daughter, minus her flowered pinafore, on the swing as Katie shrieked, "Higher, Daddy! Higher!" He looked relaxed and easy, as if he'd never seen a computer or an airplane in his life—a doting father from a kinder, simpler time.

Gwen turned to her young friend and looked at her sympathetically. "On second thought, Carrie," she said, "you'd be wasting your time."

"Okay, Katie—kiddo—you asked for it! Sky-high!" Nat threatened, pushing her ever so slightly harder. His laugh—rich, ringing, content—sent shivers of joy through Helen.

Linda would love to see this, she thought, and then wondered whether Linda wasn't seeing it after all. It seemed to Helen that her spirit was part of the benign, gentle mood that pervaded the schoolyard: in some form, in some magical way, she was there, a broken-hearted mother longing to push her daughter on the swing just one more time.

From one mother to another, Helen said in a silent aside

to Linda Byrne, *I'd say your little girl's in pretty good hands right now*.

Mrs. Lagor was wiping her son's hands with her fifth or sixth Wash'n Dri.

"Don't put your hands in your mouth, Alexander. How many times must I tell you? And after you touch the swings or the slide or anything else, you must come right back so that I can wipe your hands clean. Germs, Alexander! They're everywhere."

"That's so true," said Peaches, pausing alongside during Mrs. Lagor's little sermon. "Between all these terrible viruses and scary bacteria, I don't know how we're going to keep our children safe."

Mrs. Lagor looked up from her son's sticky hands. "I'm glad to hear you say that," she told Peaches. "Everyone thinks I'm paranoid, but—well, really. Read the papers."

"Exactly."

"You look familiar," said Mrs. Lagor, tossing the used towelette into a trash can. "Have we met?"

"I don't think so," said Peaches in her friendly, outgoing way. "I would've remembered someone with the same standards that I have." Smiling, she reached into her canvas carryall and pulled out a giant-sized container of moist towelettes.

It was like exchanging a secret handshake. Mrs. Lagor gave her a conspiratorial look and said, "Isn't it terrible? Flesh-eating bacteria! Rabies! Lyme! Hanta! Ebola! E-coli! Who can keep up with it anymore?"

"I know, I know," said Peaches. "And yet we must. I can't understand how some people can be so casual about these threats. Maybe they're just too busy to pay attention."

"Other parents may be too busy, but I'm not. I've made a point of having no other demands on my time. My son . . ."

She turned to Alexander and said, "You can play for a bit more. But no roughhousing. And don't play with Tyler. We don't like him." Turning back to Peaches, Mrs. Lagor finished her thought. "My son," she said calmly, "is my life."

You didn't have to be a rocket scientist to be able to figure that out, thought Peaches. She'd been watching the woman haul out one Wash'n Dri after another, disinfecting everything in sight. A quick trip back to Nat's car for the container of towelettes there, and Peaches had her entree into a conversation with Mrs. Lagor.

She remembered the day Alexander hurled his little blue train engine at Nat in the lobby of The Open Door; how suspicious and hostile Mrs. Lagor had seemed of Nat in particular and the world in general. She was exactly the kind of mother Peaches was looking for.

They chatted for a while about the dangerous times they lived in, and then Peaches said casually, "And let's not forget television. Look what it teaches today's kids: sex, violence, perversion. Is it any wonder that teenagers are so twisted nowadays?"

"You don't have to tell me," said Mrs. Lagor without taking her gaze from her son. "Alexander! No, no, no! No jumping!"

She added, "Alexander has teenage cousins who live in Boston, and I must say, they scare me to death. Fortunately we rarely visit."

Peaches chose her next words with care. "I think the problem with teenagers is that they have no one at home to watch over them. Their parents both work—either by choice or by need—and the kids are left to roam."

"Yes. That's exactly the problem."

"And it doesn't matter if the parents themselves are good or bad people." Peaches lowered her voice and inclined her head to Mrs. Lagor's ear. "For example. Do you see that girl in the black dress?"

"The one in the straw hat and work boots?" asked Mrs. Lagor, clearly disapproving of Becky's taste in clothes. "How could I miss her?"

"Someone just told me that she was arrested for spray painting a statue in town."

"Awful brat! Wait. I know her . . ."

"That's not the worst of it. I understand that the symbol she painted—her mother went back at once to wipe it away—was a star with two points in the ascendant."

Mrs. Lagor gasped. "Two points!" She added in a whisper, "What does that mean?"

"Well, it's pretty common knowledge," said Peaches, plucking a towelette from her big yellow container. She beckoned to Katie to come away from the box-castle and get cleaned up. "I saw it on the news once." She lowered her voice still more. "A pentagram with two points up . . . is the sign of Satan."

Mrs. Lagor clapped her hand to her mouth. "Oh my God," she croaked. "A cult."

"You think so, too?" asked Peaches with a distressed look on her face. "I did wonder."

Mrs. Lagor gasped again. "Now I recognize her. She's the director's daughter. Betty—"

"Becky."

"—Becky Evett. Oh dear God. She watches the little ones all the time. And now that I think of it, she always wears black. Look at her now, playing ring around the rosy with them. For all we know, it's some kind of ritual. Someone should do something!"

"There's no proof," Peaches reminded her. "The markings were cleaned up too fast."

Mrs. Lagor gave her a wide-eyed look. "Doesn't that tell you something? Anyway, I can find out. My husband's a contractor; he knows everyone in Salem. Wait till he hears about this. I never should've let him talk me into this place. It's not even convenient.''

She looked around restlessly. It was obvious that the news was burning a hole in her tongue.

Peaches decided to free Mrs. Lagor to do her mischief. "I promised the person who told me this that I wouldn't say anything," she told the goggle-eyed mother, "so . . ."

"Naturally. I understand."

Of course you do, you self-righteous blabbermouth. And it won't make a damn bit of difference, will it?

Peaches laid her hand lightly on the woman's arm. "Thank you so much," she said in a confidential murmur. "I feel such relief, now that I've been able to tell someone. It's a terrible thing to have to keep to oneself."

"Well, something's going to have to be done about it," said Mrs. Lagor grimly. "But don't worry," she added. "I won't bring you into it."

You couldn't if you tried, thought Peaches. But she smiled bravely and said, "Thank God for parents like you."

Peaches was chatting with a young mother when a child exploded in a howl of pain that ripped through the laughter like the crack of thunder.

"Oh, dear," said Peaches with a gasp. "Not a scraped knee, that's for sure."

A few seconds later, they had their answer. One of the toddlers had fallen and gashed her leg on a piece of broken glass that lay hidden in the grass.

"Oh, no," Peaches said, visibly upset. "She must not have picked up all the pieces."

The young mother wanted to know: "Pieces of what?"

"It was nothing, really; a little gift I brought back with me from England. It had such an interesting history, and I thought Mrs. Evett would be charmed by it."

She added lightly, "Have you ever heard of a witch ball?"

Naturally the mother had not. Peaches said, "It's a glass ball that folklorists say you hang in your home to protect you from evil. I thought it was a quaint, rather pretty little gift. I was surprised, and a little hurt, that Mrs. Evett didn't agree. She seemed quite upset—almost offended—when I handed it to her."

"Really? That's so rude," said the mother, surprised.

Peaches shrugged and said, "Well, whatever. She dropped it as if it were a hot coal, so of course it shattered—it was very fragile—and I suppose one of the pieces got separated from the rest."

There wasn't a doubt in Peaches's mind that it had; she'd dropped it precisely where someone was bound to roll over it. It was even easier than making sure the glass ball slipped through Helen's hand.

The mother—young, pretty, and usefully naive—frowned and said, "Well, if there's broken glass around, I think we should've been told." She went off to collect her child and spread the warning.

Peaches turned to check on Nat. He was behind her, with Katie in tow.

"Would you mind taking over, Peach? I want to ask Helen if anyone needs a ride to the emergency room."

"Someone said it was just a scratch," Peaches said in a quick lie. "And the parents are here, after all."

"Not the dad, and he's got the car," he said shortly, and walked off.

Peaches stared after him. This morning a cook, now a chauffeur. What the hell next?

Helen had finished bandaging poor Sarah and was saying good-bye to the little girl and her mother when Nat strode in with an offer of a ride.

"Ah, thanks," she said with more emotion than she'd intended. "But James's parents were leaving now, anyway."

"How bad was it?"

"Deep enough to bleed, not big enough for stitches, thank God. I still feel awful about it. I had Becky go over the grass so carefully. That's why we never allow glass outside," she said, disgusted with herself.

"Hey, c'mon," he said, surprised by her intensity. "Don't go beating yourself up over this. Accidents happen."

She wondered whether he'd feel that way if it were Katie who'd fallen on the shard. "I don't believe in accidents," she said stubbornly. "Ask my kids."

He smiled and said, "I keep forgetting. You're a psychology major. I suppose you think the shard got overlooked on purpose. Isn't that what Freud would say?"

"Laugh if you want to, Nat, but I mean it. I take this place absolutely seriously." She put the bandages and Betadyne back into the medicine locker that was built into the bathroom of her office.

"I still don't know how I could've dropped it," she said, closing the locker door. "I was so aware that it was glass. . . ."

"Stop," he said, touching his finger lightly to her lips. "Stop."

Helen looked into his eyes, so blue, so intense under the shock of brown hair, and said, "Okay. You're right. I will let it go." She took a deep breath and forced herself to sound light. "So other than the bloodcurdling screams, did you have a nice time?"

"Yeah," he said, sounding surprised by his own answer. "I did. This has been the first full day off I've had in a long time."

"Now wait. Be fair. Subtract the time you spent cooking."

"Why? That was fun."

"Plus, the day's not over," she reminded him. "You may yet end up in your study."

He had an oddly serene smile on his face. "I have no desire."

"Yeah, but the . . . the . . . stock market opens bright and early tomorrow," she said, totally hung up on the way he'd said "desire."

"It'll open whether I work tonight or not," he said without lowering his gaze from hers.

They were apparently in some kind of contest. He wanted to show he could be ordinary; she was determined to make him prove it.

So she hit him with the big one. "Your shareholders," she murmured in a low, perverse taunt.

"Oh. Them." He sighed heavily, like the old woman who lived in a shoe. "Well . . . I have my eye on a new company. It has a good price-earnings ratio . . . a high barrier to entry . . . and an ability to generate a lot of cash. I think."

"You think?"

He shrugged. "Corporate managers lie."

"*No.*" She was truly shocked.

"They do. You look pretty when your face gets flushed that way. So we ask the same questions over and over, and then we search through the answers for inconsistencies. That's what I'd planned to do tonight."

"Oh," she said, flushing still more as he drew nearer. "And now?"

"—I'm not so sure. What are you doing tonight?"

Her back was to the heavy paneled door, originally designed for a bank officer's privy. In a faint, faint voice, she said, "You're asking me to help you look for lies in your notes?"

He laughed softly. "You, spot a lie? I doubt it." He leaned his arm on the door, over her head. He wasn't exactly cornering her; but he wasn't exactly not cornering her.

He began to lower his mouth to hers in a kiss. Helen could've mumbled something perfectly reasonable about it being the wrong place for that sort of thing, but instead she blurted, "I can't do this! It would be cheating!"

That made him blink. "Cheating? On whom?"

"On . . . on Linda. On her spirit—the memory of her, I mean."

"That's nuts—and more than a little ironic," he added.

He surprised Helen by tilting her chin up and going through with the kiss; but there was an edge to it that made her back away from it perceptibly.

With a quick, exasperated exhale he said, "Look. We need to put some things behind us. And we will. But for now—can't you see?" he said in a voice that begged for understanding. "I'm attracted to you because you *are* so scrupulous."

He cradled her face in both his hands and said softly, "You're a breath of fresh, clean air in my life, Helen. Everything else is stale and dirty."

"That's so cynical," she said to him, distressed. "You have Katie, for one thing. And besides," she felt bound to add, "you don't know me enough to say if I'm fresh or if I'm stale."

And yet she knew—with hardly any specifics at all—that she loved him.

"Let me find out who and what you are, then," he said simply. "Let me spend time with you."

She laughed at that. "Time! The one thing you don't have to spend!"

"Now who's the cynic?"

Flushing, she said, "You're right. I'm prejudging."

"This evening. After the social. We'll meet for supper at Genevieve's. I'd come over to pick you up, but I'm afraid that Russ'd bar the door."

"He'll get over that," Helen said without much hope.

"He's going to have to."

Nat was still less than a breath away when they heard a loudly polite knock on the outside wall of the office. Helen's daughter popped into the doorway and said, "Hi! Sorry to bother you, but everyone's leaving—all at the same time, it looks like—and I thought you'd want to be there for the farewells."

Becky was looking directly at her mother, pretending that Nat was nowhere around. It took real ingenuity.

"Thanks, honey," Helen said. Turning to Nat, she said, "Will you excuse me?" She waved pointlessly at the biggest bookcase in the office and said, "I think the book you want is over there."

"Seven?" he asked, ignoring her improvisation.

"Yes, okay."

She beat a retreat with Becky, who surprised her by having other things than Nathaniel Byrne on her mind.

"I'm sorry about the glass, Mom," she said, obviously taking Sarah's injury personally. "We went over and over the grass. Stupid gift—I wish she'd left it on the other side of the ocean!"

"Ocean? What ocean?"

"Elaine told me that Peaches got the glass ball when she was in London," Becky explained.

"Huh. She must not have heard right. I had the impression that Peaches bought it especially for me."

"Since when are you two such chums?"

"Beats me," Helen said, shrugging. "A bribe, so I'll be extra nice to Katie?"

They had reached the graveled parking area, where the

last few rhododendron blossoms were barely hanging on. Becky was right: Things did have the look of a stampede. Parents were hurrying their children along as if a thunderstorm were on the way.

"Janet must be doing a brisk business at the sink," Helen said as she watched a steady stream of parents leave the basement kitchen with clean Tupperware tucked under their arms.

The good-byes seemed hurried and perfunctory. Helen was disappointed. Just about everyone seemed to have someplace to go, something to do. True, it was four o'clock, but the Ice Cream Social always ran late.

"Everything's like that nowadays, Mom," Becky said to console her. "You know how you used to ferry us all around, all day, until I got my driver's license. These kids just aren't old enough to drive themselves around yet."

"Neither is Russ," said Helen suddenly. "So what's he doing behind the wheel of Nat's Porsche?"

Becky laughed nervously and said, "The door was unlocked?"

"I'll brain that kid," said Helen, making a bolt for her son. She stopped short when she saw Nat saunter up to his car, apparently amused to see a monkey impersonating a human being inside. Helen couldn't hear what Nat said, but she could tell, even from a distance, that Russ was mortified at having been caught drooling in the driver's seat.

She watched as her son shook his head at something Nat said, then, without looking up, got out of the front seat and melted away.

She wanted to shout, "Don't slouch, damn it! Stand up straight and take your reprimand like a man!"

Instead she found herself uttering a silent, flippant prayer: *Please don't let Russ ever steal the Porsche. Please. Any car but that one.*

Chapter 19

$\mathscr{H}$elen returned to find a disturbing message on her machine: the Baers were withdrawing their daughter Molly from the summer session. No reason was given, no apology made. It was a complete about-face from their enthusiasm that afternoon. Mrs. Baer's voice sounded timid, almost fearful, as if she were afraid Helen was going to hunt her down and scratch out her eyes.

"For Pete's sake, it's your choice," Helen muttered at the machine.

She played the message several times, then made a quick return call. No answer. In the meantime she was already half an hour late for her rendezvous at Genevieve's. After taking out a couple of Stouffer's frozen dinners for the kids, Helen sped away in her Volvo, feeling a little like Bonnie going off to meet Clyde.

The line for Genevieve's went out the door. Couples milled around the two iron benches, both full, that had been placed under the awning of the restaurant for the inevitable summer overflow. Type As did not care for lines; Helen expected Nat to be long gone.

Once again he surprised her. True, he was looking at his watch and true, he was drumming his fingers on his thigh—

but he was still there. And when he looked up and saw her and his face creased into a relieved and ardent grin—well, she loved him, that's all.

"Sorry, sorry, sorry," she said, once for every fifteen minutes of her delay. "It always takes longer than I remember to clean up after the Social."

"Are you late? I hadn't noticed," he said with self-mocking humor. He glanced at the crowd with no enthusiasm, then said, "Why don't we pass? I've got a bellyache from too much Toasted Almond Sauce anyway. You're probably not hungry, either?"

"Not very," she said, and hoped he couldn't hear her stomach growling.

Apparently he could. Smiling, he added, "On my way in I did see a clam shack on the Wharf . . ."

"Great."

He steered her across and down Derby Street in the direction of the array of shops and eateries on Pickering Wharf, the jewel in the crown of Salem's waterfront redevelopment.

Helen said, "I hope my son wasn't in your car long enough to break anything."

"Actually," Nat said, "I offered to take him for a quick spin around the block. He wasn't interested." He laughed and said, "Maybe if I had just handed him the keys . . ."

"Don't even joke about it," Helen said, shuddering. "I don't know where his endless fascination with fast cars comes from. It must have something to do with the ones his father drove as a trooper."

"Hmm, yeah, they're pretty fast. I've been up close and personal with them more than once."

"Speeding tickets?"

"More than once."

She was thinking, *Well, here's the perfect role model for*

my son. "Probably you can guess how I feel about going too fast," she said.

He smiled ruefully and said, "I'm guessing you're not for it. Am I right?"

She gave him the same rueful smile back for his answer. He laced his fingers through her hand and gave it a little squeeze. "Speeding is addictive," he said. "But—scout's honor—I'm trying to stay nearer the limit. I look on it as therapy."

"Good for you," said Helen, her spirits rising again. "And in the same vein, I'll try to be punctual next—"

Oops.

He laughed and lifted her hand to his lips and said, "Next time. Yes. Tomorrow. Do that."

"No, Nat," she wailed. "Not tomorrow. I've got two kids! I don't have *time* for this relationship. Neither do you. Katie—"

"Katie's in bed," he said smugly. "Hey, a thought! Make your kids go to bed at seven."

"If I knew how to do that, I could write a book and retire on the royalties," she said as they sidled up to the fast-food kiosk.

She ordered a clam roll; he ordered a hot dog. Iced tea for her, beer for him, fries to share. They wandered off toward the boardwalk with their bag of cholesterol and found a vacant bench, just as the sparrows hoped they would.

Nat threw the beggar birds a bit of his roll and took a monster bite of his hot dog. "Mmm. Mmm. Yeah. This is good. Wonder what's in it?" he said between chews.

"Ground clam bellies, without a doubt," said Helen, dangling a breaded version in front of him. She popped it in her mouth, relishing the squish of it.

It felt so much like a date. Every other time she'd been with him had felt, somehow, like business. But this was theirs alone—the junk food, the sparrows, the boardwalk, the boats.

All theirs.

"This was a good idea," she said with a companionable sigh.

"Mmm," said Nat between slugs of beer. He burped, groaned, and said, "God, I'm gonna be sick as a dog tonight. I haven't eaten food like this since I was a kid."

She gave him a skeptical look. "I suppose you eat beansprout sandwiches at your desk?"

He surprised her by saying, "Or a salad. Something healthy, anyway. Workaholics die young, and I've got a lot to live for: Katie . . . and more, maybe, someday."

Helen felt an entirely inappropriate wave of heat wash over her. He could've been talking about anyone or anything; but she chose to believe he was hinting about her.

Careful, stupid, she warned herself. *Women make mistakes at moments like these.*

"Well, junk food or not," she let herself say, "I still think this was a good idea."

"Here's another one," he said suddenly. "Will you go with Katie and me on a nature walk next Saturday evening? Katie wants to learn about owls. She's fixated on the subject, ever since that owl showed up in the yard."

"It's still there?" Helen was surprised to realize that she was troubled by the fact.

He shrugged. "It seems determined," he said, tossing a piece of french fry to the ground. The sparrows ignored it. "Our neighbors came back for the summer and cleaned out the seed from their potting shed, so the mice are gone; but the owl's hanging around anyway. God only knows what it eats. Katie, by the way, is turning out to be a ruthless little bugger. She wants me to buy mice at the pet store to feed it. She says if I can't find mice, maybe hamsters will do."

He crushed the last of his hot dog roll into crumbs and threw them all out at once. Sparrow pandemonium. "Looks just like the commodities pit," Nat said with a snort.

He turned back to Helen. His look was tentative, almost defensive. "So? How about it? Saturday at eight?" Taking a cue from her, he added, "Very low impact on your day."

Nothing that involved him was low impact, but Helen said, "I could do that."

"Good. We'll come get you half an hour before," he said, quietly pleased.

The mood between them turned quiet. He finished his Coors, then bent the can over on itself, and then again. Helen wondered briefly, wildly, whether they'd run out of things to talk about. But that wasn't it. He simply wasn't bothered by what radio and TV people called "dead air."

She remembered Gwen's reading of him: a shy man who only acted at flirting. If Gwen was right, then at that moment Helen had every right to feel flattered—because there was neither banter nor flirting coming from him. Just pensive silence, pierced by the chirps of brawling sparrows.

"You're not much of a people person, are you?" she ventured.

"I work at it," he said briefly. He pitched the crushed can into a nearby trash bin. It bounced on the edge, then fell in. "But I was an only child, raised in a marriage of convenience. I'm not that great at baring my soul."

And that, at bottom, was what this date was supposed to be about: baring his soul.

She tried another approach. "How did you end up in the stock market, anyway?"

He laughed softly. "Funny you should ask. I've thought about that a lot, lately. I search my childhood—what I remember of it—for a defining moment. And all I can come up with is one. One lousy epiphany in forty years."

Helen had the sense that they had begun to tiptoe together into a dusty corner of his soul. She stayed very still, like a hiker who's stumbled onto a fox at dawn, as she waited for him to continue.

"I was five, maybe six," he said, letting his gaze settle on a powerboat that had begun to back out of a nearby slip. "I was summoned to the bedside of my great-great-grandfather, Joseph Bentley Byrne, who was near death. Since I hadn't been allowed to see him for a week, I knew something big was up.

"His bedroom, once the master, is now Katie's. I remember his bed: massive, carved, ornate. Like many of the furnishings, it came over from China on one of the family's ships during the early eighteen hundreds. Above the bed, where Catholics hang crucifixes, there hung a portrait of Houqua, the senior hong merchant in Canton and—if you remember your Salem history—the richest man in China back then."

"The portrait that's now in the hall," she said, recalling the gaunt, balding man with the droopy Mandarin mustache.

"Yeah. Houqua was a real hero in my family," Nat said.

Helen couldn't quite tell how he meant that, so she waited for him to go on.

"The thing is, by the time my great-great-grandfather Joseph was born, Salem was through as a seaport. His—my—ancestors had been adroit at moving their ships from the China trade to the more profitable India trade; surviving Jefferson's embargo in 1807 and then moving into the Baltic trade; surviving the war of 1812 and then moving into new markets in South America and Zanzibar.

"But ultimately, they blew it. The railroad went to Boston and New York, empowering them as key ports. The Erie Canal gave New York an even bigger boost. But Salem? No railroad, no canals, and worse than that, the silting of the harbor made Salem unnavigable for larger ships.

"But Joseph stayed here anyway. He'd made a promise to his dying father that he'd stick with Salem, and he did, struggling to make a profit in coastal shipping with smaller vessels."

Nat got up from the bench, took a step or two, and pitched the brown paper bag into the trash can. He scanned the harbor, much as his ancestors must have done. But there were no lofty clipper ships, no majestic Indiamen to be seen—only small and rather precious powerboats that slept six and huddled in the harbor if the wind blew over ten knots.

To the southeast lay Derby Wharf, once the heartbeat of it all, once thick with stores and warehouses and crammed with wooden ships with lofty masts and tangles of rigging, and brawny men—boys, really, some no older than Russ— who thought nothing of spending months at a time on the killer sea, then braving pirates, shoals, and disease at their destination, only to return, if they were lucky, over the killer sea again.

All that was gone now. What remained of Derby Wharf was a long spit of grass-covered dirt, and the ghosts of all the rest.

Nat turned his back on the scene and said, "I had the history down cold when I was five; the saga of maritime trade was a big, big deal in my family. Which is why, when I was summoned to Joseph's deathbed, I took his last words to me so seriously. As I say, it was the one true epiphany of my life."

Helen waited.

He smiled, apparently impressed with her patience. "My grandfather was a hundred and three. There wasn't much left of him by then: skin, bones, a few white hairs. To me his agedness made him look all the more formidable. I knew that old Houqua had been a very important, very wise man; but my great-great-grandfather was even skinnier, even grayer, even more used up with wisdom.

"I remember him calling me closer, crooking his index finger, twice, in slow motion. I remember walking up to the bed as solemnly as I could, just the way I had the week before when I was ring boy at a wedding. Joseph was propped up on three fat pillows, I suppose to make it easier for him to breathe. He spoke just four words to me . . . four words . . . but they were the last he ever uttered on earth."

A small, bleak smile deadened the lines of Nat's face. " *'Go where money is,'* he told me."

"Ah-h," said Helen. It explained so much.

Hands in his pockets, Nat sat back down on the bench and stretched his legs in front of him. Lost in thought, he stayed that way for a long moment, then said, "Actually, since he wasn't wearing his teeth, the words came out 'Go where money ish.' "

Helen didn't know whether to laugh or cry. She said, "So you went to Boston."

"That's where money ish."

"And instead of tea and silk and pepper, you trade shares. Instead of clipper ships, you move around on 747s. The tradition goes on."

After another long moment Nat said, "I used to wonder: why did Joseph target me, and not my father? But my father had always been perfectly content to live off the interest; if he had to, the principal. I expect the puritanical Joseph at some point washed his hands of him."

"What about your grandfather and great-grandfather? Why didn't Joseph put the money curse on them?"

Nat shrugged. "I never knew either of them. One died in a riding accident; the other got tripped up in the Depression. I don't think either one ever had the ability to make real money."

"But you do," she conceded, trying not to sigh.

"It's a knack," he said with laughable understatement.

"How ironic," she mused. "You're being driven by ghosts of your past, while I'm being prodded by—"

She pulled back suddenly from the confession. It would've been so easy to blurt out something about the bizarre events that had been plaguing her, but what would that prove? That *her* ghost was better than *his* ghost?

No. He was opening up to her at last. No.

"I never thought of it before, but a talent like yours must be a huge responsibility," she said, completely without irony.

"Lena—"

Helen looked at him, surprised to hear the name. He said, "I overheard your aunt call you that. Do you mind?"

"No," she said, although no one besides her aunt Mary had ever done it. The name sounded so different on his lips, so completely, utterly erotic. Her response to it was almost embarrassing: a hot, wet rush of desire.

"You seem to've said the magic word," she confessed with a stricken smile.

He had taken her by the shoulders; his eyes burned bright with obvious desire. "Lena," he repeated, shaking his head. "Oh my God. Lena. How did we get here?"

His mouth descended on hers, and it was the kiss of her dreams, the kiss she'd imagined during every empty night of the last four years, the kiss that made her forget, if only for now, how much she'd loved her husband. Long and deep and full of aching need, it left Helen wanting more. Her lips opened and her tongue met his, as she slid her arms around his back and returned the kiss with a breathlessness that left her light-headed.

Dizzy from him, drunk from him, she gave herself up completely to the sensation of being wanted again by a man. Satisfied and frustrated all at the same time, she found herself staggering along a high-wire of emotions without a pole.

Get down safely while you can, a voice warned her from the ground. But who could hear it above the roar of her desire?

"We ... can't ... do this," she said in panting snatches between more kisses. "We're ... on a ... bench."

"The sparrows don't care," he said, nuzzling her neck, kissing the lobe of her ear. He brought his soft lips back to hers, tasting her, heating her, driving her mad.

"Ooo-ooo-ooo," came a taunting voice from a pack of kids as they walked by, nudging and elbowing one another.

That did it.

"They care," Helen said, her warmed cheeks burning with a whole new heat. She began to pull away, afraid to look at the kids for fear there'd be someone she knew. Hard on their heels came a frowning older couple, not at all amused.

"And those two definitely care," she added, averting her face from them. Reluctantly, she took hold of Nat's wrists to unhand herself from him. "If either of my kids behaved like this in public, I'd feed 'em to the gulls," she said, sobering up at last.

He laughed and said, "You'd rather they did this in private?"

She thought about it and said, "God, I hate teenagers."

"C'mon," he said, standing up and offering her his hand. "Let's walk."

They went back to Derby Street, then walked out to the end of ghostly Derby Wharf to see what they could see and feel what they could feel. Nat knew an astonishing amount about Salem's maritime history and brought it all to life for Helen, who became shivery and teary-eyed as he described the mind-boggling hardships of life aboard a full-rigged ship.

They sat on the grassy finger of land and looked out at the twilit sea; and they kissed, and eventually they strolled back down the empty wharf, stopping to kiss again along the way. The night, warm and still and the shortest one of the year, had descended at last, wrapping itself around them like a soft black veil.

The dark has come too late, Helen thought, deeply moved by all she'd seen and heard. *I have to go home now.*

Nat was telling her of an argument one of his merchant-ancestors supposedly got into with Nathaniel Hawthorne during the time the author, strapped for cash, worked as surveyor in the Custom House just across the way from where they stood.

They stared appreciatively at the elegant Federal-style brick structure with its massive stone steps, tall Palladian windows, and eight-sided cupola. Helen had seen the building thousands of times in her life; and yet, before tonight, she had never really seen it at all.

"If Mr. Hawthorne were at his perch there now," she mused, "I doubt that he'd be too impressed with our behavior."

"Hey, he stuck up for Hester Prynne," Nat said. "I don't think he'd mind."

He kissed Helen again, just to prove his point, and Helen thought of Hester and her scarlet letter and shivered unaccountably. "Poor Hester," she said, brimming with emotion when he released her. "They were so cruel."

Nat became more thoughtful as he caught her hand in his and they resumed their walk. "The Puritan ethic produced some damn good capitalists," he said, "but I guess we know the downside."

Repression. Intolerance. The infamous witch trials.

He'd pressed one of Helen's hot buttons. "Who could forget?" she said. "No one in Salem, that's for sure. Every time you turn around, you bump into a witch on a broom handle. The damn logo is everywhere: on our paper's masthead, souvenirs, stores, restaurants—the doors of our fire engines, for pity's sake! We seem awfully proud of that summer of hysteria," she said with her usual distress. "What an image to cultivate!"

"You're one of the sensitive ones," he said, wrapping his arm around her shoulder and stealing a kiss. "Why doesn't that surprise me? Look at it this way. The Puritans were the original capitalists; and now the capitalists, with their cartoon witches, are exploiting the Puritans. I see poetic justice there."

"But there's so much more to Salem!"

"Oh, admit it," he teased. "The occult is fun."

Helen felt the blood drain from her cheeks. "I don't think so," she said faintly. "Not 'fun.' "

He tried with a light touch to kiss away her seriousness, but Helen protested. "It's not that I'm down on tourism—"

"Helen, you don't have to apologize," he said, laughing. "Lots of Salemites are ambivalent about the witching trade. But if it shores up our tax base, I say—go for it!"

He took her in his arms and rubbed his chin in the curve of her neck, taking a long, deep breath of her. "You smell divine," he said.

Don't tell me Enchantra, she thought. *Don't.*

"Earthy and sexy and—God, Helen," he said, his voice catching in his throat. "You're making me crazy."

Of course she was, she realized; he hadn't had sex in months. It wasn't hard for her to convince herself that Nathaniel Byrne was simply deprived and on fire. But there was nothing she could do to convince herself he believed in ghosts.

She wanted, suddenly, to get away. She was playing with fire and in danger of being caught with the matches. If he had any idea that she believed she'd been contacted by his dead wife . . .

"Wow," she said, sighing. "I'm beat. This has been just
. . . an incredible day."

It was the verbal equivalent of wriggling out of his arms.
Nat looked surprised and rebuffed, but he said softly, "You
must be. I'll walk you to your car."

Becky was waiting for her. She took one look at Helen and
said, "*Mother!* You *did* it with him!"

"I did *not*!" Helen said, scandalized. She thumped her
bag on the hall table and marched past her daughter into
the kitchen.

Becky was right behind her. "Your mouth is all puffy
and your face is flushed," she noted with glee.

Helen pumped soap lavishly into her hands and began a
surgical scrub at the sink. "I'm exactly the same as before
I left," she said, scowling. *And why the hell am I washing
up in the kitchen?*

Frustrated that she couldn't have a second's privacy once
she walked through her front door, Helen added, "I'm going to use some of this soap in your mouth, young lady,
unless you get out of here while you can. Beat it."

"Okay, you don't want to talk about it. That's cool with
me," Becky said with a lofty air. On her way out she lifted
a fold of her mother's dress in back and let it drop. "But
you'd better get some Wisk on those grass stains before it's
too lay-ate."

Chapter 20

On Monday the Stickneys withdrew their son from The Open Door. On Tuesday it was the Comfords. Neither couple offered a reason. Helen had never been faced with three successive withdrawals before—it was like being fired three days in a row—and so she forced herself to say to Mrs. Comford, "May I ask why?"

Mrs. Comford's smile was brisk, her manner brief. "We've decided against an urban preschool. It's too . . . urban. You will let me know about my registration fee?"

"Of course," said Helen blankly, dropping back in her office chair as if she'd been slapped.

Mrs. Comford was barely out the door when the phone rang.

"Hi," Nat said. "It's me. I waited a day so that I wouldn't seem anxious; but now, of course, it's made me anxious. When can I see you again?"

It was heaven to hear his voice; heaven to be desired instead of rejected. But Mrs. Comford had left an aftertaste like a sour pickle, and it must have showed in Helen's voice.

"Something wrong?" Nat said quickly.

Helen sighed and said, "Just another day in the preschool trade." She explained what had happened. "I have this godawful fear that a salmonella rumor's cropped up again. Someone always gets a stomach ache from eating too much ice cream at the Social; who knows how it's being interpreted. Now that I think about it, everyone heard Becky's friend Laurie going around moaning and groaning at the end."

"She ate enough ice cream to sink the *Lusitania*," Nat said, laughing. "What did you expect?"

"I know, but it doesn't take much to bring down a pre-school."

"Look, I'm a numbers man," he said. "Three withdrawals is not an anomaly."

Helen wanted to believe him. "Thanks, Nat," she said, letting herself feel relieved. "You're good for the soul."

His voice was amused and insinuating as he said, "Right now it's not the soul I'm thinking about. Lena—let me see you tonight."

She knew this had to come. She had bounced between thoughts of him and worries about the withdrawals for three days now. "Nat . . . no. The owl walk is one thing, but Derby Wharf was a big, huge, giant mistake."

"Oh, I agree. Absolutely. Pure misery, the whole time," he said with an edgy chuckle.

"No, really. There are things about me that you don't know."

"Let me find them out."

"Beliefs I have that you don't share."

"Convert me, then."

She wanted to scream, *You're on the rebound, nitwit! You're horny and hurt and I don't mean a tinker's damn to you! Leave me alone! Don't torture me with wanting me!*

Instead she said softly, "Nat, we can't go any farther with this. We can't. I have two teenagers. My daughter has made me her role model for sex and is watching every move I make; my son is just itching for me to get a life so he can grab a can of spray paint and run. In a couple of more years I'll be through this crisis of teenage timing—I hope—but for now . . .''

Her sigh was brimming with frustration. "For now, any dating I did would be strictly hit-and-run."

There was a long silence. Finally, in a voice as low and tense as her own, he said, "I've taken a hit from you, Helen. Please don't run."

Biting her lip, she looked up at the ceiling above her desk, as if a solution were scribbled there in chalk. It wasn't. She closed her eyes and let out a long, wistful sigh. "Can we just go slow, then? Can we just do the owl walk for now?"

He didn't say yes; he didn't say no. She hung up, half-convinced that he was calling on his cell phone from the parking lot of the preschool. But he was in Atlanta, she knew, and wouldn't be home until the next day. And meanwhile, who was there to put poor Katie to bed?

Peaches knew that Nat was planning to be home from Atlanta by three, which worked out well. Katie's play date with Amy was scheduled to end around then.

When Nat walked into the music room in his loosened tie and rolled-up sleeves, he found Peaches deep in conversation with Amy Bonham's mother.

Peaches could tell at a glance that he was disappointed to find visitors. His smile was polite and weary. Clearly he wanted a beer; Atlanta in summer was no picnic. Whatever energy he had was saved for his daughter. His gaze softened when he spied her at the far end of the room, playing dress-up with Amy.

"Look at this. Daddy!" Katie cried, running up to him with her new stick-on earrings. She held her curly hair back from her ears. "Amy gave them to me. See?"

Nat dropped his briefcase and squatted down to give her a hug. "Well, you look just gorgeous in them, buggles. Can I try them on?"

Katie let out a shriek of laughter and clapped her hands over her ears as she goose-stepped back from him. "No-o! Daddies don't wear earrings!" She turned and fled to the other end of the room.

"I guess you're right," he told her, smiling. "Well, after I change clothes, you have to dance with me, because you look so pretty. Okay?"

She turned back to her father and said, "Okay, Daddy. But first I hafta put this . . . this long thing on," she said, grabbing a thrift shop shawl that Linda had bought for the dress-up box. "An' a hat." She began rummaging through the box for suitable millinery.

Constance Bonham had been burning Peaches's ears off with preschool gossip. Now she turned the heat on Nat.

In a grimly discreet voice she said, "Nat, have you heard about this Satanism business? Is there possibly anything to it? I want to say no—it seems so unlikely—but nowadays nothing is unlikely. I mean, these cults are everywhere. Why not Salem? It's a natural fit."

Nat had been about to slip away. Now he stood there, obviously dead tired, suit coat slung over his shoulder, briefcase in his hand, and said, "Connie, I have no idea what you're talking about."

"Mrs. Evett's daughter, for God's sake! She was arrested for spraying Satanistic graffiti on the statue of Roger Conant!"

Even Peaches was surprised at the change in Nat. His stance turned rigid and a dark flush suffused his face. His brows came down hard over his steel blue eyes as he said sharply, "Who the hell said that? Becky was there to stop her *brother* from tagging the statue!"

Constance gasped and said, "Her brother, too?"

"No, no," Nat said impatiently. "I mean yeah, he sprayed paint on the statue. That's all. Regular graffiti stuff. There was nothing Satanistic about it."

"What did he spray on it, then?" Constance asked him.

Nat snorted and shook his head. "I don't know. Just . . . stuff. Jesus. Helen was right. This town has witches on the brain," he said, not bothering to hide his disgust.

Peaches had been watching his reaction with growing annoyance. Bad enough that he was intrigued by the Evett woman; but now he was defending her. This, after slipping away on Sunday night . . . She never expected him to move that fast. She bit her lip, pondering her next move.

Nat misinterpreted the look on her face. "Peach?" he said, scowling. "*You* haven't heard anything?"

"Not a word," she said, acting as if she were trying to seem calm. "I'm as distressed as you are."

"I'm not distressed," he snapped. "I'm goddamned pissed." He turned on his heel. "It's dumb gossip, Constance," he said over his shoulder as he walked away. "Ignore it."

Rebuffed, Constance turned to Peaches. "He doesn't want to know," she said flatly.

Peaches lifted her finely shaped eyebrows in the barest suggestion of a shrug. "He's a man. Do they ever?"

The weather forecast was terrific right through the weekend, which meant that Helen's one possible excuse for not seeing Nat—rain—would be denied her.

Not that it mattered. In their last phone call he'd announced his intention of getting into her life one way or another. He planned to attend the monthly meetings, to volunteer his time (and considerable talents) at fund-raising, to help chaperone field trips when the occasion arose, to crotchet potholders for the Penny Fair if he had to. Whatever it took.

It was a very grand vision. "Whom do you hope to impress?" she had wanted to know.

"Her initials are Helen Evett."

"You're doing all the right things for all the wrong reasons."

"I'm doing all the right things for two great reasons: Katie and you."

And on it went, until finally, worn out by his relentlessness, Helen had thrown up her hands and said, "If you do half the things you say you will, I'm going to end up paying *you* to have Katie come here."

And now it was Saturday, and her heart was doing its *thumpa-thumpa* thing at a one-two clip, and she was obsessing over frizzy hair, baggy khakis, and the wrong shade of lipstick when the real issue, the only issue, should have been: *Where on earth can this possibly go?*

Even assuming that his attraction for her was genuine and not a knee-jerk response to biological needs; even assuming that he had time, and she had time, to squeeze a relationship into their already harried lives; even assuming that they could figure out a place to even *have* the damn affair—what then?

He'd love her and leave her and break her heart. Or he'd love her and want her and she'd have to come clean: *By the way—Linda Byrne? Have I mentioned we've met? Very nice lady. Oh yes; we're still in touch. Did you have a message for her? No problem; I'll pass it on for you the next time she haunts me.*

If Nat backed away slowly and then broke into a run, could Helen blame him?

And yet, there was reason to hope. The encounter or ordeal or whatever it was that Helen had experienced in her office on Sunday seemed to have a finality to it. Maybe Helen had simply passed through a phase, an ultrasympathetic reaction to poor Katie's loss of her mother (Helen had been just four when her own mother died).

What else could it be? Helen hadn't suffered a trauma to her head; she didn't have a brain tumor; and as far as she knew, her family had no history of schizophrenia. Mass hysteria? But where were the masses? She was all alone in her nuttiness.

Okay—maybe not completely alone. Both Becky and Nat had sniffed *Enchantra* when they shouldn't have. But that was such a small thing, compared to the profound events that Helen had experienced.

She was in a last-minute change into a denim skirt when the doorbell rang. Alone in the house for once, Helen had to answer the door herself. Russ was off at a birthday party, and Becky had graciously agreed to pick him up at ten (anything to help her mother find romance).

For tonight, only little Katie stood in the way of their falling into one another's arms—and Helen was actually grateful for it. *We have time on our side,* she thought. *The longer we wait, the better for us.* Her feelings for Nat ran far, far too deep to squander them on some quick wild fling.

She opened the door and fell in love all over again. He was holding his daughter; they came as a pair. It was unbelievably easy to love them both.

Katie was dressed for the occasion in coveralls with an owl appliqued on the bib. "We're gonna see some ahls," she said, cutting right to the chase. "Big, big ones!"

"Well, that would be exciting, wouldn't it," Helen told her.

It was a crazy idea, expecting a three-year-old to stay awake through a twilight nature walk. They'd be lucky to hear an owl, much less see one. But Helen hadn't been able to make Nat understand that. He'd given his word, he said. And the new Nat meant to keep it.

"All set?" he asked Helen. His look was carnal and

innocent at the same time, a tough combination for her to have to resist.

Damn you, she thought. *You aren't making this any easier for me.*

"You bet," she answered. "Do you have mosquito repellent for Katie?"

He groped around in his aqua-blue diaper bag. "Check," he said. "And juice. And a change of pants. And a hat. A jacket. Extra shoes. We can take Everest if we want to."

"Welcome to ParentWorld," she said with a wry smile.

She locked the door behind her and they all piled into his Porsche which, Helen had to admit, was an extraordinary vehicle. Glove-soft leather, discreet electronics, the faint hint of a fine cigar—it was a machine that Batman would be proud to own.

Helen said something to that effect and Nat astonished her by saying, "I'm thinking of maybe trading it in for a van. You can fit camping equipment in a van."

She turned to him and studied his clean-cut, clean-shaven profile. He was too lean, too aristocratic to qualify as a Marlboro Man; and yet she could picture him easily with a five-day-old stubble of beard, frying a freshly caught fish over a campfire while his daughter toasted a predinner marshmallow on a stick.

She could picture it only too well, and it made her heart ache.

To sound supportive she said, "I have a sea kayak—it was Hank's—that I've been meaning to sell."

"Maybe you won't have to," he answered, reaching over to stroke her cheek with the back of his fingers.

Thumpa-thumpa.

"Daddy, I wish I could see the ahls right away," said Katie from the backseat.

"Pretty soon," her daddy said.

Helen turned around. The child was yawning heavily,

fighting to keep her eyes open. Helen put her hand on Nat's arm, then hooked her thumb a couple of times toward the car seat.

"All right," he admitted. "So she finds us boring. It doesn't mean anything. Katie? Tell Mrs. Evett what a nice long nap you took today."

"Uh-huh."

"And tell Mrs. Evett how excited you were when we were getting dressed to go on our hike tonight."

"Mm-hmm."

"And tell Mrs. Evett what kind of owl we have in our yard. You remember—what did we see in your *Big Book of Owls?*"

Gone. Katie's head was drooping forward and to one side; her mouth was a little ajar as she drew in long, deep breaths of sleep.

Smiling, Helen said softly, "Maybe we should just turn around and go home?"

"Not a chance; she'd never forgive me," Nat said. "She really has been fixated on this trip—I'm telling you. Anyway, Peaches said she slept almost twice as long as usual today. She'll perk up."

"She's exhausted," Helen said, but there were worse things to do than drive around in a Porsche with a handsome man and a sleeping three-year-old, so Helen sat back and enjoyed the short ride north to the Ipswich River Sanctuary. Nat, who'd tracked the place down through the Audubon Society, said it was the best kept secret in Massachusetts: 2,800 acres of wilderness—eight miles of river and forest—hidden behind rural suburbia off Route 1.

They talked of childhood pleasures and favorite vacations, staying away from the subjects of their marriages and their careers, and in a short while they were pulling into the parking area behind a modest, rustic outbuilding where the staff naturalist was in the process of briefing a small group of adults that had gathered for the hike.

Nat, carrying his droopy-eyed daughter, nudged his way up to the front of the gathering.

"We'll be taking our time, walking very slowly," said the naturalist, a big man with a beard and a laid-back slouch that made him look a little owlish himself. "Naturally we'll keep our voices to a minimum."

He looked at Katie and translated for her benefit. "We must be very, very quiet.

"We'll keep an eye out," he continued, "for a tree covered in whitewash. With any luck, we'll find owl pellets below it on the ground. Unlike eagles and vultures, the owl swallows its prey whole, so it has to get rid of the undigestible parts. It regurgitates a pellet with the bones in the center, tightly packed and surrounded by either soft fur or down feathers. That way, the owl doesn't gouge itself on the sharp bones as they come back up."

He led the group to a small glass case and said, "Here's an example of a pellet that's been carefully pulled apart for examination. You can see the intact skull—the best way to identify the prey—which in this case belongs to a field mouse. Other prey are birds, shrews, voles—whatever's on the menu that night."

All of it was very interesting, but not to Katie. She sighed; she plucked at her father's jacket in boredom; she yawned repeatedly.

Nat and Helen exchanged glances. He grimaced. Maybe they should bag the whole thing, his look said.

The naturalist was telling the group that he'd be calling to the owls, who he was convinced heard the calls. "Some may call back," he said. "Definitely the screech owl will, and maybe the barred owl. If we're lucky, we'll hear the saw-whet owl. I doubt that we'll hear a great horned owl; they're later in the night."

Katie interrupted him. "We have a short-eared ahl. In our yard."

"Really!" he said, genuinely interested. "That's very uncommon. Where do you live?"

Katie automatically looked at her father. "Right in the heart of Salem," Nat said proudly. You'd think he was the one who'd given birth to the bird.

The naturalist said, "They prefer marshes and prairies. Is the owl hurt, do you think?"

"No," said Katie confidantly. "It goes like this: *kee-yow*," she said, dipping her head in imitation of a sneeze.

Smiling, the naturalist said, "Well, *we* won't be hearing a short-eared owl; they tend to move around in late afternoon."

Katie's face registered massive disappointment. Her brows came down and she stuck out her lower lip.

Her father recognized the signs. "Do you maybe want to go home, honey?" he murmured. "Are you tired?"

"Yes," she said, fed up with the tour, the tour leader, and the grown-ups who'd duped her.

Nat smiled an apology to the rest of the group and backtracked out of the room before Katie began what he clearly thought was going to be one of her fits. Helen, falling in behind him, was still listening to the group leader's remarks on her way out.

"There's an old Indian legend," he was saying in his quietly interesting way, "that says when a person dies, the soul of that person enters an owl; and if that owl happens to look you in the eye, it means that the soul has made contact with you, and you become his friend."

Helen stopped in her tracks. The hair on the back of her neck stood up, just as it had on the day that she'd first approached the Byrne mansion. On the same day—very probably, the same hour—that Linda Byrne had died, an uncommon owl had made uncommon contact with Helen by flying at her and looking her straight in the eye before it veered away, eventually to take up residence outside of Katie's bedroom.

My God. That's it, then. That's what this is all about. Even Katie ... Katie knows, in some subliminal way. ... Somehow she's connected, still, to her mother ... and that's why she wanted to come. ... Not to look for owls, but so that we could hear the legend. That was the whole point. Linda has made her daughter—made me—*come here so that I would understand.*

Wave after wave of goose bumps rolled over Helen as she stood there, caught in time, fearful and awestruck and overjoyed all at once. She realized that what she now possessed—what she'd been missing up until then—was a simple explanation to extraordinary events.

If Helen had been a Native American, if she had had access to a tribal shaman, she would not have stumbled around in the dark for so many months. But she was not a Native American; she was a Salem Yankee with little time for her spiritual side.

Linda Byrne has made me her friend. Her loves are my loves. Her pain is my pain. If I fail, she will mourn. If I triumph, she will rejoice. We will celebrate together, or we will grieve together. Because she is my friend. I've known it all along; and yet I haven't understood it at all.

Chapter 21

"Excuse me, miss, are you all right?"

It was the naturalist, who'd sent his group on ahead while he paused to take the measure of Helen.

Tears were rolling down her cheeks. "Oh, yes—truly, I'm fine," she said. "Your Indian legend has touched me very deeply, that's all."

He sounded a little wistful as he said, "I've had it happen to friends—confronting an owl that way—but not to me. Maybe someday."

Smiling through her tears, she shook his hand. "Thank you. You'll never know how much this meant to me. Thank you."

They went their separate ways. Helen caught up with Nat at the car; he was wondering where he'd lost her. He put a finger to his lips, then pointed into the back seat of the Porsche where Katie sat slumped in her car seat, out to the world.

Smiling, Helen slipped her bag through the open window and whispered, "She knows more about owls than they do, anyway."

She and Nat lingered outside of the car for a moment, listening for sounds of night birds, hearing only the last, aching notes of a robin singing its evening song.

Nat turned to Helen; slipping his hands behind her head, he lowered his lips to hers in the kiss she knew would come. It was tender, erotic, another step closer to bed. There was no longer a question of *if* between them, just when.

His tongue slid over hers and she caught her breath in her throat. Helen knew the taste of him now, savored it; and she knew she wanted more. Never mind all her good intentions. It wouldn't be long; it *couldn't* be long. She wanted him too much.

He ran his hands down the curve of her back and caught them under her buttocks, pulling her hard against him as he kissed her mouth, her jaw, the skin exposed by the curve of her scooped-neck top. With her neck arched, her eyes closed, Helen clung to him, with one thought filling the recesses of her heart: *I can't let him go, I can't.*

Her one wild wish—that they could be in bed just then—couldn't be granted; but she returned his kisses as if it could. Hot, wet, wanton—she was making a fool of herself in the parking lot of an Audubon sanctuary.

"I'm sorry . . . this is . . . oh God . . . I'm sorry," she said in whimpering gasps between kisses.

It was insane. He whispered, "Helena, Helena," combining versions of her name, pounding her with it in a drumbeat of desire. "Make love with me!"

"How, Nat!" she murmured, angry with frustration.

Suddenly he broke from his embrace of her and in a low growl said, "I'll show you how."

He led her a few steps away to the edge of the wood, practically in spitting distance of the Porsche, and then behind a wild, unkempt shrub that had sprung up beneath a weedy maple. In deepening darkness he leaned against the tree, then pulled her back into his arms.

"*This* is how," he said, kissing her hard and deep.

Somewhere in the racking thunder that rolled through her mind, Helen heard the sound of a zipper and then felt the folds of her skirt being lifted, exposing her thighs to the cool air of the night. She stepped out of one side of her underpants as he pulled them away, and all the while her mind was thinking, *There are a thousand reasons not to do this*.

And then all thousand fell away like the last dim rays of light as he hoisted her on top of himself and they succumbed, with hot, passionate sounds, to this one wild thing.

It was wordless, breathless sex, primitive and focused. He came quickly, after a few deep thrusts; but not so quickly as she. Panting and spent, Helen collapsed on his shoulder, then let her legs slide slowly down the outside of his as she tried, feebly, to stand on her own feet again.

Wildfire. She'd burst into flames and then been quelled, all in the space of two or three minutes. And now that it was over, Helen, dazed, almost in shock, could think of only one thing to say.

"Katie."

Never mind where they were, whom she'd been with, *how* she'd been with him. The only word left in Helen's vocabulary as she slipped her underpants back on was *Katie*.

"I know," he said, still trying to catch his breath. "I kept . . . an eye . . . on the car."

Helen was appalled that he'd been able to do that. But she would've been appalled if he hadn't. The first inkling of coming misery flashed before her like a flare shot off at sea, and then she was left in darkness again.

Dismayed, she said, "I never even thought of watching the car."

"You were facing the tree, dope," he said in voice that was meant to be breezy but sounded as shaken as her own. "How could you?"

He took her by the shoulders. She was just able to make out the features of his face, but not to read them with any accuracy as he said, "I didn't mean for it to happen this way, either."

"But it did." She said it sadly, knowing there could not be a second first time.

He tilted her chin and gave her a breathless, utterly gentle kiss. "Are you all right?"

She began to say something, then stopped. With a small ache of a laugh, she said, "Sure. I guess."

Enfolding her in his arms, he whispered a second time, "I didn't mean for it . . . this way."

They went back to the car, both of them subdued, and Nat began retracing the route to Salem. The raw magic of the sanctuary had touched the wild creature in them; Helen left it behind with more fear than regret.

What had she done? Her plan to build a gradual, solid, lasting relationship had seemed so reasonable. She had wanted him to come to terms with the death of his wife, to test his commitment to parenting, to put his career in some kind of perspective. She thought of his earlier, poignant plea: *I've taken a hit from you, Helen,* he'd said. *Please don't run.*

In the silent darkness of the car, she smiled bleakly to herself. The only thing hit-and-run about her was the sex she'd just had.

Another thought flashed across her brain, sending chills through her: What if she became pregnant? Unprotected sex in a wildlife sanctuary? It *had* to have been her fertile time. She tried to remember when her last period was, but drew a blank.

She shuddered, knowing that the night would be the first of many spent in second-guessing.

Nat saw her distress. He said softly, "It's not the end of the world, Helen."

"I've never done anything like that before!"

His voice was low and sad and pained. "I didn't think you had."

"I don't know what came over me," she said, hugging herself.

"It was nothing we could fight," he said, sounding as abashed as she felt. "It was . . . God. It was incredible."

Isn't that what the man always says?

She made herself sound brisk. "We should have tried harder not to give in."

"Now you sound like Hester Prynne."

"Yes, well, look what happened to her."

He reached over across the gearshift and took Helen's hand in his. "I understand what you're saying, but—"

"I know. You're a numbers man. You're going to tell me that the odds are against it."

"No, I was going to say, if anything comes of tonight— I'll be there for you, Lena. No matter what happens, no matter what you decide, I'll be there. I promise."

Ignoring the fact that she had misread him completely, Helen zeroed in on his tone instead. He sounded more than determined; to her he sounded almost grim.

It's because of Linda, she decided. *He was never there for his wife, and now he wants to make up for it.* But did she want a man to "be there" who was spurred by guilt?

She did not. "You don't have to worry that I'll become pregnant," she said in a proud lie. "It's not the right time of month."

"You sound angry."

"I am; at myself. How can I expect my daughter—inexperienced, with hormones surging—to practice some self-control if I can't do it myself?"

He said nothing for a moment. Then, softly: "Have you been with anyone since Hank?"

The question took her breath away. How could he possibly assume that she'd go four years without a man? It was . . . insulting.

"No. I haven't."

He amazed her by sounding disappointed with her answer. "In that case, there goes my theory of destiny, all shot to hell," he said quietly.

Her laugh had a dangerous edge to it. "You're saying the real reason I joined you at a tree in the woods is because I haven't *been* with someone in a while? Ha. Guess what? That's my theory about *you*."

"Are you kidding? What do you think I am? Some tom—"

Katie stirred in her car seat, which instantly reduced him to a whisper.

"—some tomcat?" he finished. "Listen to me. I'm driven to you the way a starving man . . . a thirsty man . . . oh, Christ, I don't know how or why I'm driven to you, Helen. I just am."

He lifted her hand slowly to his lips in a kind of silent homage. "Whatever is happening between us is way, way bigger than anything that's happened to me before."

Helen sighed deeply. It didn't seem possible to be so unhappy about happiness. She said, "We need time to talk, really talk, Nat. We seem to make time for everything else . . ."

He thought that was funny; even she could see a certain lunatic humor in the remark. "But it would be nice if we had more than two minutes," she said dryly. "There are things I want to tell you . . . and things I want to know."

"About Linda." It wasn't a question. "Sometimes I feel as if we're in a kind of *ménage à trois*—you, me, and her ghost," he said, unwittingly hitting a bull's eye. "She's more in my thoughts now than ever—and yet you're always there, too. It's an odd, odd thing," he mused.

They rode for a while in silence, reluctant, still, to come to grips with that ghost.

Eventually Helen turned to another worry altogether. "Two more parents withdrew their children, this time from the fall session. Is that still within the range of normalcy?" she asked him lightly.

She assumed that he'd come back with a resounding "absolutely!" Instead he said with a troubled air, "Is anyone offering a reason why?"

"Nothing that makes sense," she admitted. "They tell me the program's too structured; the program's too loose. The setting's too urban; there are too many shrubs. That's why I think it's really the salmonella thing. When we had that false alarm three years ago, I had to write and then call every single parent to reassure them. Even then I could tell some of them were reserving judgment."

"I don't think it's salmonella this time."

"Maybe, but one of the parents is particularly paranoid about that kind of thing; she might've gone too far in her speculations."

"Helen. There's another rumor going around," he said. "I had no intention of telling you—I'm still not sure I'm doing the right thing here—but five withdrawals is too many. Unless someone's decided that the preschool's been built on a toxic dump, five is too many."

"What . . . is it, then?" she said with a sinking heart.

He hesitated, then said, "Someone's been mouthing off about Satanism in connection with Russ's graffiti."

She was dumbfounded. *"What!"*

"Yeah. Apparently one of the neighbors across the Common saw the boys at the statue, then called the police. Supposedly, after the kids were hauled off she sent her husband out to look at what they'd done. The woman told someone who told someone who told someone—you know how it goes—and a Satanist version, with Becky as gang leader, slithered onto the grounds of the preschool during the Ice Cream Social.''

"I don't believe it," she said flatly. "Who told you?"

"Eventually the story ended up in the lap of Constance Bonham, who's a neighbor of mine. She's the one who came to Peaches and me with it. It's so asinine. I've had Peaches working overtime trying to track this thing down."

Still in a state of shock, Helen said numbly, "What did she find out?"

Reluctantly, he answered her. "It seems your aunt was telling some people at the Social about how you made your kids go back and clean off the paint; she was very proud of that. Her story must've got merged with the Satanist crap and . . .''

He shrugged unhappily. It was obvious that he didn't want to be doing this.

For the rest of her life, Helen remembered everything about that moment: the black, moonless night, the black leather of the car's interior, the black hood that clawed the road ahead of them, even—bitter irony—"That Old Black Magic" on the FM.

Black. Round and round it went, down and down it went: black, black rumors. A rumor of Satanism, no matter how absurd or unrelated, would bring down the school in no time flat. Every preschool director in America knew that. A lifetime of work, a career dedicated to caring for children she loved—gone. The prospect was mind-boggling.

"But . . . there was nothing Satanistic," she said, dazed. "There was an initial R. And the usual—well, the f-word, only it looked like f-u-c-h. And last of all, the word Sarah. That was it."

She turned to him and said helplessly, "You do believe that, don't you?"

"God—you have to ask?" But he added in a depressingly grave voice, "You've got to confront this head-on,

Helen. Call a meeting of the parents and deny it.''

"No," she said, shaking her head. "If I do that, it'll look like I'm protesting too much. I have to hope it blows over. I can't believe that anyone would seriously believe such trash. Anyone who knows Becky . . .''

An image of Becky popped up in her head: sweet, lively, generous Becky, with her funky black clothes, clodhopper shoes, and sunflower hats. Becky: outgoing, gentle, loved by all. Becky, who related to kids so well that parents fought over having her sit on Saturday nights for them.

Becky, a cult leader and Satanist.

"How could anyone do this?" Helen said, appalled. "How could they?"

"Call the meeting, Helen."

"*No*. I won't have Becky's name dragged on stage for any reason," she said vehemently. "She'd die if she knew I'd done that."

"She'd die if she knew about the rumor."

"It's true. This is horrible," Helen said, as one ugly implication after another came oozing out.

"We've got to find out who started this thing," Nat said angrily.

"We can't. That would just keep it going longer. God in heaven," she said, pressing the palms of her hands over her mouth. She shook her head in disbelief. "This is too much; too much for one night."

"I shouldn't have told you, Helen," he said instantly. "It was dumb. You didn't need this."

"No, no, better to have heard it from you than a parent. Oh, it explains so much. The looks . . . the contempt—even fear—in their voices . . . I couldn't understand it."

She bit her upper lip, trying to keep her emotions under control. "What do I do? What *can* I do?"

"Helen, we'll get through this. You're innocent. Becky

is innocent. People don't willingly destroy the lives of . . . the innocent.''

But even as he said it, Nat's voice faltered. He was from Salem, the same as Helen. They knew full well what could happen to the innocent.

He pulled up in front of her house, then got her door for her. Katie woke up and began to fuss, forcing Nat and Helen to part after a hurried embrace. He said, "The graffiti rumor was bad luck, but it will pass. You're too well liked, too well respected. You've got the most level head of anyone I know. No one who's met you can possibly doubt you."

He kissed her softly and said, "At the sanctuary—I've never known anything like that, Lena. Never. Please believe me."

He left and Helen went inside and directly to the shower, where she stood under the showerhead until the hot water ran out. Then she slipped into a T-shirt and jeans and went downstairs to wait for her children. She was desperate to have them in her arms again; to keep them safe from harm.

They didn't deserve this. No one did. Russell was a handful, yes, but no more than that. And Becky . . . Becky was a complete innocent. Helen's anxiety turned to anger and then to frustration and then to rage again. How dare someone slander them that way?

She closed her eyes, trying to control her emotions—but as soon as she did that, she was back in the sanctuary, under the tree with Nat.

Think about something else.

She opened her eyes and stared at the clock, waiting for Becky to bring Russ home—Becky, who should be having a postmovie pizza with a nice boy, but instead went to an early show in her own car so that she could be free in time to fetch her brother. Becky would be crushed by this.

Think about something else.

She closed her eyes and was back at the sanctuary.
Think about something else.

She opened her eyes and remembered the owl. That, she could think about. Somehow, in some way, there was a connection to Linda in all of this. Linda had been a mother, too. Linda had loved her firstborn child; she would've loved her second one as much. Linda would understand what Helen was going through.

Get me through this, Helen begged her friend. *You're a mother. You know what this is like. Help me.*

"Mom? You home?" yelled Becky.

"In here, honey," said Helen, forcing herself to sound composed.

Becky wasn't fooled for a minute. She stomped into the sitting room, still in her combat boots.

"What happened?" she said, pulling up short at the sight of her mother's tearstained face.

Helen couldn't possibly tell her. Instead she pointed to Becky's shoes in a diversion tactic. "Shoes. Off. Now. There are rubber marks all over the hall floor," she said, in a poor imitation of her usual scolding.

Becky dropped onto the hassock in front of her mother's chair. "You had a fight," she said, unlacing her heavy shoes. "*Please* don't tell me you had a fight. I *knew* something would happen to screw this up! He made a move on you and you decked him."

"Not even close," Helen said faintly.

Becky stopped midlace and looked at her mother. "He didn't make a pass?"

Helen gave her a pitiful fragment of a smile.

"You didn't deck him? You—? Ohh-h . . ."

Russ chose that moment to make one of his rare appearances in the sitting room. "Ma, I told Becky to wait in the car but she came inside the house to get me anyway. In front of everyone!"

"Oh, horrors," said Helen, reassured by her son's mundane lament. It was so normal. *He* was so normal. She loved them both so much.

Becky was able to study her mother and taunt her brother at the same time. "I baby-sit there. Why shouldn't I go in?" she said. "I suppose you wanted everyone to think you were going home in the Porsche?"

"I wouldn't be caught dead in it," Russ said fiercely. He gave his mother a furtive look, noticed that her eyes were red-rimmed, did a double take, and promptly started backpedaling out of the room.

Helen said, "Wait. I need to talk to you both."

Becky, shoes in hand, stayed where she was on the hassock. Her face, always lively and curious, settled into an expression of thoughtful repose. She looked captivatingly beautiful; it made Helen want to cry again. Her Rebecca; innocent Becky—how dare anyone?

She said, "I know I told you both not to go around bragging about your spray-paint caper, but I have to ask you. Did either of you tell anyone about that night?"

Russell's logic was impeccable. "If we did you'd kill us, so what's the point?"

Becky had none of her brother's flippancy. "Mom, how can you even ask me that? It was the worst night of my life," she said, her face turning a lighter shade of pale.

Becky was looking for some kind of reassurance that the night wasn't coming back to haunt her. Helen couldn't give it. Instead she turned to Russ and said, "Would any of the other boys have said anything?"

She'd only met one of them since the night of the arrest: a more or less presentable kid who was Russ's age but who was being sent by his parents to private school in the fall, apparently to shape him up. (Helen, on the other hand, preferred to keep her son in public school and shape him up herself.)

Russell was taking his time to think his mother's question through; he seemed to understand that the answer was important.

"Martin wouldn't say anything," Russ decided. "He'd be laughed outta school. Kurt wouldn't bother; it wasn't a big enough deal. And Binny—well, you met Binny. He said he didn't tell, but he likes this girl," Russ said with a philosophical shrug. "Anything's possible with Binny."

"Which of the artwork was Binny's?" Helen asked drily.

"I *told* you. He likes this girl. Sarah. But he's too dorky for Sarah."

"Takes one to know one," Becky got in.

Russ gave his sister a slanty look and sighed, clearly uncomfortable speaking of Matters Sexual. "Kin I go now?"

"Thank you very much for your patience and your thoroughness," Helen said with the irony she reserved exclusively for him.

He got away, but not before whacking a chair with his way-too-big feet, which made Becky roll her eyes and Helen sigh. One look at Russ and anyone would know: He was much too clumsy to make a decent Satanist.

Becky turned to her mother with an intelligent, troubled look in her green eyes. "Who else has found out?" she asked, already blushing a speculative shade of pink.

"I don't know that anyone has—for sure," Helen hedged. "There's talk going around, but it's so garbled that it's hard to make heads or tails out of it."

"Oh, that's great," she said morosely. "I just know this story's going to follow me to college."

"Honey, it won't."

"I'll have to go to the West Coast . . . leave Salem forever . . . it'll be too embarrassing to stay. . . . If this gets to any of my friends . . ."

She stared at the middle distance and blinked once or twice. "Jessica's mother looked at me really weird the other night," she said suddenly. "Oh, I'll die. Although, Jess didn't say anything, but she wouldn't, to me. But she would to Nicole. *Mom!*" she cried.

"Becky, Becky, get a grip!" said Helen, trying to make her daughter feel silly. "I only asked you both about it because I heard that a local journalist is researching a story about gangs and graffiti," she said, coming up with a plausible lie. "I don't even know what publication it's for. But I didn't want you two volunteering to do an interview, thank you very much."

"Oh." Mollified, Becky said, "Really, Mother. You're the one who should get a grip. Russell and Binny, palming themselves off as gang members? Puh-leeze."

She stood up, obviously relieved, and said, "I'm going to bed." With a tired sigh she added, "I can hardly wait for Russ to get his own license."

"Oh, me, too," said Helen dryly.

Becky hesitated, then said, "Mom? It's okay, you know, about . . . y'know. You're over the age of consent."

"I suppose you're right," Helen acknowledged, blushing at her daughter's uncanny perceptiveness. "However . . ."

"I'm not," Becky finished for her. "I know. G'night, Mom," she said, throwing her arm around Helen and kissing her on the cheek. "Sweet dreams."

"I'm sure," said Helen. But she knew her dreams that night would be anything but.

Chapter 22

𝒯wo more on Sunday.

Helen tried halfheartedly to press the parents for the truth behind their withdrawals; but she couldn't bear to hear it, any more than they could bear to tell it.

"It's an impossible situation," she told Nat that evening when he came by. "Part of me wants to confront them, but a bigger part of me—"

"—is too proud," he said as they sat on the chaises in the garden, speaking in subdued voices.

Helen didn't deny it. She'd spent the day in a pendulum-swing from anger to helplessness and back to anger again.

"What can I do?" she said. "The rumors are beneath contempt. There are no facts. It's infuriating. Doesn't my reputation have any value at all? What about Becky's? She's baby-sat for years. Kids adore her. There has never been a single criticism about her."

Helen pulled her knees up and wrapped her arms around her shins. "It gives me chills, to know there are people willing to believe garbage like that about my children. As for the ones who spread the garbage—well, let's hope I never meet them in a dark alley," she said grimly.

"I'd like to have a piece of that action," Nat said in a

voice that was, if anything, more grim than Helen's.

Something about it made Helen turn to him and say, "Have you heard anything more?"

"Yeah. I don't know whether you're going to laugh or cry at this one. It turns out that my neighbor Connie Bonham's hairdresser is married to your plumber. Are you ready for this? He says your house is haunted. Something about your hearing knocking in the pipes, and he couldn't find a thing."

Helen's heart dove straight through the chaise lounge. In all the agonizing hours since Nat had told her about the rumors of Satanism, she'd never once considered the effect her *plumber* could have on her career.

"This is unbelievable," she whispered. Her mind was racing ahead to a new and even more terrifying scenario: what people would think if they knew about her profound awareness of Linda Byrne's . . .

Ghost.

Nat had stood up and was extending his hands to her. "C'mon," he said. "We'll go for a walk."

Helen let him drag her out of the chaise, but a walk was out of the question. She was far too shaken by this latest twist in the ongoing drama. She shook her bowed head and said, "I'd be really, really lousy company right now, Nat."

"You'd be really, really fantastic company," he argued softly, slipping his hand under her chin and tilting her face toward his. He kissed her very gently, a kiss that she knew was meant to reassure, not to excite.

"Listen to me," he said, drawing her close and stroking her hair in a comforting way. "Since you refuse to defend yourself, you're bound to lose a certain number of parents. That's a given. You have to be willing to let them go."

"You're right," she said unhappily. "But I would so much rather they stayed."

"I know, darling, I know."

In the meantime she was thinking, *Only Aunt Mary knows about Linda Byrne. She won't say anything. As for me, I'll go to my grave before I tell another soul.*

Nat added, "I want you to know, though, that I reserve the right to defend your honor if someone comes gossiping to me."

She smiled. "Just don't go challenging anyone to a duel. I'm pretty sure there's a law against that in Massachusetts."

"Fine. I'll meet 'em in Rhode Island."

She laid her cheek against his chest, breathing in the scent of him. The roses were in full bloom in the garden, and so was an umbrella of fragrant red honeysuckle nearby. No matter. It was the scent of *him* that was leaving her drunk as a bee. She lifted her face to him, filled with a wistful desire that they could just meet, and court, and make love like everyone else in ordinary life.

But Helen's life just then was anything but ordinary, and so as soon as their kiss reached flash point, she drew reluctantly away, her lips still in a slow burn.

He understood. "Not now . . . not tonight," he agreed without her having to say a word. "But soon, Helen," he whispered. "Because I want you very much. And I know that you . . . Well. Soon."

"Will I see you tomorrow?" she said, immediately contradicting herself.

"On Katie's first day of school? A thousand-point rally couldn't keep me away."

She laughed at the absurdity of it; but he was making her feel better by the minute. *This is what I haven't had for the last few years,* she realized. *Someone in my corner.*

She walked with him to his car, and they kissed goodnight. Her last words to him were, "And thanks for not bringing up . . . the sanctuary." Even as she said it, the slow burn on her lips spread through the bones of her cheeks and then to the tips of her ears.

"I'm still too overwhelmed," he said, sounding almost baffled. "But don't think it isn't always on my mind."

He got in the Porsche and drove off. Helen, still wrapped in the heat of him, went back inside her house. She put the kettle on and waited for it to boil, her mind so filled with concerns that they cancelled one another out and left her catatonic.

On top of all else, she was desperately worried about her aunt, who'd seemed listless and out of sorts all week, complaining of the cold despite temperatures in the eighties.

This morning Helen had finally insisted that her aunt go in for tests. Aunt Mary, fearing she'd end up under the knife, had refused. Eventually the two women ended up in the still unresolved cataract-operation argument.

It took the shrill whistle of the teakettle to jolt her out of her daze.

Pay attention, jerk! the teakettle cried. *Make the tea, then see your aunt, then look over the waiting list for The Open Door. And while you're at it, stop brooding over that guy Byrne. You don't have time for him now. Pay attention, jerk!*

Helen took a deep breath, then blew it out, then poured the tea. She was walking out the kitchen door with it to go across the hall when she noticed, on top of the fridge, the framed wedding photo of Hank and her that usually sat on her bureau.

Putting the teacup aside, Helen went back to the family room, looking for her son. The television was droning but Russ wasn't watching. His nose was buried in a copy of *Hot Rod Magazine*.

He didn't look up right away, which gave Helen a chance to look at him and size him up as any stranger would. Motherly bias aside, she was amazed that anyone could look at him and see evil. It simply wasn't there.

She'd seen hardened fourteen-year-olds—kids whose

emotional lives had been deadened by repeated blows to their bodies or minds—but Russ wasn't one of those children. She studied the boyish lines of his angular, softly freckled face. It was a moody face, a troubled face. But not a hardened face.

"Hey, kiddo. Are you the one who put the wedding—?"

She looked around and blinked. A steel-framed photo of Hank in his trooper's uniform sat on top of the television. Another of Hank, her, and the kids in a rowboat at Lake Kennebago had been set on the lamp table next to the blue denim-covered sofa. Another one of Hank with a basketball—this one filched from Becky's room—was sitting on the drop leaf table under the far window. The room had been turned into a regular Hall of Fame for Trooper Henry Evett, husband of Helen Evett and father of two.

She picked up a small, paper-framed high-school graduation photo of Hank that had been placed strategically on the steamer trunk in front of the sofa. "I think maybe this one is pushing it a little, honey," she said wryly. "Don't you?"

It had been years since she'd seen the photograph. She wondered how Russ had managed to find it, since he often couldn't find the milk carton on the refrigerator shelf.

Russell looked up from his magazine with round green eyes. " 'Scuse me?"

Helen sat the frame, with its blunted cardboard corners, back on the trunk. "I think it's wonderful that you respect and miss your father so much, Russ, but . . . truly, you don't have to worry. No one could ever take his place; not in the same way."

"Yeah, but what about some other way?" Russ retorted. His young face, so naive, so desperately melodramatic, was poised on the verge of tears.

Helen sat back on the rolled arm of one of the easy

chairs, trying not to crowd her son with intimacy. "It's true that Mr. Byrne and I have started . . . seeing one another. But that doesn't mean that I've forgotten your father, or that I ever want you to. Why would we do that?" she asked simply. "When he was such a wonderful person."

"You talk about him as if he's—gone," her son said, setting his full lips in a straight line of resentment.

Helen folded her hands in the lap of her pale-print skirt. "Oh, honey, he *is* gone," she said softly. "Not the memory of him; not the sound of his voice, or his laugh, or the way he used to guess the questions on *Jeopardy*. But he is gone. And no matter how much we want to change that—no matter how much we want to hug him or arm-wrestle him or shoot a few hoops with him—we can't. We have to hold on to the memories, and talk to him in our thoughts, and concentrate on hearing his voice—which is hard; we have to work at it or we'll forget."

With a breathtaking effort, she beat back the sudden image of Hank laid out on a slab—an image that she had managed to keep at bay for several months now—and said, "But, Russell, we can't bring him back. Don't you think I would if I could?"

The tears that Russ had been holding back broke and made a run for it, mortally embarrassing him. He looked down at his magazine, then at the television, then around the room in dismay. His father was everywhere, and yet nowhere.

"I loved my dad!" he said, throwing down the magazine and jumping up. "And I'm not ashamed if someone knows it!"

He ran, crying, from the room. Helen picked up the tattered paper-framed photo of her high school lover and held it to her breast.

She had spoken the truth to her son when she said they couldn't bring him back. But for the first time, she understood that Hank had never gone away; that no one ever did. In some way, in some form, part of them stayed behind to watch over those they loved. Occasionally their voices were shrill, but often they were faint—in which case it was up to those they loved to listen hard.

Hank, she said silently, *I love him. A little in the same way I loved you . . . a lot in a different way. Tell me it's all right.*

She listened, as she had so many times in the last four years, for the sound of his voice. And now, at last, she heard it: in the steady beating of her own heart.

Helen stayed up late with schoolwork and, quite amazingly, overslept the next morning, the first of the summer program. She threw on a challis sundress of deep maroon with tiny flowers the color of wheat, slipped into a pair of low-heeled shoes, and grabbed a straw hat on her way out with Russell. What the straw hat was for, she had no idea. In the back of her mind was the thought that Nat would be there not only to drop off his daughter, but to pick her up again after school. Maybe they could all go for a walk on the Common.

As for Russell, Helen could tell by his face that last night never happened as far as he was concerned. He kept to the subject—basketball—and expected his mother to do the same. She drove across town and dropped him off at basketball camp (part of the deal she struck with him after the spray painting), then continued on her way to the preschool.

Part of her was expecting no one but the staff to be there. They knew nothing of the rumors—not from Helen, anyway. She'd agonized over it but in the end had refused to legitimize the gossip by discussing it, even with the staff.

Helen was relieved to see plenty of parents milling around the parking lot, talking in small groups. Then she noticed that some of the kids were in the playground and some of them, still with their parents. Apparently no one was inside, which is where they were supposed to go directly.

Was The Open Door still closed? It didn't seem possible. Helen pulled into a staff space and got out of the car, then waved to the closest of the parents and said, "Has no one arrived to open up yet?"

"They're inside," said one mother, and then she turned away.

Stung by the rebuff, Helen hurried with a sinking heart along the flagstone path that led from the parking area to the front door. So distracted was she that she didn't notice the graffiti until she was nearly on top of it—and then it hit her with the force of a two-by-four across the face.

SHE'S ANOTHER.

The foot-high words, all in capitals, were scrawled on the old red bricks in Day-Glo pink next to the main door. You couldn't miss them, although the color was far more shocking than the sentiment.

Helen's first thought was, *Another what?*

Her second was, *Paint thinner won't work this time.*

Furious at the vandalism, she swung the door open and strode inside, determined to call the police—and aware that they might find it ironic.

What goes around comes around. Thank God the vandal had run off before he finished the job; it might've been a lot worse. Or maybe he'd been caught? She found herself praying that he had. Either way, the deed was done and tongues were wagging all over again. *Hell.*

Janet was on the phone in Helen's office, calling hardware stores for advice on how to get the paint off. Kristy Maylen, who taught the older three's, was there, too. And so was a police officer.

He'd just finished taking a statement—such as it was—

from Janet. She'd come in, found the scribbling, and called the police. End of story. Almost.

Helen said, half in relief, "I guess the kid got spooked by something before he had a chance to finish."

But the officer, a middle-aged man with a sympathetic manner, shook his head. "You're not reading it right. The message reads SHE'S AN OTHER. Three words, not two. The 'Others' were a Satanist gang we shut down in the late eighties."

It was another two-by-four, right across the face. Helen had to struggle for breath as she said faintly, "I don't remember anything about it."

"It was in the paper; but we don't go out of our way to publicize that kind of thing. It's bad for tourism, and we don't need copycats. Someone's just pulling your chain, I expect," he said, seeing Helen's distress.

"Can you find out who did it?" she said, reeling.

He lifted a shoulder in a half-shrug. "It's hard. Graffiti is very frustrating to stop. It's all the rage now—as anyone who walks around a city can see. My guess is it'll get worse before it gets better. Once in a while an irate owner will offer a reward for information. You could try that."

Just what she wanted to do: advertise. "Thanks," she said, dismissing the idea out of hand. "But I was hoping for a more discreet solution."

The officer looked at her curiously but said nothing. Helen thanked him for his time and walked with him to his patrol car, which was parked smack-dab in front of the school—more advertising.

She was about to retrace her steps down the flagstone path to the parking area, with every intention of shepherding the parents inside like some border collie, when she saw her first parent approach: Nathaniel Byrne, holding Katie by the hand.

Helen greeted them with more enthusiasm than she felt.

It was too late to drape a black cloth over the offensive scrawl. She had to stand and watch while he stopped and stared.

He fell into the same trap she did. "Another? Another what?"

"An Other," she corrected, saying the words separately.

"Who's another? Another what?"

"Becky, I suppose. Another Other."

Scowling at the Abbot and Costello routine, he said, "Let me try it one more time: What's an 'other'?"

She took a kind of morose pleasure in giving it one last twist. "What's another nail in the coffin of my career? This is," she said, running a finger over the disgustingly dry pink paint.

Lowering her voice and turning away from Katie, Helen explained what she'd learned. "The Others were apparently a local Satanist 'cult' in the eighties. They turned out to be a gang of midteen kids with a penchant for cutting up rats and woodchucks. I didn't ask what they did with the parts," she added wearily, "and the officer didn't tell me."

Both of them glanced over at the parents still hanging back in the parking area. "Maybe they were all just waiting for the police to leave," Helen said hopefully.

Even as she said it, two or three mothers broke away from the rest and began walking hurriedly down the flagstone path with their little ones. Maybe they had faith in Helen; maybe they just wanted to get on with their day.

Nat turned to his daughter, who was deep in conversation with her teddy bear, and said with hearty enthusiasm, "C'mon, Katie-kins, time to go to school, just like the big kids!"

He gave Helen a last, burning look. "Call a meeting of the parents, damn it. Get it all out. Clear the air once and for all."

"No, Nat!" she said. "I haven't done anything, and nei-

ther has Becky. I refuse to—well, hello there, Merielle,"
she said as the child, running ahead of her mother, drew
near.

Exasperated, Nat took his daughter inside, leaving Helen
to face little Merielle's mother, who took one look at the
graffiti and said, "That's what all the fuss is about? I've
had worse on my storefront, believe me. Try selling lingerie
sometime." She glanced at the scrawl again and said, "The
worst thing about it is that the colors clash," then gave
Helen a wry smile of sympathy and went into the little brick
bank.

How could I have bumped her to the waiting list? Helen
thought. *She's the bravest woman here.*

Helen stayed right where she was, in front of the spray-
painted wall, forcing the incoming parents to look at her
instead of it as they straggled in. Some were friendly, some
were reserved.

And some drove off with their children.

Helen tried not to let it upset her. Nat was right. She was
bound to lose some parents if she chose not to confront the
rumors. She waved forlornly to him on his way out as he
passed behind some of her stauncher supporters, who were
busy telling her how wonderful she was. No one actually
used the word *Satanism,* but it was clear from their flattering remarks that they were trying to tell Helen they were
on her side. Helen drank in their compliments like a thirsty
camel, knowing the ride ahead might be long, hot, and dry.

Eventually the last parent left. "Hold down the fort,"
Helen told Janet without waiting a second longer than necessary.

She drove off to the nearest hardware store, had them
mix a quart of brick-red paint, bought a throwaway paint-
brush, drove back to her preschool, and got to work. In
twenty minutes the pink letters were covered by a red rec-

tangle of paint—not the most sophisticated camouflage job in the world, but good enough for now.

After that, she sat back and waited for the next shoe to fall.

Chapter 23

On a street of grand Victorians, one house was grander than all the rest. It had a columned veranda that curved from front to side, an octagonal turret, and multiple gables fitted into its steeply sloped roofs. Meticulously restored, the house was painted a dark but pleasing brown, with accent shades of copper and sienna highlighting its intricate, extravagant trim.

The wide, inviting porch was festooned with massive pots of pale ivy geranium and highlighted by an old-fashioned, wood-slatted swing suspended from chains. On the swing sat Rebecca Evett, dressed in black bib-top overalls over a white shirt. Next to her sat a four or five-year-old girl with cherry-blond hair, wearing a blue gingham sundress.

On the little girl's lap was a young white cat.

The child was having trouble getting the frisky cat to stay. Rebecca took the animal from her and showed her how to pet the cat in a soothing way. She began to stroke the animal under its chin. The cat stretched its neck, begging for more. Rebecca put the cat back on the little girl's lap. The girl rubbed the cat's throat and giggled at the ease of her success.

The child's mother, dressed in dinner clothes, came out of the house, spoke briefly with Rebecca, hugged her daughter, and walked down the steps to the Lexus that was parked on the street. Her husband took off with a squeal of tires; they must have been late.

It was getting dark. Rebecca swatted a mosquito on her arm, then stood up. She looked down at her black overalls and let out a cry of surprise. Wiping away what was obviously a layer of white fur, she led the little girl, carrying the cat awkwardly, inside the house.

Peaches waited until the door was closed, then turned the key in the ignition of her car and shifted into drive.

Almost two weeks had passed without any more shoes falling, and Helen was beginning to allow herself to think about possibly breathing easy again sometime soon.

"I still cringe as I approach The Open Door every morning, but I think whoever had a grudge against me must be satisfied," she told Nat.

They were slouched together on the blue denim sofa in the family room, eating popcorn and watching a rented video. Nat had wanted something mindless; Helen, something happy. They settled for a French film which had turned out to be both cerebral and sad—and badly dubbed besides—so they'd simply shut off the sound and admired the scenes of Provence while they talked and waited for Becky to come back from baby-sitting.

"You're thinking that this person just wanted you to take some kind of hit financially?" Nat asked, sounding unconvinced.

Helen wrinkled her nose. "Not exactly. You're gonna laugh, but . . . what if someone on the waiting list really, really wanted to get her child into The Open Door? Wouldn't the Satanist scare be a quick and easy way to do it?"

Nat did laugh. "Come on. I know preschool is serious stuff with today's yuppies, but—come on."

Helen tossed a kernel of popcorn at him. "Hey. If a Texas mom can hire a hit man to take out her daughter's competition in cheerleading. . . ."

Throwing his hands up, Nat said, "You win. I forgot. This is America. Who was on your list of suspects?"

"Well—Merielle's mother, for one. As we feared, Merielle herself is a real terror; I wonder if any school would've taken her. The point is, her mother wasn't the least bit put off by the graffiti. She runs a lingerie shop, incidentally."

"Hmm. Lingerie. I see your point. A woman who understands lingerie is a woman who knows how to get what she wants."

His ironic tone was just suggestive enough to make Helen's cheeks flush. She was painfully aware that they hadn't made love since that one wild night, which she was convinced had all been a dream, anyway. But they had managed to steal some torrid moments in her office, in his car, and—if Becky only knew!—on one of the kitchen chairs. It couldn't go on this way.

Echoing her thoughts, Nat said wryly, "Will I ever see you in lingerie, do you think?"

"If both my children are sent to prison, maybe," Helen quipped. "But in the meantime . . ." She pointed to the ceiling, which was vibrating in tune with a Pearl Jam recording.

"At least Russ is sticking close to home," she added, turning sideways and pulling her legs up on the sofa. "And he did let you make popcorn for Scotty and him." She slid her bare toes under Nat's thigh and wriggled them tauntingly. "I call it progress."

Nat snorted and said, "Progress? He scarcely comes near me. It's like taming an ocelot."

"You've tamed one?"

"I had a friend. Anyway, now that Scotty's piped up and said he'd like to take a whirl in the Porsche sometime, I'm hoping your son will condescend to go along for the ride."

"I thought the way to a man's heart is through his stomach."

"The way to a man's heart is actually through lingerie," Nat said, wrapping his hand around her ankle. "The way to a boy's heart is, of course, through a hot rod."

"I see. Now that I've got that straight, I guess I can stop baking chocolate chip cookies for all of you."

"Hey, hey, hey! Let's not be rash," he said, giving her an impromptu foot rub.

Helen laughed seductively and said, "I'll show you what's rash," and redirected her other foot to where it was bound to get Nat's interest.

Which is exactly when Becky decided to arrive through the front door, letting it slam behind her.

Up went the leg, down went the feet on the floor. When Becky walked into the family room, what she found was her mother and her mother's friend Mr. Byrne sitting demurely in front of a muted television watching a hilly village in some other country.

"How'd it go?" Helen asked in a ridiculously casual voice.

Becky had the kindness to pretend her mother really cared. "Oh, fine. Kayla's such an easy sit. She has a new—"

Suddenly she let loose with half a dozen violent sneezes, then finished the sentence. "—cat. And I think I'm aller—"

Four more big ones. "—gic to it. He sheds like crazy. Look at my clothes!"

"You could always wear white," her mother said, hoping against hope.

"But that wouldn't stop me from snee—"

Off she went on another round of explosions. She left the room in misery, clearly in search of tissues.

Nat said, "Poor kid. But you guys have a cat."

"White cats shed much more than black ones."

"Mmm; that explains the jillion black cats in Salem. And here I thought they were just tourist props."

"You mean—"

"One for every witch," he said, taking her hand and kissing the knuckles.

The smile on Helen's face softened into a thoughtful pursing of her lips. "We're so schizophrenic about that, aren't we. We have this very real—and justified—fear that crackpot Satanists are going to be drawn here because of the city's history. But then we turn around and slap those witch silhouettes on everything we own. And meanwhile, Wicca is a serious, ancient religion that doesn't get the respect it's due. Even here."

Nat leaned back into the sofa with his hands behind his head and gave her a long, appraising look. "Helen of Salem—you care too much about this town. Salem is a brand name now, and brand names sell; just ask the Chamber of Commerce. There's nothing you can do to change its image. It's set in granite."

"I don't want to change it. I just want to understand it," Helen said, troubled by the speculative look in his eyes.

"Do you know what I mean?" she asked him. "You must have felt it when you walked around some of the 1692 sites: the burial ground on Charter Street, the victims' houses in Danvers and Peabody, the Corwin house here in Salem. There is such . . . sadness everywhere . . . such a terrible sense of fear and dread."

She shivered and rubbed her arms. "Innocent men and women hanged by a mob of well-meaning hysterics. I've practically heard the moans . . . felt the shivers of terror. Haven't you?"

"A little, I suppose," he admitted. "It's been many years since I've done the tour. Even then, it wasn't as intense as what you're describing. How do you remember it all so vividly?"

Helen was reluctant to say that she'd been going out of her way to drive past the sites when she was out on errands. And she had no intention of telling him that she felt prodded to do so by the spirit of his dead wife.

"I've been researching," she settled for saying.

"Helen, you're taking this too much to heart," Nat said softly. "We both know why."

He took her hand in his. She closed her eyes and let the warmth of it pass through hers, like a reassuring current. There was no question about it: He was keeping her battery charged. If it weren't for him . . .

She shivered again and said, "Anyway, I guess the shakeout you predicted is over. No one's withdrawn in almost a week."

She opened her eyes and looked at him with such warmth, such gratitude, that she was afraid he'd see how desperately she loved him and flee. "I'm glad you've been with me through this, Nat," she whispered. It was all she dared confess.

His response was a look as burning as her own. He said her name in a low, husky voice and drew her close. "Ah, Lena, Lena," he said. "These last two weeks . . . they've been a kind of wonderful agony. . . ."

He slid his hand up the inside of her thigh and under the fabric of her shorts and kissed her hard, his mouth covering hers, his breathing itself hard with frustration.

She wilted under the heat of his kiss, under the hot wet caress of his tongue, as she felt his hand working the fabric away from her body, well on the way to tormenting her still more. Alarm bells began ringing loudly inside her head: She didn't care.

Fingers touched flesh, sending a jolt through her. She sucked in her breath in a rage of desire for some release, for an end to the tension. Almost two weeks since the sanctuary . . . two long, frustrating weeks . . . a wonderful agony. She felt the first ripples of an orgasm, unexpected, out of the blue . . .

And incomplete. The muted sound of Russell's big feet thumping down the carpeted stairs was like the sound of cold ocean surf breaking over her head. She pulled away from Nat's kiss and clapped her hand over his wrist.

"Stop," she whispered, jumping up from the sofa. She began fiddling with the tape in the VCR as she listened, heart still pounding, to her son say good-bye to Scotty and then close the front door.

She felt like a fool, but she couldn't help herself; the charade went on as she called out in suspicious motherly tones, "Russell? I didn't hear his father's car out front."

Russ said in a loud, bored voice, "His dad was beepin' his horn for five minutes. *We* heard it."

"Well, why did you take so long to go down, then?" she shot back, trying to save face. She rolled her eyes at Nat and got a comical cringe from him in return. There they were, with three-quarters of a century between them, scared to death of a fourteen-year-old snot.

Russell tore back up the stairs without bothering to answer her silly question, which was fine with Helen. The last thing she needed was a face-to-face confrontation with him.

She stood up, and Nat stood up, and they held hands, leaning their foreheads into one another.

"Close call," she said, blowing out air.

"Jeez. I never heard him. This is nuts, Helen. I understand that you want to be home for your kids, but . . . can't we go to a nice dinner at a nice hotel?" he asked. "I'm not asking for the night," he added wryly. "Naturally I know better than that."

She took a wincing, hissing breath of air. "Oh, Nat . . . I don't know . . . a hotel? What if someone saw us?"

"Who would know? Who would care?" he said, nuzzling the curve of her neck.

Off and running went her heartbeat. "No . . . wait . . . wait," she objected, trying weakly to evade his caress. "It's just that right now all I want to do is . . . hide."

He drew back and looked into her eyes. She expected to see frustration there, maybe even annoyance. But his gaze was completely sympathetic, his smile forbearing. "Hide. Right. Okay. I'll see what I can do."

The next morning, Nat called and said, "Cancel the video. The house is ours."

"No, it isn't. Becky's having a couple of friends over to study, and Russell—"

"*My* house. I gave Peaches a weekend on the Cape. There's a great bed and breakfast there that Linda and I once stayed at. I had hopes that it would be you and I who—anyway, Peaches is gone and here's the plan. Katie and I do some heavy-duty bonding at the Knights of Columbus carnival. I wear her out. You arrive around six-thirty. We put Katie to bed. We dine. We make wild, abandoned love until eleven. Twelve, if I can keep you. You return home. Tomorrow we do it all over again. I'll take Katie to Nautilus or something. So? Pure genius, am I right?"

After a too-long pause, Helen said, "What did Peaches say when you sent her away?"

"I did not send her away," Nat said, miffed at Helen's tepid response. "I just . . . gave her an early birthday present. As a matter of fact, it was her idea. She'd mentioned recently that the bed and breakfast sounded like a wonderful getaway. Actually, I think she had in mind a family outing for all of us, but this'll be even better for her. No nannying. Maybe she'll meet a great guy."

You are the great guy, dope, thought Helen. In the last two weeks, Nat had spent every minute he could with Helen, bringing Katie along if the hour was early enough. Technically, Peaches should've been thrilled with her new free time. But Helen understood, as Nat did not, that no woman likes giving up territory to another. Was Peaches in love with him? Helen didn't know. Nat would've laughed at the notion; it was better left unsaid.

In any case, Helen didn't really care what Nat did to get rid of the ever-hovering Peaches. He could've put her in a rocket and sent her to the moon—whatever it took for Helen and him to be alone, if only for a few hours.

All day Helen savored the thought of the evening to come. Late in the afternoon she took a long shower and deep-conditioned her hair, then pumiced, buffed, polished, and lotioned every surface of her body. She hadn't lavished such attention on herself since—well, since Hank. She chose her laciest underthings and an easy-to-remove dress. She tried on earrings, then took them off. They'd only be in the way.

She was standing in front of the full-length mirror, pinning a tortoiseshell comb into her thick black hair, when Becky came in with an armload of just-folded towels for her mother's bathroom.

"Yikes, Mom. Why the gray dress?"

No way was Helen going to say why. "Because I like it."

"No, no, no." Becky plunked the pile of white towels on the wicker hamper and went to her mother's closet. "You look better in color." She pulled out a pretty rayon dress in a flattering shade of mauve. "Wear this one."

The dress had a million buttons down the back. "Nope,"

Helen said serenely. "The gray looks fine on me."

Becky scrutinized the dress for flow and cling and decided it would have to do. Sitting cross-legged on her mother's bed, she said, "Is it serious? I know it is for you. Is it for him?"

Helen felt no need to hide the truth from her perceptive daughter. "I think so," she said softly. "I hope so."

"I'm really glad. It's just so cool that you're in love."

Helen glanced at the open door. "You don't have to shout it from the rooftop."

"Mom. Stop babying him. Russell can handle this. He's not a little boy anymore; why treat him like one? Are you really so worried he's gonna freak out? Or is it more that you're afraid to move out of mom-mode?"

"Darn good points, Becky," said Helen, giving her daughter a yank on the collar. "Go away."

"Okay, okay." Becky untangled her long, tanned legs and hopped off the bed. "So where're you going to dinner?"

Helen shrugged, carefully avoiding her daughter's gaze. "Someplace quiet."

Becky studied her mother for a long moment, then smiled. "All I can say is, Mr. Byrne had better make an honest woman out of you after all this. Take an umbrella."

She flounced off, leaving Helen to stare at a thoughtful-looking reflection of herself. As for Mr. Byrne: what, exactly, *were* his intentions?

She wished she knew.

By the time Helen pulled up in front of the green-shuttered mansion, she hardly cared. She expected to feel shy, or to have scruples or reservations or stupid second thoughts. Instead she was amazed to see that she was on fire for him. When he opened the door it was all she could do not to throw herself into his arms.

He'd dressed more casually than she, in khakis and

crumply white linen shirt. It gave him an air of slouchy elegance that she found desperately appealing. Once she was in the hall, he took her in his arms and kissed her; she threaded her fingers through his shower-damp hair and let herself enjoy the first sweet taste of the night to come.

He said in her ear, "I've been obsessing on you all day long. On the Ferris wheel, on the merry-go-round, at the milk-bottle toss . . . I wish you'd come along."

"No, you were right to be with Katie on your own. Did she have fun?"

"She loved it," he said as they headed automatically for the music room. "It was a little touch and go after the candy cotton and ice cream, though. Maybe I shouldn't have done both."

"Maybe," Helen said, smiling.

Katie was in her pajamas at the far end of the room, kneeling next to the low table on which she liked to draw and paint. At the moment she had her big crayolas out and was immersed completely in her work. Helen was a little disappointed that the child hadn't come running. In the past two weeks—and especially during the two days that Helen had taken over Katie's preschool class—they'd become delightfully at ease with one another.

"Hey, kiddo, look who's here," Nat finally said.

Katie kept on coloring. Puzzled, Nat prompted her again.

The child looked up at Helen with blue-eyed reproach. "You made Peaches go away," she said. Without waiting for an answer, she returned to her drawing.

"No, honey, I—"

"Katie, what're you talking about?" her father said, amazed. "I told you. Peaches went for a little vacation on Cape Cod. She'll be home tomorrow night."

Helen saw that his cheeks were flushed. *Guilt.* Somehow he must have implied to his daughter that he was sending Peaches away so that he could be with Helen. Distressed,

Helen sat on the sofa where Katie was working and, resting her arms on her thighs, clasped her hands and said, "What're you drawing, Katie? May I see?"

Still on her knees, Katie edged away from Helen. But she didn't reposition her drawing, which Helen studied with some interest. It was a murky arrangement of lines and shapes, but one aspect of it seemed clearer than the rest: a stick-figure inside what looked like a cage or basket.

Helen took a shot. "Is this a drawing of a zoo?" she asked.

Katie shook her head gravely. "That's Peaches. She can't get out."

Helen looked up quickly at Nat, who was standing above them, hands hooked in his front pockets. "Katie, that's silly. Peaches is fine. She needed some quiet time to be by herself. Just like you."

Katie stuck out her lower lip and said, "Is she coming back?"

"I told you—tomorrow night. C'mon, Rembrandt," he said, lifting her in his arms. "Time for bed. You've had your milk; your teeth are brushed. I'll read you a story and—would you like Mrs. Evett to read it to you instead?" he suddenly asked.

Katie, who just two days ago had sat mesmerized in the classroom circle while Helen read a tale from Beatrix Potter, decided to decline. She shook her head, lifting her arm over her eyes in the universal sign of rejection. Children did that, Helen knew; but she wasn't prepared for the pain she felt when the child was Katie.

"Well . . . good-night, then, sweetie," she said with a re-assuring little wave.

It was good that she hadn't risked blowing Katie a kiss, because the child turned away and buried her face in her father's shoulder and wouldn't have seen it anyway.

She's afraid of me, Helen thought, dismayed.

"She's tired," her father said, offering a more reasonable explanation. He nodded at the liquor cabinet and said, "Why don't you pour while I. . . ."

He lumbered off with his cranky cargo and Helen, feeling a bit dispirited, walked over to the glass-fronted cabinet where a bottle of French chablis stood uncorked and ready. She poured herself a glass, then wandered into the kitchen to see whether anything there needed tending.

It was all under control: a casserole of lobster thermidor, ready to pop into the Viking oven; two bowls of undressed salad in the Sub-Zero fridge; a crusty baguette on the Corian counter. Despite the elegant simplicity of the meal, Helen's guess was that Nat had had it catered, and she was right: a canvas sack with *Christine's Catering* stenciled on it lay on top of a small plastic cooler tucked away in a corner.

A note on the stove said fifteen minutes at 350 degrees. Good. They'd get the meal behind them in no time. Startled by her own brazenness, Helen returned to the music room to wait. She was feeling more and more restless and edgy, almost driven. She paced the width and length of the room, pausing to stare through the floor-to-ceiling casements at the damp and gloomy garden that lay beyond. The open east-facing window panels were spotted with rain; she drew the casements most of the way closed, then opened them again after she felt the air flow cease.

She wanted so much to seem in control of herself. But her nerves were jangled, her emotions on fire. *What is wrong with me?* she wondered. It couldn't just be the need for sex. No, it was Katie looking at her that way—it was disconcerting. Nat was probably right about her being worn-out, but still. And her drawing of Peaches in a cage— even more disconcerting. Could Peaches really have replaced Linda so soon in Katie's eyes?

Why not? Wasn't Helen hoping to do the same in Nat's eyes?

Too soon, too soon, she thought wildly. *He's still angry at his wife, he's confused. Too soon.*

The more she waited for Nat to come down, the less resolve she had. She'd been assuming that her edginess was eagerness; in fact, it was just the opposite. She wasn't ready for this. *He* wasn't ready for this.

She heard a sound and whirled violently around. He was standing at the far end of the room, his hands slung across his hips. She didn't understand his body language at all; was he angry?

"You won't believe this," he said, walking over to the glass-fronted cabinet and picking up the glass of wine she'd poured for him. He came over to where Helen had been standing and listening—she now realized—for the sneezing sound of the short-eared owl.

"Katie made me call Peaches," he said, shaking his head. "To prove she hadn't gone to heaven." He stared out at the garden with Helen. Together they listened to the sound of rain dripping on the ivy that clung to the bricks around the casements. "It was the damndest thing," he said after a moment.

"She's afraid of me," Helen murmured.

He was amused by that. "Two days ago she wasn't. She came home thrilled to have you taking care of her class. She hardly ate a thing at dinner that night; ask Peaches. No, it's not so much that she's afraid of you as that she's afraid Peaches will go away."

"She connects the two."

"She doesn't. Anyway, she talked with Peaches, was reassured, and is fast asleep. The night," he said, taking Helen's wineglass from her, "is ours. Finally."

He put the stemmed glasses down and took her in his arms. And suddenly, nothing else mattered. Helen remembered why it was she'd come; why it was she'd dressed with such care. She loved him, and wanted him, and nothing would be right until she felt him inside her again.

He slipped the tortoiseshell comb from her hair, letting her hair fall in a heavy slide to her shoulders, then pooled the shining black mass in his hands and inhaled deeply from it, as if it were rose petals. Smiling, pulling her close, fitting her hard against him, he said in a rueful voice, "Supper . . . I did promise you food . . ."

"Turn off the oven," she whispered.

"My thoughts exactly."

They detoured through the kitchen. He flipped off the preheating oven while Helen, explaining one more time about food left out at room temperature, tucked the glass dish in the fridge for safekeeping. After that they went up the graceful curved staircase, the same staircase that generations of his people had ascended with just the same purpose in mind.

The same staircase that Linda Byrne had ascended.

For a moment Helen faltered.

Nat noticed at once. "What?" he said.

She rallied. "Nothing." Nat had a different bedroom now, a different bed now. It would be all right.

They passed the door to Peaches's room. Helen had to resist an urge to throw it open, making sure she wasn't there. Then Katie's room. Automatically both of them paused to listen. They heard the sweet, blissful sound of quiet.

And then, at last, they entered the room that Helen hadn't been in since she fainted. It was a beautiful room, neither masculine nor feminine, but of good classic design, from the walls upholstered in chinoiserie toile to the needlepoint rug in tea-stained tones of ivory and faded red.

In place of the canopied bed where Linda had died, there was a simple bed with a padded headboard covered in the same chinoiserie as the walls. The canopied bed, she knew, was on permanent loan to a West Coast museum; Nat had told her he could not deal with the memories.

"So. Here we are," said Nat behind her. "Why do I feel as if it's my first time?"

Helen turned from the bed to him. "Because in a way," she said, "it is."

He was leaning against a walnut tallboy, with his arms folded nonchalantly across his chest and an edgy smile on his lips. His dark hair had gone too long uncut—probably because he was so occupied with her—giving him a laid-back air at odds with the tension in his voice. As for the look in his ocean blue eyes—it was unfathomable. Desire, yes; but bafflement, too. He was looking at her as if she were part apparition.

"Helen of Salem," he murmured. "You have me in your spell."

"No, don't," she said, abashed. She went up to him quickly and put her hand over his mouth. It was a melo-dramatic gesture, to be sure; but she was in a heightened state.

She took her hand away almost at once, embarrassed by her response. "I'm Helen Evett," she said. "No more, no less."

"Whoever you are," he said, amused by her distress, "I love you dearly."

"I—"

What could she say to that? They were the words she longed to hear, at a time she could not trust them. She put them aside, like cut flowers in water, and promised herself to arrange them later in her heart.

She bowed her head and took a deep breath, then let it out. "You must know how I feel, Nat," she said, too over-come by emotion to tell him.

"It would be nice to hear the words," he prompted in a soft, coaxing voice.

But the words would not come. Instead, she raised her arms around his neck and lifted her face to his, inviting him to kiss her and find out.

He took up her offer, kissing her with a warmth that quickly became heat, a heat that boiled over into abandon. His hands slid up, then down the curve of her spine—and then back up, to where the zipper began. He caught hold of it and pulled it down easily; the sound was music to her ears.

The dress fell away in a puddle at her feet as Helen became another step unbound. Nat took her by her shoulders and eased her down on the bed, then, gazing down at her, said in a voice slurred with desire, "Stay right . . . there. Don't go . . . anywhere."

Dazed with a sense of her own power, at the same time almost helpless with love for him, Helen watched as he jiggled a drawer in a small commode that stood alongside the bed.

"This time I'm prepared," he said, then let out a soft curse of exasperation and added, "except that the damn drawer sticks."

The hazy smile on Helen's face sharpened into something else altogether as he finally got it open with a sharp knocking sound.

Jiggle. Knock.

Jiggle knock. Jiggle knock, jiggle knock, jiggle knock!

"*Oh no!*" Helen cried, jumping up from the bed. "It can't be . . . Linda, Linda! Oh *no!*"

Chapter 24

$\mathcal{S}$tiffly, blindly, Helen lunged for the drawer, slammed it shut, then tried to jiggle it open again. Yes, yes, it was the sound, the exact sound—and then the sharp *knock* as it broke free. After Linda's death, she'd been haunted by that sound for weeks. It was the sound that the plumber couldn't trace—and no wonder.

"What do you keep in that drawer?" she said to Nat. "Tell me what you keep in it!"

He stared at her as if she'd gone mad. "Condoms," he answered.

"Always? Always in that drawer?"

"Christ, no. I haven't used 'em since I was eighteen. These are for tonight—for you. For me . . . for us," he said, angered and confused by her outrageous behavior.

"*Before* tonight! I mean *before*," she cried.

"Before—? I don't know. Stuff. What does it matter? She kept stuff there. Dental floss. Paper, pencils, that kind of thing. For making notes to herself as she was dropping off to sleep."

"Why would she do that?" Helen demanded, more of herself than of him. "Why would she want a paper and pencil?"

"I just told you why, Helen. Jesus! What's wrong with you?"

She wasn't listening. "What was so important that she had to write it down *then*?"

"Then? When?"

"When she was dying, Nat!" Helen said, whirling around to him. "Why did she bother forcing this drawer instead of calling you—or 911?"

His voice became quiet, his face, as still as a pond at midnight. "How do you know that she opened the drawer?"

Helen made a tisking sound of impatience, as if one of her kids were asking her how to ring a doorbell. "Because I heard it—how do you think? I heard it. Over and over and over."

"Helen—"

"No, no, I know what you're thinking. I *did* hear it, Nat. I did! You have to believe me. Becky knows."

"Becky!"

"She didn't hear it, exactly; but she saw me hear it!"

"When? Where?"

"After Linda died. In my bedroom. Why do you think the plumber said the house is haunted, Nat? Because it is! She's there!"

"In your house? But—you never even met Linda; you talked to her only once!"

"It was the owl. I saw the owl in front of your house on the day she died. The *owl*, Nat. I told you about the legend I heard at the sanctuary—"

"You sure as hell didn't tell me you believed the legend!"

"You thought it was charming enough when I related it to you—"

"Charm is one thing, but this is nuts! You're nuts!"

She recoiled from the blow, but kept on charging forward. There were doors to be knocked down; she'd have to ignore the pain. "Tell me how she died, Nat—tell me!"

"No!" he said, his voice rising dangerously. "It's over! Done with!"

"Don't you understand? It's not over! She's not over!" Helen cried. "She's still here—and she's in *pain*. Tell me how she died, Nat," she pleaded. "Please, please tell me what you saw."

Tears were flowing freely now; Helen let them flow unheeded. He let out a furious oath, then grabbed her by her shoulders and brought his face close to hers. "You have to know? It's so *fucking* important to know? All right—I'll tell you! I went into the bedroom to change my shirt—the door was locked—she didn't answer—we'd been fighting—I came back down to my study to get a key—went back up—unlocked the door and found her. Dead. Of an overdose. Ergotamine. The drug that so fascinated you the last damn time you were here. *God*!" he said, investing a wrenching bitterness in the word. "Are you happy now?"

Helen blinked back more tears. "Was the drawer open? Was she holding a pencil?"

Another escalation in his anger. His hands gripped her shoulders ever more tightly. *"There was no pencil!"* he said in a furious voice. "Damn you! Only the bottle of pills, spilled on the rug!"

"Why was the drawer open, then?" she asked, wincing from his hold.

"Why? Because that's where she kept the goddamned pills—in the goddamned drawer!"

Her voice was a mere croak. "But are you sure?"

"No, I'm not sure!" he said, throwing his hands in the air so violently that Helen staggered back. "What do you want from me?" he shouted. "What do you want? Every gruesome detail? Is nothing sacred to you? All right! Linda was pregnant, you understand? *But not by me*. She tried to

abort the fetus and ended up killing herself in the bargain! And yes, they did an autopsy! Is that what your next—?''

''That was *your* son who died, not anybody else's!'' Helen shouted, rounding on him. ''How dare you accuse your wife that way?''

He scowled, then suddenly stopped as if he'd been stabbed. He stared at her with something like fear and said, ''How do you know it was a boy? Even Linda didn't know.''

Helen blinked. ''I don't know how I know. I—''

''Mom-meee-e-e,'' came a wail from behind her. Instinctively Helen snatched her dress from the floor and held it to her breast.

''The monitor,'' Nat muttered, waving away her gesture.

The wail—heartwrenching, pitiable—evolved into a loud, sorrowful cry through the speaker on the commode.

''Mom-mee-e-e-e . . .''

Nat was standing with his legs apart, arms at the ready, watching Helen intently from under partly lowered lids— as if, she thought, he were expecting her to metamorphose into some kind of evil old crone. She watched the muscles of his clenched jaw working as he waited for her next move. His breathing was as labored as her own.

The wail grew louder.

''I have to go,'' he said abruptly.

''And so do I.''

He turned on his heel. Before he was through the door of the bedroom, Helen had slipped her dress over her head and was pulling up the zipper. She glanced at the opened drawer with its unopened condoms, and then at the bed. It was not a bed she would ever lie in; of that she was sure.

Then she, too, left the room.

The silence of Sunday was deafening. No one called, no one came, no one apologized, no one withdrew, no one did

anything. All day, Russ and Becky draped themselves listlessly over various pieces of furniture, as oppressive to Helen's spirits as the damp and muggy weather that refused
to clear out. The garden was buggy, the house was hot.
There was no place to go and nothing to do, nothing to do
but wait. The sense of imminence was profound.

In the evening Helen, hoping to bring down her feverish,
anguished state over Nat a degree or two, poured herself a
tepid bath. She piled reading material high alongside the
claw-footed tub, and brought in the first cup of tea she'd
made all day.

The top book in the pile was a home reference manual
that listed symptoms for various illnesses. Helen turned
straight to "dementia" and decided, all in all, that nothing
came close to describing her state of mind. What she had
was not in home reference manuals.

That left Aunt Mary's worsening condition. That afternoon she'd given everyone a scare by forgetting, for at least
fifteen minutes, what day it was and what had happened on
Saturday (she'd gone to a slide show on urban gardens at
the senior center). Half an hour later, she was fine again.
Most frustrating of all, the episode was completely unlike
her other lapses—forgetting words like *afghan*, or how to
use a waffle iron.

Helen was scheduled to see a doctor about her aunt; but
that wouldn't be until a week from Tuesday, and that was
too far away. After some reading, she was more confused
than ever. She sighed and put the book aside, then moved
on to her next terrible concern: the outburst of near-hysteria
that had prompted a dozen children to be pulled out of The
Open Door in little more than a week.

Nat had been right, of course: Helen was obsessing over
Salem. Now she'd found a collection of essays that tried to
interpret the witch hysteria of 1692. Surely there'd be an
answer in there somewhere. If she could just understand

the past, she felt that she'd be able to understand the present. Wasn't that the whole point of history?

And so Helen read of Betty Parris and Abigail Williams, the nine-year-old daughter of a minister and her eleven-year-old cousin, who one day suddenly began weeping and staring and running around on all fours making strange, guttural sounds.

Bewitched, said the examining physician.

The hunt for witches began. Soon the girls named the minister's servant, the Barbadian slave Tituba, and two other lowborn women, Sarah Good and Sarah Osborn, as their tormentors. Tituba, terrified by her interrogators, eventually confessed to flying through the air and being a handmaiden of Satan.

The hunt continued. More women were accused. More women accused. Soon men were blamed, including a former minister. Neighbors came forward. Old grudges were satisfied. Trials were instigated. Those who admitted their guilt were put in prison. Those who proclaimed their innocence were hanged.

Nineteen died on the gallows. Four died in jail.

One man was braver and more adamant than the others; he refused to plead at all. For his convictions, Giles Cory was pressed to death under a weight of stones. In his death agony, his tongue protruded from his mouth. The sheriff shoved it back with his cane.

Why?

He looked haggard and tense and fiercely distracted.

"*Peaches?* What're you doing back here already?" Nat glanced at his empty wrist, as if it could tell him the day of the week, and then looked blankly at her again.

He hadn't shaved; hadn't showered; probably hadn't slept.

"The weather. And something's wrong," Peaches added

as she swept past him into the hall and dropped her leather travel bag on the marble-tiled floor. "I heard it in your voice on the phone this afternoon. Is Katie all right?"

"Of course she is," he said, annoyed by the mere question.

Had he been drinking? She searched the brooding features of his face for evidence of it but found nothing there but raging torment.

Helen Evett. It was as she hoped: He was beginning to doubt her at last.

Peaches put her hand on his forearm and said softly, "Then what is it, Nat? Tell me. I've been in agony all day, worrying about you."

"Unnecessary agony, in that case. I'm fine," he said bitterly.

Despite his mood he grabbed hold of her bag and said, "I'll take this up for you. Katie's in the tub, getting her bath. She'll be glad to see you," he added as they made their way up the stairs. "She's been whining for you all day long."

"I missed her," said Peaches simply. "I'll be glad to put her to bed if you like."

"If you're not too beat. The housekeeper quit, incidentally. And I couldn't find the phone number for that market that delivers—we're out of milk. And why the hell can't anyone make a decent sweater? Katie's red one—which she insisted on for school tomorrow—turned everything pink when I tried washing it. You're gone a day and a half," he said, "and the whole house falls down."

Peaches laughed and said, "That was *your* idea, Mr. Mom."

"Well, next time I get one of my bright ideas—stop me."

They were in Katie's bedroom now. Katie heard their

voices and called out excitedly, "I'm in the baftub, Peaches!"

Peaches turned to Nat and gave him a look much warmer than anything she had before. "It's wonderful to be back home, Nat. Shall I take over from here?"

"God, yes," he said abruptly, and he left her to it.

Suppressing a grimace of disappointment, she watched him leave, then went into Katie's bathroom with a cheerful smile on her face. Katie was all enthusiasm; she needed someone to push her boats through the tub while she tried to sink them with her washcloth. In a minute or two, Peaches was extracting what she needed from the child.

"And after the carnival, then what? Did you have any visitors?"

"Uh-huh. Mrs. Evett. And Daddy was mad at her and he was yelling and I waked up."

"And did you eat breakfast with that bad Mrs. Evett?" Peaches asked softly, watching the door.

"No. I diddent."

"Well, good. Now I'm back and I won't go away anymore. We won't let that bad Mrs. Evett do that to me, will we?"

Katie shook her head, apparently without comprehending. No matter. The seed was planted; it needed only occasional watering. Peaches wrapped a big blue towel around Katie, then lifted her solid little form out of the tub, stood her on a thick chenille rug, and patted her dry. Nat had laid out Katie's pajamas, mismatched in two different patterns. Katie wanted Snow White on the bottom and the top, so Peaches went out to the dressing room to make the exchange.

When she came back, she found Katie in her father's arms. "Hey, pumpkin," he was saying in an obviously contrite voice. "How about if I tell you an extra long story tonight?"

"And Peaches, too? Two stories?"

His voice was warm and amused as he said, "Okay—if you still want to hear another one. But my story is very long and very exciting: all about the adventures of Percy the Porcupine and how he got mixed up with a bunch of horses," he said, rubbing his unshaved chin on the open palm of his daughter's hand.

"Daddee-e! You scratch!" she said in a giddy squeal. "Like a por . . . por . . ."

"Porcupine," he said, lifting the Snow White pajama tops from Peaches as he passed by her, chuckling.

"I'll just dash out for milk," Peaches told him.

"Great," he said. "I'm sorry about that. And—well, for the surly reception, Peach."

She tried the warm look on him again. This time, it seemed to take. His own look was melancholy, but that was all right; she could work with melancholy. She got in her car and backed out of the cobbled parking area just as the first rumble of thunder rolled through. Good. There was always the chance that the cat would be huddled in the gazebo, waiting to be let inside.

If not today, then tomorrow.

Violent thunderstorms pounded Salem until midnight and then moved east, leaving the city scoured and clean in its wake. By morning, a bright sun and cool Canadian air helped lift Helen's spirits out of the ditch where they'd spent the night.

Helen hauled Russell out of bed and loaded him into the Volvo, then picked up Scotty on her way to The Open Door. She'd hired the boys to paint some playground equipment, and today was the first good drying day they'd had in a while.

She hadn't expected to see the Porsche.

It was parked, lights flashing, in front of the school

where the patrol car had sat so recently. Nat was behind the wheel, obviously in too big a hurry to go into the parking lot. Helen caught a glimpse of Peaches—who wasn't due back in Salem until that evening—taking Katie into the preschool.

Helen's spirits surged, then sank, then collapsed altogether, leaving her in emotional chaos.

Suddenly Scotty said, "Mrs. Evett, stop the car!"

She slammed on the brakes close behind the Porsche. "What? What is it?"

Scott threw the back door open. "Mr. Byrne promised us a ride," he said. " 'Member, Russ? C'mon! We got time."

"No way," said Russell sullenly.

"Hold it right there, Scotty," Helen said, but it was too late. The boy was making a beeline for the passenger side of Nat's car.

"I'll get 'im," Russ said suddenly, jumping out of the Volvo.

"Russell—the door," Helen said, exasperated that both boys had left both doors open. She was leaning over to close them and move out of the way of the beeping car behind her when she saw one of the four-year-olds from the preschool being rushed across the street by her father.

Alarm bells went off. The Rosdicks were in the middle of a bitter custody battle; as far as Helen knew, Mrs. Rosdick hadn't given anyone else permission to accompany her daughter. The fear was confirmed when Lisa Rosdick came running from the parking area, screaming hysterically for someone to stop her husband just as his car screamed off in the opposite direction down the avenue.

While Helen watched in astonishment, Scotty dove headfirst into the Porsche, with Russell right on top of him, and Nat threw the car into a sharp U-turn across oncoming traffic and roared off after the fleeing car.

Leaving her own Volvo standing, Helen rushed out to drag the hysterical mother from the middle of the road. They ran to her office to call the police. Helen's hand was shaking violently as she punched in 911. She thought, *I'll have to put it on speed dial if this keeps up.*

She gave a brief description of the crime, then handed over the phone to Lisa Rosdick for the rest. Parents piled up, agog, in the hall outside her office. Another thought occurred to Helen: *Will they blame this on me, too?*

And then the most horrible, belated, unbelievable thought of all.

My son is in that car, on a high-speed chase after a lunatic. My son!

She ran back to the street, more filled with shock than with rage, more filled with rage than with confidence. *How could he? How could he endanger my son?*

For an agonizing eternity she waited for the Porsche to return, shepherding an embarrassed Buick. But no one came back. A police car pulled up. Helen realized, for the first time, that Lisa Rosdick was alongside her, crying, incoherent; had been there the whole time.

My son. Helen scanned the avenue up and then down, straining for sight of the Porsche.

The officer and a couple of parents tried in vain to get Lisa Rosdick to calm down. Finally the officer—the same one who'd come about the graffiti—gave up and turned to Helen for information. She told him what she knew in a voice as calm as soft rain, afraid that if she lost control she'd never get it back again.

The officer was reassuring but cryptic, telling Helen only that everything was under control.

Peaches was there now, too. She was smiling as she said to Helen, "There's a call for you in the office."

Helen felt a sudden rush of loathing for her. "I'm busy," she said, and turned away.

Peaches tapped her on the shoulder. "It's Nathaniel Byrne," she explained.

Whirling back to face her, Helen said angrily, "Why didn't you say—?" She bit back the rest and said, "Thank you," then ran back to her office, seizing her phone in a death grip.

Nat's voice was passionless, careful. "I'm sorry I couldn't get through to you sooner; your phones have been tied up. We're two or three minutes away."

"I hope my son enjoyed the ride," she said coldly.

"I'm sorry about that, too. I made a judgment call."

"Your judgment *stinks*," she said, losing it at last. She slammed down the phone, taking out all her pent-up emotion on AT&T.

By the time she got back outside, she could see the sleek black car bearing down on them. Helen stood on the curb like a prison matron, arms folded across her chest, trying to decide whom to pummel first: him or her son.

The car pulled up alongside and the boys jumped out, oblivious to her fury.

"Oh, man, that was so-o cool," crowed Scotty. "I'm not gonna forget that as long as I live!"

"Yeah, but my dad was in lotsa chases better'n that," Russ argued, loyal to the last.

"Man, I'm savin' up for a cell phone. Gotta have a cell phone. The cops got 'im, just 'cuz of us. Can that guy drive or what?"

"It was the Porsche," said Russ. "It practically drove itself."

"Oh, like you know—"

Helen wasn't really listening. She was watching the driver, shadowed by the low roof of the car, for some sign, some . . . anything. The passenger door was still open. Out of nowhere, Peaches slung her lithe body gracefully into the bucket seat and closed the door. The Porsche took off, leaving Helen in its dust.

She rounded on her son. "What's the matter with you?" she said, whacking him on the shoulder. "Are you crazy? Jumping in a car like that on a high-speed chase through the city? What's the matter with you?"

Russell, mortally embarrassed in front of the gathering, rallied to his own defense. "We didn't even run a light! He just kept behind the guy and called the cops and told them where he was!"

"Yeah, Mrs. Evett," said Scotty, dimly sensing disapproval through his euphoria. "He even used his turn signals."

"I don't care what he used! When you see something dangerous going on, you're supposed to jump *out* of the way, not *in* the way!" To Scott she said, "Wait till your mother hears about this!"

She began shooing them toward the school building like a couple of errant lambs until she realized, quite suddenly, that both the boys were taller than she was. When had that happened? Here they were on the cusp of manhood, and she was still treating them like ten-year-olds—treating them like the boys they were when Hank died. Becky was right.

It had to stop. "I'm sorry for losing my temper in front of everyone," she said to both of them outside her office.

Scotty, suspecting a trick, looked at Russell for his reaction.

Russ said tersely, "It's a little late now."

"Yeah," said Scott, still with a wary look.

"I know it is," Helen admitted, suddenly tired of it all. "Go see Janet and she'll set you up with the paint you need."

After the child was returned to her grateful mother, Helen spent the rest of the day aching to pick up the phone and call Nat. But she resisted, preferring to wait to see who came for Katie after school.

Peaches came. Suppressing a sense of disappointment that bordered on despair, Helen watched from a classroom window as Peaches, with an animated Katie skipping alongside, steered the child to her own car, a two-door Toyota. Next to the Toyota was parked a silver Mercedes convertible with its top down. Peaches settled Katie into her car seat, then paused for a long, admiring once-over of the sleek silver automobile before slipping into the driver's seat of her Toyota.

She'd rather have the Mercedes, Helen realized.

Or, for that matter, the Porsche.

The thought came out of nowhere, but once formed, it lingered.

The Porsche, the mansion, the diamond bracelet. Peaches wanted it all. She didn't give a damn about Nat; she certainly didn't give a damn about Katie. She was after the money, pure and simple.

Suddenly it all seemed so clear. How else to explain the nanny's unending pleasantness; her constant, hovering manner? It went beyond mere professionalism—beyond sainthood, even; Mother *Teresa* scowled more often than Peaches. All this time, Helen had assumed that Peaches was genuinely in love with Nat. Those adoring looks, that smitten laugh—lies! She was after the money. Helen knew it, now, in her soul.

The question was, how far would Peaches go to get it?

Helen spent the next half hour on the phone, tracking down herbalists in the area. She'd formed a crazy little theory, almost on the spot, as she watched Peaches drooling over the Mercedes convertible. Ironically, it came as a result of the research she'd done into the possible causes of the 1692 Salem hysteria.

At least one scholar had theorized that the girls who'd been bewitched had in fact been suffering the effects of a fungus that had contaminated their bread. The disease was called *ergot*, caused by a grain fungus of the same name. The effects of the poison were far-ranging: everything from extreme headaches to convulsions, psychosis, and death.

Ergot. Naturally the word had jumped out at Helen. Last night, amid the thunder and lightning and driving rain, it had seemed merely a bizarre, eerie coincidence that Linda Byrne had died of an overdose of a prescribed ergot derivative. But now, after the Mercedes, Helen was not so sure.

After dropping off Russ and Scotty, Helen sought out her herbalist. She'd been told that the owner of the Health and Happiness Food Store, tucked away in a dingy side street in nearby Peabody, would be back at four-thirty.

She was there waiting at four-twenty-five, trying to look as if she shopped regularly in the funky, dark, unfashionably dreary store with its two crowded aisles of mysterious roots and herbs and limp, untreated vegetables.

At the half hour, an ancient wall clock with a neurotic tick let out a burp of a chime, and an old Chinese man, older even than the clock, pushed open the wood-framed door and shuffled inside. Small, dark, as wizened and dusty as his store, the owner was dressed in traditional garb, from the small cap that fit snugly over the white hairs of his skull, to the black cotton slippers on his small, delicate feet.

"You find you want?" he asked Helen with a shopkeeper's concern as he passed.

"Not exactly," said Helen, feeling her way into her strange request. "I'm looking for certain information. They told me on the phone that you would know ... if anyone would ..."

The shopkeeper's expression remained impassive.

Helen smiled ingratiatingly. "Ergot," she said. "Is it still around nowadays?"

"Sklorshum?" he said.

"I'm sorry?"

"You want sklorshum?"

"No, I'm talking about the disease—ergot. In rye bread. Is it still possible to get bread that's infected with ergot?"

"Ah . . . sklorshum."

"No," she said, feeling as if one of them was speaking martian and one of them wasn't. She tried again. "When you buy commercial rye bread from a supermarket, it's made from flour that's free of any fungus—ergot, that is. But I want to know if someone could get hold of flour that's bad. If someone could make bread from it, say, that would get someone else sick."

The shopkeeper's eyelids lowered an infinitesimal amount. "My flour good flour."

"Oh, no, I didn't mean to imply . . . I just meant, is the fungus still around that was such a scourge for so many hundreds of years? You know, in France; in the rest of Europe; maybe even in . . . Salem?"

A veil came down between the shopkeeper and Helen. "You from FDA?"

"No, not at all," said Helen, annoyed with herself for not anticipating the language barrier. She condensed her quest to its essence: "I'm only trying to find out whether it's possible to get hold of ergot. If an evil person could still do that."

"You want sklorshum, you go Bristol-Myers," he said gruffly, and then he shuffled to the back of the store and disappeared behind a curtain.

Chapter 25

"Sorry I'm late, kids," Helen yelled to no one in particular as she dropped her purse and briefcase in the hall. When no one in particular answered, she paused, still holding the bag of groceries she'd picked up after her farcical visit to the herbalist, and said, "Anyone home?"

Becky was on the kitchen phone. Her voice, louder than usual, sounded puzzled and animated. The pitch, the tone, the speed of it were unlike anything Helen had ever heard from her before.

Helen went straight to the kitchen.

Becky hung up the phone, took one look at her mother, and blurted, "Someone killed Anna's cat!"

"Oh, no," said Helen. The floor beneath her feet seemed to sink halfway to hell. "Oh, no."

Becky stood there, making quick fluttery motions with her hands, like a baby bird flapping its wings in distress.

"And her mother thinks I did it! Mom! She thinks I did it! That was her on the phone. She called and said they found the cat behind the house and its throat was slit—and I was like, Oh my God, and she says, what do you know about it, Becky? like I knew something about it, and I said, nothing, and she says, Becky, tell me the truth and I said

I *am* telling you the truth and she just . . . *freaks*. Like, she just started *screaming* at me on the phone, Mom—screaming! I didn't hear half of what she said, it was all about Satanists and dead chickens and black clothes and things like that and oh my *God*—what is going on, Mom? And she said, she said she knew about our house being exorcised and I said what are you talking about? And she said that we cooked blood and the police had to come because of the smell and—''

At that point Becky finally stopped for a breath and burst, instead, into tears. She threw herself into her mother's arms and clung to her. "What's happening, Mom?" she cried, racked with sobs. "What's going on . . . what's going on? I'm not a devil worshipper . . . what does she mean?''

"Oh, honey," Helen said, holding her daughter tight, trying to stroke away her appalling bewilderment. "Oh, honey, never mind, never mind. It has nothing to do with you . . . nothing at all. You've been caught in this . . . this *evil* and we . . . we have to get out of it somehow, we have to make people understand we haven't done anything.''

But all the while, Helen was thinking of nineteen others with the same dead hope.

Becky shuddered violently and said through chattering teeth, "Who could d-do that to a p-poor little cat . . . who could d-do such a thing?''

Her wail turned loud with new misery; she loved animals too much to be able to handle this. It was Becky who'd insisted on adopting one-eyed Moby from the shelter; Becky who was forever finding homes for strays. She'd paid for ads, paid for shots, given her time at the shelter.

Even now, Moby was perched on a kitchen chair, waiting for the wailing to stop so that he could have his supper. He decided to nudge Becky along, planting his paws on her hip and giving her a soulful look. Becky picked him up and pressed him to her shoulder, rubbing her tearstained cheek on his flank, as if she could amend someone's cruelty to Anna's cat with kindness to her own.

Becky, a Satanist.

It was too much.

"Damn it to hell!" Helen cried, slamming an open palm on the mable counter. "Why us? What have we done to deserve this? There's no logic, no reason for it!"

Through the curtained window of the kitchen door she caught a glimpse of movement in the back hall—Russ, no doubt, backing away from the bloodletting of emotions that was going on inside. Somehow his reluctance to face their agony infuriated her; it made Helen say something she regretted for the rest of her life.

"It never would've happened—none of this ever would've got started," she said loudly, "if it hadn't been for that stupid, damned graffiti! One dumb stunt—one moronic episode—and our lives are ruined! We're going to lose the school, lose our good name, lose everything!"

"Mom, don't yell like that . . . ," Becky said, aghast.

"No, damn it, I'll yell all I want! It's the only thing I *can* do; don't you get it? Don't you see how trapped we are by this? We can't win! We can't say we're innocent. No one ever believes that. But we can't say nothing or they'll think we're guilty! What choice does that leave? Should we just make up something, the way the poor fools did the first time around? Should we just lie and say, yes, we're Satanists, we've done despicable things and please forgive us? Gee! With any luck, maybe we can avoid a trial and imprisonment. Maybe we can just stand around in pillories on the Common for a while. Maybe that'll do the trick!"

Becky fell back into a kitchen chair, blasted by the force of her mother's fury. Moby hunkered down in her lap, still hungry, still begging, still purring.

In a broken, tragic whisper, Becky said, "I didn't know."

The image of her daughter sitting there burned itself into Helen's mind and heart. Every tiny detail of it, from Becky's wet lashes and runny nose to the small black cat who was purring so hard that Helen could see his shoulders trembling. It was a picture of innocence: innocence defiled.

Overwhelmed, Helen fell to her knees alongside her daughter and laid one arm on her shoulder, the other across her lap, encircling her. "Becky, Becky . . . I love you and Russ more than life itself, you know that. I would do anything for you. That's why I was so angry now . . . because I feel so helpless to stop this. But I promise you: One way or another, I *will* put a stop to it."

Helen forced herself to smile as she smoothed away a long, golden band of hair that had broken free from the single braid into which Becky had bound her hair. Then she stood back up, desperately needing to shower and put on something different, something fresh and clean—something unrelated to the day's awful events. On her way out of the kitchen she saw a can of cat food still jammed in the electric can opener, half-opened.

She left it there, knowing full well that Becky would not let Moby go unfed.

The calls began coming that night: hate calls, hang-up calls, and finally, at three o'clock—the witching hour itself—a death threat. Helen disconnected all the phones and, after reassuring her children that it was just a drunken prankster, sat up at the window of her bedroom, watching the street for cross-burners and fire-bombers.

It was the longest, most harrowing night of her life. She had known grief, and she had known fear; but she'd never known such stark, lonely apprehension before. It seemed to Helen, in her hyperalert state, that she could hear the rumbles of the approaching mob; smell the creosote of their burning torches. Would they come and drag the children and her from their beds? It seemed all too possible.

At one point, shortly before dawn, Helen thought she saw something move in the privet below. She slid the bedroom screen up, ready to throw down a needlepoint stool—her only weapon—on the possible intruder. But then the night became quiet again, and the air became still, and she decided that the mob had not yet reached her doorstep.

She told herself that she'd read too deeply; that she'd taken Salem too profoundly into her heart. But then she remembered other preschools, other hysteria. Other trials. Some of the recent accused had been found innocent and their reputations handed back to them, charred and tattered. Others—others still languished in prison. Were they guilty? Innocent? Helen didn't know. She could only know about herself, about her children. And they were innocent.

And she was alone, all alone, in her fight to prove it.

Eventually the first dull light of morning made its reluctant appearance, halfheartedly chasing away the specters of the night. Aching and sore, Helen stood up and stretched and decided before anything else to reassure herself that her children were safe. After that she'd make coffee. After that, a shower. A cheerful dress. A nourishing breakfast for all of them. Because that was how big hills were climbed: one small step at a time.

She walked quietly down the hall, careful not to wake either exhausted child. Becky's room came first. The door was ajar. Helen pushed it open a little farther, wincing at the squeak. Becky was deep in sleep, her head cocked awkwardly on the pillow, her mouth slack. Helen listened to the sweet, rhythmic sound of her daughter's muffled snore, taking immeasurable comfort in it.

One small step at a time.

Pulling the door quietly shut, she tiptoed across the hall. Russ slept much more lightly than his sister; Helen didn't dare risk turning the doorknob and intruding on his space, so she simply stood there, wishing good sleep and long life for him.

She turned to go, then paused; then turned back to the door. Russell's DO NOT DISTURB sign wasn't hanging on its hook. Last night had been traumatic enough so that the usual rules of order might not prevail, but: Russell's DO NOT DISTURB sign wasn't hanging on its hook.

Helen took hold of the doorknob, gave it a sharp turn, and swung the door wide. Her son's bed was its usual jumble of clothes and blankets; the sight sent a sigh of relief surging through her.

And then she saw that he wasn't in it. Foreboding gave way to panic as Helen ran up to the bed and snatched a sheet of notebook paper, raggedly ripped from its spiral, from the middle of the deep blue bedsheet.

Mom,
It's all my fault, I know it. How could anyone blame Becky? It's stupid. If they want to blame somebody, let them blame me. You can make up anything you want. It doesn't matter. It really doesn't. And then maybe they'll leave Becky and you alone.
Your son Russell x

PS. Tell Becky she can have my CDs. All except Sonic Youth. Those go to Scott.

She read the note again.
And again.
Nothing so far had prepared her for what she was feeling. The dreadful events of the last few weeks suddenly seemed like small bumps in the road compared to this. Russell: *gone*. The pain was numbing. For one long hellish instant she thought she'd been knocked unconscious.
She read the note again. It had never occurred to her that

Russ would react to the episode by running away. She'd imagined him in danger from drive-by shooters, marauding gangs, vicious muggers. She'd never imagined him in danger from his family.

Had he run away? She read the note again. Suddenly the words seemed ambiguous, ominous.

It's all my fault.

Helen had warned Russ—over and over—about drink. She had talked to him—knowledgeably and calmly—about drugs. But never, ever had she brought up the subject of suicide. The idea was simply too taboo. She hadn't wanted even to put it into his head.

It really doesn't matter.

Words of despair.

Oh, God—would he? Helen raced to the phone and punched in the infernal three numbers to get the police. Instead of the coffee, the shower, the dress, the breakfast—the police. Before searching . . . praying . . . crying—the police.

"Find him," she begged after telling them everything they wanted to know about her missing son. "I'll be there in twenty minutes with the photos. Find him."

His name was in the computer now, connected to thousands of other computers. Pray God the system worked.

Helen ran down the hall and rousted Becky out of bed. "Find him!" she said after waving Russ's note in front of her. "Check all his haunts. The video parlors, the movie theaters—check Salem Willows Park. He could be there, sleeping under a tree. Take this photo with you. I'll drop the others off with the Salem police, then go on to the state police. Aunt Mary can cover our phone. He can't have gone far."

Becky wasn't a morning person. Droopy-eyed and clutching the photo in one hand, she stared at the note in her other, trying hard to focus on the urgency of it all.

"He called you 'Mom,' " she said at last.

"You're right!" Helen snatched the note back. *Mom*, it said; not *ma*. "He wouldn't do that unless he were feeling—"

"Already homesick," said Becky with a sleepy smile.

Despair, Helen thought, then shoved the idea away. "Homesick," she agreed, almost fiercely. "Yes. Already."

"And look at that tiny *x* next to his name," Becky added, her natural optimism shining through her weariness. "You know how Russell feels about words of love. He only uses them in code."

Helen was ashamed to admit that she thought the "*x*" was an allusion to Generation X—the lost generation, as some of the kids liked to tag themselves. "You're right . . . ," she said again, but this time she was even less sure. "It doesn't matter. We've got to find him, Becky!"

Helen sprinted down the stairs and across the back hall to her aunt's apartment and, despite the hour, banged on the door and then let herself in. Through the open door of the darkened bedroom she could see her aunt still trying to struggle into a bathrobe.

"Aunt Mary—it's me." She apologized for waking her aunt up, then helped her into a fuzzy pink robe and sat her down at the ancient enamel-topped table in the kitchen. Sliding a cordless phone across the distance between them, she said carefully, "I'm expecting a call from Russ sometime today. I'll be in and out, and I'm afraid of missing it."

There were mornings when Aunt Mary had trouble getting into gear mentally; but this wasn't one of them. "It's six-thirty A.M.," she said, fixing a surprised look on her niece. "Where is he?"

Helen clasped her hands together in a prayerful pose, then pelted her chest softly with them. Her gaze was fas-

tened on the July sheet of a calendar that hung on the pale
yellow wall next to the door: a serene view of a country
cottage, its perennial border abloom with daylilies, daisies,
and black-eyed Susans. The idyllic setting was so at odds
with her life that Helen closed her eyes and looked away,
as if she'd stumbled across a mangled body.

She took a deep breath to steady herself, then came up
with a tiny smile of dismay. "He's . . . ah . . . he's run
away, Aunt Mary. You remember that weird scare over the
Satanism? Well, it's back. Someone killed a cat that be-
longed to a little girl that Becky baby-sits and—"

"Oh my lord. They think Russell did that?"

"No, actually it's even dumber than that. They think
Becky did it."

The elderly woman stared blankly at her niece; it was
too early in the morning for such drama. Helen felt a surge
of protectiveness for her aunt, sitting there puffy-eyed and
shivery in the early morning sun. But she had no choice;
there was no one else to cover the phone.

Fearing one of her aunt's memory lapses, she asked gently, "Did you understand what I said?"

"But . . . then why did *Russell* run away?"

"Ah. Good point," said Helen with a wan look of her
own. "I said some things yesterday . . ."

Her hurtful words fell back down over her like concrete
blocks, crushing her spirit. "And Russell took them personally."

She stood up, aching to be on her way, but paused and
said, "You know the movies where the sidekick runs in
front of the bad guys to draw their fire away from the people he loves? That's what Russ is doing."

He's pleading guilty to please the mob.

"The poor thing," said her aunt, drawing her robe
around her more closely. She looked so terribly, terribly
tired. "Where would he have gone? Not far?"

"No father than the mall, anyway," said Helen lightly. She knew that to Aunt Mary, running away meant hiding out in a friend's basement all day.

She was determined not to alarm her aunt any more than she had already, so she added, "I'm just afraid he'll get stuck somewhere without carfare and call home. So if he does, be sure to get an address and tell him not to move, would you? And meanwhile, I'll keep checking with you. We should have this all worked out by the end of the day. You know how temperamental kids can be."

Seventy-two hours later, what was left of Helen's world was being methodically dismantled.

Every cop in the city, every trooper in the state was on the lookout for Russell Evett, a black-haired, green-eyed cop's kid with two pierces in his ear and a great grin, if one of them was lucky enough to see it.

He wasn't dead. That was the big, overwhelming thing. He'd called Scotty—*that* hurt—and told him to pass the word that he was okay. The call had been quick, Scott said; Russ had been afraid it would be traced. That was another blow: her son, acting like a fugitive from her.

But she cheered herself with the news that he was alive and hopefully not far from home: Boston was her best guess. Helen loved Boston; but the thought of Russell roaming its streets with nothing but the clothes on his back and a few dollars in his pocket was nothing short of terrifying. She sent Becky and a couple of her friends to search for him in the Cambridge area, which Russ knew pretty well, while she stayed home coordinating the search in the manner of a military campaign, with a private investigator as her aide-de-camp.

But despite the army of friends, relatives, and mercenaries that surrounded Helen, the plain truth was that she herself was under seige: The Open Door was teetering on the brink of collapse. After the cat episode, another dozen or so parents panicked and fled the summer program; classes were now down to less than half their original size. A teacher gave notice. The cook quit. The afternoon person simply didn't show.

All of the rest of the staff, as well as the remaining parents, were ready and willing to rally around Helen—but she wasn't there to lead her troops. How could she be, when her son had gone missing?

It came as no surprise to her when Janet called late on Wednesday morning. "Two reps from the Office for Children are here on an impromptu inspection. Is it possible that it's coincidence?" she asked wryly.

Smiling bleakly, Helen said, "Be nice to them. We have nothing to hide."

"I heard Mrs. Dunbar went straight to them after she heard about the cat."

"That was bound to happen, Janet. You and I discussed it."

"Well, excuse me, but I don't understand what someone's dead cat has to do with this establishment."

"It doesn't take much to bring down a preschool," Helen said almost absently. Her mind was on the search. "Janet, when you call, call me on my aunt's line, would you? I need to keep this one free."

"Anything new?"

"Not so far."

Janet's sigh was heavy and unanswerable. Helen knew that her assistant was ready to charge over hot coals for her and the preschool. "Janet? I'm sorry, I truly am, but I have to stay here."

"Don't apologize," Janet said firmly. "I'd do the exact same thing. It's just too bad, that's all. You and your children don't deserve this. First Hank, now this ridiculous hysteria. And all because of some idle gossip and a tragic coincidence—well, it's not right. It makes me wonder who's running things up there.''

Helen hurried off the phone before Janet's plainspoken sympathy reduced her to weeping. It was hard to read phone books through tears.

Tears or no tears, one particular phone number kept throbbing in place on her yellow pad. It was the only one Helen hadn't crossed off; the only one she could not bring herself to dial. Her hand hovered over the phone.

Leave no stone unturned, she told herself. *Not even that one.*

The phone rang shrilly as she reached for it, sending her heart cracking against her breastbone. "Yes?"

"Mom, it's me. We couldn't find him. I'm sorry. We went through every record store, every arcade, every bookstore. We saw a kid go into the Harvard Coop who looked a little like . . . but he wasn't. We were thinking of maybe checking around the Charles River; you know, where they have those little swan boats?''

"No. I don't want you driving around Boston after dark. Mr. Merkle will take care of that part. You did your best, honey. Now come home. And drive safely. How was traffic going in?"

"No sweat. Bobby's a real good driver.''

"I know. Thank him—thank everyone—for me.''

Again she had to hurry off before the tears started up. Becky and her friends—and Helen was amazed to see how many were coming forward—were all trying so hard. Everyone was.

It made Nat Byrne all the more conspicuous by his absence.

Helen bit down hard and picked up the phone. He could help or he could go to hell.

Chapter 26

$\mathcal{P}$eaches was trying on a ruby necklace, one that had come down to Linda through the Swiss side of her family, when the phone rang. She considered not answering—she'd already spoken with Nat—but it was seven-thirty; anyone who mattered would know that Katie would be in bed, and her nanny at home with her.

"Peaches? It's Helen Evett. May I speak with Nat, please?"

Well, well, well. She was swallowing her pride after all. "I'm sorry, Helen," Peaches said, "but he isn't here."

"Do you know when he'll be back?" Helen asked. Her voice was surprisingly businesslike for a woman whose only son had run away.

"Nat is out of town."

"Ah. Of course," Helen answered.

There was a pause that Peaches didn't bother to fill. By now everyone knew about the cat; everyone was entitled to have reservations about Helen.

"When will he be back?"

Ooh. Pushy. Interesting. "Probably by the end of the week. Is there a message I can give him?"

Peaches heard a sigh. "No," Helen said, not so briskly

as before. "I guess he can't do anything. . . ."

It was time to sound concerned. "Really, I'll be glad to give him a message; he checks in all the time when he's away."

"Yes . . ." Another sigh. It was obvious that she was agonizing over whether to tell Peaches—presumably about her son—or wait for Nat.

"It can wait," Helen said at last. "Is Katie all right?" she added. "She hasn't been in school since Monday."

Peaches lied and said, "She's a little under the weather."

"I'm sorry to hear that. Is she running a temperature?"

"She'll be fine," Peaches said cooly, preempting further discussion.

Helen got off the phone quickly after that. It was wonderfully convenient. Now Nat wouldn't have to hear about either the cat or the kid until he returned home. By then he'd be tired and glad to accept a glass of wine from Peaches, and happy to relax in the company of his sweet and adorable daughter.

The rift between Nat and Helen was already wide and deep. With the right presentation, the latest events in the Evett family would seem bizarre at best, abhorrent at worst. Nat would pull Katie from the preschool; Peaches was ready to bet the farm on it.

She unclasped the ruby necklace from her throat, put it back in its case, and put the case back in the safe. All in all, she really did prefer the emerald.

Helen laid the phone down as if it were a bird with a broken wing. Whatever feelings Nat had had for her, whatever reforms he'd promised to make for Katie's sake—they were over. He'd gone back to his career the way a man backslides into drink or gambling. And the worst part was, she was the one who'd driven him there.

Helen stared at the phone, her mind adrift. For the moment things were almost eerily silent. She began to wander through her shockingly empty house, waiting: for Becky to come, for Russ to call. For some sign, any sign, that her life had reached a low point. She couldn't bear the thought that it might go lower.

The hardest place to be was Russ's room. Helen paused at the door, then made herself go in. She hadn't been able to bring herself to make his bed or change his sheets, which were still the way he'd left them. She wanted him simply to show up, as if he'd been to basketball practice, and go into his room and crank up the music to some deafening volume. She'd give anything to feel the walls of the house shaking again.

She stopped in front of Russ's shrine to his father and fingered the trooper's badge that lay propped against the photograph of Hank. It seemed inconceivable to Helen that during all the recent traumas, she hadn't once had a sense of Hank . . . being there for her, somehow.

It was too ironic. A virtual stranger had been able to figure out the trick of crossing the veil and confounding her life; but her husband—the father of their two beleaguered children—was sitting it out on the other side. There was only one man alive who could comfort her—but he was busy making money.

She sat on Russell's bed, staring blankly for a long time at the picture of Hank, and then she began to cry. It was both her curse and her blessing that no one was there to hear her do it—not Hank, not Becky, not Russell, not Nat. She could wail as loud as she wanted. And she did.

It was a release that was long, long overdue. Tomorrow—tonight—she would be strong again. But not now. The tears were as vital to her survival as spring rain to a good strong crop.

When Helen finally heard the front door slam, that's

when she hastily wiped her eyes and called out, "Who's home?"

Because it was always possible that he'd decided to come back. Far stranger things had happened lately.

"It's only me, Mom," Becky called up. "Sorry."

"Don't be sorry, dope," said Helen, coming down the steps to hug her daughter. She held her for a long, emotional moment. "Don't you know how glad I am to see you?"

Helen *was* glad. In her yellow T-shirt and white shorts— Becky hadn't worn black since Russ left home—the girl was as cheerful a sight to behold as the five-foot sunflowers that looped around the birdbath.

Becky had brought home half a dozen doughnuts. Helen took the cordless phone over to Aunt Mary's, where the three women drank tea and ate all six pastries while they insisted to one another that Russell couldn't have gone far, because no tollbooth attendant or bus driver would've let him pass—he was a cop's kid.

No one brought up the possibility of hitchhiking.

And then it was time to try again to sleep. The nights so far had been endless; but tonight, no doubt because of her good long cry, Helen dropped off at once into an exhausted, dreamless stupor.

Until the rapping sound.

It was a single, sharp crack, nothing at all like the persistent jiggle and knock that had haunted the nights of her spring. Disabled by sleep, Helen sat part of the way up and tried to track the sound. Someone was trying to communicate; she hadn't dreamed it; someone was out there.

The clock in the hall struck three. There was another sharp crack. This time she heard it clearly. Something was being pitched—or pitching itself—against the windowpane. Fumbling for her flashlight, Helen ran to the window and threw up the sash, then the screen, and hung over the sill.

If he doesn't have a key . . .

But it wasn't her lost son who was standing below her window in the misty black of the garden, and it wasn't the prayed-for ghost of Hank Evett. It was flesh and blood that Helen never thought she'd see at the house again, much less standing in the ivy at three in the morning.

She aimed the flashlight directly down on him. In the narrow beam he looked drawn and haggard, even fiendish, as he squinted in the focused penetration of light. His hair was unkempt, almost wild; the expression on his face was urgent and intense as he called her name in an undertone.

"What're you doing here?" she asked, shocked by his appearance.

He gestured to the front porch, signaling her to take him in.

"Yes. Wait," she whispered, although she felt she must be dreaming. She threw down the flashlight and, without taking the time to grab a robe, ran down the stairs and swung open the door.

The man who stood before her was not the man from whom she'd fled. He looked thinner, older, worn with care—a carbon copy, she thought, of her own suffering. She was baffled; *he* hadn't lost a son. And then she realized he had, and—like her—so much else besides. "Oh . . . Nat . . . ," she said in a voice wrenched by emotion.

He caught her in his arms and held her fast, as if he were afraid someone was going to snatch her away. "Helen . . . Helen, I'm sorry. Oh my love, I'm so sorry," he said hoarsely, over and over. His breath felt warm on her night-cooled skin. After all these nights: he was so real. It was a measure of her love for him that she didn't know or care what he was sorry about; she only cared that they shared the heartache.

"Nat . . . I'm so glad . . . oh, Nat, that you're here," she said, shutting her eyes, absorbing the reality of him. He was a dream come true. She was ecstatic at his return; if one dream could come true, than so could another.

Through the thin gauze of her cotton gown she could feel that his clothes were damp from the night air. "I thought you were away . . . that you were never coming back to me," she said in joyful confusion.

"Let's go inside," he said. "You're shaking like a leaf."

He closed the door and she led him by the hand to the denim sofa in the family room, where she curled up against him, her arm looped across his chest, her cheek pressed over his heart. This was the important thing, to feel him there, to know he was there. All else could wait.

"Tell me everything," he said simply.

She said, "When did you find out?"

"I got back a couple of hours ago," he told her. "Peaches wasn't expecting me until tomorrow; she was asleep. I was glancing through my mail and saw an envelope from Rhea Lagor. I remembered her—I remembered her son—from my first visit to The Open Door. It's not every day I get a train engine thrown at me. So I opened the letter and read it.

"It was incomprehensible," he said. "Something about an eviscerated cat and animal worship and would I be willing to attend a meeting of concerned parents. Apparently she'd tried to leave a message through Peaches, but Peaches told me—when I woke her up to ask her what the hell was going on—that Mrs. Lagor was a nut and she'd assumed I wouldn't want to be bothered. Which was at least partly true.

"So then," he said grimly, "I got Peaches's version. And now I want your version, the true version. I love you, Helen. I'm so sorry I wasn't here for you." He stroked Helen's hair away from her cheek. "Forgive me, and tell me what happened. And then we'll find Russ."

Overwhelmed by his simple declaration of faith and love—and hope—Helen told him everything, beginning with the call from Anna's mother to Becky. From Becky's reaction of horror to her own frustrated outburst, from Russell's note after the night of hate calls to her indifference to the collapse of her preschool, she told him everything.

She tried hard to stick to the facts; to keep emotion out of her voice as she did so. But by the end of her account, tears were rolling unchecked down her cheeks.

"I'm sorry," she said, trying to brush them from his shirt. "I'm just . . . an emotional mess right now."

"That's all right. When you're ready." He held her close, and kissed the top of her head, and stroked her hair, and waited in silence for her to become more calm.

Eventually Helen sighed deeply; she was in control again. "What did Peaches say?" she murmured.

He shrugged off the answer. "It doesn't matter."

"She told you she believes it all, didn't she."

"It truly doesn't matter, Helen. I'm not interested in what she believes. All Peaches knows is what she hears. Never mind her now," he said, dismissing her in a voice that was surprisingly harsh.

Immediately he apologized and dropped his voice back down. "I don't want to wake Becky."

Helen burrowed more deeply against him. "Becky asleep is anyone else in a coma," she said, smiling. She yawned herself; her eyelids were becoming heavy. It would be so nice to nod off in his arms, right then, right there. In the morning she just knew everything would be back to normal.

"And so you threw some stones against my window," she said dreamily. "Instead of using the phone. I'm glad."

"I didn't want to alarm your house. I was out . . . I was walking around . . . I . . . my original plan was to call you first thing in the morning. I went to bed . . . but then . . ."

He was rubbing her upper arm idly as his voice meandered around, groping for words. "Something happened, Helen," he said unsteadily. "Something that sent me out of the bedroom, out of the house . . . and straight here. There's no one I can tell this to. No one but you."

There was, in his voice, a low note of awe that spoke to her more profoundly than mere words could ever do. Helen shivered, and pressed against him, and when he seemed reluctant still to speak, she sat up and took his hand in hers.

"What happened in your bedroom, Nat?" she said, returning the gravity of his look. "Tell me what you saw."

He sucked in his breath, then seemed to forget about it as his eyes darted from right to left, focused on something she couldn't see. He might have been reading a ticker tape. He let out his breath in a rush, then shook his head.

"Not what I saw. What I smelled. *Enchantra,* Helen. The room was redolent with it. I must've been dozing; I know I was agitated . . . restless . . . but I think I dozed off. And the scent . . . the scent was overwhelming enough to wake me up."

He had become restless all over again. He needed to stand up; to pace. "Linda rarely went into that room; the bedroom we used is now Katie's," he explained. "I had the new room completely done over to suit me. Almost nothing in it is from . . . before."

Here, Helen could not help correcting him. "The commode alongside the bed . . ."

Wincing, he paused to say, "Yes. That's from our old room." His face turned suddenly querulous, as if he couldn't remember how it had got there. He rubbed his temples wearily, then abruptly resumed his pacing. "But more than that . . . there was something more . . . something intense going on. I could feel it, Helen," he said, more to himself than to her.

He was rubbing the back of his neck, stumbling through his spiritual encounter all over again while he paced and

talked. Helen watched him closely, unable to look anywhere else. He was wearing beat-up khakis and an old blue
shirt, the kind of thing he might've worn to clean leaves
out of the gutters. With his stubble of beard, uncombed
hair, and—Helen couldn't deny it—a turbulent look in his
eye, he might easily have passed for a street person.

"I didn't see her or anything, not in any clear way. But
there was a sense of her, a . . . a presence. Ah, hell, I can't
describe it," he said, and then proceeded at once to try
again.

He turned to Helen and said, "It was . . . she was . . .
benign. I mean . . . it wasn't like *Nightmare on Elm Street.*
She was filled with sorrow . . . but she forgave me. That
was somehow clear."

"Forgave you?" Helen whispered.

He was standing above Helen now; suddenly he fell to
his knees in front of her and slid his arms along the outside
of her thighs, and dropped his forehead onto her lap.

"I wronged her, Helen," he said, dragging the words out
in a moan. "I wronged her in a way I can never forgive
myself for. I loved her . . . and then I turned on her . . . and
you were right: Linda was perfectly innocent. Whatever
happened, she didn't mean to take a life, hers or anyone
else's. Whatever happened, that was *my* son who died with
her. God in heaven!" he said in a choked voice. "How can
I ever forgive myself?"

His agony was shocking, unbearable; it tore Helen up in
a whole new way. She laid her hands on the back of his
head in a kind of benediction and said, "No, no . . . it
wasn't your fault . . . not in the way you think . . . you were
misled . . ."

He seemed not to hear; he was completely focused on
pouring out his heart to her.

"In my wildest dreams I wouldn't have known I could
experience this. Any of this," he said in a voice twisted

with pain. "And yet—God help me—I love you more, Helen. I love you still."

And then he sighed and said in a low bleak whisper, "Forgive me, Linda."

He looked up at Helen then, his gaunt, handsome face streaked with tears. "I'm sorry. I love you. I'm sorry."

There was so much Helen wanted to tell him, so much he needed to know. But the moment was sacred; she would not defile it. "I love you, Nat," she whispered. "With all my heart. My soul."

They went upstairs after that, and made love. He came into her with more sorrow than passion, more stillness than joy. And Helen held him fast and would not let him go— or come—because in all the wild ferment of rumor and loss and squandered emotion, this, at least, was real. He was real, and she was, and their love for one another.

They lay without moving for a long time, he in her, she around him, until the obvious, the inevitable, happened: Their need to be released overcame their desire to hold on. In utter silence, he brought her to a deep, rhythmic climax, and then he himself shuddered, and sighed, and lay still.

Relishing his weight on her the way she would a heavy, comforting blanket on a bone-chilling night, Helen touched her lips to his shoulder in a gossamer kiss.

"I love you," she whispered.

"We'll find him," he said again.

Their limbs locked together, they passed what was left of the night in a kind of desperate sleep, gathering strength—because now they knew that the most dangerous demons prowled around in the day.

The sun was bright; the air was clean and fresh. While Nat showered, Helen—energized and filled with the sense that they both had Linda's blessing—sneaked down the hall into her daughter's room.

"Becky . . . honey . . . don't be alarmed," she said, shaking her gently by the shoulder. "But I just wanted to warn you."

Becky moaned and buried her nose in her pillow. "Mmmmph . . . what about," she said in a muffled voice.

"Well . . . about Nat. He's in the shower."

Rolling her head to one side, Becky opened one eye in a squint. "Whose shower?"

"Whose. Mine. Whose do you think?"

"Did he run out of water at his house?"

"No-o-o."

"Are we taking in boarders?"

"No-o-o."

"Mmmph." She closed her eye again. "Okay . . . I'll sleep in."

"Thanks, sweetie," said a blushing Helen, bending over to kiss her daughter's cheek. "That'd be so much easier, for now."

Helen was halfway out the door when Becky called her back. "Mom?" she murmured with a sleepy smile. "Would you like me to put a spell on him?"

"That's not very funny, missy," Helen said, grimacing at her daughter's black humor. "And besides," she added with a relenting smile of her own, "you'd be a little late."

"Mom?"

"Yeah, snot?"

"It's nice to see you happy again. Even this much."

Helen said softly, "This much is pretty much," and closed the bedroom door shut.

She went down to the kitchen and began rummaging for something to cook. The cupboards were bare: three slices of bacon, a few tired blueberries, the last of the Bisquick. She hadn't shopped all week; but then, no one had eaten all week.

Aunt Mary had brought over some chicken soup, with

apologies for messing it up and making it thin. And without salt. Or carrots. The soup, still in the fridge, was a constant reminder to Helen that she had to get her aunt in to a doctor, and fast.

If I have to drag her kicking and screaming, Helen thought, *I will.* It all seemed suddenly so much more doable.

The bacon was sizzling and the pancakes, fashionably thin, were stacking up in the oven when Nat came up behind Helen and slid his arms around her waist.

"Mornin'," he whispered in her ear. "I love you."

Despite her agony—*because* of her agony—Helen needed desperately to hear those words. "Tell me again," she whispered without turning around. Her eyes stung with tears. In the middle of so much joy, she was feeling so much pain.

She turned to face him. "Please. Tell me again."

He cradled her face between his hands and murmured, "Let me start at the top, then. I love your black shimmering hair—it reminds me of the way night falls over a crystal clear lake in winter. I love your gray-green eyes, and the way your lashes stick together when you cry. When you cry you're so heartbreakingly beautiful that I want to cry with you.

"I love your nose," he said, continuing his journey south. "It has character, and a certain regalness that makes me want to fall to one knee and beg you to make me your knight. And I definitely love your mouth. It wants to be kissed."

To prove it, he kissed her.

"Your chin has strength; your neck—well, if a neck can show kindness, then that's what yours does."

She laughed, despite herself, and he kissed her again to silence her. "Your shoulders have a set to them that tells me I want you always on *my* side. Which brings me to your breasts," he said with a devilish smile, cupping his hands under them and skimming over her nipples with his thumbs through the thin fabric of her shirt. "Ah, those breasts. I'm repeating myself here, but—"

The rest of the compliment was overtaken by the shrill ring of the kitchen phone. It was early, six-forty-five; Helen broke from Nat's embrace and tore the phone from its cradle on the wall.

"Hello? Hello?" She waited in agony. "Who's there? Who is it?"

Silence. "No, please . . . Russ, if it's you, please . . . please talk to me."

Silence. And then a dial tone.

Biting her lip, Helen hung up slowly, needing the time to beat back the tears. Head bowed, she turned around into Nat's waiting arms.

He encircled her and held her tight. "I have a call out now to the guy I told you about," he said. "The father of the Lollapalooza kid."

"The one who never came back from the concert?" she murmured into his shirt.

"That's the one. I'm telling you, who could be harder to track than that? But this guy's a whiz at locating missing kids. He's the best there is. We'll find Russ, Helen," he whispered in her ear. "I promise you."

The bacon, burning black, set off the fire alarm, which Nat charged out to disengage. Helen moved the cast iron pan to a cold burner and began salvaging the three charred strips. She was thinking, *How can I love Nat when I don't have my son back*? As for the preschool, she couldn't even think about it. And yet every day it became a more compelling crisis.

Nat returned shaking his head. "Geez, Becky is a heavy sleeper."

Helen looked up from her reverie and gave him a dis-

tracted smile. She was back in her agony, big time. It was
even worse now, because she had the added guilt of having
felt happy for a couple of hours.

Nat gave her a thoughtful look, then went over to an
open plate rack and took down plates and mugs. He said,
"I called Peaches after I showered, incidentally, and talked
to Katie, too."

"So early?"

"Katie's a morning person—as you'll see. Anyway,
she's fine. She'll be going to school today."

"Did Peaches ask you where you were?" Helen asked,
swinging open the oven door with such surprising force that
she nearly took it off its hinges.

"Peaches wouldn't do that," he said quietly.

"I suppose not." She took out the warmed plate of pancakes, put out napkins and a bottle of syrup, and they sat
down to their forlorn-looking meal. Helen didn't bother to
apologize; she knew Nat would understand.

In the meantime, her mind had veered suddenly and completely over to Peaches. She wanted fiercely to believe it
had been Russ who'd called—just to hear his mother's
voice—but the call had felt like Peaches. It could've been
just another infuriated parent, but—the call had felt like
Peaches.

Helen couldn't explain that sensation to Nat, any more
than she could explain her bizarre theory of the ergot. She
didn't dare. As much as she distrusted—even despised—
Peaches, she knew too well what unfounded charges could
do to the heart and soul of a human being. She would not
give voice to her suspicions; not yet.

Nat broke into her reverie with a gently worded query.
"Are you thinking of going to The Open Door today?" he
said. "Because I can stay here for you—"

"No, no. Becky will be in all day. Or Aunt Mary can

stay here, in a pinch. Besides, don't you have to be at work? Eventually?''

He said, ''I've told you, Helen; I'm winding down on that. This was my last trip.'' Then he gave her a wry smile and said, ''But of course I can't expect you to believe something I said in the heat of passion. So I'll say it again, over pancakes: I'm winding down.''

She sighed, then said, ''Whereas I have to put in an appearance. Janet can't be expected to do my job for me. It's so unfair to her. If anyone's going to be stoned, it should be me.''

Nat's wry smile faded as he reached across the table for her hand. ''Is it really so bad as that?'' he asked her seriously. ''You honestly think you may lose the school?''

The words, coming from someone else, made it sound all too possible. Helen nodded, not trusting her voice. Then she said, ''You don't think like a woman, Nat. You don't think like a mother. If my child were in a preschool in a situation like this, I'd have second thoughts. I know I would, no matter how well I trusted the staff. Even now—even after what's happened to me,'' she whispered, ''I know I would.''

Nat said, ''Maybe you should try talking to Anna's parents.''

''I did try talking to them—as soon as Becky told me about the cat. They referred me to their lawyer. God only knows what they're planning.''

''Suppose I find out,'' he said grimly.

''No! Your job is to nail down the new investigator,'' she said, picturing Nat on a white horse charging up Anna's front porch. ''I'll go to school later and . . . I don't know. See how bad it is. But, God, I don't want to,'' she added, dreading it.

She knew that Nat had been in favor of the direct approach all along. Now he said, ''You *should* want to, damn

it! That school is as much a part of you as Russell; as much
a part of you as I plan to be. You can't turn your back on
part of yourself!''

Suddenly he stood up, went behind her ladderback chair,
lifted it from the floor—with her still in it—and turned it
toward the door to the hall. ''Put on a dress and get out of
here. You've got call forwarding now; you've got a cell
phone. You're not going to miss his call. C'mon—up!''

Helen let Nat haul her from the chair, then promised him
she'd go back into the rubble of The Open Door and sal-
vage what she could. He left after that, and Helen—well,
she stalled. What if the call forwarding didn't work? Or the
new cellular phone? So she did the dishes. She looked over
her list. She checked on Aunt Mary. She gave instructions
to Becky. She fed the cat. She fed the cat again.

And all the while, when she wasn't staring out the front
windows, she kept staring at the phone, willing it to ring.
It finally did, at nine o'clock; but it wasn't Russell. It was
the second of the three herbalists she'd originally contacted.
He spoke perfect English.

And he was able to get Helen up, dressed, and out the
door in no time flat.

Chapter 27

The bastard! Where did he get off, walking away in the middle of the night? Bastard!

Peaches had got up early, made a gourmet breakfast for two, and waited. When Nat didn't show up in the kitchen at his regular time, she ventured to knock on his door, then to throw it wide open. He was gone. His bed had been slept in, all right; but he'd left before dawn: a four A.M. thunderstorm had ripped through one of his open windows, soaking the Oriental carpet below it. She hadn't heard the Porsche. In fact it was still parked at the house.

Bastard! When he called, it was all she could do to sound surprised and civil. "Oh, Nat, I assumed you were sleeping in," she'd said mildly.

Sleeping in was exactly what he'd been doing. The question was—in whom? He hadn't bothered to say, of course; just asked to talk to his daughter and to make sure that Peaches was taking her to school, even if it was for the last day of the week.

Bastard. He'd been besotted from the start with the Evett woman. Peaches had watched with growing disbelief. Nothing had seemed to shake him. At one point Peaches really did believe she had him backing away from Helen Evett, after which the cat episode should've provided the coup de grace to the relationship.

But she'd misread Nathaniel Byrne. He wasn't like the others. She'd tried every trick she'd ever used to bring well-bred men to their knees. Hints of decolletage, eye contact, carefully indiscreet remarks, accidental brushups against him—shit! *Nothing* worked on him. She should've been more direct. No doubt that's how the Evett woman snagged him. Shit. All that work—wasted. She'd have to take what she could and cut her losses.

But first she wanted to be sure that he was with Evett. The call Peaches had made just before seven told her only that the boy was still missing. She couldn't be sure that Nat was there, and the stakes were too high to make easy assumptions. Now it was almost nine, and there was still no sign of him.

She shoved another candy bar at Katie Byrne and dialed the number of Helen Evett.

The voice that answered was old, frail, uncertain: obviously, the aunt. Peaches put on a professional smile and said, "I wonder if I could speak with Nathaniel Byrne, please."

The old lady sounded even more muddled than at the Ice Cream Social. "Nathaniel? Now let me think. I do know that name. Oh! Nat. I'm sorry; you must have the wrong number. He doesn't live here."

"I know he doesn't live there. But is he there?"

"My dear, I've just told you," the old woman said in a sweetly patient voice. "It's a workday, you know."

"Yes, I—well, never mind. Is Mrs. Evett in?"

"Helen?"

"Yes," said Peaches, grinding her teeth. "That's the one." It was always possible that she and Nat had gone off together. "I tried The Open Door," she lied. "But Mrs. Evett wasn't there."

Now the old woman became suspicious. "Are you one of those parents that keeps calling and saying cruel things? Because if you're trying to hound my niece—or my grandniece—"

"No, no, not at all. I'm sorry. I should've said who I was. This is Peaches Bartholemew," she said in a reassuring way. "Mr. Byrne's nanny?"

"Oh, for goodness' sake," the old woman said, relieved. "Why didn't you just say so? We've never met. I'm Helen's Aunt Mary."

The introductions behind her, the aunt said, "No, I haven't seen Mr. Byrne. As for Helen—well, she's supposed to go to the school *some*time today, but the girl went tearing off just now to see some herbalist. As if she doesn't have enough on her mind!"

Peaches became very still.

"An herbalist? My goodness," she said lightly, "what on earth for? Some special blend of tea leaves?"

The aunt began working herself into a fret. "Well, that's just it. I don't understand it at all. Why go there, when there's a nice organic food store nearby with good fresh vegetables and hard-to-find spices that I go to all the time—well, I don't go to it very much anymore, not since—well, the summer's been so hot, I haven't done much cooking and of course with Russell gone and then this business with the witches is taking everybody's time and—now where was I?"

Peaches said slowly, "Helen Evett. She's gone to an herbalist. You were about to tell me why."

"Oh, yes. To find out about a fungus in rye bread. It's such a strange thing to do! I'm a bit worried about her, between you and me. She was very excited, overly excited. With all the strain, well, even though she's a levelheaded girl—actually, a woman, I suppose, but she'll always be

my little girl—well, actually not mine, but almost as well
as . . ."

It was like being hit in the face with a hammer by a
ninety-pound invalid: The swing wasn't much; it was the
hammer that hurt. Peaches interrupted the babble to say she
had another call and got off the phone.

Shit. Way worse than she thought. Sooner or later Helen
would hit the right herbalist.

Peaches headed straight for the wall safe in Nat's study.
Unhooking the Butterworth painting—it should've been
hers!—from the wall, she quickly spun the safe's dial to
the left, the right, the left. She heard the satisfying click of
the tumbler, then swung the door open and began removing
Linda Byrne's jewels, old and new. It was no coincidence
that after Katie handed Helen Evett a diamond bracelet
from a drawer of the commode, Peaches had encouraged
Nat to consolidate everything in the wall safe. She had in
mind an emergency scenario like the one she was playing
out.

She had a dozen of the most valuable velvet-encased
pieces on the desk when she heard Nat's surprised greeting
to his daughter in the hall. Shit! She grabbed the booty and
flung it under the leather cushion of one of the matched
wing chairs—she knew where he sat; he never sat there—
then closed the safe, hung up the painting, and dashed over
to the bookcase on the opposite wall just as he reached the
open door to his study.

"Peaches."

The word sounded cold, almost threatening, on his lips.
Nat didn't ask what she was doing there; obviously it
looked as if she were searching for a book on finance,
which he'd freely lent her in the past. Instead he said,
"Would you mind telling me why Katie isn't in school?"

She'd jumped at the sound of her name, closing the book
with a snap. "Oh! Nat," she said, clapping an open palm

to her breast. "You frightened me! I thought I'd left the front door unlocked!"

"I'm sorry," he said with an icy stare, and waited.

Discreetly ignoring his tone, Peaches said, "Katie's still a little sluggish." (With three candy bars in her, she could hardly be anything else.) "I have a call out to the pediatrician," she added in a lie.

She put the book back on the shelf and said, "I tried to let you know. I even called Helen Evett, because I thought she might have heard from you. But Helen wasn't home, and her aunt," Peaches said with a bland look, "said she hadn't seen you. And with your car still here . . ."

She gave Nat a baffled shrug, though her heart was still hammering loud enough for a deaf man to hear.

But Nat was suddenly somewhere else entirely. "Yeah . . . I was sure I caught a glimpse of Russ as I walked past the Common. I've been combing the area since then, asking about him. How even a dimwit like Mrs. Lagor could take the boy's running away as proof of anything," he burst out, and then he remembered where he was and returned to the business at hand.

"Well, never mind. That isn't what I want to talk about now," he said with a distracted look. "Will you have a seat?" He indicated the leather chair with the jewelry under the cushion.

"Thanks, I'll stand," Peaches said quickly, drawing his focus away from the chair.

He went over to his Regency desk, the desk that had cost him an arm and a leg at Christie's, and sat on one corner of it. Folding his arms across his chest, he said, "The Evett family's in a crisis, as you're well aware. You know that I care deeply about all of them, and yet you said things to me last night about them that were vicious and perverted. You amazed me, frankly. You're entitled to your own opinion, Peaches, but I think that at this point it's best you leave my employ.''

Just like a businessman: make it quick; make it clean.

Peaches merely stared.

Businessman or no businessman, Nat responded to her stare with a dark flush of angry guilt. He went around to the back of his desk and sat down in the leather swivel chair that Linda, with Peaches's help, had bought him for his thirty-eighth birthday.

Pulling out the wide flat binder that held his personal checks, he said, ''You've put in long hours at the job since Linda's death; I'm perfectly aware of it. I think half a year's severance would be fair compensation.''

He began writing a check. Peaches gave him an ugly smile which was wasted on him as he filled out a blank, tore it from its record, then held it out to her.

His face was impassive as he said evenly, ''You have an evil mind, Peaches. If I ever hear you say another malevolent word against Linda, or anyone else that I hold dear, I promise you: It will be your last.''

She glanced at the amount, then folded the check and tucked it in one cup of her bra, exposing gratuitous flesh to him as she did so. Lifting her chin and arching one brow at him, she asked, ''Are you throwing me directly into the street? Or will I be allowed to pack my things and take them with me?''

''Take what you need,'' he said shortly. ''I'd prefer that you send for the rest.''

She could see that it filled him with loathing simply to have to speak with her. It made her want to drag him down to her level; to engage with her. She said with a sneer, ''My performance here has been nothing less than stellar. May I use you as a reference?''

But he refused to acknowledge that she was any longer in the room.

Flushing a deep, dark shade of humiliation, Peaches turned on her well-shod heel and left the room.

It was all the fault of the Evett bitch. *Damn* her to hell.

Helen Evett drove home like a madwoman; her trooper husband would've been shocked. She'd got the information she needed from the herbalist to confirm her goofy theory, and now she was ready to share it with Nat, because it didn't seem so goofy anymore. After that, they'd decide about the police. Helen had no proof, still; only the theory. But at least it was plausible.

The first words out of her mouth as she flung open the front door were, "Who's home?"

Out toddled her aunt. "Only me, dear," she said with a sweet look of sadness. "Becky's at the store, food shopping."

Helen didn't have to ask whether Russell had called. Nonetheless, she was fiercely optimistic. The day so far had been filled with amazing things, and it wasn't even noon.

"Aunt Mary, I have to go over to Nat's. I shouldn't be long. But I have to—maybe I should call first," she decided, and she ran to the kitchen phone and punched in his number. Busy.

She turned to her aunt, then frowned with concern. "You look awfully hot," she said, noticing the beads of perspiration on her aunt's rather fuzzy upper lip. "Are you feeling okay?"

Aunt Mary sighed and sat down on one of the oak chairs. "It's awfully warm today, isn't it?" she said unhappily. "Maybe I shouldn't have put on panty hose." She was wearing sky blue polyester pants and a floral blouse to match, because she'd rather melt than be caught in creased clothing. She slipped off her Cobblers and wiggled her toes, trying to create a breeze.

Helen, who was carrying a glass of cold water over to

her aunt, stopped and stared at her feet. Her aunt was wearing two pairs of panty hose, one on top of the other. *Oh, no,* she thought. *Please. Please don't slip any more than you have.*

"Aunt Mary . . . you were in such a hurry," she said softly, "that you doubled up on your panty hose. I've done the same thing myself. Why don't you take them both off? You'll be so much cooler."

The elderly woman looked at her feet with astonishment. "For heaven's sake." Her lined, pale cheeks rouged to pale pink. She looked at her niece, her eyes watery with tears, and said, "It's the same at the Senior Center. I can't remember any of the steps to the dances . . . any of the rules to the games. Lena," she said fearfully, "what will I do? Tell me what to do."

Helen stooped down to eye level with her aunt and took her trembling hands in hers. "You can go with me to the doctor on Tuesday," she said urgently. "You can get tests . . . this isn't as bad as you think. Sometimes there are perfectly good reasons for people to be forgetful. Plus, look at all the stress we're going through! My God—half the time I don't know if I'm coming or going!"

"Yes . . . yes," Aunt Mary said vaguely. "It's so hard to remember everything nowadays. Such a busy summer . . . so many people. Oh! Peaches Bartholemew called," she said, suddenly remembering. "She was looking for Nat. At nine in the morning! Here! It was almost rude."

Now it was Helen's turn to rouge up. "Did she say what she wanted?"

"No. She asked for you, too, but I told her you'd gone to the herbalist's. You know . . . her voice is so familiar. I'm sure I've heard it before. But I know I haven't met her. Have I?" she added timidly.

Helen shook her head, then said, "Unless it was at the Ice Cream Social."

Her aunt pursed her lips. "I don't think so. I would've remembered her name. It's so unusual. 'Peaches.' What does she look like?"

"Very beautiful. She dresses well. Long, auburn hair; she sometimes wears it in a braid, or a twist. She's tall. Good figure."

It was amazing, in fact, that Nat had been able to resist her.

In the meantime, Helen's aunt was frowning fiercely, her nose scrunched up, her mouth pressed firm, trying to place the voice with the face that Helen was describing. She looked like a contestant on *Jeopardy*.

"I know!" she cried, clapping her hands together. "I remember!" Her face became utterly joyous, younger by twenty years.

"It *was* at the Ice Cream Social. I thought she said she was someone's mother, not their nanny; but maybe I misunderstood her. She was, oh yes, I remember now, very interested in everything. And she said nice things about you, what a good mother you seemed to be; and I know I was bragging, dear, but I told her how you were bringing up the children so well by yourself . . . how you made Russell do chores for his allowance, and how Becky had to help with her car expenses by baby-sitting—I even told her you made them clean up the statue! Oh, I went on and on about you, dear. I think I bored her to tears. She hardly got a word in edgewise. I remember now! I do!"

The rumors about Satanism: Peaches was there.

The rumors about Linda: Peaches was there.

The rumors about Nat: Peaches was there.

Helen jumped up. "My God! How could I have been so stupid! It never occurred to me that *she* might want to bring me down. I'd never have guessed her motive! But she must have seen, way before I did, how Nat felt. Compared to what she'd already done, the Satanism—the cat—was child's play! An amusing way for her to get me out of the picture!''

She had another thought. "Aunt Mary! Did you tell her about all those weird soups you make? Did you tell her about the duck soup?"

"The *czarnina*? I may have. I remember she was curious about my last name . . . but then, she was curious about everything. We did talk about Polish food . . .''

"Oh my God.''

"Was that the wrong thing to do?'' Aunt Mary said fearfully.

"No, no, no. Don't worry about it. You've helped me a lot.''

She ran back to the phone and pressed the redial button. Busy. Damn it!

Turning to her startled aunt, she cried, "Stay right here. I'm going to Nat's. We've got her, Aunt Mary! We've got her!''

Helen ran out of the house with no more explanation than that. In the few minutes that it took to negotiate summer traffic between her house and Chestnut Street, she had more than enough time to work herself up into a belated fury. What had been mistrust, then loathing, now turned into a kind of full-blown outrage. Helen was beyond itemizing the injustices by this time; all she knew was that Peaches was evil, and she had to be locked away.

She rounded the corner onto Chestnut Street, which as usual was free of traffic. Her view of Nat's mansion was unimpeded. She could see Peaches ahead of her, loading a suitcase into the trunk of her Toyota.

No. She couldn't leave—she had to be stopped. Helen roared up alongside the Toyota just as Peaches dropped into the driver's seat. Leaving her own car door open, she ran around the front of the Volvo and up to the Toyota.

Peaches, catching sight of her, scowled and rolled up her window.

Furious, Helen slammed her hands against the window glass and shouted, "You murdered her! I can prove it! And all the rest! You evil, evil woman!"

With a squeal of her tires, Peaches tore literally out of Helen's grip, wrenching Helen's right hand in the process. Appalled at the thought that she was getting away, Helen ran up to the deep green door of the mansion. She lifted the brass knocker with her left hand and rammed the ship down on its pad. Nat had heard the commotion. He swung open the door with a look of wonder on his face.

"Where's Katie?" Helen said, charging past him.

"Upstairs, lying down. She has a stomachache. Why?"

"Oh my God, we have to get her to a hospital, then!" cried Helen.

"It's not that bad. She said Peaches gave her three candy bars, God knows why. What's wrong?"

"Call the police, call the police!" Helen said, dragging him over to his hall phone. "Do you have her license number? We have to stop her. She killed Linda!" she cried. "She's running away!"

"No, I booted her out," Nat said, amazed at the state Helen was in. "Calm down, calm down. What's going on?"

"I have to see Katie first!" Helen broke away from his grip and ran up the stairs. Katie was fine. She was sitting on the floor, playing with her drink-and-wet doll. Her reaction to Helen was a surprised grin.

"Hi, Mrs. Uhvett. You wanna play wif me?"

The sight of the child in her pink Oshkosh bib overalls and bow-topped hair was so at odds with what Helen feared she'd find that she felt, briefly, like a fool.

She made herself smile and blow a kiss to Katie and say, "I'll be back in a little while, honey," after which she backtracked into the hall where Nat was waiting to usher her into a quiet corner of the house. "C'mon," he said. "My study."

But Helen couldn't wait that long. "She'll get away!" she kept insisting to Nat on their way down the open, curving flight of stairs. "Don't you see? Linda didn't die of an overdose of prescription ergotamine. She was poisoned, somehow—with ergot!"

"What're you talking about? Ergot; ergotamine—they sound like the same thing."

"Yes, the drug is derived from the fungus ergot—from the dried sclerotium of the fungus is how the herbalist explained it. The first guy knew that, too, but I couldn't understand him, and—"

"—and I don't understand *you*, Helen," Nat said, more and more alarmed by her.

"What don't you understand? Peaches poisoned her! The autopsy showed the presence of an ergot alkaloid, but it didn't say where it came from—how could it?"

Helen picked up the phone on the priceless sycamore side table that graced the hall and handed it to him. "Call them!"

It seemed almost like a dream. In this perfectly exquisite environment a jungle snake had bit and poisoned, and now it was slithering away.

"And tell them what," he said, slamming the phone down in its cradle. "To put out an APB on Peaches because she murdered Linda by talking her into swallowing half a bottle of pills?"

"She didn't do it that way! She did it some other way, obviously—with a syringe or something. She tampered with something Linda ingested; maybe she even injected it directly—"

"Why for God's sake? Why would she murder Linda?"

"For you, of course—no, that's not true," Helen said.

She swung her sore hand in a wide arc around her. "For *this*, Nat! For all of this."

Obviously it had never occurred to him. "That's insane!" he said. "How could she think I'd offer it to her?"

If the situation weren't so tragic, it would almost be laughable. He was so naive. "She looks like an empress, Nat; all she lacks is the empire! She wouldn't be the first woman to do what it takes to get one."

He was still incredulous. "I can't believe she'd do something that . . . speculative!"

"For God's sake, you work in the stock market," Helen cried. "Does The Great Depression mean anything to you?"

"Jesus."

They were wasting time. "Nat . . . you know and I know that Linda is innocent. She didn't overdose, and she didn't commit suicide. Nat—you *know* that. After last night—you know!"

It was the first time since he'd come to her in the middle of the night, devastated by grief and remorse, that Helen had alluded to his experience. It was too sacred to invoke lightly, but Helen was invoking it now.

Some of what he'd felt last night came back to him in a rush; she could see it in his face. He bent his head, deep in concentration.

When he looked up again, his face was grim. "The police won't be able to do anything this fast," he said. "But I can call my bank."

They went into his study and he looked up the phone number, telling Helen what he'd paid Peaches, explaining to her that the only place where she could cash a check on the spot for that size was the bank the check was drawn on.

"I'll tell them there was a problem," he said, punching in the number. "I'll get them to try to stall. I'll go to the bank; you call the police. Get them here. You can keep me posted on my cell phone.''

The meander through the bank's hierarchy took an agony of minutes. Helen spent them pacing between the twin leather wing chairs that flanked the desk. Once, she stopped to stare through the floor-to-ceiling windows that looked out on the lush garden and vine-covered bricks of one wing of the house. Was the owl still there? She wished she knew.

Finally Nat hung up. ''Okay, we're set. When she gets there, they'll take their time. I'm on my way. Keep an eye on Katie, would you?''

Helen nodded, eager to have him off in pursuit. He was walking past the sycamore table in the hall when the phone rang. ''Maybe the bank,'' he said, pausing to answer.

But it wasn't the bank. Nat's face looked startled, then glad, then calm by turns. ''Hey,'' he said casually. He gave Helen a fierce look, then put his index finger to his lips before he said, ''How's it goin', Russ?''

Chapter 28

Russell. It was all Helen could do not to cry out his name. With a wrenching effort, she made herself keep silent as she crept up to Nat's side and tried to overhear what her son was saying.

But this was Russell. He wasn't saying much. Between Nat's "uh-huh's" and "mm-hmm's," she wasn't able to make out a single word, only that it was definitely Russ's voice, mumbly and reluctant.

Was he hungry? Was he safe? Was he near? Helen tried to mouth the phrases for Nat to ask, then abandoned the attempt when he turned his back on her to concentrate.

"Yeah, I thought it was you . . . yeah . . . sure, I don't blame you. Mm-hmm . . . okay. See you soon."

Nat hung up. Helen grabbed his arm and cried, " 'See you soon'? He's coming home? What does that mean, 'See you soon'? Is he all right? Is he—?"

Nat cut in quickly to say, "He sounded okay, Helen. Tired. Disheartened, maybe. But he sounded okay. He wants to meet with me to talk."

"Meet with you! Where? When?"

"Right now. I can't tell you where; he asked me not to."

"*What*? You *have* to tell me!"

"I gave him my word, Helen; don't ask me that."

"Nat—I'm his *mother*. You have to tell me, Nat!" she cried, cut down by his impossible demand.

Nat frowned, then shook his head with an anguished look of his own. "Don't look at me like that, Helen. If Russ and I are going to have any kind of life together, then he has to feel he can trust me."

"Yes," she said numbly. "I understand." She was almost to the point where she did understand. Instead she bowed her head and whispered, "All I ask is where he is. That's all."

Nat let out an exasperated, tormented sigh. "All right! I'll tell you, but on God's honor, you can't ever let him know that I did. He's at the Common. With any luck I can bring him back here to you and still make it to the bank in time to intercept Peaches."

Peaches! Helen had forgotten completely about her. "Yes . . . hurry," she urged.

He left her and she rushed to the salon that fronted the street, throwing open the inside shutters in time to see him tear off in the Porsche. Light poured through the formal, empty room, highlighting the subtle patina of well-polished wood, the bleached antiquity of the patterned rug, but making the room look, somehow, more unused than ever. Too many ghosts. Helen shuddered and fled upstairs to tend to poor, neglected Katie, an innocent pawn in a game to which only Peaches knew the rules.

But Helen found that she could no more focus on Katie than she could memorize the Constitution. Her concentration was somewhere else entirely, with her own lost child. The decision she made to call Becky was no decision at all; it was an act of pure, driving instinct.

"Becky!" she said when her daughter answered the phone. "Thank God you're home. Russell's back. I'm at

Nat's. How fast can you get here? Don't ask questions, honey—move!''

Becky, loyal soldier, said excitedly, "I'm on my way, Mom!"

Helen waited and paced, beside herself with anxiety. What if Nat couldn't persuade Russ to stay? Only mothers could do that. No one was closer to a son than his mother. Nat couldn't understand about Russell and Hank. He said himself he hadn't been close to his own father. And in any case, she was the one who'd said the hurtful things that drove Russ away; she was the one, the only one, who could take them back.

Before Becky got the chance to put a foot over the threshold, Helen was out the door.

"Watch Katie!" she cried over her shoulder to her astonished daughter. "I just want to make sure Russ is okay. I just want to see. I'll be back . . . few minutes, tops. Watch Katie!"

She ran to her Volvo—amazingly, still in the street with its engine running and driver-side door open—and got in . . . racing toward the rendezvous spot . . . trying out excuses in her mind to account for her presence on the Common if she were seen.

A block away on Summer Street, Peaches watched from her car as the white Volvo streaked through the intersection.

Goodness. Everyone's in such a hurry today, she thought with a grim smile. She pulled back out into traffic, ready to make the loop back around to Chestnut Street.

All in all, it had been a good decision not to race them to the bank. Why risk everything for six months' wages when there was a whole damned pension plan, wrapped up in velvet, waiting under a seat cushion in Nat's study?

*   *   *

If Helen had been born two hundred years earlier, she might have been going off to the Common—known then as the Swamp—for no other reason than to fetch the family livestock after a day of grazing. But she was a thoroughly modern woman on a desperately modern mission: to reconnect with her son.

Surely the Common was the place to do it. The family shared a lifetime of memories there, all of them happy. Concerts, kites and ice cream; May Days, Haunted Houses, and caroling—nothing bad had ever happened to them at the Common.

Pray God today was no different.

She pressed forward on her mission, leaning over the wheel like a jockey over his steed, urging the car forward. Pointless: traffic was bumper to bumper. Worse still, there were no parking places anywhere near the Common. Since it was midday on a Friday, it should've come as no surprise; but Helen was moving in a dream, where neither time nor days had meaning.

She crept along Hawthorne Boulevard and then, in desperation, brazenly fell in with the cars looping around the Common, scanning the triangle of green for signs of Russ and Nat. She passed almost under the shadow of the memorial to Roger Conant, the site of the mischief that had started it all; but her mind, heart, and soul were focused on the park.

She saw them before they saw her and slammed on her brakes. They were sitting on a bench at the north end, as far from the crush of tourists milling around the Witch Museum as they could get. Helen let out her breath in a burst of relief, like a diver who's been under water too long. *He's home . . . alive . . . safe . . . with Nat.*

Her heart went out to both of them: to the man and to the boy, both of them feeling their way gingerly through the conversation, both of them in clothes that could use a wash. Nat was turned part of the way around to face Russ, listening intently to him. He was leaning with his right forearm on his thigh, his left hand gripping the backrest behind Russ's shoulder. Russ was sitting bolt upright, his palms flat on the bench alongside him, the toes of his Nikes lifting and falling alternately. Once or twice he lifted one hand to make a point.

It was clear, even to Helen, that they were connecting on some level; that Russ was ready to come home. She had to smile. She'd already seen him say more in the last two minutes than he'd said in the last twelve months. It was like a dream, a dream come true.

And like most dreams, it ended abruptly.

The car behind Helen, patient so far, decided that she had no real point in stopping there and gave her a couple of polite toots. No big deal; but Russell turned around, saw the Volvo, and jumped up, clearly outraged. Then Nat saw her and stood up, just as outraged.

And then, perhaps because she'd been jolted out of her euphoria, Helen suddenly remembered the biggest outrage of all: Peaches was still at large.

And Becky and Katie weren't afraid of her.

In an agony of decisiveness, Helen took off in a rush, leaving her son to fend for himself. What was she doing, skulking around the Common? She should be at Nat's house, guarding the children. Her heart went flying into her throat and there it stayed, nearly choking her as it hammered home the simple, pounding thought: She knows we know.

Helen rejoined the procession headed vaguely in the direction of Chestnut Street. Cursing the crosswalks, gnawing her lip, pounding on the wheel with her hand in frustration—none of it did any good. The cars continued to creep along, one behind the other, like a row of fuzzy caterpillars going as fast as they can. She stopped at a red light. A UPS

truck, turning out of the intersecting traffic, pulled in front
of her as her light turned green, further adding to her torment. Now she was not only paralyzed, but blind, seeing
nothing ahead of her but a vast brown wall.

Almost in self-preservation, to keep herself from going
mad, she reverted to a dreamlike state where neither time
nor distance had any relevance at all. Only the goal mattered: the wish that had to be fulfilled if the dream were to
stay a dream, and not crumble into a nightmare.

She tried to make herself think the way Peaches would
think, and she succeeded only too well. *Half a year's wages
is nothing to her. Her appetite is more voracious than that.
She knows where the valuables are kept; Nat said so himself. She'll use her key. Becky will be upstairs, playing with
Katie in the nursery. She won't possibly hear Peaches come
in.*

Nightmare thoughts. Helen picked her way through them,
turning them over, looking for glimmers of light. *If the
jewelry, the securities, whatever, are in Nat's study, she
may just sneak in, take what she wants, and leave.* It was
one small ember of hope.

Helen's next thought was like a bucket of cold water on
it: *If the things are in Nat's bedroom, Becky will probably
hear her.*

Suddenly she remembered the tea party: remembered Katie, running into the room clutching a diamond tennis bracelet in her hand, and Peaches, stepping in to relieve the child
of it.

She should've known then! The evidence was all around
her; but it was in shards, like the wreckage of a broken
mirror, and she was too blinded by fragments to see.

Helen tortured herself with reminders of missed signals
and wrong assumptions all the way to Chestnut Street. But
when she turned onto the broad, quiet avenue and saw the
Toyota parked in the drive of the mansion three doors down

from Nat's, that's when she knew. Her latest, worst fears were right on target.

She's back, and she knows Becky's in there. By now Helen had no doubt that Peaches recognized the car Becky drove. By now Helen assumed that Peaches was practically omniscient. She was giving Peaches, too late, the credit she deserved.

She parked her Volvo across the rear end of the Toyota, blocking it from being able to back out. Fear clawed at her heart as she ran down the street to the red-brick mansion, then took the steps in a bound. Without much hope, she tried the door. Locked.

Her one recourse was to frighten Peaches out the back. Noise; it was the only weapon she had. She thought of a blueberry farm she'd once gone to, where a cannon boomed every fifteen minutes to scare away crows.

Her mind was working on some new, unplumbed level as she glanced frantically around, then snatched up an iron boot scraper that sat on the stoop. Taking aim at the elegant deadlights that lined either side of the door, she began smashing through the intricate pattern of lead-framed panes of delicate, aged glass, setting up a horrendous, SWAT-like racket. If the alarm went off, so much the better.

But it didn't. She heard nothing inside—no screams of panic, no slamming doors, no fleeing footsteps—as she fumbled with the broken glass, gashing her arm in the process, and then threw open the deadbolt from inside. She pushed at the heavy door with her wounded arm, leaving a slash of blood across its deep green surface, and burst into the hall, more terrified by the silence than she would be of gunfire.

She ran straight to the study, foolishly holding her arm up to slow the flow of blood on the Turkish carpet there. In one sweeping glance, she took in the marine painting tossed carelessly on the desk; the wide-open safe on the wall; the long brown envelopes and blue-bound documents scattered beneath it. A hoarse groan of anguish caught in her throat.

Where was Becky?

She fled from the study back into the hall and took the curving stairs two at a time, her breath coming in long, ragged gasps, her brain spinning light-headedly. She no longer knew or cared if she was behaving rationally now; it was irrelevant. She ran into Katie's room: the feed-and-wet doll, alone on the bright blue rug.

Where was Katie?

Nearly blinded by fear now, she turned, stumbling, and fled down the hall to Nat's room.

No one. Nothing. Not even the scent of *Enchantra*, which deep down inside she'd been hoping to detect.

Sobbing with frustration, she ran back out into the hall, then threw open the door to Peaches's room, but it, too, had nothing to say and no one to show.

I didn't look in the music room, she realized. She ran back out to the second-floor landing, peering over the mahogany handrail and past the enormous chandelier into the vast expanse of the hall below.

But she could see nothing beyond the rich kaleidoscope of Oriental rug that seemed to shift and pulsate below her. She whipped her head back, afraid that she was going to faint and pitch headlong over the rail, and closed her eyes, taking deep draughts of air, trying to reverse her giddiness.

She opened her eyes. On the landing above her, across the open expanse of extravagantly empty space, stood the woman who had taken profound and obscene liberties with Helen's life and the lives of all she held dear.

She was dressed in a short loose shift of teal silk and, as always, she looked nothing like a nanny. Anyone would've thought that the petulant child in pink overalls that she held in her arms was her daughter.

"Where is she?" cried Helen. "Where's Becky?"

Peaches smiled. "Your daughter is refreshingly naive for a sixteen-year-old."

"If you've hurt her," Helen said in a shaking voice, "I'll kill you."

"Ta. What kind of talk is that for a pillar of the community?" Peaches asked, letting the nylon carryall that was slung over her shoulder slide to the floor. She shifted Katie from one hip to the other.

It was such a mild response; Helen made herself believe it meant Becky was safe. "Why did you come back?" she asked, almost in a wail. "Why couldn't you just keep going—away from here, away from us?"

Again the nanny smiled. "You're not stupid, Helen. You know why."

"Take what you want, then! Take it and go!"

Katie began to squirm. "Pee-e-ches," she whimpered. "I wanna get down."

"In a minute, sweetie," Peaches crooned. She gazed down at Helen from behind the third floor balustrade, its painted balusters standing like short white sentinels in front of her. In a pleasantly musing voice she said, "Do you have any idea, Helen, how awkward you've made things for me?"

"I've done nothing to you," Helen said. "And neither have the children. Especially the children. Please . . . put Katie down."

"Yes, Peaches," Katie pouted. "I wanna go down. Put me down," she said, trying to squirm out of the nanny's grasp.

"All right, Katie," Peaches said suddenly. "Here. Sit." She twisted Katie to face forward and flopped her down on the banister like a rag doll on a Christmas mantel.

For a second, the child was too stunned to say or do anything. Then she looked down over her shoes at three stories of open space and began to wriggle and scream. In a panic she tried to turn back to Peaches—her little arms were groping wildly—but Peaches held her pinned to the rail.

It all happened so fast. Helen stared wide-eyed and disbelieving at the drama playing out on the landing above hers. It was beyond dream, beyond nightmare, beyond anything her imagination could possibly conjure. "Oh, Peaches . . . don't . . . please . . . I'm begging you," she cried as the child became more and more hysterical.

"Begging? That must be hard, for a woman like you," Peaches said loudly over Katie's screams.

"If you want me to, I'll beg. I'll do anything. Only tell me what you want."

Where was Katie's mother? What good was a ghost if it had no power? Why wasn't Linda smiting Peaches with one fell cosmic blow? The question, then the answer, zipped through Helen's mind like consecutive flashes of lightning. *If Peaches is felled, then Katie will fall.*

"What I *want*," said Peaches with a sudden, devastating shift in tone, "is to get the hell out of here!" She added more calmly, "I'd prefer that you didn't follow me."

Helen said, "I won't! I won't! As long as I can have Katie." She was becoming more and more lightheaded, presumably from loss of blood; every second counted now.

Katie was almost totally unmanageable, screaming and kicking to be let off the rail. It was a wonder that Helen was able to hear Peaches say above the din, "You want Katie? Why didn't you say so?"

Her smile, evil and merciless, told Helen more plainly than a billboard what was to follow.

Peaches lifted the terrified child from the rail. Holding Katie by the armpits, she swung her back and alongside. "Here. Catch," she said, then bent low, twisted, and hurled the child, like a sack of grain, over the banister and high into the air.

Helen's mouth dropped open in horror. She couldn't scream, couldn't run, couldn't do anything except grip the rail with a kind of righteous force as she watched Katie, in slow motion, arc up and up and then crest and then begin, in even slower, more horrible motion, her descent.

An unholy fury possessed Helen. It wasn't right, destroying the innocent. It was cruel, it was wrong, she wouldn't stand for it any longer. Filled with a power she never knew she had, filled with a blinding, limitless resolve, she felt her whole being, every atom of it, lift in place, then come down hard against the balustrade, parting it in two, sending herself hurtling into the same empty space as the child above her had been; trying, ludicrously, to catch the child in flight.

Helen landed on the floor of the entry with sickening speed. Somewhere in her consciousness she heard a major bone break and felt searing pain rip through her leg. She blacked out from the agony of it, then made herself revive. *Katie.*

Groaning with pain, she forced her eyes to flutter open, then peer around the floor. *No Katie.*

And no screaming. The only sound Helen heard was a small, whimpering plea, like a puppy left too long in the cold. Helen rolled on her back, nearly blacking out again from the pain, and opened her eyes.

Two stories above her, hanging from the exquisite chandelier by one pink strap of her OshKosh overalls, was the three-year-old whose life, Helen now knew, meant more to her than her own.

"Oh, Katie," she said in a breathless moan. "It's all right . . . just . . . shhh . . . it's all right . . . shhh . . . I'm coming. . . ."

She rolled back on her side and began to drag herself to

the infinitely finite circle directly under the chandelier. Each new inch of ground was a new and bloody skirmish in the monumental battle to get there. The urge to black out was as powerful as the equal and opposite urge to get to the circle before something gave way—the OshKosh strap, the chandelier, the child's small beating heart.

There were no sounds now, not even Katie's random broken sobs; only the slow, swishing hiss of Helen's clothing dragging across the pile of the Oriental carpet. Helen had no idea if Katie was conscious or not. She only knew that she had to reach the shadow of the chandelier.

She was nearly there when she heard the sound of tearing metal. Helen stopped, despite herself, and looked up. She saw that the sconce that had hooked Katie's overalls was hanging at a hideous, asymmetric angle. Above and beyond it she saw Peaches, still on the third floor landing, staring down at the unfolding drama.

A car door slammed outside. It was like the hushed call of a director: *action*.

Katie began suddenly to scream. Peaches turned and fled from the balustrade. Helen crawled a last handful of inches before the sconce tore free from the chandelier and Katie came dropping like a stone onto Helen's broken thigh, sending her, finally and against her will, into the sweet release of prolonged unconsciousness.

Chapter 29

When Helen came to, she half expected to see Katie playing pony-boy on her shattered thigh: the pain was unbelievable.

But Katie was gone. In her place, two paramedics—the burly one looked kinder—were in the process of rearranging Helen's leg fragments in a splint. In a near-swoon, Helen rolled her head from one side to the other, looking for other, more beloved faces.

Becky was standing a little to the left, pressing Katie close to her shoulder, stroking her cheek, soothing her whimpers. Next to her stood Russell; even through her tear-blurred vision, Helen could see that his nose was red from crying. To Helen's right, Nat was on his knees, doing for her what Becky was doing for Katie.

All safe . . . all alive. Helen's smile, so barely there, was profoundly joyous. "I feel . . . like Dorothy . . . in the *Wizard of Oz*," she whispered.

"Oh, Mom . . . oh, Mom," Becky said, tears running freely down her cheeks. "I saw it . . . I saw what happened."

"You coulda died," said Russell in a voice as pallid as his face. "You almost could've."

"She'd never do that," Becky said in distress to her brother. "How can you say that?" She turned back to Helen. "I got free out of the closet . . . I saw you. . . . I saw the banister just . . . split in half . . . ," she said, covering her hand over Katie's ear and pressing her close. "Mr. Byrne said the glue in the joint must've dried out. It almost looked like you were pushing it apart—"

Nat cut her short. "Hey, kids, c'mon . . . let these guys do their job. You're not making it any easier."

He turned back to Helen and said in a low, shaken voice, "Everyone's fine. *You* kinda took it on the chin, darlin' . . . ," he said, trying to manage a smile. "But it's over now, Helen. It's over."

"Peaches . . . ?"

"It's over."

After that he hustled the children into the music room and cleared the way for the paramedics to get Helen onto a collapsible stretcher and into the ambulance.

"As soon as Janet gets here," he told Helen last thing, "she'll take the kids back to your house and I'll follow you to the hospital. I wish I could come with you now, but—"

"No," Helen said faintly. "Stay . . . until Janet." In a groggy, pain-drenched voice she said, "How did she die?"

"Later . . . it can wait," he said, more somber than ever.

She motioned to the paramedics for a moment's more time. "Please, Nat," she begged. It seemed to her that she had to know. That she had to put Peaches Bartholemew behind her before she could begin the rest of her life.

Nat seemed ultimately to understand that. He said in a flat-calm voice, "She was climbing down the ivy that's trained up the back of the house. Her carryall was slung diagonally across her chest. It got caught in the growth when she lost her footing on the way down. The handle caught around her neck, breaking it."

Helen closed her eyes; tears surprised her by spilling out. "Who found her?" she whispered, dreading the answer.

"Thank God, the police. They didn't see her at first. They saw the jewelry, splattered on the ground below her. It fell out of the bag as she . . ."

"Hanged there. Oh, God."

"It's over, Helen. Go. I'll be there for you as soon—ah, there's Janet now. I'll be there for you, Helen. Period."

Six days later, Helen was out of the hospital. Her doctors called her spunky and Nat called her nuts; her insurance company was thrilled. Her aunt thought it was scandalous, but Helen didn't care. She had minds to soothe and hearts to fill, at home and at school.

Her shattered femur had been expertly rodded; she'd been able to avoid the dread cast-brace. All that remained was to master the use of crutches. It wasn't easy. She hadn't given her son nearly enough credit for his earlier nimbleness on them.

Russ teased her often about her awkwardness; it gave him great joy. (Without asking her, he'd also painted her crutches bright yellow, because he was afraid that someone might not see them and knock them out of his mother's grip.)

Helen stayed at home for a full, luxurious week, surrounded by flowers and fruit baskets and the good wishes of the parents who'd stayed loyal through it all. It seemed to her that after months of stop-and-start agony, her life was moving into a smoother stretch, like a river that hits sudden rapids and, just as unexpectedly, flattens and becomes serene again.

The first good news had come early. While Aunt Mary was visiting in the hospital, a sharp-eyed surgeon had taken one look at her and, after a few questions, suggested that she be tested for hypothyroidism. Aunt Mary's puffy eyes, her facial fuzz, her distressing bouts of forgetfulness—all were symptoms, he ventured, of the eminently treatable disease. There was dancing (well, hobbling) in the hospital halls that night.

There was more good news. Nat had decided to leave his job and work at home. He couldn't give it a hundred percent anymore, he said, and it didn't seem right to give it any less.

As for the brick mansion with its bloodstained door, it would be sold.

"Too many traumas; too many brutal memories for Katie and for me," he'd told Helen in the hospital. "I can't go into the garden, my old bedroom, my new bedroom. Katie—well, I wouldn't think of taking her up the stairs again."

"It's been in your family so long," Helen had said, though she agreed completely.

Nat had merely shrugged. "It's time to move on."

Go where money is, his great-great-grandfather had commanded. The words were like a curse that had hung over the majestic, sorrowful house on Chestnut Street. They had sent Nat away from his home in search of a fortune and had drawn Peaches into its midst on the same wretched quest.

And like any curse, it had left in its wake death and destruction and burned-out dreams.

So Katie had stayed at Helen's house for a couple of days; but by the time Helen was out of the hospital, she and Nat had moved into a small, charming Victorian rented out by an elderly gardener who'd decided to move to Vancouver to be nearer her daughter.

"I'm really getting the hang of this parent thing," he'd told Helen one afternoon on his way to pick up Katie from

The Open Door. "And the house is working out great. It's just the place to crank up a new career. They say everyone has at least one book inside him. Mine happens to be a common-sense guide to investing—not the Great American Novel—but what the hell. Maybe the novel will follow."

Another blessing: The Open Door was still open. Not many parents and preschoolers went through it anymore, but it was still open. The appalling death of Peaches Bartholemew had sent another round of parents withdrawing, of course; violence to them was violence, and Helen couldn't blame them.

"At least the halls aren't buzzing with all those false rumors anymore," Janet had told her boss on the phone.

"Why bother," Helen had answered wryly, "when the real facts are so much more sensational?"

A version of those facts had made it into the Sunday paper; but much of the story was too painful to tell. Helen had declined to give interviews, so the world would never know the whole, sordid truth: that Peaches had somehow poisoned Linda Byrne with ergotamine, either in pharmaceutical or natural form.

It seemed likely that the nanny had doctored some of the old Tylenol capsules that they'd found in the medicine cabinet. Her fingerprints had been found on the bottle, along with Linda's. But the fingerprints weren't proof, and in any case the question was moot, because Linda was dead and so was Peaches.

The real question was, how could an innocent like Linda have allowed a demon like Peaches to touch her soul? Not an hour had passed in which Helen hadn't pondered it. But like most dark mysteries, it was fated to drag through time unsolved.

But now it was Monday morning, and Helen, with Becky's help, had dressed in her favorite sundress, the pale yellow one dotted with blue cornflowers, and was waiting

for the arrival of Nat to take her to school for the first time
since Russ had run away.

Becky wasn't very happy about it. "The doctors wanted
you to stay home for a month, Mom," she insisted as she
cleaned away the breakfast dishes. "The best you could
whittle them down to was three weeks. Why are you going
back in two?"

"Because I want to thank the parents who've hung in
there," Helen said, draining the last of her coffee. "This
has been a long and bumpy ride for them."

"*Them?* What about *us*?"

Helen gave her daughter a melancholy smile and said,
"We knew we were innocent. They didn't."

Becky was having a harder time than Helen with the
parents' faintheartedness—but then, Becky wasn't a parent.
"The school was almost empty last Thursday when I
picked up that stuff for you," she said indignantly. "I
didn't see any great show of faith."

Helen shrugged and said, "When you're older, you'll—"

The mellow toot of Nat's new van alerted them to start
Helen on her way. Fending off her daughter's offers of
help, Helen slung her handbag across her chest, took up
her crutches, and began her awkward step-thump to the
front door.

By the time she reached it, Nat was on the other side,
with his bright-morning grin that perfectly matched hers.
They spoke the same language, those grins: *I'm so happy
that you're alive.*

Helen waved to Katie, sitting in the backseat, and Katie
waved back with both hands.

"She's been wild with excitement that you're coming,"
Nat said as he hovered over Helen while she poked her
way slowly down the steps. "She brought you her favorite
barrette to wear. Look thrilled."

Helen flashed Nat a look of pure love. "I *am* thrilled."

With his help, she got herself into the van, then made a big fuss over Katie's gift and promptly clipped it to her hair.

"It looks pretty," Katie said, clutching her hands together and cocking her head appraisingly. "Pink is pretty. I like pink best. Don't you like pink best?"

That was the opening theme in a happy monologue that lasted most of the way to school. There was one brief pause, during which Helen said to Nat, "I've been trying to prepare myself for today, but—"

"But baloney. The school's still standing. I say, that's a miracle in itself." He reached over and took her hand. "Give it time, Helen. You'll build your business back up."

"I've been thinking of maybe changing the location . . . maybe even the name," she conceded, blushing to admit it.

"Don't you dare."

She didn't have the heart to tell him she'd been thinking of selling out altogether. In any case, they never got a chance to get another word in edgewise.

By the time Nat pulled up in front of the little brick bank, Helen was ready to stick her crutch on the gas pedal and send the van off again. A crowd had gathered, and it didn't look kind.

Curiosity seekers. She averted her gaze from them.

Nat helped her out of the van. "All set, darlin'?" he murmured. She nodded and the three of them—Helen on her crutches, Nat holding his daughter by the hand—began their march to the front door of The Open Door.

Helen scanned their faces, all of them looking either sheepish or frankly curious. They were faces she knew. She hadn't seen some of them since the first wave of panic after the picnic. There were the Baers . . . Mrs. Stickney . . .

Lynn Comford. Apparently *everyone* had come to stare. An air of awkward embarrassment seemed to hang over the gathering. No one, obviously, knew what to say.

In the meantime, a group of mothers and their children were rushing to the front from the parking area, unwilling to miss a thing. The scene had the look of the Academy Awards—but the feel of Gallows Hill.

Flushing with emotion, Helen smiled bravely and kept her eyes fixed on the wide stone step that lay at the threshold of the big glass door. She had no desire to trip and fall—if the pain didn't kill her, the humiliation certainly would.

She worked her crutches through the crowd and onto the stone step. Then, from behind her she heard a single loud clap. Followed by another. And another. The clapping became steadier, louder, evolving into a slow, sad drumroll of applause. Helen glanced at some of the faces. More than one had tears rolling down.

She was stunned: clever Gwen Alaran—in tears. Little Sarah, gashed at the picnic, there with her mom and dad. Candy Green, bearing flowers . . . Henry holding their daughter Astra . . .

All applauding: not in jubilation; not with any hip-hip-hoorays; not with grins, or backslapping, or fists in the air. What Helen saw, all around her, was a community expression of regret and apology. Completely unprepared for it, she felt goose bumps lifting the hairs on her arms. She had to bite her lower lip and fight back tears. On the wide step she turned on her crutches and said in a trembling voice, "Thank you, everyone."

Inside, more tears, many smiles, more applause. Preschoolers from other years—now young boys and girls— were there, and their mothers and fathers. Nannies—loving, tender nannies whom Helen respected and liked—were there. Russell was there! Becky! She knew! And Aunt Mary, blowing her nose.

And Janet—steadfast, loyal Janet—was there, standing by her office, tears flowing freely. She threw her fleshy arms out wide, then remembered to restrain her enthusiasm and caught Helen, balanced on crutches, gently by her shoulders.

"Welcome back, Helen Evett," she said with quivering lips, and kissed Helen on her cheek. She pointed to a banner overhead: WELCOME BACK.

Helen managed to whisper, "Janet, was this all your idea?"

Janet smiled and nodded toward the tall, grave man riding shotgun alongside Helen's crutches. Helen whipped her head around. "Nat!"

His eyes were dancing with pleasure but his expression was bland as he said, "Hey . . . my kid's gonna be late for school."

Helen continued her step-thump down the hall toward her own office. Teachers, mothers, fathers . . . and everywhere, the children she loved; had always loved; would always love. At the door Helen turned again to say thank you, but it was hard. The words were tangled around her heart, and her heart was caught in her throat.

From behind his mother's skirt appeared little Alexander Lagor, clutching his Thomas the Tank Engine in one hand, thrusting a clump of white lilies at Helen with the other.

"These are for you, Mrs. Evett. B'cause you got hurt."

"I gave Mrs. Evett a barrette," Katie chimed in. "A pink one!"

"Yes, you did, Katie. Thank you, Alexander," Helen said softly to the shy little boy. "They're very beautiful."

Alexander shuffled backward toward his mother and didn't stop until he was hidden safely behind her skirt again.

Janet announced cheerfully, "Everyone? For those who don't have to go on to work—and for those who do—there are milk and cookies, coffee and doughnuts in the assembly room."

The little brick bank had room for them all.

Epilogue

Helen's moan of passion turned into one of dismay.

"Oh, no! Here they come. Hurry, Nat!"

"Lena," Nat groaned in a voice more hoarse than amused. "You think I can turn it on and off like a water spigot?"

Helen wound her fingers through his thick hair and gazed up at him. The blue eyes under his glistening brow were a little unfocused.

She knew the look. "Yeah," she said in a sexy, lazy taunt. "I do."

She pulled him down to meet her kiss, bringing him to exactly the level of passion that was required to make the spigot flow freely, then pushed him away with a giggle. "Hurry! Clothing!"

Nat jumped out of bed and into his brand-new Bermuda shorts while Helen grabbed a handful of tissues, slapped them between her thighs, and made a dash for the bathroom.

"For a lady with a rod through her femur, you move pretty fast," Nat said in admiration. "And you don't look bad doin' it, either."

She laughed at the pun and slammed the door in his face.

Just in time, too. The predictable knock at their door came within seconds, and Becky ushered Katie into the room.

"Daddy, Daddy!" cried Katie. "I saw a starfish, but it was dead and Becky said it would stink if we took it back to Salem."

"Hi, Mom!" Becky called through the bathroom door.

Helen opened it. "Hi-hi," she said, knotting a batik pareo around the bathing suit she'd slipped on. "Where's Russ?"

"In the game room with the kid from two-sixteen."

"An' I saw a crab—it walked like this, backward," Katie said, sticking out her behind and shimmying in reverse. "And then I saw . . . um . . . this black thing with . . . like a porcupine has?" She turned to Becky for help.

"Sea urchin, sweetie," said Becky.

"Aunt Mary called," said Helen. "She says hi."

"I bet she's sorry she didn't come."

"With the backgammon tournament this week at the center? Are you kidding?"

"An' those things could stick you if you stepped on 'em!" Katie said, tugging at Helen's pareo. "I didn't go by them, though. Becky carried me so I could see them in the water."

"How was the beach?" Nat asked Becky. "Empty? Crowded?"

"Great! I met some kids my age. They want to meet me down at the pool," Becky said. "If you want me, that's where I'll be. Just shout."

She flounced out of the room, then turned back at the door that separated the suite. "Y'know—I never knew a honeymoon could be such fun."

Her mother and stepfather exchanged a look. "Yeah. Neither did we," Helen said dryly.

"Oh. Do you want me to watch Katie some more?"

"No, no . . . you go ahead. Have fun," said Helen, sighing.

"Okay," Becky said uncertainly, and left, a little less bouncy than before.

She left the suite and Nat and Helen burst out laughing.

"I heard that!" Becky said from the hall.

When he was sure she was out of earshot, Nat shook his head and said, "Whose idea was this family honeymoon, anyway? Katie, wait . . . not on the bed . . . let me wipe the sand off your feet first."

"Oh-h-h, come on," Helen coaxed. "It's Bermuda! The kids are loving it. And it's the last break we'll all have together for a while. You like it, don't you, Katie?" she asked her newest child.

"Yes!" said Katie, standing unsteadily on one foot as her father brushed the sand out of her toes with his fingers. "Especially the starfish. I wanna go back and get it."

"This little piggy's in trouble *now*," said Nat, wriggling her toe menacingly.

"Oh, Daddy! I'm too old for that game."

"Oooh, Miss Hoity-Toity! I hope you're not too old for a nap?"

"I'm *definitely* too old for a nap."

"That's what I thought you'd say. What about some quiet time instead?"

"How about a snack and then some quiet time?" Helen asked.

A deal was struck. Helen settled Katie in the adjoining room with a glass of milk, a Bermuda tea biscuit, and a Dr. Seuss, then came back to see Nat bending over the balcony rail, looking down at the pool.

"I'm glad she didn't see you leaning over like that," Helen chided softly.

Nat sighed. "I know. I wonder if she'll ever get over the fear."

"In time."

He waved—obviously at Becky and her new friends—then came back inside. "I don't like the look of the fella she's talking to. I wish she'd wear something more . . . modest . . . than that bikini thing."

Helen laughed and said, "They all dress like that. Heck, if I looked like her, *I'd* dress like that. At least she wears both pieces."

Nat sighed again. "Why do you think I didn't want us to go to a *French* island?"

He made it sound like a fate worse than death.

Helen wrapped her arms around him from behind and leaned her cheek on his back. "You are so sweet. Fatherhood is going to make you an old man in no time flat."

"Well . . . it's a whole new set of worries, a seventeen-year-old. It makes four look easy."

"And don't forget Russell."

"Ah . . . Russ," Nat said, his voice swelling with affection. "My man. That boy is so cool."

"What, cool. He's a typical fifteen-year-old," she said, utterly grateful for it. "Except taller."

"Did I tell you he beat me at the gym four games in a row? Michael Jordan could take lessons."

Smiling contentedly, Helen ducked under Nat's arm and together they stood and looked out at the serene vista before them. It was a perfect Bermuda day. Soft breeze, bright sun, pink sand, blue sea . . . the whole idyllic scene, framed by soaring palm trees to the left and to the right. The gentle rollers that slid over the sand seemed—to Helen, in her present mood—to have come from a great, great distance; from somewhere where angels cavorted with dolphins and spirits rained blessings on all living things.

"I see a basketball scholarship ahead," Nat said dreamily. "I see Duke . . . Seton Hall . . . Notre Dame . . ."

The words tripped off his tongue reverently, a father's litany of hallowed places.

"We'll go to all his games," Nat said, lost in his fantasy. "We'll cheer him on. We'll get thrown out of motels for having rowdy victory celebrations. We'll—"

Helen gave him a squeeze. "We'll do the best we can, my love," she said, gazing out at the sea. "We'll do the best we can."

Only in his dreams has Burke Grisham, the once-dissolute Earl of Thornwald, seen a lady as exquisite as Catherine Snow. Now, standing before him at last is the mysterious beauty whose life he has glimpsed in strange visions—whose voice called him back from death, and the shimmering radiance beyond, on the bloody field of Waterloo. But she is also the widow of the friend he destroyed: the one woman who scorns him; the one woman he must possess...

A Glimpse of Heaven

Barbara Dawson Smith

"An excellent reading experience from a master writer. A triumphant and extraordinary success!"
—*Affaire de Coeur*

KAT MARTIN

Award-winning author of *Creole Fires*

GYPSY LORD
_____ 92878-5 $5.99 U.S./$6.99 Can.

SWEET VENGEANCE
_____ 95095-0 $4.99 U.S./$5.99 Can.

BOLD ANGEL
_____ 95303-8 $5.99 U.S./$6.99 Can.

DEVIL'S PRIZE
_____ 95478-6 $5.99 U.S./$6.99 Can.

MIDNIGHT RIDER
_____ 95774-2 $5.99 U.S./$6.99 Can.

Against the backdrop of an elegant Cornwall mansion before World War II and a vast continent-spanning canvas during the turbulent war years, Rosamunde Pilcher's most eagerly-awaited novel is the story of an extraordinary young woman's coming of age, coming to grips with love and sadness, and in every sense of the term, coming home...

Rosamunde Pilcher

The #1 *New York Times* Bestselling Author of *The Shell Seekers* and *September*

COMING HOME

"Rosamunde Pilcher's most satisfying story since *The Shell Seekers*."

—*Chicago Tribune*

"Captivating...The best sort of book to come home to...Readers will undoubtedly hope Pilcher comes home to the typewriter again soon."

—*New York Daily News*